The Death
of
Rock'n'Roll,
The Impossibility
of Time Travel
and
Other Lies

JOHN,

I AM QUITE CERTAIN
GLASS TIGER DOES NOT
MAKE AN APPEARANCE IN
THIS BOOK! BUT STRANGER THINGS
HAVE HAPPENED, NO?

LONG LIVE THE MUSIC
OF MUSIC!

RW

ISBN: 1489534784

ISBN 13: 9781489534781

Library of Congress Control Number: 2013909819

CreateSpace Independent Publishing Platform

North Charleston, South Carolina

Dedication:

To Nicole and Spencer, who give me inspiration and resolve, as well as all those who take a stand regardless of how difficult or trivial doing what's right may be.

Author's Note:

The Death of Rock 'n' Roll, the Impossibility of Time Travel and Other Lies is a work of fiction. There are references to well-known people, events, bands and places, however all dialogue, interactions and context has been fabricated and embellished for the purpose of being fictitious. Any resemblance to current events or locales, or to living persons, is entirely coincidental.

Cover Art Credit:

"Strolling Bones", original art by Peter Wyse. Rights reserved. www.peterwyse.com

Cover Art Design C7 Design www.cseven.com

Contents

Part 1

Transmission

Transmission:

A verb for the action of passing radio waves from a source to a destination. The fundamental basis upon which radio is built and operates.

A verb describing the act of moving something from one place to another, or otherwise being moved from one place to the next.

In communication models, the initiation of a message or communication.

A song by Joy Division, from their debut album *Unknown Pleasures*, released in 1979, ushering in the age of goth and a darker shade of punk. Some claimed this was the coming of the Death of rock 'n' roll. They were wrong.

Radio, live transmission...

It was the transmission of Joy Division songs that forged the way for what would become the subset of rock 'n' roll referred to as "goth." Music created by this band was inspired and borne out of an age in which the youth felt isolated, disengaged, and hopeless. These were the sounds of music that articulated and amplified the anguished screams of a youth facing the specters of high unemployment, massive industrialization and inflation. It was a time in which there were few prospects for a better life. Even meaningful employment after university was unlikely, and yet the politicians of the world focused on nuclear arsenals and regional conflicts rather than less significant matters, such as social conditions or the disassociation of the youth.

Transmission. The phase of communication where a message is sent, but confirmation of receipt has not yet occurred. If a tree fell in the forest, it would transmit a sound, and even if that sound might not actually be heard or acknowledged, it would still constitute a transmission. This represents the threshold between philosophy and science.

Transmission. The phase in which most communication between generations remains stranded.

Listen to the silence, let it ring on...

Transmission. The phase in which expression of values is conveyed from one place to the next.

Transmission. A means by which energy is produced and then transferred from a source (such as an engine) to a target (such as an axel) while being converted to power, in order to provide movement.

Transmission. An act of moving an object between points.

Dance, dance, dance, dance, dance, to the radio...

Joy Division – *Transmission*

Transmission. Did I mention it was also the name of the radio show that I've had since I was seventeen?

1 – About a Girl

This is Radio KQSF FM 91.1. The show is L'émission: The Transmission, and I'm Sid. It's now one thirty Monday morning January thirtieth, and I'll be here until I give up or until the jazz guy starts at six o'clock. Yeah, the name is French, sort of cultured and highbrow, so pay attention.

Kurt Cobain was right, and so were Lloyd Cole and Sid Vicious. Stories are always about a girl. Regardless of anything else in the story, it is always about a girl. Maybe that's why things always turn out differently than you expect.

Music lets us travel through time, so why don't we see the breadth of influence of women? What they've altered along the way. Let's see, all the pasts that have been altered and outcomes affected. Up next is the track you're expecting from Nirvana, taking us to 1989 when the song first appeared on the album Bleach.

FCC transcript KQSF 91.1 FM 01.30.2017 0130
Operator comments redacted

About a girl. "It's true", I decided. I suppose the story is always about a girl, even when it isn't that type of story. This is a story about the things that are important—not just important to me but important to everyone. And when I mean everyone, I mean the world.

My best friend, Kenn, and I were experts in the important. And as far as important things went, girls didn't usually rate all that high, at least not to Kenn and me. Rock 'n' roll, however, did. In fact, Kenn and I would rate rock 'n' roll as the second most import thing to us, with only breathing air ranking higher. And just slightly higher at that.

Kenn and I had been best friends for a long time, so long that we actually had the sort of relationship that you'd think would never end. A sort of friendship that always had an immediate comfort and familiarity, where all the problems of the day and plights of humanity were discussed. Our relationship was like this because we did discuss everything. One perfect piece of vinyl at a time.

Well, usually it was vinyl, but failing the unspoiled expanse of a record, our discussions always had some form of rock 'n' roll in the background, regardless of the media selected. Of course, our preference was long-play vinyl, but I will discuss the nuances of why later.

Rock 'n' roll was our sanctuary. Our lifeblood and our solace. Sure, oxygen was physically more important, but once it attached to our blood, it flowed through our bodies to a rock 'n' roll beat in 4:4 time. Besides each other, rock 'n' roll was the one thing that Kenn and I could always rely upon and understand more than anything else. It was the sun that our world orbited around.

As kids, music planted seeds of an obsession deep within our fertile minds—seeds that grew into enlightenment. Something that permeated every thought, regardless of whether our state was conscious or asleep. Of course, I had a job and whatever else that was required in order to function in society, but the highlight of my day was always meeting up with Kenn to listen to music and discuss what was going on in the world. And when I say "world," I mean the world of music.

We actually discussed all things…girls, beer, politics, people we knew, pizza. But the only topic capable of holding our interest continually, like the gravitational pull of the sun, was rock 'n' roll. Because all things either started with or ended with rock 'n' roll, like tides crossing to foreign shores only to later return.

Driving to Kenn's one particular evening, I reflected on my day. It could have been any day, really, because with the exception of the music that I listened to, they were mostly the same—uneventful, with my underachieving existence blurring together like fence boards seen from a passing car. I would plod along doing just enough to get by, striving to be a satisfactory employee or student or son…but usually falling short. I would tend to what was necessary, and then my attention would return to rock 'n' roll. I guess that's the problem with an obsession.

That day was mediocre, just like the days prior—and the days before that and even many since. Just like classes at public school and then later in college. Although I would never consider myself a failure or substandard, that was exactly what my transcript usually showed. Probably more substandard than an outright failure, but then again it's often a thin line. And there's a thin line between substandard and average and another between average and exceptional. So in fact, I was really only a couple of thin lines away from an exceptional life. Kenn concurred with this view, but probably because these lies also applied to him.

Even as I replayed some random day in my mind, I thought about the exceptional world of rock 'n' roll. A world that was in contrast to my life, a contrast as clear as black and white stripes. A world not like the harsh wasteland I so often found myself in, but rather one that I understood and that nurtured me through compassion and acceptance. I remembered such a harsh world personified by a Spanish class in school. It wasn't just Spanish that seemed foreign to me. I struggled in math as well, but math had a tendency to follow me into other classes.

Here I was in Spanish, bracing my fears against probabilities that I only possessed a practical understanding of, without appreciating the underlying statistics, with my math skills hiding in the hallway, as the teacher started turning toward me. Intuitively I knew that she was going to ask me a question.

Turning to me with kind eyes but a stern and demanding disposition, she said, "*¿Quisiera bailar conmigo?*"

I could feel the blood rushing to my face as though the eyes of each of my classmates were mirrors reflecting the heat of the sun. Inescapably I was the center of attention, which I despised, especially since I had overlooked reviewing my Spanish lesson, considering it unimportant. I fumbled for what I could only guess might be the answer. "*Mi nombre es…*" It wasn't that I thought Spain or Spanish didn't matter, but I just ended up being distracted by the Clash song "Spanish Bombs" and spent the night reading about the band and the Spanish Civil War. It seemed like a good idea at the time, like so many others. What obsession gives, such as learning about the Spanish Civil War, it takes in other forms. Today's sacrifice for obsession was my Spanish oral recitals.

Laughter erupted through the classroom, cutting off my reply and reinforcing my positioning in the bottom social caste in the American public school system.

It was a position that I occupied, along with Kenn, throughout my life. More than a position, maybe it was our lot. Even though Kenn and I weren't in all of the same classes, we had both been around enough to witness similar humiliations of each other. Sometimes we would think that we had the correct answer, so we would volunteer, and other times we were called upon. Eventually, we would discover that whether we answered the question correctly or not didn't matter. Our lot had been cast, and accordingly we were indefinitely condemned to a specific caste. If we provided a correct answer, the collective reaction was that the question was easy or that we were weenies. Of course, errors and missteps always resulted in laughter and ridicule.

"Kenn, please name the planets, starting with the farthest from the sun," Mr. Ward would inquire during a science class early in the school year.

"Huh?" Kenn would reply with distracted ambivalence.

Once Mr. Ward restored order, he would brace himself on his desk with one hand and rub the balding spot of his head with his other hand. Staring at his desk, he would repeat the question to Kenn.

"Well, there's Pluto and then *Planet of the Apes* next and then that place where Sean Connery filmed *Outland,* but I think that was a moon…" Kenn would start. Laughter and groans would ensue, relieving Kenn of his participatory obligations for the day.

What else did they expect kids like us to do in those circumstances? That's right, nothing. So we checked out and quit engaging in class. Increasingly we would be distracted, either genuinely or feigned, when our turns for questions came about.

Playground sports were worse than any classroom. Kenn and I went from being picked last to not being picked at all. It didn't matter what the game or contest was. We were excluded as if we were invisible. Something as easily dispelled as a gas in a gale. For many of the stormy days of our youth, invisibility was a blessing, but even that took some time to realize.

In fact, all the time Kenn and I thought we were unique and alone in our suffering, we really weren't. Alone for sure, but unique? Hardly. Still we were stunned when years later we realized our lives bore a distinct resemblance to the song "The Ostracism of Vinny Lalor" by Darren Hanlon. It was a profound revelation that spurred me to ask the local library to find a copy of *A Descant for Gossips*, by Thea Astley, which I read voraciously.

I understood that for every action there was a consequential reaction. Intuitively I knew that a body in motion caused friction. I understood that Kenn and I caused friction with people and that usually that corresponding motion left a bruise or a cut on Kenn or me. This wasn't something that I needed science to explain. By the time I had finished the first few of Astley's chapters I understood that life imitated art and that the themes that ran through music and literature were as much about human expression as the act of reciting them. Rock 'n' roll seemed to borrow ideas from the other arts but also seemed to reflect my experiences. This enlightenment would stay with me. Later, when I heard Mike Ness sing "When the Angels Sing," I would think of Dante's *Divine Comedy*. I still hear it in the sets on my radio show and in my interventions setting up the playlist for the night.

Originally, the realization came through a pause in the conversation one evening at Kenn's, while we were listening to a new album that I had brought over.

"Hey, I bought the new Darren Hanlon album *Fingertips and Mountains*," letting myself in, I announced over the music I could hear from the speakers that I knew were located throughout Kenn's house. He never locked the door, believing that if someone wanted in bad enough, locking a door would never be sufficient.

"Any good?" came Kenn's reply from some unseen recess of his home, which I knew to be his basement. Even with music everywhere, Kenn rarely spent much time anywhere else. Sometimes he'd even sleep down there.

"I was waiting to add it to the program tonight, so let's find out. Does that work for you?"

Kenn was always game for a theme or a structure to sculpt our nocturnal music sessions around, so new music always presented new ideas for him. "Come on down. How about starting with the new album and then rounding the night out with some Lucksmiths and Hanlon's other albums?"

It was a rhetorical question, really. I knew that Kenn would already be culling music for the evening's program. In fact, I could already hear the beginnings of "Hiccups" getting louder as I descended the stairs. At one point Kenn and I had quit discussing the morality of "sharing music" and focused instead on the music itself. The lines in the debate continue to shift, but just to be safe, Kenn and I cross-registered our various Apple devices to allow access regardless of whether the music was "his" or "mine." Plus, the only limit to the music that we legitimately purchased was the amount of money we had, so at least in our minds we were on solid footing with any sharing that occurred.

"Here, sync my iPod, and we'll give it a listen," Kenn said.

Such was both the informality and priorities of our relationship. Greetings, salutations, shaking of hands and other forms of acknowledgment that friends often shared gave way to the passing of music, beer, or falling into a conversation midstream. After all, there was always time for checking in, once the music was playing.

Kenn and I quietly talked about the small matters during the first half of the new Hanlon album. New music was always treated with more reverence than anything else. It was the first listen that was going to plant the seed of our opinions of the album and even the current stature of the artist. Like Christmas morning, it was a potpourri of hopes, expectations, and fears of efforts falling short and watching the reactions on other people's faces. While we had a basic frame of reference to work with new music, the greeting of the new offering was always an auspicious time, fraught with emotion.

"What are you doing?" I asked Kenn when I finally noticed him, rather than the music.

"Eating pizza."

"Given that your mouth is full and you've got a slice in your hand, I could have guessed. But what are you doing with your slice folded over?"

"What's the big deal?" Kenn said. "This is how you eat New York-transplanted European-style slices. You know, if you're in the know."

"*New York Style? In the know?* What the Hell are you talking about? When did you start to claim to be *in the know?* Besides, I had pizza with you last night and you ate it like a normal guy from Oregon rather than some yuppie metrosexual from Manhattan." A stream of questions flowed from my mouth gathering ideas and thoughts like errant skiers and trees in the teeth of an avalanche.

"Yeah, well, if you can't be bothered to keep up with the world around you, dude…," Kenn said, trailing off, with his condescension taking on a casual aloofness. "Besides it wouldn't kill you to read *GQ* from time to time. There's an entire article about the pizza of NYC this month. You should give it a try. Not the pizza, but, you know, reading."

Kenn. *GQ.* Both subjects not only appearing in the same sentence, but without a disjunctive clause? It seemed as unlikely as "sustainable peace" or "a cool Canadian band." But there it was, taunting me like a "wet paint" sign needing verification.

"Seriously, Kenn, when in the Hell did you start reading *GQ?*" I considered asking him *why* also, but I was still suffering the effects from the shock of hearing that my buddy had secretly taken to reading men's style and fashion mags.

"Try it," Kenn instructed. As he watched me take a slice, administer Frank's RedHot, and then fold the pizza in half, he continued. More sheepishly, he admitted, "Yeah, well, the pizza article was on the page across from a piece about the Beastie Boys that I was reading. What do you think?"

After some deliberation, I replied, "I think the loss of Adam is a damn shame. Both for the band and for rock 'n' roll."

"Of course, but I meant about the pizza."

"Oh," returning from my lament about the Beastie Boys, "it sort of sucks. All the hot sauce settles into the middle. But that's not as disturbing as you reading *GQ*. And I guess it makes eating it faster, too."

"Yeah, totally faster," Kenn added, his sheepishness departed, leaving only a wolf and his slice. "That's why I tried the thin crust tonight, too. Also, less pizza goo runs onto your hand, making it easier to keep the vinyl clean."

The night wore on like that. Conversations ranging between the inane and the solemn with subjects like "how best to eat pizza" or "how cancer had become a cancer upon rock 'n' roll" occupying the ends of the spectrum. That's probably how Kenn and I spent most of our time together, ranging across topics, completing each other's sentences and generally giving each other a hard time. But always, there was music and tonight it was a new offering from Darren Hanlon.

So, Kenn and I quietly commented and chatted, mostly about the new works we were discovering, as Darren Hanlon filled the basement. But then, at track 7, "The Ostracism of Vinny Lalor" started and all commentary stopped. It wasn't because it was the best track on the album. In fact, by the time you consider, "Hold On," "Old Dream," "Couch Surfing," and "Elbows," there is barely room in the top five for track 7, but that wasn't it at all. It was the story that the song told and what that story meant to Kenn and me.

It was Kenn who dispelled the stunned silence. "That could be us in that song, dude."

Sure, perhaps not the "sounds of burning zoos" or "watching dancers catch fire," but Kenn was right. Just like Kenn and me, the denizens of a town that was tiny enough that it didn't rate a presence on a national map ostracized Vinny Lalor. While we were in a college town, it still struggled to find reference on maps that were any larger than regional. Certainly, no national maps would locate us.

Presidential hopefuls never passed through our town (governors rarely did), and good bands would never end up there unless they had been taken hostage. But it wasn't that we were victims of geography, it was that we shared an experience with a character in a song, who we would later learn made her first appearance in a novel. What life might have been like for Vinny in a small regional Australian town we'd never know. But because rock 'n' roll told a story relating to our lives, Kenn and I understood one of the fundamental elements of Vinny's existence.

"Wow," I replied in slack-jawed contemplation, "Kenn, you're right. I wonder if there's a connection. Hanlon has moved to Oregon now you know. Maybe he's trying to communicate with us."

"Yeah, right," Kenn replied. "Like Hanlon has nothing better to do with his time than track us down."

Whatever schedule or motivations Hanlon might possess, the fact was that this was the first time Kenn and I noticed music talking to us. This realization set off an inundation of discovery where we scoured other albums in our collection to listen with a renewed understanding of how music could tell the stories of the world around us. Just another life changing rock 'n' roll discovery for Kenn and me.

But how did I come to learn about rock 'n' roll in the first place? Well, that's a good question. The scientist, that Kenn would later claim to have become, taught me about rock 'n' roll. I suppose that this was well before Kenn became a self-proclaimed scientist, and maybe it was more of an introduction that sparked an evolution rather than a tutorial of instruction. Kenn and I were always learning and evolving so that our knowledge of rock 'n' roll could expand, because rock 'n' roll is important. This evolution was how we found our place in the world and solidified our understanding.

That's where I was heading tonight, to the one place in the world that Kenn and I had made. A place of rock 'n' roll nestled into the safety and sanctity of his basement. At Kenn's there were three constants: pizza, beer or Mountain Dew, and rock 'n' roll. Kenn and I would consume all of it until we wearily retired for the night. I would go home and the music would be silenced, if only temporarily.

Listening to music was like traveling through time. Everything else would stop and blur, a phenomenon frequently found in science fiction movies or to simulate when someone was dreaming. That's how it was for Kenn and me. Everything but the music was paused. Even as the music continued, we would discover that the music would take us back to other times and teach us about the world. It was Billy Bragg and the Clash that taught us about the Sandinista in Nicaragua. We learned about places where fascism reigned, repression ran unchecked or other things were happening without Kenn and I being aware of the world beyond our sheltered existence. Rock 'n' roll helped us understand culture and history. Band names like Midnight Oil, Hunters & Collectors, NWA, and Public Enemy were all cultural references to people and places that were beyond our comprehension in Oregon. I wondered what else could we learn about our connection to the world around us from art?

Have you ever wondered what it would be like to travel through time? I suppose you have, because everyone does. Or at least I have assumed everyone does, because I always did.

Once we understood rock 'n' roll, Kenn and I remained focused on the important things. The big issues. That's how it was and that's how it would always be with Kenn. It could be anytime we got together to spin records at his place. Not time travel or girls, but rock 'n' roll, and our conversations merely peppered the audible ambience created by the music we played into the nights of our youth.

"Hey, did you see the *Spin* article? Looks like Iggy Pop got the Stooges back together with the *Power* album lineup," one of us would ask.

"Yeah, I'd love to see that show," the other would answer.

"Look, there is a review of the New Christs latest album in *Rolling Stone*."

"Really? After a hiatus of seven years, I hope it's good."

"Should be great. I mean really, it's The New Christs."

This was the ebb and flow of our existence. Kenn and I were the alpha predators patrolling the world of rock 'n' roll knowledge.

Like sharks along a reef, if something happened, we were on top of it. We seamlessly carried conversations set to the music of the session. I'm sure that anyone witnessing the exchanges would quickly lose track of whose comment was whose; Kenn and I were of one mind, especially regarding music.

We knew the tours, the album releases, the band compositions, and the set lists on the live albums. It didn't matter when or where; Kenn and I knew the date of the release of the Lou Reed and Metallica collaboration and followed the Internet frenzy that it unleashed, back when buzz marketing or viral releases still hadn't run their course on the Internet. This was our world, and we were fully plugged in. We were like the CIA, Mossad, MI5, the NSA, and Julian Assange all rolled into one dynamic team. An entity of singular focus. A two-man team dedicated to rock 'n' roll. A duo destined to be heroes.

"This is cool, it looks like Shriekback is polishing off a new album."

"Really, I thought that Billy Bragg had seconded some of the band's members for his efforts."

Kenn and I knew better than anyone else about music and often found that we were frustrated by this knowledge.

Flipping through a seemingly endless and also seemingly random collection of articles, Kenn asked, "Did you see this piece on censorship? It's like the *Dawn of the Dead* but with the PMRC." We knew that while people like the Parents Music Resource Center were wrong and at the end of the day they really didn't get rock 'n' roll, frankly it was an abomination that they tried to curtail what they didn't like. It takes all kinds to keep this world running, so you've just got to let things take their course and hope for the best.

"Ridiculous. Look at this quote: *My little boy has become a sociopath listening to Megadeth and Trent Reznor.* No, your little boy is a sociopath because you're a shitty parent. You know, Kenn, it's always the same. It's easy to make music the culprit. But it's mistaking the symptom for the disease."

"I'm mean look at how Lindsay Lohan and Miley Cyrus have turned out, growing up with Disney."

"Well, and Disney and Billy Ray."

"True. And Lohan was better in *Machette.*"

"Of course, Rodriquez is a genius; but what ever the influences *were,* rock 'n' roll or even rap music wasn't the problem." I tried to conclude.

"Really, it's like what McCartney said: *Live and let die.*"

 In fact, this story is also about what happens when you don't live and let die. It was the story of our lives.

While I've never been a big fan of the Beatles, McCartney, Lennon, or any of their incarnations (and frankly McCartney should have been sent to Pluto with nothing more than bottled water and crackers for his stint with Wings) the Beatles were the real thing and if nothing else they're a good place to start. If more people listened to the Beatles and their various derivatives (except for Wings) rather than admonishing music, the world would be a better place.

Even the breakup of the Beatles, including whichever account you believe, or your thoughts on Lennon and Yoko Ono, didn't really matter, because it was a reflection of the human condition and our freedom to make choices. This was another topic that Kenn and I discussed at great length.

"But don't you think that people should have the freedom to make choices, Kenn?"

"Well, yeah. But seriously, when people make choices like joining Wings, you just can't help them. How could a friend let that happen? Didn't McCartney have any friends, good friends? Maybe even people nearby who just didn't hate him? Even a stranger would stop you if you were walking out of the bathroom with toilet paper stuck to your shoe." Kenn could and would run this tangent until it circled back on itself, but sometimes that was a point approaching infinity, but fortunately not this time.

My only chance of getting him back was to say, "Don't worry, buddy, I'd never let you join Wings. "

"Yeah, me neither, dude."

With that settled, I could let my guard down for other candid discussions, such as admitting that it wasn't really the Beatles that I was tired of but their treatment on the radio that I grew weary of.

"Really, can't radio stations find anything to play other than 'Hey Jude,' 'I Want To Hold Your Hand,' and 'Can't Buy Me Love?' How hard can it be to program a good radio show? It's the same with the Clash being remembered only by 'Train In Vain' or 'Rock the Casbah.'" Good songs, to be sure, but we aren't discussing bands with a couple of EPs or a handful of singles. These are bands that made a difference. Stood up when things were hard and blazed a path for others to follow.

"Hang on right there," Kenn would interject. "You're not really comparing the Beatles to the Clash, because the former was merely all right, while the latter was truly awesome. And the Clash made a more obvious difference to music, rather than just producing estrogen-pitched screams for walking across airfields or whatever other trivial thing they might have done."

While this was the slightest of tangents, the acts that made their mark, like the Clash, the Beatles, the Rolling Stones, Marvin Gaye, or Elvis are important as part of our collective history. Just like the Federalist Papers and the Constitution. Knowing that underlying importance motivated and focused Kenn and me in our tireless pursuit of rock 'n' roll. And as important as these milestones and great acts were for rock 'n' roll, it was these things that consumed our conversations.

"Buddy, you're sounding a little paranoid again." I would suggest to Kenn.

"Sure, I've been told that I was paranoid or delusional or had a complex like the Spanish guy with the windmills, all of which is totally ridiculous. I've never even been to Spain, and I've got nothing against windmills. All of this aside, how else do you explain that the United Nations doesn't protect the rights of rock 'n' rollers? There's no local police force, no government agency, there isn't even a help line or a support group. Why? When it comes to the lack of support for rock 'n' roll there is simply no other explanation but that of a conspiracy."

"OK, you're sounding very paranoid." Like I said, everyone has his or her reasons for wanting to travel back through time. A kiss to take back, to help a friend or to say something that wasn't uttered. A regret to repair. For me it was always about what I had missed with rock 'n' roll.

Unfortunately, rock 'n' roll is typically a misused term and an overly broad classification of music and far too often includes pariahs such as Bon Jovi, Motley Crew, John Cougar Mellencamp, Huey Lewis and the News, Tom Cochrane and Red Rider, and Brian Adams. Abominations. Infidels. Clearly then, any proper definition of rock 'n' roll would exclude these artistic blights, but then what does it include?

Simply put, rock 'n' roll includes anything that Kenn and I like. Rock 'n' roll includes everything from Alien Sex Fiend to Zeke and everything else in between. It wasn't just important issues that were discussed during these record-spinning sessions; it was a learning environment, too. Kenn and I had a game that we'd play during the early days of organizing our record collections. One of us would call out a letter, and the other would have to name a band.

"V?" I would inquire.

"Verve. You can do better than that."

"Ok, how about W, then buddy?" I would counter.

"Seriously, dude." Kenn was good at this and usually at least a step ahead of me. "Wilco, the Waco Tragedies—Brian Wright's band on his first two albums, the Weather Prophets, Wall of Voodoo. Try again. See if you can stump me."

I would pause thinking of something that would unseat him. "Z?"

"OK, not bad, but still I've got Zeke and Zappa, Frank. My turn, names with "Q.""

I was ready for him and always tried to mix sub-genres or stay with a theme. "Q" was good for that. "The Queers, Queen, Queen Latifah, Queens of the Stone Age." All derogatory terms for homosexual men, words I would never say, but still a theme, at least in my mind.

"K," Kenn would continue.

"Please Kenn, that's an easy one." It was, so rather than a theme I tried to impress him with range of acts. "The Killers, Kate Bush, Killing Joke, King Apparatus, Kiss." We would do the same thing with numbers. But even though this sharpened our memory and recall of various bands, an A-to-Z listing of bands doesn't define rock 'n' roll, even for us. A listing is merely that, an enumeration of acts that contribute to the overall rock 'n' roll fabric, but such a role call doesn't *define* anything, but merely points the way.

Kenn once said, "Rock 'n' roll is about the human experience." And I think he's right. Rock 'n' roll is the reflection of the human experience, about hopes and dreams. It has the ability to convey a message that transcends class, religion, language, and culture. The Ramones played to a raucous crowd of Spaniards in Barcelona, opening the show with Morricone's timeless movie theme, "The Good, the Bad, and the Ugly." Listening to the album you can hear the crowd losing control and shouting "Hey, ho! Let's go!" in English...the chant that characterized the Ramones and served as their rallying cry at the start of shows or the inevitable *encore*.

There was probably an argument to be made that the views that Kenn and I tightly held about rock 'n' roll was like the line from Jonathan Richman's "Monologue About Bermuda," "Nothing snotty about that, is there?"

Well, it is complicated to define something that is so nebulous and uncharacterized. Also, rock 'n' roll has changed throughout time. Originally it had its roots in blues and the American South and was then adapted (or plagiarized, depending upon your views) by artists (or thieves, depending upon your views), such as Buddy Holly, Elvis Presley, the Big Bopper, and the rest of the righteous souls who followed in their footsteps in whatever manner or form.

This story is about some of the events that threatened to destroy rock 'n' roll and the actions Kenn and I took that protected it for future generations. A story about lies that we discovered.

This is a story about the contribution that Kenn and I made to ensure that the music that guided our lives survived without decline. Of course we had to travel great distances and face perils of every sort in order to vanguard rock 'n' roll, but someone had to stand up to the Man, and Kenn and I were just the heroes charging to the rescue in this hour of need.

Some would call this an obsession, others misguided. Kenn said it was science and that his pursuit of rock 'n' roll knowledge made him a scientist. I think that it was simply in our blood, and of course that is also why Kenn and I were incapable of retaining (paying) jobs or girlfriends. Actually, outside of the relationship between Kenn and me, we didn't really have any friends. As for girlfriends, well, that is more a deliberate choice. Like I said, the story is always about a girl. This is just a different story.

Let's start with Kenn's discovery. After all, Kenn claimed that he was a scientist.

2 – The Scientist

For those of you who don't know what you're listening to, you've dialed up Radio KQOR FM 89.9, and I'm Sid. For those of you who've intentionally tuned in, thank you. It's two oh-five a.m., and this is rock 'n' roll. There is some debate as to whether music is an art or a science. But is it really much of a debate? Probably more like a personal monologue, much like a radio intervention. Those claiming that rock 'n' roll is art are those who find it creative or who have made it beautiful. Others point to the harmonics, the audible frequencies, tangible forces that can be measured and predicted by the bounds of science. I think music has to be both art and science. Certainly there are limits to how far music can go in either direction, just like there are limits to what art can represent and science can measure. Above all, there are some things that we just know, without the illustration of art or the explanation of science.

What is all this talk of science and life? Here, listen to this. This is a perfect example of what I'm saying. The beauty of art, the precision of science, and a scientist who's caught in the middle. Here. Let's listen to Coldplay.

FCC transcript KQOR 89.9 FM 11.18.2011 0205
Operator comments redacted

The scientist was calling me. I knew who it was because my cell phone was banging out the drum lead from the Ramones's "Do You Remember Rock 'n' Roll Radio?" It was the ringtone that I had set for calls from Kenn. No, not the live version of the song recorded in Barcelona on the *Loco Live* album. Does it matter? It's just silly ringtone. It's not the genuine article. And it was just the drum lead, not the vocals; that would have been over the top. But it was the ringtone for Kenn, my best friend and self-proclaimed scientist.

"Dude, you've got to get over here now," Kenn pleaded. There was always something with Kenn. Some conspiracy. Something to rush to. An emergency of some kind. Some emergencies were real, some imagined, but there was always *something* with Kenn. And for Kenn, whatever it was, it was always real, even if it was really imagined. Time was always of the essence for him. Me? Not so much.

"Kenn, I'm coming by later tonight anyways. I've got a couple things to do now," I tried to explain.

"Man, you've got to get here now. This is really important." Then he hung up.

Kenn Ramseyer has been my best friend since we were about ten. Certainly well before we knew that we were destined for the greatness that comes with saving rock 'n' roll. Well, not just rock 'n' roll, but also the world.

He always went by Kenn, "with two 'n's," he would say. Why? Because that made him different. The truth was that Kenn was different enough, even without spelling his name differently. From time to time, I'd call him "Junior" just to piss him off and he'd call me "Dick," but no one else got away with that sort of thing with us. These were the monikers that would immediately cause us to bristle, the sort of thing that only the closest of friends would dare attempt.

Our initial interactions were inauspicious enough. We lived in the same neighborhood; we went to the same school and played in the same playgrounds, probably for longer than we actually knew each other. Most of the time, our conversations were limited to a mutual exchange of grunts and nods that in vague grade school language meant "hi." Sometimes we would talk about *Scooby Doo* or exchange rules to a game that was being made up on the fly…the things that you expect from kids on playgrounds.

Kenn and I were both scrawny, unhealthy-looking kids whom, for whatever reason, didn't manage to have a great number of friends or even just a few. Nor were Kenn and I really given over to the many outdoor pursuits that Oregon seems to foist upon its youth. Notwithstanding this early common ground, we didn't have any real reason to become friends, so we didn't. Until we did. We needed a catalyst to drive us together, to forge us into friendship and to anodize us into heroes. Some form of evil catalyst that would spur us into taking a stand. An action that would cause a reaction.

This particular adversity occurred at the hands of the typical all-American playground bully and his crew of friends. The one that everyone is familiar with, even though he isn't listed as one of *the people in your neighborhood* or discussed by *Mister Dressup*. Every community had such a bully, just like there was a fire chief and a baker. On one unspectacular day, the sounds of torment and anguish interrupted whatever imaginary game I was playing. I saw the hulking figure of Harvey McCloy, the neighborhood bully, with his motley crew of supplicant minions, towering over Kenn, taunting and raining threats upon him. What did he want? Lunch money, humiliation, dominance, stature that only comes through degradation of others? I suppose it could have been anything. Kenn always had lots of lunch money and no friends, so the combination was alluring even without Kenn being scrawny. Contrasting the slight physique and lack of athleticism that Kenn and I were cursed with, McCloy was large. Large for his age, but neither lean and muscular like the kids whose fathers worked in the mountains, nor fat like the car dealer's son. McCloy was some sort of hybrid between the two. You could see a certain softness about him, but it was his girth that was unmistakable, and McCloy knew it. In fact, he effectively used his bulk to throw his weight around in such a manner that immobilized the weaker of the species. It was a special sensitivity that bullies seemed to have, a talent to understand their strengths and the weaknesses or vulnerabilities of others, even among children who lack awareness in other forms.

As is often the case with these types of bullying episodes, there was no crowd present. This wasn't a fight between two kids that was cause to stop playing and gather to watch, cheer, and place bets. This was something that no one wanted to witness and deliberately avoided seeing. Kenn would be perfectly isolated.

Because of a similar experience earlier in the week, I was still sporting sore ribs, a split lip, a bruised eye, and a feeling of humiliation that seeped through me like the urine that had stained my pants. What I felt most was shame. Shame of a memory that pained me even more than the rib pain that flared every time I moved. Unlike the ribs, which only hurt with each cough, sneeze, drink of water or deep breath, the humiliation followed me like a shadow. The degradation was like a specter that lingered around me like the smell of blood in a carpet or the sting of astringent on a wound. I told my parents that the bruising was from playing tackle football at school, which made my father proud and my mother quietly pat him on the shoulder. "It's good to see you being rougher, growing into a man," he said. My mother said that as long as I was having fun and being fair, the other kids would spend more time with me. "That's how to make friends, honey." I just nodded, mentally confirming that my parents would never really understand me.

On that prior occasion, I was unprepared for McCloy, but the beating changed me, and while I lied to my parents and to my teachers about a bicycle accident or sports injury or whatever, my imagination attacked the problem. I always had a good imagination. I just need to engage it with a problem.

During this interval, I did what so many of us do. I considered what I should have said, berating myself with questions. What I would have said if I had been clever enough or quick enough. What if I could travel back through time? What would I have done? Although I wasn't initially prepared for the confrontation, I knew that I *would* be the next time.

With bullies there is always a next time, and as it turned out, the next time was now. There I was watching the same scene, this time in the third person.

I could hear the free-form jazz of schoolyard taunts: wimp, faggot, chicken, weakling, pansy, Commie. Words rather than notes. Bullies, not musicians. Words that were disjointed and random, words that gathered around a central riff to build a theme, and a theme to build a song. Words that told a story when heard together but lacked any meaning on their own and were without context. Words laced with intention and emotion but with meaning not understood by the mouths that spat them. Words like the bullies themselves: useless, pathetic, and weak in isolation, but collectively indomitable.

I had been exposed to my uncle's jazz records before and never really liked the sound, but what I'd heard now was different. This was a human abomination producing an artistry of hatred and malice. The free-form jazz dialogue continued and became punctuated with the percussion of fists and kicks falling upon Kenn, who among all the labels hurled upon him, became the one not uttered: victim. At that moment I realized that the past had prepared me for the future, but I couldn't turn back the clock, and all I had was the present to set things right.

I could change the future, if I dared. If I had the courage. If I could summon the resolve to make a choice now that would prevent my and Kenn's victimization.

"Hey, sissy, leave him alone," I shouted in the most strident tone I could muster, notwithstanding the efforts of my fear to choke all sound from my throat.

It was the quiet after a jet takes off from an airport. The bully circle stopped its seething noise and opened, allowing Harvey to turn and face me.

"Well, now," he said, with contempt filling his eyes. "I thought you would have learned your lesson the other day. Why don't you come and join your girlfriend here." Some of his minions grabbed me, tripped me to the ground and then kicked my already tender ribs.

"Harvey," I said, with a confidence that startled even me, "you're going to let us go. In fact, you're going to give me my money back and make sure that no harm ever comes to us again." I may as well have slapped him with the wings growing out of my back for the shocked expression on his face.

"Right. Sure, I'm going to make sure you and baby boy are safe. Why?" he said, asking the obvious question.

"Because you don't want to face the consequences of continuing this." Looking around I understood two things: there would be no help for me and that I was committed to my course of action. My lack of retreat founded my resolve.

"Why? Are you going to tell your mommy, little baby?" His fiendish colleagues giggled at this.

"No. Not at all. I'm actually not going to tell anyone…well, at least not for a while." I could see that McCloy was struggling to control his confusion, which was threatening the bully's bravado.

"But I'll tell you how this will go. Kenn and I are good kids. Teachers like us; we do well in school. That's going to stop today. We're going to start being distracted, falling asleep in class, sitting alone during recess, and refusing to change for gym class." This was actually another lie, sort of. Kenn and I weren't really good students, but we were well on our downward spiral to scholastic mediocrity. This would simply be the justification.

"I don't care," Harvey said, his grip on the situation becoming tenuous.

"Yeah, well, Harv, that's not all. We'll continue with our refusal to cooperate until the school counselor gets involved and asks us what's wrong, after weeks of being called into her office and the principal's office as well. I'll finally tell them that you had only quit beating on us after we agreed to give you blowjobs."

I had an idea what a blowjob was, sort of. I had heard about it in a movie that my father watched one night when my mom was working late. My father didn't know that I was listening at the door, but it sounded like something that girls did for boys, and I was pretty certain that most dads in Oregon didn't want their boys doing it for other boys.

"So?" Harvey responded, sounding less sure of his footing. Even the members of Harvey's intrepid band of minions seemed to be losing their resolve. The more they started to weaken, the more assertive I became. Courage is like that. It's liquid. That's why some find courage in a bottle, sometimes with a tidal force. This was the first time I had felt the tide of courage washing upon me to give me strength rather than pulling me into a sea of emotion that inspired helplessness. I found the sensation exhilarating. This new flood of courage straightened my posture and planted my feet more firmly. I closed my hands into relaxed, but confident fists.

"Well, Harv," I continued derisively, knowing that he hated being called Harv, "then the police will come, and while they may not charge you, they will certainly tell your parents." His and Kenn's faces indicated that they understood my plan. "What do you think your father would say about you forcing other boys to give you blowjobs? Your dad is a judge, right? Does your mother still drag you to church with her? After months of trying to get to the bottom of our problems, no one will even question us. But you will be questioned. Do you think your father will have questions for you?"

My recollection today probably makes the story sound more sophisticated than it really was, but it really did involve a threat about us lying and about the blowjobs.

We never did get our money from Harvey, but from that day forward, if either Kenn or I fell or tripped, Harv would appear as though on wings to help us up. It was my first stand against a bully. I felt a rising sense of pride, excitement, and fear. I suppose fear is always there, isn't' it? Fear and excitement walk hand in hand. But as Kenn and I were walking away from Mc-Cloy, I could feel the effects of the adrenaline rush that I had just experienced starting to wane, leaving me feeling drained, anxious, and more than a little scared that Harv would call my bluff.

"That was awesome, man," Kenn said, with true awe in his voice. Being kids, that was as close as he got to thanking me, but being kids, that was enough. "Hey," he said, "do you ever listen to the radio?"

"Only with my parents." It was 1990, and popular radio was something of a wasteland. Vanilla Ice, Soul II Soul, Janet Jackson, Bryan Adams, and Celine Dion, the latter two laying the foundation for my contempt for Canada and the musicians it produced, dominated most of the radio I had heard. I know that we were taught in school that Russia and China were our enemies, but I couldn't understand why. Canada was right next door, across a virtually unguarded frontier and sending a veritable landslide of music across the border. Canada and its actions with regard to rock 'n' roll represented a clear and present danger, but no one seemed to care.

"I've got my own radio and found some stations that are way cooler than what my parents listen to," Kenn said. "Maybe you want to come and listen with me after school today." Even at that young age, Kenn was a music scientist. Exploring, learning, and seeking. Maybe that was how he thanked me after all. Come to think of it, I'm not sure I've ever heard him say "thank you" in all the time I've known him, but maybe that's how things go with friends.

Without anything else to do, I took Kenn up on his offer, and after school Kenn and I went to his parent's house, which seemed fancier than mine. Rather than playing on the house's expansive grounds or racing through its wide halls, Kenn and I listened to rock 'n' roll on the radio. It turned out that Kenn had found a couple of college stations that would open a new world to us. Like Columbus returning to Italy with the spoils of the New World, my imagination ran wild with possibilities. I suddenly understood the power of radio. A power utilized by Tokyo Rose and by Radio Free Europe to communicate ideas beyond words. An ability to stir emotions. Suddenly the radio wasn't background noise or something for my parents to talk over in the car, but something important. Important to me. From then on when I turned on a radio to awaken the programming that was magically processed inside, something awakened in me as well. A call to action. A reason to believe. Radio was the first medium that allowed rock 'n' roll to reach me in a meaningful way. It was a discovery that Kenn shared with me, as though he had invented it himself, for which I would always be grateful.

We all have the first indelible moment. A point in time where we discover something that moves us to a new enlightenment. A painting that awakens a love for art. A story or a poem that unlocks literature, leading to a lifelong relationship with words. For me, it was listening to a radio in Kenn's basement, crackling and impossible to tune perfectly; it was at that time that I first heard David Bowie's "Five Years." Five Years. The same length of time I would later spend vacillating around the university to complete my first degree. Five years…the length of Stalin's ambitious but horrific plans for social and economic change. The period of time in which you could achieve something significant…an Olympic dream perhaps, but not an entire lifetime, unless you were a squirrel. This was the start of five years of change for me, all because of David Bowie, Kenn Ramseyer, and Harvey McCloy. What came next was defined by songs like Nine Inch Nails – "Head Like A Hole" and Jane's Addiction – Caught Stealing, the Cure – "Pictures of You" and of course Nirvana – "Smells Like Teen Spirit". It was 1990 and I finally understood that there was music that spoke to me.

Although my reaction to radio and the rapture induced by rock 'n' roll so many years ago was profound, the details remain etched in my mind with clear lines as though cut into a metal plate. While it seemed like a few days ago that Kenn and I had listened to his radio together, so much had happened since then. But time is like that. Time looks different when you are looking toward it or back upon it. Regardless of how much time had passed and all that Kenn and I had done during those years, I still had no idea that so much more was going to happen to us. How could I? I couldn't see the future any better then than I can now.

Now, it was seventeen years since that radio show and the time seemed to have disappeared. In contrast to the time that dragged like tectonic plates against each other since Kenn had first called today. Seventeen minutes, three pleading phone calls, and seventeen SMS messages (or maybe just one SMS resent sixteen times) later, I arrived at Kenn's house. I let myself in and grabbed one of the last three Mountain Dews from the fridge, which hissed open as I carried it to the cavernous basement. Kenn's fridge represented the philosophical question "is it half empty or half full?" of leftover pizza and takeout food, beer (whatever was on sale), and Mountain Dew. No milk, no fruit, and no vegetables, unless these items were component parts of the leftovers. Oh yeah, and Frank's RedHot sauce. It couldn't be Kenn's without Dew and Frank's.

Half empty or half full? I was the philosopher. The Che Guevara to his Fidel Castro, the Karl Marx to his Lenin, the Peter Buck to his Michael Stipe and the Brian Eno to his Brian Ferry. If I had been more practical and realistic, I would have recognized that the contents of his fridge were past their expiry dates, filthy and inadequate, but after long enough it becomes part of the setting, much like a stain that remains even after it has been scrubbed clean or painted over.

It was odd how things like that worked. There were things that we would never see, like the dirty fridge or the rust stains in the bathroom sink, and others like stains in carpets that we would always see, even after the carpet had been replaced. Even all these years later I know that Kenn would still hear taunts from bullies or admonishment from his father. Furniture that had long been replaced would still appear broken and strewn throughout a room.

A lot of things had changed in Kenn's life and in particular with his home, but some things never did. I don't know if it was merely for sentimental reasons, but even now, having a complete house at his disposal, we were always set up in the basement. Maybe the climate was better for the vinyl, or maybe we could play music loud without neighbors complaining, not that the neighbors were really close enough to hear, but you never know. But maybe it just felt right. Equipping the cavernous basement with all the accoutrements of a shrine for rock 'n' roll. Speakers, amps, Kenn's iMac, turntables, cassette decks and CD players, iPod docking stations, power cords, a large flat-screen or plasma T.V., a couple of overstuffed couches, a scattering of coffee tables, and desks. No fancy art on the walls, just gig posters or photocopies of album covers taped to the walls and the white board, which proved useful for lists and also plotting out Kenn's many conspiracy theories.

"OK, buddy," I announced, as the caffeine from the Mountain Dew took hold, "I'm here. What's on? What's so important this time that it couldn't wait another fifty seconds?"

"This is awesome," he exclaimed triumphantly. Of course it was awesome. Everything, good or bad, triumph or conspiracy, in Kenn's mind was always awesome. Kenn continued in a softer tone. "Nice of you to take your damn time." Kenn's moods could swing with the range and predictability of a metronome. Reaching his limit on one end, he started swinging back to the other. Unable to contain his excitement, he said, "I just saw MC5."

"Yeah, so what, they're back together, they're touring," I said, unimpressed. "We were talking about it weeks ago. Give me something new, or admit that you just had another panic attack. What, were they on *The Tonight Show* or something, or maybe it was just a spider shadow on the album cover again?" I asked with as much palpable condescension as I could channel.

"Fuck you," he retorted. "It looked like a real spider that time." It was true, the cause of his panic attack looked like a spider the size of a hubcap, but then again, Kenn isn't known for his housekeeping prowess and now that his parents weren't around, well, let's just say he didn't have the motivation. "No, dude. I saw them live!" he exclaimed.

"No. You, fuck you," I said, engaging in our usual discourse of lowbrow fencing, a form of discourse that was admittedly easy. "OK, did you see them on YouTube or TV? This isn't such a big deal." I knew that the MC5 tour wouldn't be passing anywhere near Oregon, as few tours ever did.

"I created a time machine and saw MC5 at CBGB's in New York." Kenn's enthusiasm overflowed. While prone to inspire fantasy, which often inspired conspiracy, Kenn usually tempered these wild departures from reality with some form of drug or alcohol consumption. Oddly, however, a quick survey of the basement revealed no indication of either activity having recently occurred. But for some reason, he had me intrigued. There had to be something beyond Kenn's nonsense.

Ordinarily Kenn wasn't convincing about anything other than music, but now, about time travel, he seemed certain. He always had opinions and theories, but they always lacked credibility and usually stank of conspiracy worse than his basement the day before the cleaning service arrived.

But still, Kenn had me at CBGB's, and I was intrigued. We had always talked about going to a show at CBGB's in New York. The bar was legendary. The Taj Mahal of rock, the Carnegie Hall for punk. A place where all the good bands wanted to play, and the best did. Some of them, like the Ramones, got their start there, while others, like the Talking Heads, Operation Ivy, the Cramps, Died Pretty, and Huevos Rancheros merely added to their cred.

Unfortunately for Kenn and me, the dream of going to a show at CBGB's had died, like many of our rock 'n' roll dreams. After a protracted licensing and rent fight in 2006, the bar closed with much celebrity and fanfare. CBGB's was consigned to history not with a moment of silence but with the din of rock 'n' roll that it was known for. There had been talk about moving the bar, its urinals, sinks, lights, all of it, lock, stock, and barrel to Las Vegas, but Kenn and I knew that this was just an attempt to chase butterflies and it would never be the same. These plans also fell through when the owner lost his fight with lung cancer in 2007, less than a year after the bar closed. Perhaps this was simply another example of the old couple that has come to personify codependency. CBGB's and Hilly Kristal, the old couple that couldn't exist without each other.

But for Kenn and me, the demise of CBGB's was always just a stark reminder of all that was beyond our reach. The clubs, the bands, the gigs, the entire rock 'n' roll scene passing before our eyes with ambivalence, leaving us like voyeurs lurking in the shadows. Watching, fantasizing, wondering, but living a life completely inchoate as bands broke up, destroying our dreams that we would one day see them in concert. But CBGB's was something that Kenn and I clung to as the life preserver floating in the icy waters of what would always be unfulfilled dreams.

"OK, Kenn, seriously…you want me to believe that you've created a time machine?" Buying time, I tried to plot a course for a response, but was struggling, as one might. "It would be cool to travel through time to see gigs, but—"

"I'm not sure that you'll understand. It's sort of a science thing," he interrupted, "and...well...I suppose I sort of discovered it and didn't really create it."

"While I'm following you on the bit where you said that you 'didn't create a time machine,' you've got your work cut out to get me any further along in this discussion. Besides, buddy, you barely escaped high school with your diploma," I reminded him.

"Yeah, but I passed my sciences, with honors."

"But the only reason you passed science—"

"With honors," Kenn inserted.

"With honors...is because you threatened to tell the cops that Mr. Ward offered to sell you the drugs he had in his desk. Incidentally, the drugs that were in his desk were the very same drugs that he'd confiscated from you earlier that week."

"Yeah, well, after the cops raided the school, he was singing a different song, wasn't he," Kenn added.

"Sure, but that doesn't make you a scientist."

"Look at the transcript, dude. I've got potential. Besides, Albert Einstein failed science." Kenn never let this discussion go.

"OK, science guy, then you'll also know that any body at rest has potential as well," I continued, preparing for Kenn's dogged insistence of his science pedigree, without a degree.

"Huh?" Kenn asked, but really he was simply stalling.

"I said that I agree you've got potential. OK, so then how does it work?"

"It works great!"

"No, I mean what causes it to work?"

"Me. I cause it to work."

"OK, Kenn, so what you're saying is that you don't really know what triggers or controls the time machine?" I should have been used to these types of conversations, as they represented a fairly normal course of dialogue with Kenn, but still it was tiring and often served to obscure the original point.

"Of course I do. It's easy. It's like that dude Al said, E=MC5."

"What? Who's Al?" I asked in quick succession, my confusion mounting.

"You know the guy with the crazy hair that made all the nukes."

"You mean Albert Einstein? The guy who failed science because he didn't extort his teacher with drug possession charges?"

"Yeah, him."

"OK," I said as I rubbed my temples. "First, OK, crazy hair, fair call. But, he never actually made any nuclear weapons. He theorized about the energy that would eventually lead to the development of the nukes. The Manhattan Project made the weapons. Also, just a nit to pick on your formula, because I know that your experience with physics is mostly limited to falling out of bed, but it's E=MC^2. Energy equals mass times the speed of light, squared."

"Yeah, well, you're wrong about some of that shit," Kenn stated with authority. "I know for a fact that the nukes were built in the desert and not in New York. What kind of fuckwad would build shit like that in the city? As for the formula—wrongo bongo. It's E=MC5. The rock 'n' roll chord "E" applied to MC5 songs. MC squared? Seriously. Never was there such a band, and it's a lame name anyway. Maybe you're thinking of L7, from the slang for a "square." But it's MC5 from Michigan, forbears of punk and defenders of rock 'n' roll. And you're supposed to have finished college. Waste of fucking money, if you ask me."

But yet I hadn't asked. I knew better than to ask Kenn's opinion on college.

"And time," he continued, "time you could have used seeing gigs."

This was my life. These were the conversations that I found myself having. Of course Kenn was right. Unfortunately on both counts of the time and money wasted during college, and I had been on both sides of the argument before.

According to my parents I wasted my time at college going to gigs, programming a radio show, collecting music, socializing, and drinking beer. My parents didn't know about the money spent on drugs and merely assumed that I was wasting my time with girls. Disappointingly, this wasn't true. There simply was no opportunity to waste time on girls. Kenn and I seemed like a weapons-grade girl repellant. Probably because we were too complicated for girls to like us.

According to Kenn, however, by attending classes, completing my courses, and getting a degree, at the expense of not taking on more radio spots or going to more gigs and spending more cash on music, I was also wasting my time. However, for Kenn, the cash I spent on drugs and beer was more of a gray area than it was for my parents. Yes, my soul was often pulled in opposite directions.

"More like Lou Reed's 'Paranoia in the Key of E,' than the chord 'E.'"

"Huh?"

"Nothing. You were saying that I wasted my time at school, but you've fixed that now."

"Yes. Yes, I have. How are you going to repay me?" Kenn asked, seemingly forgetting our rich history together, but also managing to carry a conversation along two tracks, one being his alleged discovery of time travel and the other remuneration from me for sharing the discovery.

"I'll start by discontinuing this conversation," I concluded.

"I accept," Kenn agreed, but not graciously.

"So back to making this thing run. How does it work?" I asked, not unrealistically and trying valiantly to change the subject back to the original issue.

Kenn spoke with the confidence of sharing an observation that was so pedestrian that even a child could see it, as though it was a law of physics as simple as water flowing down hill due to gravity. "Yeah, you just load up *Guitar Hero* with MC5 tracks. Then we hit the 'E' chord, and off we go. You play a few chords and then we're hittin' the gravel off to a gig."

By this time, I am staring at Kenn, nodding patiently, as though I were actually following and even believing what he was recounting. "All right, I'll try anything once," I said. "Can I shout, 'Kick out the jams'"? I asked ambitiously.

"Next time," he replied quickly, as if he'd anticipated my question. I mean, who didn't want to yell, "Kick out the jams!" to start a song? For a rock fan, that's as good as being Moses and reading the Ten Commandments to the Israelites.

"OK, is this part of the payment?" I said, trying to bargain the best that I could. But how do you negotiate with a guy who's managed to convince you he can travel through time?

"The smallest part," he replied, conceding nothing.

"I'll count you in...," I offered. "One, two, three, four."

Kenn started the *Guitar Hero* track, hit and held the "E" chord, and the room started to shudder. The music seemed to reverberate from within us, and I started feeling disorientated. The walls started splitting at the seams, and light poured in and washed us out as if we were standing in an overexposed picture. Then I felt the force of a strong push as my body jerked backward. I started to worry that Kenn was right about being on the road. I started feeling like I was being pushed through pavement, instead we were just hitting the gravel.

3 – Hittin' the Gravel

Travel. It's something that we all do. We travel for obligations, like seeing family or seeking employment. To and from work. This is Radio KQPR FM 92.1, and I'm Sid sitting in this week for Fu Flux Flam, the self-described martial artist arsonist who normally fills this slot with culinary tips and rock 'n' roll. I can offer you good music, but don't count on me to help you be well fed.

Travel inspires us, teaches us, and binds us. We're a society that loves our cars, road stories, the nostalgia and romance of journeys short or long, and all types of transportation. Springsteen, Cormac McCarthy, Hunter S. Thompson, the Talking Heads, and the Killers take us through themes that are at once familiar and interesting to us because they relate to being on a journey. Even if travel is only a metaphor for the experiences we find around us.

Up next we've got the Supersuckers, who are Hittin' the Gravel. Fasten your seatbelt.

FCC transcript KQPR 92.1 FM 03.14.2008 1321
Operator comments redacted
Flag as: Watch

Hitting the gravel. Getting traction. On the road. Any one of these phrases were used to start our road trips with…well, at least until we had heard *The Sacrilicious Sounds of the Supersuckers* album; then it was always Hittin' the gravel. Like so many things in rock 'n' roll, it just made sense after we heard it. The phrase seemed to articulate, even embody, the act of going to a rock 'n' roll show. It was a course that was coarse. A general sense of where we were going and why. It was rough and dirty, which suited our circumstances. We were in a car that was barely roadworthy, littered, soiled with fast-food wrappers and soda bottles. It was all simply base. A part of the rock 'n' roll landscape and experience: It was just as we liked it.

"Watch-tha-fuck-out-asshole." I heard the voice with a distinctive accent, but couldn't see the person, as I was being shoved against a wall. I was disorientated and confused. It was dark, loud, and smoky. Where was I? As I started to steady myself, the floor seemed to fall away from the weight of my foot each time I set it down. There was a voice I could hear, apparently belonging to a rather large, surly, and longhaired guy with a well-worn leather jacket and Boston Bruins T-shirt. "If you can't handle your beer, ya betta get tha fuck out or at least watch where yar walking."

"Sorry," I begged off, "must be the beer. Sorry." I held my hands up with my palms facing him, in submission. Submission in the face of physical threats was a response that I had a good deal of experience with. Usually if the aggressor wasn't too belligerent, submission would work, but weakness in front of someone like Harv, well, that was just spraying naphtha into a fire. Gaining some space and figuring out why I was being pushed around seemed like a good idea, especially since I didn't know what was happening and my head was reeling in upheaval. Fortunately the hockey-cum-rock 'n' roll fan seemed to be more interested in making sure I didn't walk over him than giving me a beating. Consequently, he began to regard me with caution rather than with the potential for violence, as his attention drifted back to the front of the bar, and he allowed me to surrender space between us.

I was starting to remember what had happened, that I had been with Kenn in his basement listening to music. And we were discussing MC5 and…time travel? Kenn was showing me his time traveling discovery in his basement. Could it have worked? I certainly wasn't in his house any more, not that you could tell by the odors alone. Although the smell of stale spilt beer and human sweat was familiar, I didn't remember the smoke at Kenn's. In fact, we never smoked anything inside at Kenn's. The music was loud, but that wasn't uncommon for Kenn's house or mine or really anywhere civilized. Just like beer had to be cold and pizza warm, rock 'n' roll had to be loud. Smoke would damage and degrade the stereo equipment, so the little that we smoked, we always did elsewhere.

It wasn't just the smell of smoke and the aggravated dude who was preparing to do the mashed potato with my face that was different from being at Kenn's. There was something else, something about the music, not the volume, but the sound itself. The sound was different here. It wasn't just louder than it had been at Kenn's, but I could feel a certain rawness, of speakers being pushed to distortion or abused and worn out. Whatever the case may have been, the sound system certainly didn't engage Dolby noise reduction. Heathens.

Then, as my eyes began to focus better and my senses returned to me, I realized there was a band on stage. The music was live. I was at a gig. Somehow I had been flushed from the bowels of Kenn's house to the bowels of a rock 'n' roll bar. My steadiness and control over my senses started to wane again. Confusion and curiosity mixed as seamlessly as the guitar and bass line that I could hear, my heartbeat erratic, unlike the beat coming from the drum kit. Where could I possibly be? Not a MC5 gig like Kenn had promised, the sound I heard wasn't theirs.

The sound was raw, stripped back, but more finely crafted than the MC5. MC5 was to rock 'n' roll as the caveman was to the club. MC5 was primal and powerful, roughly hewn from whatever materials were at hand, but what I was listening to was more than just raw. Maybe *minimalist*? Still a club, but one fashioned from hand chosen materials and worked on a lathe or by a craftsman. Refined, but left feral. The contrasts only added to my confusion, sounding familiar and in fact known to me, a face that is recognized but seen out of context, preventing you from identifying or naming the person. My head felt as though it was going to splinter open.

Peering through the smoke and throng of bodies, I could see the band, but barely. Who were they? Why were they so familiar? It looked like there was a woman on stage, and three, no four, guys. The guitars were jangling, and the woman's voice was haunting. Was this the Velvet Underground? I thought that we were going to an MC5 show. I knew that the bands had a period of crossover during which they were both active and setting the groundwork for what would later be an important period in rock 'n' roll. But did they ever perform together? I didn't know. I was confused and still disoriented. Had I eaten anything out of Kenn's fridge? That usually set me off and was prone to cause anything from nausea to hallucinations, sometimes both.

Then, as I looked around and started entertaining the idea that Kenn had found a way to travel through time, I remembered that MC5 opened for the Velvet Underground in Boston sometime in 1968 or 1969. But I hadn't even been born yet in 1968. And I was born in Oregon, where Kenn and I still lived. Boston was on the other side of the country. My confusion and disorientation complete now, where was Kenn?

"Hey, buddy, ya a'right?" asked the guy in the Bruins T-shirt, suddenly concerned, although perhaps only slightly. At least his initial aggression was quickly subsiding.

"Yeah, not sure. I've got to find my friend, I don't really know where I am," I replied in a daze, rubbing my temples.

"Look, I don't want to have to bust your skull, I'm just here to see the show. Why don't ya get some water and sit down. I'm sure your pal will come find you. Or maybe one of those Panther hippies, if you're with them. But lay off the fuckin' beers," he said as he directed me to the bar and then disappeared, likely happy to put as much distance between him and whatever condition that I was in as possible, and hey, the Velvet Underground was on stage. This would be a historical night. Who wouldn't want to bask in that light?

I sat down beside one of the support beams that was located alongside some shallow riser steps that elevated the back of the bar about eighteen inches above the front and tried to force myself into believing that I was witnessing the Velvet Underground live. As predicted by the Bruins fan, before long Kenn walked over to me and asked, beaming, "How good is this?"

I thought about saying something about missing MC5, but then again I was watching the Velvet Underground at a period between their first and second albums, years before I was born and was facing such overwhelming emotions all I could do was shake my head. "Lou Reed," I said with an exhale.

"I told you it would be awesome. Drink this," Kenn said, while handing me a beer. In the first of what was to become a series of strange experiences, I realized that the term "awesome" was falling short of a proper adjective to describe traveling over twenty-five hundred miles and over two decades through a video game. Awesome could describe leaving Kenn's basement without a serious infection, but this?

40

Between songs, Lou Reed spat through his mic, "I'd just like to make one thing clear. We have nothing to do with what went on earlier and, in fact, we consider it very stupid." Sterling Morrison shook his head, and Nico looked distracted or embarrassed, maybe preoccupied, but certainly not impressed. Maybe she was just high.

"The White Panther Party debacle?" I said to Kenn.

"Yeah, people were talking about it at the bar. Talk about a gong show. I'd like them to try that shit at a Public Enemy gig."

"Well," I said getting sucked into the conversation the same way goldfish get trapped in an emptying drain, "I suppose that the name could have been considered insulting to the Black Panthers, but White Panther Party were in fact an anti-racism group that endorsed the Black Panther's platform. Also, its not as though Public Enemy would stand in the way of a bunch of seditious white guys."

"Yeah, I was thinking more about them getting on stage and interrupting a show," Kenn replied knowing that he was setting me off and deliberately trying to miss the point.

"Funny. You know this gig might have been the beginning of the end for Sinclair and MC5."

"Just as well," Kenn added, finishing a swig of his beer. "Do you remember what happened?"

It was an obvious question because we had missed seeing the actual events, but knew enough about the two bands to have read about the evening. Especially given the fact that the gig had been listed in various places as one of the most notorious performances in alternative music history. But more than playing catch-up, I think that Kenn was also trying to gauge my lucidity, which, given how I must have been acting, was also fair enough.

"Yeah, basically, some yokel commandeered the mic in order to exhort the audience to tear down the venue and burn it to the ground. It was unclear if the arson-baiting orator was actually affiliated with the Panthers, a friend of Sinclair's or just some random drunk. All the same, it was a lame thing to do. Just like the local anarchists back in Oregon that claim some laudable social objective to justify destroying property."

It was another example not just of how rock 'n' roll so often walked hand in hand with politics and social dissent but also of how hooligans can ruin a good time. American poet John Sinclair managed MC5 at the time. I'm sure initially Sinclair seemed like a good choice, with his deep interest in art and music. However, Sinclair was also sympathetic to Huey Newton's call for white people to assist the Black Panthers and thus became a founding member of the White Panthers. Unfortunately, his strident politic views caused disharmony and conflict rather than the social change that was sought. Incidents like that of this evening showed the White Panthers to be like any other dissent group, just like the G8 and World Trade Organization Summit protests and the "Occupy Manhattan" movement merely highlighted the common problem. Social dissent groups are effective at attracting members who want to take a stand, but more often than not the people participating are less invested in the issues and more interested in merely being antisocial. I had read about Sinclair, Newton, and the Panthers of the '60s, and while I understood their position, I could never understand it without experiencing the social context of the time. It was an aspect of history that I could never fully get over, but there we were, on the cusp of it now, but still lacking an understanding of the context.

"There is a difference between being antisocial and seeking social change," I said. "I wonder if people will ever learn that anarchy isn't the same as dissent."

"Would have never happened at a Public Enemy show," Kenn reiterated.

"OK," I conceded, feeling confused, elated, disorientated, invigorated, and in complete disbelief. "But it's still lame. It looks bad for rock 'n' roll and makes for an easy target for the Evil to identify that kind of behavior. It's inexcusable." Then changing the subject, I asked, "So, how do we get back?"

"After the show," he responded, transfixed by the stark minimalism of the Velvet Underground.

"Yeah, of course," I said. "I'm certainly not leaving *this* gig early, but I meant *how*, Kenn. How does it work to get us back?"

"I know what you meant. Like I said, after the show we just sort of end up back at my place."

Strangely, Kenn's answer actually made some sense, given our history with rock 'n' roll. After all, that was how most gigs ended for us, back at Kenn's. Even while he lived with his parents, we would return from a gig, buzzed out either on beer and a bit of weed or simply on a high from seeing a great show. We would convene in his parent's basement, spin music and bask in the afterglow of the rock concert.

This had been the usual practice, and it was only once that we had regretted returning to his parent's place, late, after seeing the Blasters. Even after that night, we would continue to end up at Kenn's because it was comforting or helped anchor the night for us. But we didn't discuss it. Some things simply just continue as they always do.

His parent's disapproval was obvious and resolute, probably as intractable as Kenn was himself. But it didn't change our behavior; it couldn't. This was rock 'n' roll, an energy that was vital to us. Kenn didn't seem to mind at the time, but then I suppose he didn't talk about it much either. Very little had changed since those first gigs. Of course our music collections grew and his place was his own now, and he didn't have to worry about what his parents...well he didn't have to worry about his parents.

Despite how much of a routine going to gigs may have been before, time travelling to a gig was significantly more complex than taking a bus to the university or piling in one of our shitty cars and catching whoever was passing through town. I needed a better answer about getting back to Kenn's, but as I sipped my beer more slowly than I ever had before, I also knew that I could wait. A lot of explanations from Kenn required waiting. This one seemed worth the wait, especially being in the audience seeing a young Lou Reed live.

It was an unfortunate part of my personality that always required an answer in order to process a situation or a set of facts. So, knowing how we'd get home was an important aspect of my evening. It was like deciding who was driving or what we'd do if we got separated. Not only did these decisions govern my conduct, but other considerations included how much we could imbibe or what would happen if Kenn or I hooked up with a girl from the bar—something that we hoped for but was such a long shot that bookies wouldn't even give us odds. However, this wasn't a night like any other, and some things simply are without explanation. Like the possibility of time travel. The Velvet Underground.

In fact, even later, crossing back to see the Velvets, I would be stunned into silence at what I witnessed. I would often wonder if I possessed the capability to recognize the influence that they would come to bear upon rock 'n' roll, if I didn't have the benefit of hindsight. It was very possible that I could be the kind of guy who would look around and say, *"Yeah, that Martin Luther King Jr. guy sure is a compelling speaker. Hey, look at all the people that have turned out to hear him..."* but then really think nothing of the greatness that I was beholding. Again, experiencing history without the proper context or the sense of how things will turn out. But now with the benefit of hindsight, I would go back and soak up so much more of the speeches or the energy of the marches.

Because you *know* what Reverend King stood for and because you *know* the impact that he made, if you traveled back through time, it would mean so much more. Wouldn't it? Everyone had dreams. It was the articulation of a dream, a dream of such scope and nobility that inspired so many others. The Velvet Underground may have started out modestly enough, but they had to be considered a Big Bang that started other bands. This wasn't a Million Man March; this was just a gig in Boston with a few hundred people. A gig that Kenn had brought me along to. An event that Kenn and I traveled through time and space to see, a fact that sounded outlandish when he first told me, but was now proving to be true. Whatever else was going on, it was clear that my little brain couldn't cope with the idea that Kenn had conveyed us through time and space. I had no basis upon which to process this information. How could I?

So, Kenn and I sat nursing our beers and finished our first Velvet Underground show without any further words. The gig in its own way stripped down to basic minimalism, a style that Lou Reed would later become legendary for. A style that, at least that night, mirrored the interactions between Kenn and me: There was nothing to say during the gig. Nothing to do at all but watch. No singing along, no dancing in the bar. For us there was only silent awe as the band performed, like cats watching birds through a window, transfixed but removed.

In the span of the evening, I barely finished the single beer that Kenn bought me and didn't move from my impromptu seat on the riser. I wish that I could say that I enjoyed the show, that like a dry sponge thrown onto a wet counter I soaked in the experience, but the truth is that I was so absolutely blown away with it all. I was more like a piece of granite. My mind simply couldn't process having experienced time travel, being in a Boston bar and being in front of a band that would spawn and motivate so many others. I was too overwhelmed to absorb more than the fewest details.

What songs did they play? Good question. I could tell you it was some of the first two albums, but you would know that by the date of the show, even if you weren't there. What was the bar like? I couldn't even tell you if they served beer, except I suppose they must have because Kenn brought me one. It was like suffering with the flu at an art gallery—you're so focused on your lack of physical control and the distraction of your body rebelling against you, that you couldn't comprehend anything else that existed around you, but had a vague sense of the color on the paintings. Lou Reed and Nico could have been singing naked, and I probably wouldn't have registered that it was weird. Sure, it was only rock 'n' roll, but how do you process time travel when you experience it firsthand? Trying to recall the bar, I suppose I remember some of the physical features, like the riser that I was sitting on, the dude in the Bruins shirt who I seemed to have antagonized, Kenn's quiet self-contentedness, the beer he gave me and the band. I remember all this in general terms, but like a black-and-white movie playing in the background. Context without detail or detail without context. Like such visual art, I knew where I was; I just couldn't process what I was witnessing.

Kenn was right, this was awesome. This was lightening in a bottle. This was learning that the earth was round. Inventing the gramophone, a cure for syphilis, and Gutenberg's press all rolled into one. Time travel. Science fiction's Holy Grail, now delivering rock 'n' roll to Kenn and me. There are things that are awesome like the Grande Canyon or sunsets; then there are things that are fucking awesome like sunsets over the Grande Canyon; then there is time travel granting you unfettered access to rock 'n' roll. No words to describe this at all.

The band finished performing "Here She Comes Now," so I guess that I remembered *one* song, and as you would expect, the house lights came on. People started to leave, and a few others remained at the bar ordering drinks as Lou Reed and John Cale lingered

45

onstage unplugging their instruments, talking to the throng of girls and getting ready to leave. I lost track of Kenn and felt a momentary panic of being alone in a strange city. But this was worse, because I was in a strange city *and* a strange time. My mental anguish and anxiety gave way to a more immediate physical concern as I felt a sudden unyielding constriction on my chest and pressure on my temples. Beneath my seat, under what I thought was a safe stair riser, started to lurch and heave. I was losing control over my senses, and everyone around me looked like they were spinning into a drain. What was happening?

Where was Kenn? I could feel air being crushed out of my lungs and what felt like a five hundred-pound monster standing on my sinus tract and temples, but taking care not to crush me. Thoughtful monster. I suppose it's a luxury that one has with a certain girth, but again I seemed distracted.

Suddenly, as the monsters tentacles were reaching into my chest to pull out the essence of my life though my nose, the air in the bar started feeling hotter, and I felt the ignition of a burning sensation that ran like a lit fuse down my spine. I wasn't actually in any physical pain, just debilitated by the constriction coupled with a hot sensation that ran the length of my body like a rolling marble. I could feel the pressure, but the impression simply moved along from one point to the next. The bar started to roll end over end, forcing me down to my knees in order to steady myself, closing my eyes and fighting for breath.

Slowly, I opened my eyes again and saw my hands clenched so hard that my knuckles were turning white and my palms were cramping. My lungs were pounding out heaving, deep breaths, on the cusp of hyperventilation, my pulse racing. I looked at what I was holding and saw the corner of the coffee table in Kenn's living room.

"Pretty cool, hey dude?" I could hear Kenn say in the distance. We were back.

I left Kenn's without a word, just a nod and a wave. Maybe it was a thumbs-up sign, I don't really remember, but I recall that Kenn let me go, handing me a Dew.

"The cold liquid and caffeine will help. Let me know when you're ready to talk about this, buddy."

Of all the things that Kenn and I had been through...

Kenn knew enough to let me go and knew I had a lot to process. Go figure, time travel. Actually time travel and rock 'n' roll. Processing the revelation of Kenn's discovery and potential implications actually took me three full days, after which I went back to his house to talk to him again. My understanding of the universe, albeit limited, had just been reduced to a seething mosh pit that was considerably difficult to reconcile.

But I knew that I had to talk to Kenn. We always returned to that, like the records that we played, regardless how long the song was, Kenn and I always got back to the start. Just like we did with other matters, we would with time travel.

I let myself back into Kenn's house, with a case of beer and two massive pizzas, one Hawaiian, perfect in its minimalistic simplicity, the other what we had affectionately called "The Kitchen Sink" or just "The Sink," because it had everything, except olives and those black anchovy fish things.

"OK, that was pretty cool," Kenn said, answering the lingering question from days ago. Strangely, I managed to match Kenn's initial characterization of "awesome" with my own understatement.

"We've got to give this some thought though, dude," I said, putting the pizzas down and handing him a beer. I opened my own beer and grabbed some paper towel, a couple of plates, and a slice of The Sink. We always had paper towel around; after all, our hands had to stay clean if we were going to handle vinyl. Oils from our hands and stains from food could be fatal to records.

"First of all," I said, "I thought that we were going to see MC5, but we didn't. Were they even in the crowd? The fact that we didn't see MC5 would seem to me that there is other potential for traveling to gigs, because ultimately we know that they opened for Velvet Underground."

"Yeah, I thought of that, too," he said. "But even limited to MC5 gigs I figured that time travel was pretty cool and we could live with it"

Did Kenn just say "limitations to time travel?", and with such a defeated and regrettable tone? Strangely, not as many limitations as I would have thought a week ago. Somewhere Jules Verne was spinning in his grave, or maybe he was walking over to tell Elvis, *"Hey, dude, seems like you really haven't left the building…"* I don't know if Verne would have said "dude," but I'm sure he and Elvis would have some interesting conversations.

"Maybe we can figure out a way to see other bands and not just those at the same gig."

Suddenly, a conversation with Kenn about time travel was as natural as eating Hawaiian pizza drizzled with Frank's RedHot. I thought about The Smith's final studio album, *Strangeways, Here We Come.* Strange ways indeed.

"I dunno, I can only get it to work with the MC5," Kenn replied with a mix of resignation and contemplation. Almost like he had somehow failed or fallen short, in creating time travel that was limited. Fucking guy. Rather than reveling in perhaps the greatest discovery of all time, here he was feeling like he had failed, because his time travel discovery could only interact with MC5 gigs. A twinge of pain for Kenn welled from within me. His ability to achieve remarkable things had always accompanied critiques of the shortcomings rather than the success. It was usually around his parents that I had seen this occur, but still now, after having discovered a limited form of time travel, he was counting thorns, not smelling the rose.

"How many times have you gone out or over or across, or… what do we call it?"

"Seven or eight. Not many," Kenn replied, "but except that time with you, I've always seen MC5 actually play. I think we'd call it 'across,' because we're crossing time and space. I know it's supposed to be a continuum and all, but to say forward and back sounds lame."

"Yeah, lame."

First, combining Frank's and pizza and now time travel with MC5. Surely there had to be a Nobel Prize in here waiting to be found. So we eventually decided, in our vernacular—time travel would be referred to as "crossing."

We talked about crossing and the feelings of going across for a while. Crossing was always the same for Kenn. He didn't feel the same disorientation, but he noticed that the room started to shudder and that the music seemed to resonate from within him. During the show he said that it helped if he had a beer—"you know, something to hold on to," he would say.

Surprisingly, at least to me, he said the first couple of times he went over he didn't drink anything. I tried to imagine Kenn at a gig without a beer, but simply couldn't. Rock 'n' roll without beer was like Hawaiian pizza without Frank's hot sauce. You could do it, but why would you? I mean we hadn't lost a war or anything.

I suppose I was going to have to expand my imagination now. There certainly was a lot happening. Maybe it wasn't my imagination that needed to be expanded, but rather my interpretation of the world around me. After all, it is the understanding of our world that creates the constraints that we in turn impose upon our imagination. It might have been the same as if I had just learned to walk on water, if I had learned to do the impossible.

"Hey, what are you doing? You can't walk on water." "But dude, I am." Of course I couldn't travel through time, yet Kenn and I had. But how? Because, dude, we were time traveling. We were discovering that the impossibility of time travel was simply just another lie.

Kenn's explanation started innocuously enough and with me nodding and smiling at him. I was nodding the way you would at an angry tourist who is trying to explain something to you, in an incoherent language, long after you've lost interest in trying to understand him. What quickly became obvious was that Kenn was startled the first time that he happened to find himself traveling through time (fair call) and didn't really know what to expect (also a fair call), so he thought it prudent not to drink during his journey. However, Kenn discovered that once he did have a beer or water or soda—something to hold onto—it made him feel more grounded, which is why he brought me the beer in Boston. Not only did this make sense, it actually worked. It probably worked better on me, because I tended not to travel even by car as well as Kenn did. In fact, even the few hours of time zone changes seemed to hammer me when I'd go on the rare family vacation when I was younger. So, you can imagine how I would be completely laid to waste gaining and then losing decades of time. Like always, I was glad to have Kenn as a friend to help me through this. Once again it was Kenn who was leading me into rock 'n' roll to a degree that I could never have anticipated.

Coming back after a show was different for Kenn than it was for me. "Yeah, I don't know dude, it's just like the show is over, I go to leave or walk through a doorway and then hey! I'm back, looking through my fridge because I'm usually hungry by then." In fact, he claimed that he would often try to leave the bar or hall or wherever the show was being played, through the door, and then find himself exiting his bathroom at home. Weird, but I suppose time travel would have to be.

We talked about the experience we had that night with the Velvet Underground and the potential options, until the pizza was cold and the beer exhausted.

"OK, science guy," I challenged, now feeling better and more capable, "you up for an experiment?" Somehow I always felt more empowered, more creative, and even more daring after a belly full of pizza and a few beers.

Kenn agreed and I proposed that we continue to try to time travel to gigs with the basic MC5 / *Guitar Hero* setup that Kenn had discovered, but with different modifications. MC5 was great, but if we could find a way to get to other gigs, this would be a truly inspired discovery.

With our expertise and knowledge of rock 'n' roll, we were motivated to see all that time travel could offer us…different periods of time, different bands, festivals, anything that involved rock 'n' roll. We tried a seemingly exhaustive series of combinations such as playing *Guitar Hero* while listening to other music or having the sound off on the game, trying demo mode; thinking about other bands that played with MC5 and trying to get to those gigs; wearing T-shirts from other bands; putting posters or concert fliers over the TV screen, but the result was always the same.

Regardless of what we tried, Kenn and I always ended up at a random show, with MC5 either on stage or having been. The venues were usually different, sometimes in Detroit, New York, or LA; others in London, Belfast, Paris; and others where we had no idea where we were. Sure, it was a little weird, a little frustrating, and sometimes disconcerting, but it just wasn't the outcome we were looking for. Not what we wanted but still not such a bad outcome. We saw MC5 a multitude of times as well as other bands such as Primal Scream, Cream, Big Brother, Blood Sweat & Tears, the Motherfuckers, the Stooges, the Doors, and the New York Dolls. Pretty tough to complain when you're seeing lineups like that. Oh yeah, and we were traveling through time and space through a video game, a pretty stellar discovery in its own right. Unlike the feral nature of rock 'n' roll that was part of it's appeal, we wanted to control time travel. We wanted to pick the gigs we'd see and when; a discovery isn't really much good until you can control it.

"I totally agree dude," Kenn commented. "It's cool that rock 'n' roll can't be controlled; it's like no one can ever claim dominion over it. But damn, I wish we could see other bands."

Ultimately, our relationship with music was symbiotic. Rock 'n' roll nourished us, provided the energy to pump our hearts to drive blood and oxygen through our bodies, and in turn we cultivated a knowledge of music and imparted our knowledge every chance we got.

"You know, I think our efforts make rock 'n' roll stronger. More accessible, vital, vibrant, and viable to the masses. Dude, this is an important job. Crossing is going to revolutionize our understanding of rock 'n' roll. Really, it's the least we should do considering the full life that rock 'n' roll has given us." Kenn enthusiastically continued.

I liked the idea of his world view and agreed that we should learn more now we had a vehicle that afforded us deeper access to rock 'n' roll. Like a backstage pass but to *any* gig or time period. If only we could control the travel, but in its current state, or perhaps due to our current understanding of crossing, it was an insolent child that refused to mind its parents—Kenn and me. What could be more frustrating to a parent? Kenn and I resolved to find a means to expand the potential of his discovery.

Sometimes we would enter into the venue right out of our crossing and others we would find ourselves outside having to pay to get in. It fascinated me to realize that we never ran out of cash, and if the gig wasn't too far in the past our credit cards would work, but cash was easy for access and beer and anything else really. Another great discovery, because our cash balances seemed to remain unaffected when we returned, as though the money had never really been spent, since we made sure only to use currency that was relatively new, on the premise that if it hadn't been printed yet, then it couldn't be spent in the past. The same theory applied to credit card purchases…well, at least after the first couple of times when Kenn happened upon another related and impressive discovery that would change our lives.

Returning from a crossing in which Kenn had used his credit cards for some beer, concert shirts, trying to impress girls, more beer, and an assortment of pizza and nachos, Kenn and I realized that we had just experienced the most expensive night we had ever endured. It was then that Kenn lighted upon the idea of challenging his credit card charges from our time travel. His idea was genius in its simplicity. He would call Amex and complain that they had an error in their system that allowed him to be charged for something with a date however many years in the past, sometimes even before he owned the credit card. It was impossible to argue against logic, that their system either missed a charge for years or was charging something to an account that didn't exist at the purported transaction date. OK, perhaps this wasn't as big a deal as time travel, but the two are related, and you have to admit it's still pretty good. Crazy like a fox that Kenn. Crazy like a fox.

It was weeks later nearing the end of my workday when I was listening to the Public Enemy / AC/DC – Black is Back / Back in Black mash-up that a solution dawned upon me that could expand the frustrating limit of our crossings. One of the only things that I liked about my job was that I could plug in and listen to music relatively uninterrupted. From time to time, my supervisor, Eunice, would require my attention, and she would trespass upon the musical oasis that I had manufactured at work. Eunice would come by with her dated '60s shag-styled hair and equally dated polyester suit skirt. However, it appeared that Eunice thought the key to her salvation was to be found in boxes full of baked breads and donuts. I could often smell the sugar and yeast on her and see the stains of various pastry fillings or brewed coffee on her clothes. Amazingly, she was almost physically fit, or so she insisted. To me, she looked like the adolescent hippo in polyester tailored to fit a forty pound lighter version of herself.

But it wasn't just about the baking for Eunice. To show all of us minions that she was "hip," on Fridays, when our corporate dictates regarding our dress were relaxed, Eunice would wear acid-washed jeans with a matching denim mini vest. While other employees mocked her for her fashion choices, I (ever reticent to join in on what could only be construed as bullying) assumed that acid-wash meant that they had forced you to eat LSD first and that in having a bad trip, the rest of her fashion decisions were explained. Even forgiven. Still, deconstructing Eunice, as much as I loathed her, was something which I couldn't abide.

But on this day, I had no such interruption from Eunice, and my audible cocoon was undisturbed. I was able to keep myself occupied in the government job that my father or one his friends had helped arrange for me, by entering and reviewing data collected by forestry officers on the health of the trees throughout Oregon. It wasn't great, but it paid for rock 'n' roll, and there were relatively few hassles. And so here, today, it was the unlikely marriage of Public Enemy / AC/DC, an arranged marriage in fact, by a rather talented DJ who grafted their music together in such a way that it was amusing and brilliant. Not only was the work inspired, but inspirational, and I had just been the beneficiary.

I called Kenn and told him to stay put (no crossing) until I got back. With that, I counted down the hours to the end of my day working for Big Brother and then anxiously drove to Seattle. The purpose of my mission was to look for Brian Alex and to seek his advice, not knowing if I would be able to find him or if he would even talk to me.

Brian Alex is of course DJ Scene, considered by most as one of the preeminent DJs at work today. DJ Scene was like Mikhail Baryshnikov or that girl figure skater that got beat with the pipe by the boyfriend of the other girl figure skater. I say that "Brian Alex is of course..." like it was common knowledge and that for me, just part of the array of stunning facts that I have at my disposal, but unfortunately this was not the case. While I did, in fact, have a dazzling knowledge of rock 'n' roll, "mixing"—the term for what DJs do—was not really part of that body of information that I had dominion over. I knew *generally* what was going on, but it was like saying that I knew Australia had claimed Antarctica and was mentioned by Modest Mouse in the album *The Moon and Antarctica*, but I didn't really know much else about it, including why Australia would be interested in claiming a large uninhabitable block of ice.

Fortunately, another advantage of my data processing job was that in order to actually perform my job, I required a computer. And given that I was rarely interrupted by my polyester-wearing, profoundly styled supervisor, I was able to research things on the sly while I was still at work. Some people called it slacking off or even stealing company time, but really it was the least that the Oregon Department of Forests, (or whoever actually paid for the work I was doing) could do for the cause of rock 'n' roll. You have to realize that forestry was a government job, and government, especially big government, was bad, and so exercising my Second Amendment rights of being free to oppose government, music and rock 'n' roll research on paid time was my act of civil disobedience. So, confronted with a question of mixing, I needed to research, and in so doing I discovered so much that would be helpful, mostly that DJ Scene was an expert and close at hand.

Brian represented an unquestionable talent. One which I didn't fully understand but had to admit was impressive. While not really my thing, you have to appreciate the talent, and more importantly, I needed his knowledge on mixing and the technology required. So, I sort of had to work up the right tone and level of awe in order to be believable when I met DJ Scene.

The drive up to Seattle dragged on for hours along the winding Pacific Northwestern highways, though the fog and rain. Even when the fog cleared, I failed to notice the natural splendor of the area, an area full of old-growth spruce, influenced both by the mountains and the proximity to the Pacific Ocean. This was an area that organizations like the Sierra Club fought to preserve for good reason. It was rich, abundant, relatively underpopulated, and treed with majestic specimens of coniferous trees. Campers sought refuge in its natural beauty, clean air, and screeching eagles. But not for me. I couldn't see any of it. My preoccupation and anxiety was resonating with the background noise of Echo and the Bunnymen. The car's tires kept beat with the throbbing bass lines of Shriekback or something with David J. The ventilation fan that kept the condensation away from the inside of my windshield screamed along with the guitars of Social Distortion or the Jazz Butcher. And that strange noise that I've never really deciphered became part of the cacophony of sounds generated by the Jesus and Mary Chain, or Public Enemy. Even still, I would ordinarily notice the synergy between the sounds. I'd notice different textures or samples when I was listening to music, especially on a long drive, but not this time. I was of singular focus and more than a little preoccupied with unanswered questions. Would Alex see me? After leaving work I spoke to him on the phone, and he sounded distracted when he had agreed to meet, but I wonder if he was even listening. Would this work? If it did, would I have figured out a further refinement for crossings? Could it really be that simple? What was the extent that Kenn and I could cross for? I wonder if I would make a difference or if could I unlock mysteries that had eluded me for all my life. Would I really improve upon Kenn's discovery?

On my way to see Alex, I developed a story that was both simple and believable. Or so I hoped. Basically, I wanted to sample *Guitar Hero* tracks and mix them with other sources in my collection as a form of art. This would then become an expression of modern art mixing media and sources into an overly textured experience, allowing the viewer to encounter multiple stimuli in a new form. "Look, dude," I would later say with a casual confidence, "the hope is that I can get it all pieced together and then take it down the coast to SFMOMA by the end of the year. I can run a few days of exhibiting and then some surfing for a few as well." Right, I had never surfed, but I had been to San Francisco, so the story sounded good. Besides, I knew that the San Francisco Museum of Modern Art allowed all sorts of strange and different things to be exhibited.

Over the phone I had explained to him that I was new at it all and really didn't have a clue what mixing was all about, but was an avid collector. Like any good music lover in Seattle, Brian agreed to meet me for the price of a cup of coffee and some tips on new music. Surprisingly, DJ Scene actually showed up to meet me, perhaps for the free coffee, but I knew that it was a start, and I was very optimistic because of it.

We met at Pike Place, where I bought a couple rounds of coffee and offered up some views on the latest efforts of Australia's the New Christs, and Hoodoo Gurus, both of whom had returned to active duty after a long hiatus. Brian, like most people associated with the music industry, was immediately suspicious of me. Question the motives that may have been lurking behind my questions. He was guarded and reserved, which I expected, so I took my time. As I was talking to Brian, I thought about my father trying to teach me to fish. Catching something was about patience and timing. It wasn't so much what he said, but how he said it. Or how he would repeat questions, but in a slightly different manner, sometimes injecting other bits of information.

"So, you want to start DJing?" Or, "Where did you first hear me spin?" Some of the things that I had explained that could easily have caught me in a lie.

Although it was exasperating to endure this on my limited coffee and snacks budget, it was understandable that Alex be guarded. Anytime someone achieves success, he attracts a certain number of people who want to emulate him or try to detract from his success. But eventually Brian agreed to help me out and actually thought that the idea sounded cool. So here I was, a completely random clown asking a bunch of questions that I barely understood myself and was sure could be seen through like the plot of a Jackie Chan movie, still I let my reel spool out.

"No, dude," I would sigh, "I'm trying a new form of art. To see if there is a synthesis possible between different inputs derived from *Guitar Hero*. I've never listened to a DJ spin. I come from a small town in Oregon," I would reiterate as a partial truth. "Look, I'm desperate to get out of Oregon and to San Fran. I love music, and I think that this multimedia platform is novel enough to get me an exhibit spot. Even if it isn't, it will be pretty cool to try."

This was certainly a better truth than Kenn and I thinking that DJing was an abomination. Lures and lies are really the same. I've always been an advocate for the truth, but perhaps not bashing someone with it, especially if that would dissuade him from helping you. But this is how I gained Brian's confidence. Bit by bit, coffee by coffee, and through offering my knowledge of bands that he was unfamiliar with. I was seeking knowledge from Brian, and he knew it, but I was also sharing. It was the sharing that eventually warmed him to me.

When he turned out to be really cool, I added comments about the old rooArt label-based Trilobites, and Tales Tall and True bands, for good measure. On his advice I rushed away from our finished coffee and bought a Yamaha MW12 mixing table. Also on his advice, I was able to find an electronics shop within a few blocks from where we had met, and soon I was hurrying back to Kenn's house feeling like Santa might with a sleigh full of gifts.

Seattle is nice, but with a little luck I would be back seeing grunge shows there very soon. But way back. Back to the first Nirvana gigs to resolve a lifelong mystery of mine. Finally, I would be able to count the people who actually saw them in the little bars they frequented before they made it big with their fortuitous appearance on *Late Show with David Letterman*. Immediately after airing on *Letterman* more people had claimed to have seen the band "before they became big" than was possible given the capacity of bars that Nirvana played. I suppose people always want to be in at the beginning of a big thing, like emotional investing—buy low and sell high. For me, as long as someone was onto a band, it didn't matter when they got on. The Clash are still selling albums and creating new fans. These fans can't have all been in London when it started, and it doesn't make them more or less cool because of it.

While I was aware that I drove back from Seattle, I couldn't tell you anything about the drive. Like my drive up, and my crossing to inadvertently see Velvet Underground, I was too distracted by the task at hand and the potential that was sitting on the seat beside me in the Yamaha box. As distracted as I was going to see DJ Scene, I was even more distracted on the way back to Kenn's. My brain was reeling with the possibilities, the effects of being over-caffeinated and having spent too many hours in the rattling disaster that my Ford Escort represented. My back was stiff, my ass flat, but all I could think about was Kenn. And rock 'n' roll.

I exploded into Kenn's house to find him listening to a podcast from some university in California, maybe Riverside, but it didn't matter. "Wha' tha' fuck?" he said, looking at the box under my arm. Fear spread across his face like I was no longer his friend, but rather coming through his doorway like a member of a tactical unit or part of a zombie hoard.

"No. Fuck. Is that a—"

"Listen," I interrupted, knowing where he was headed, "you can be a hater or you can stay with me, and try to keep up. I think this will work. I know your feelings about mixing tables, but this may be the missing piece. If not, it goes on eBay."

While acknowledging their place in the rock 'n' roll universe, Kenn wasn't a fan of mixing, not withstanding that it was basically the same technology that producers used to create studio recordings, just on a smaller scale. In fairness, I really didn't give Kenn much of a chance. Having consumed my third Super Big Gulp, a mix of Mountain Dew and whatever cola was on tap, solidifying my caffeine fix of the day and adhering to my enthusiasm for my pending experiment, I was the linguistic equivalent of a rhinoceros driving a steamroller.

"Or if not eBay, you can host ravers," Kenn added with obvious disdain. I ignored him.

The theory I had was simple. DJ Scene was right, setting up the MW12 was straightforward. I commenced connecting the mixing table to Kenn's audio equipment, on different input channels, and within minutes we had the *Guitar Hero* game console with the output from the Yamaha running through the USB port on Kenn's iMac.

"OK, where do you want to go?" I asked. "Let's pick a band that never played with MC5."

Ultimately, the idea was to feed other songs through the *Guitar Hero* game console, rather than the MC5 tracks that were part of that release of the game. If it worked, then we would be able to use *Guitar Hero* as a throughput device with the mixing table and have the ultimate output device as Kenn's iMac.

"Sade," he replied.

Again, Kenn amazed me. His suggestion was genius in its simplicity. Sade would be a good show, and there was no chance that she would play anywhere near an MC5 gig. I suppose that they could both be in New York at the same time, but along with a billion other people, what was the harm?

"Nice one," I said. "Count it out."

Kenn hit the "E" chord, and again the walls started to split at the seams, and light poured in, and then I felt the floor give out under my weight. I opened my eyes to see what had happened. There was a breeze in the air that felt like a fan blowing the air from a steam room on me, and the ground was soft. Looking down I saw sand, and instead of the stale air of Kenn's home I was struck by a waft of something soft and fragrant. Flowers, maybe? A gentle hint of salt water spray as well? In the distance and over the gently rolling surf, I could hear Sade's siren-like voice crooning "The Sweetest Taboo."

We had done it. We had found a way to unlock any gig that we wanted to see. Kenn and I, through a series of trials, had kicked his original discovery wide open.

I kicked off my shoes and turned to find Kenn with an impossible smile on his face. "You go up to the show if you want, buddy," I offered. "I'm gonna put my feet in the surf and listen from here."

As Kenn headed up to the show, I laid on the sand, reflecting what we had accomplished. We had transcended time and space. I know that Kenn considered himself a scientist, but real scientists with considerably greater education and experience hadn't uncovered the puzzle of time travel. Most hadn't even seriously *considered* this puzzle. More importantly, we found a way to participate in rock 'n' roll shows that were otherwise lost to us. Now bands that were defunct in bars that were closed would fall at our feet, like flower petals at the feet of Roman gods.

I was anxious to see Sade live, but I was now in some Caribbean paradise, with her music in the background. Outdoor venues are great for music, but sometimes it's about the other experiences as well. This was pretty great. More importantly, a sea of changes that we couldn't possibly predict was coming in with the crashing waves, and we were going surfing.

Once again it was obvious that one never knew where the next innovation or inspiration would come from. In a song about the inventor of the bicycle kickstand, Darren Hanlon asked, "What chicken laid the egg from whence inside an idea hatches?"[1] One just never knows, but like the chicken and the egg, changes are inevitable. Thinking back, I have often wondered if Hanlon invented the kickstand or merely introduced it to Australia, like so much of the Greek technology taken from Egypt. I should make a note to research that the next time I'm at work.

Regardless of who invented what or which beach I was lying on, I was sort of halfway listening to Sade. It was clear that Kenn and I were on the cusp of something monumental. For the first time in my life, I realized that these events would bring to our lives a series of changes. Strange changes.

---

[1] "The Kickstand Song" – Darren Hanlon, from the album *Hello Stranger*

4 – Changes

Welcome to Radio KQSF FM 91.1. This is a change from what you'd normally expect from a radio intervention. I'm not going to talk. The FCC requires station identification and the time, which is now one thirty-three, Monday morning.

Changes are good, as long as you embrace them. You don't even have to expect them. Just welcome them, like a stranger at your door.

I'm Sid; you may not agree with me, but let's hear what David Bowie has to say.

FCC transcript KQSF 91.1 FM 04.11.2001 0133
Operator comments: compliant programming –
complaint not supported

Changes. It's true that time changes all things. Time changes people, and sometimes people change with the times. Time passes people like mountains of granite, changed but inflexible. Crossing as often as we could, Kenn and I faced an avalanche of changes. Changing our understanding of our world; changing how we perceived opportunities, situations and history; and most importantly, changing our rock 'n' roll perceptions. Crossing through time allowed our knowledge and understanding of rock 'n' roll to escalate profoundly.

Kenn would say, "Exponentially." Maybe that was true. I always struggled with math, so I simply deferred to him on such matters.

I was confident that Kenn and I would adapt to these changes and move with them together. There was simply nothing to indicate that we wouldn't. Certainly, Kenn and I had been through our share of adventures and misadventures before this. So why would this be any different? We didn't really have any other friends, and this was all about rock 'n' roll, so there was nothing to suggest that we wouldn't remain as united and strong as we had always been. Nothing I suppose, but my own arrogance and naiveté, but I guess history would judge; it always does. But that analysis would be for a different time and a different place. For now we were considering our future in the past.

Buoyed by our initial success, we eagerly expanded our musical experience from merely listening to albums to going to shows. This was really no different from how we started out so many years ago huddled over Kenn's radio listening to college radio shows. Of course everyone remembers his or her first gig. There is something wild about it. The jostle of the crowd, the din of people waiting for something to happen, but without urgency or purpose, until their anticipation is dissipated by the crackle of a guitar being plugged into an amp. Kenn and I were no different. Our first rock show was seared into us like a brand. Unfortunately for us, it was the Mountain Bends, a joke based on the fact that the band was from Bend, Oregon, a town as small and isolated as ours. However, the joke didn't end there. The band played a two-set engagement with a mix of uninspired covers and horrible original numbers. It was dreadful. A Vincent Van Gogh cutting off his ear kind of bad. The guys were out of step from each other. The guy screaming into the mic was out of key, as were most of the instruments, and the drummer continued to lose the beat like it was a handful of ball bearings on a concrete floor. In short, I struggled to find anything redeeming about the performance, and they were probably only there in an attempt to get free beer on a Friday night.

The band members themselves were individually terrible and collectively a disaster. Not unlike many local bands, the members of the Mountain Bends did not go on to better acts. They became schoolteachers, river guides, farmers, accountants, and anything but musicians. But they were five guys who loved rock 'n' roll, and for Kenn and me, that was enough. That's why we found redemption in the evening, redemption in a shared love of rock 'n' roll.

Redemption for the band was only one part of the night for us; everything else was about the rock 'n' roll experience. After all, we were at some bar with a name based on a clever double entendre, but still lame. You know the type of place with a name that actually doesn't make any sense, like "The Pot Hole" or "Pole Position," the sort of names that would make you roll your eyes and keep your distance from. Places that Kenn would call "the fairy tale distance," as in far, far away. But notwithstanding the lousy bar name and the fecal band, the energy was electric. It was a rock 'n' roll show. It was loud, boisterous, smoky, and dark, with the sour smell of human odor mixed with spilt beer and other liquids drying; becoming sticky on the floor beneath your shoes.

It was sort of like Kenn's basement but with other people there. There was a strange feeling of being anonymous, yet in an intimate setting and being part of something collective. An experience that was complete on its own like the late-night music sessions with Kenn. You didn't need to talk to anyone, but with a nod or a smile, you could communicate that you were part of the same shared experience, with a bar full of people you didn't know, some you'd recognize, and others you had never seen before or might never again.

As good as it was to listen to recorded music through a perfectly modified and setup stereo, live music was so much better. It was the difference between seeing a photo of the mountains and hiking them. Between seeing the image and breathing the cool crisp air, feeling the softness of dirt compacted beneath your feet and listening to the wind whistling through the trees and pulling at your clothes. Rock 'n' roll, like holding a loved one, needed to be experienced personally, and that's what live music has always provided. This is what live music has always meant to me. Kenn and I returned to the intoxicating embrace and pounding beat of live rock 'n' roll every chance we got.

Of course we were hooked. Between gigs and recorded music, Kenn and I simply wouldn't ever have enough money to do everything we wanted. Growing up, our parents thought that rock 'n' roll was a waste of money, so our meager allowances were never sufficient for gigs, and later we faced other financial constraints as adults. Again, an example of our rock 'n' roll existence reflecting the human condition of scarcity in the face of desire. Does anyone really have all that they want?

So, like most people, this problem was overcome by setting priorities. Kenn and I would never buy the same album as each other, except in rare cases, like when the Creeps finally released *Now Dig This!* in North America; when the Celibate Rifles released *Blind Ear*; or, when the Clash gave us *London Calling*. There were other albums, too, but they had to be colossal efforts. We're not talking about *Rattle and Hum*, but albums like *Deserter's Songs* or *Seven Seconds*. Similarly, we would never see the Mountain Bends again, even if they played again, and there was no indication that they would. We would spend our few dollars on seeing good acts when we could, and we just couldn't justify wasting money on bands that were just going through the motions. Unfortunately, not a lot of good acts came through our town and certainly nothing big. We would never host the Cure, Nirvana (at least not after they became worth seeing), Lou Reed, or David Bowie. Instead we would get the acts that lived close by or were simply hungry for gigs. These were still great bands and even better gigs. Bands like Hüsker Dü (and later, Sugar, and Bob Mould), the Supersuckers, Canada's D.O.A, who hailed from nearby Vancouver and toured like they owed Satan money, or Blue Rodeo, who, quite frankly, seemed to just love touring through the mountains and looking for an excuse to linger.

Before we discovered crossing, Kenn and I would do whatever we could to get into shows. We would save money, volunteer, or even sneak in to venues. Sneaking in seemed riskier than it actually was, largely because the acts that we managed to sneak our way into were small and relatively insignificant. But we learned a few tricks along the way, and the easiest way to work our way into a gig without paying was to arrive early, go to the loading bay, and start moving equipment. No one would ever turn down an extra set or two of helping hands. It was like we were the Samaritans of rock 'n' roll. But just in case, we would say that "we're with the band," and that would provide us with safe passage for the night. Sometimes we'd even get a laminated guest pass.

I would like to say that we would brag about this later or that it provided some cache, but Kenn and I didn't really have anyone else to tell these stories to, so really we only did it for the sake of seeing rock 'n' roll up close and personal, while stretching our chronically limited budgets as far as we could. That was how it used to be for two guys from a smallish Oregon town struggling to shoehorn as much rock 'n' roll into our worlds as we could.

But like all things rock 'n' roll, it was more than a chance to merely watch gigs. We were now actively participating in rock 'n' roll. Now it was like collecting a midstream sample of rock music any time we wanted. Suffice it to say, we were becoming immersed in our passion.

I would like to say that we started modestly enough, but that's not really true. Was there anything modest about rock 'n' roll? What about time travel? No, that's probably not fitting with what most people would consider modest, either. Perhaps the closest that we got to a modest start was crossing to see Modest Mouse, but even that wasn't modest, it was great. Big walls of sound, haunting lyrics and jangling guitars, it was all there. It was almost as though rock 'n' roll had now been laid before us, just so we could soak up as much as we wanted, and while Modest Mouse wasn't that old, the really cool thing about time travel was that all Kenn and I had to do was wait for two conditions to be satisfied: A band had to record music and they had to play live.

First, a band needed to have recorded music in some form, obviously. This would allow us to feed it through *Louis Louis*—the name Kenn gave to the mixing table.

"So, what are we doing with *Louis Louis* tonight?" Kenn taunted, doctoring his Hawaiian with Frank's RedHot.

"*Louis Louis?*" I asked, not understanding that I was taking the bait, partially because Kenn was usually obtuse and partially because I had turned my attention to the dilemma of deciding if I wanted a Dew or a beer. "Are we looking at cover versions tonight, maybe comparing the oft-covered Richard Berry classic? I think we've got the Motörhead and the Stooges versions, but I'll have to see what else. Iggy Pop did it without the Stooges, and then there are also the various Black Flag renditions. I don't think it's gonna make a long session, though. Doesn't it seem inconceivable that we don't have a version by the Cramps? Surely they must have covered that some time."

"No, Dick," Kenn smirked. "I'm not talking about the Kingsmen or Richard Berry's original. I'm giving a nod to Lucifer. As in the fucking mixing table is an implement of Satan. Are we going to cross tonight or what?" And with that, Kenn launched into an uninspired commentary on his views of mixing.

"Yeah, we're crossing," I replied, attempting to get him back to the music and away from how my mixing table came to be called *Louis Louis*.

The second condition we required was that the band must have performed somewhere. Obviously, this was so that we would have a time and place to travel to. Both conditions were easily achieved, especially as podcasts and other digital media were developing to make it easier for bands to record and circulate their music without needing to be signed to major recording contracts.

You might say that we were wasting our time going to gigs—people always said that—and perhaps wasting the opportunity afforded to us with time travel, but keep in mind two things: For Kenn and me, time travel was about the gigs, about rock 'n' roll and nothing else. Not just because that's what Kenn and I liked, but the function of the time travel was actually tied to the gig or the band. This never changed, regardless of what band we went to see. We would arrive shortly before the show and then cross back once the gig was over...well, at least initially. But for us, time travel was only about rock 'n' roll and not *carte blanche* to mess around with the fabric of history. Which is just as well. Changing history isn't something that should be undertaken lightly, even by guys as incredibly knowledgeable as Kenn and me.

Notwithstanding how clever we thought we were, and really, we were pretty clever having discovered time travel, we also knew that time was the very basis of life. It was the measure of all things. Something that provided an order, a benchmark, or means of comparison. Not only did time underscore every-thing, it was still something that we couldn't really control, even though we had managed to travel through time. Just like the weather, you could predict it to some degree, harness its energy and enjoy its fruits, and you could even prepare for it, but you were never going to control it. That's why picnics and sailing are always adventures. So is rock 'n' roll.

Weather...time travel...rock 'n' roll...all untamable beasts. May-be that's why Kenn and I loved music so much. Besides, we were just happy being able to choose the shows that we wanted to see.

So I should probably say that it was the *planning* of the cross-ings that started modestly enough. We would collate our music collection and then start setting up the mixing table. Once *Louis Louis* was in place, Kenn and I would pick our gigs, queue the music, and then we'd enter through *Guitar Hero*. How could it be any easier than that?

At first it was the classics—the Cramps, the Dead Kennedys, the Ramones, the Clash, the Four Tops, Wilson Picket, Otis Reading, and whatever else we would round up. Think of a classic act, and we were there. I even made Kenn cross for the Kingsmen just to give him some stick about naming the mixing table. No band that had left a mark on the history of rock 'n' roll remained unobserved. Then we'd pick random bands as the mood struck us, or sometimes we'd go through them alphabetically or use an approach that was more research driven…you know, maybe to confirm something that someone had said about some show, or to see who was in the lineup during which live shows. Kenn and I were dedicated, and that was the sort of information that made us better, stronger, more knowledgeable, readier to serve the great cause of rock 'n' roll. We were always crossing and expanding our knowledge, learning more and more about the bands that we loved and discovering other bands that we hadn't heard of before. We were armed to the teeth with ways to enter rock 'n' roll, and *Louis Louis* was working as hard as the devil that Kenn had named it after.

As we discovered the various combinations and permutations of live music, our experiences richened. It was as though we were becoming genealogists of rock 'n' roll. The premise was simple, really. We would select a band that we wanted to see—either from our collection or from the opening act at the gig we'd end up at—and then follow their progress. So, we would see MC5, then we would continue on to the New Race, as MC5 members split onto other projects. We were so impressed by former Radio Birdman front man, Rob Younger, when we saw the New Race, we followed him to the New Christs and into his various studio credits with Australia's Citadel records, to experience the bands he produced like Died Pretty, the Lime Spiders, and the Celibate Rifles or bands such as HITS, the Angry Mob, or Triptyched Out, that the New Christs played alongside of. Of course we also saw the Radio Birdman. You wouldn't go back in time to see ancient Egypt without trying to at least glimpse Cleopatra bathing, would you? Nevertheless, following Rob Younger was simply one example of a path we took through *Louis Louis*.

The process was similar to how genealogy paths veer off, split, and rejoin, and take you for a ride beyond anywhere mere imaginations could go. The journeys exceeded anything we could expect, notwithstanding the almost daily expansion of our ability to imagine new possibilities. We followed band members from the Cure, Split Ends, the Small Faces, Joy Division, and various others. Some were short trips like with Velvet Underground's Sterling Morrison, but others, like Elvis Costello, David Bowie, and Brian Eno seemed to have no end…at least until Kenn and I could figure out how to travel into the future. But there are no plans for future travel. There isn't really any rush for that. The past has more than enough to keep us busy.

We saw bands that were really very good opening for even better bands. In some snow-gripped city in Canada, by pure coincidence, we saw a local band, Color Me Psycho. The only Canadians that can spell "color" correctly. Yeah, fucking Canadians and their "ou" sounds. "About" becomes "a boot." And then they have to add a "u" to words like "color" and "neighbor" when the words are just fine being spelled properly. Don't get me started.

Well, notwithstanding my well-founded and completely justified contempt for Canadian bands, we found ourselves crossing to see Hüsker Dü. It just so happened that Kenn and I arrived in Canada—a fact that we only discovered when we received some silly-looking colored money as change for the beer we had bought—and discovered that not only did the beer boast a higher alcohol content but that Color Me Psycho was opening for Hüsker Dü and both bands were excellent live. Loud guitars, creepy, haunting keyboards and lyrics we couldn't comprehend. All excellent, and Canadian to boot. Again, why the fucking Canadians say "a boat," I'll never understand. But it could have just been that Kenn and I had discovered another exception to the rule that all Canadian bands sucked.

At any rate, Color Me Psycho became the Forbidden Dimension and then a solo act, and the various lineups changed through the years, with members coming in and out of various other bands. Kenn and I followed them all. Some had modest careers, and some ended prematurely. All of this seemed so inherently unfair when acts like Celine Dion (also Canadian, but without the "ou," maybe because she's French) had the benefit of titanic marketing efforts that managed to parlay something mediocre into a self-sustaining industry.

Again, the human condition found in music, life imitating art. Rock reflecting the human struggle. Isn't it true that the best don't always rise? Isn't that what Malcolm Gladwell's book *Outliers* shows us? Success is more than pure talent or luck or whatever, but rather the combination of it all in the exact proportions at the right time. How did bands become huge like U2, while other equally apt acts like the Died Pretty or the Rheostatics remained virtually unheard of? Well, I suppose that in the case of the Rheostatics, it was because they were Canadian, but they didn't suck the way other Canadian bands did. Rock 'n' roll was good for that, and that's what made Kenn and me so complicated: all the thinking that we did.

We saw some shows that changed our views of things. Like finding the only two good Canadian bands or other unknown collections of talent, bands that we had never heard of, but that were actually good. We also found out things that related to the world at large and things about other musicians, even ourselves. Not unlike most people, we had our distinct preferences and we bandied them around like a favorite Frisbee or beach ball. But soon these discussions became irrelevant. What was the purpose of picking a favorite when you had unfettered access to a vast array of options? Why pick five "must-see" gigs when your opportunities were endless?

Our views changed in other ways as well. Picking up on the list from the movie and novel *High Fidelity* of "Top Five Bands or Musicians Who Will Have To Be Shot Come the Musical Revolution,"[2] Kenn and I had our own list and our own views. Hornsby was pretty close, but we would let Simple Minds and U2 off the hook and add Tom Cochrane and Don Henley. We would add to this list and construct purges in our minds like Public Enemy storming the stage during a Vanilla Ice show and tearing out 'nilla's spine as a reminder and warning to all. In the background the rolling spoken word / jazzy dialogue of Gil Scot Heron would play, announcing that "The Revolution Will Not Be Televised" and that all impostures, poseurs, and garbage acts would not be tolerated or condoned. However, even these views changed unexpectedly during our crossings as well, teaching us to temper our judgments.

One night, Kenn and I were in a crummy little bar in Godhasforgottenwhere, Texas, with the dry cold February wind buffeting through the cracks around the windows and doors of the bar. Outside was miserable, not the snow and wet that would send you shivering to find a warm hearth or at least pizza and beer at Kenn's, but a biting wind that swirled dust everywhere, both peppering you with particles and sending a chill into the marrow of your bones. But that was outside; inside, Kenn and I were enjoying a Mojo Nixon show with a Texas-sized plate of

---

[2] Nick Hornby, *High Fidelity* (New York, Penguin, 1996), p. 160

nachos and some beer. Nachos are a fair substitute for pizza. It was a good crossing. Kenn and I had found ourselves at the back of the bar, between sets, so we didn't have to hear the warm-up act but had time to look around the bar that was cluttered with neon beer signs, stickers, old license plates, and lone star badges. From what Kenn and I could tell, this was our kind of place, except that it was in Texas. Still, it was a place that catered to rock 'n' roll and served beer and some limited selection of bar food, all without pretense or glamour. There were a couple of bartenders, but refreshingly, they were busy serving patrons and not trying to be discovered as the next big model or movie star.

By the time Kenn and I were onto our second or third, maybe even fourth beer the show was well under way. Mojo was good. Funny, with short interventions and some limited discourse with the audience, but nothing to distract from his music, and he was rolling through all his material. Suddenly Mojo rounded into his somewhat controversial hit "Don Henley Must Die," causing a fracas to erupt at a table in the far corner of the bar. Kenn and I looked past the tired and threadbare pool table over to where five, maybe six or seven guys had been sitting around a table of predominately empty beer pitchers, a couple still unfinished, in front of them. Surprisingly, the din of the guys yelling and knocking over their drinks rose above Mojo Nixon, as the bar's attention turned to the disturbance as one of the group appeared to be struggling against the restraints of his companions.

I say "surprisingly" because this wasn't really the sort of thing that occurred at a Mojo Nixon gig. Maybe All or Sons of Freedom or Soundgarden, but not Mojo Nixon. I mean if you were there, you typically knew what you were in for. Songs about "Debbie Gibson's Two-headed Love Child," a girlfriend who was "Vibrator Dependent", or the revelation that "Elvis is Everywhere." You just couldn't find yourself at a Nixon show without expecting to hear these songs, and if you were going to be offended, then why would you go? Mojo is controversial and juvenile, and Billy Graham is a Christian—if you're not interested in what they're serving up, there's no reason to stop in. So why the rowdiness now?

Suddenly the restrained patron broke free of his friends and started rushing to the stage. Kenn and I were agape with the fury of activity. Should Kenn or I intervene? Probably not, and not really our style, even if we hadn't agreed to observe history only, without interference. Besides, even someone with the most cursory of rock 'n' roll knowledge would have immediately realized that the patron rushing the stage was the object of Mojo's ridicule. Storming the stage like an FTA agent was Don Henley, who, with unbridled emotion, seemed to be of singular purpose. Kenn and I were witnessing Don Henley himself, rushing to the stage during a song about why he should die. We were going to see Mojo kick Henley's ass onstage. This was going to be awesome. Kenn and I started moving toward the stage as the crowd started forming a ring like we were at a cockfight. All that was missing was someone booking odds and taking bets.

This was a small venue, so there were no barricades or security personnel, and consequently Henley immediately found himself onstage with the ease of Hugh Hefner scoring at the Playboy Mansion. Then…silence. The bar stopped moving as though the power had been abruptly cut off. Mojo seemed trapped, staring at Henley in stunned silence like he was caught in the searchlight of an UFO, while everyone else was waiting for what had the making of a good ol' Texan confrontation, complete with the dry winter wind whistling in the background. There was no question that Henley had the drop on Mojo. In fact if Mojo had been shadowboxing odds makers would have picked Mojo's shadow and not him.

But he didn't. This wasn't *Fight Club* or Octagon fighting; this was rock 'n' roll. A place that is as wild and untamed as Texas of old. No, Henley didn't lay a hand on ol' Mojo.

Instead, Henley called out into the mic, "Hey, Mojo, may I cut in?" handing Mojo a fresh beer and replacing the mic into the stand. As Henley started to *lead* Nixon in "Don Henley Must Die." Instantly, like the returning birdsong after a rain, everything sprung back to life again, and Mojo performed an impromptu duet, albeit noticeably perplexed. The song ended, and Henley sent Mojo another beer and rejoined his table.

"Shit. Maybe Don Henley isn't so bad after all," Kenn commented.

"Yeah, bad or not, he's certainly found his way off our list for the musical revolution. I didn't see that coming, did you?"

But it was more than Henley being granted amnesty for the eventual musical revolution that we felt sure was forthcoming. His actions planted the seed that gave Kenn and me cause to rethink our views of the world. But even that seed, freshly plant-ed, would later grow for us to explore and enjoy its fruit.

Unfortunately, the events in Texas didn't change how we felt about Henley's music, although we tried going to a couple of his gigs (using CDs we'd borrowed from the local library), but just couldn't find our way to connect. But what Henley's actions should have taught us is that people need a chance and that they should be judged by their actions, not their art. We were too busy laughing about the fun of the show to see the subtle lesson at the time. But it goes without saying that you can't judge a record by its sleeve. There are so many examples of this. Just look at R.E.M., the Rheostatics, and the Ramones, just to stick with "R." All these bands have had good and bad cover art—even their names are somewhat dubious—but yet when you close your eyes and open your ears, they deliver. And deliver big.

Ironically, my father told me something like this once. It was when he tried to teach me that it's important to identify the fun-damental reason why you're holding someone in high regard. You needed to understand whether it is for their achievements or their fundamental character. If it's the former, then limit your appreciation accordingly, so you can say, "Sure Kafka can really write, but there is no way he's looking after my children." Of course this was easier for my father when he was trying to dis-abuse me of my fondness for rock 'n' roll than it was when one of his favorite baseball players was implicated in illegal gam-bling activities. "But dad…you don't really think he should be exonerated do you," I pled.

"Never mind, this is different," he insisted. Sure it was different, it always was.

But all the same, Don Henley and Mojo Nixon teamed up to im-part a new way of looking at things for Kenn and me, at least when we finally took time to reflect upon ideas of geese and ganders, and even then we needed a context not yet discovered to connect all the points, and for now more immediate questions consumed our attention. Questions such as how Don Henley ended up at a Mojo Nixon show. Rock 'n' roll has a fabric of its own, and our crossings were full of different lessons and obser-vations. Rock 'n' roll moves in mysterious ways, and we were still in the relatively early days of our crossing experiences.

One of the things that we noticed was that regardless of the gig or the band or the venue, there were always girls clamoring for the band's attention. Detached guys like Iggy Pop, Jonathan Richmond or Kurt Cobain. Strange guys like Trent Reznor, Iggy Pop or David Bowie. Angry guys like Rollins, Danzig or Iggy Pop. It didn't matter what the guys were like—if they were in a band and performing, there were always girls around like seagulls on a fish in the sun. Kenn and I simply didn't understand, but then there was so much we didn't understand about girls.

It was always about a girl. Girls. Girls. Girls. Of all the things that Kenn and I did not understand, at the top of the list was the subject of girls.

Part II

Shadowplay

Shadowplay:

A noun describing a form of puppet play or performance in which the image of the puppets is projected onto a screen by light;

A metaphor for viewing the consequence of an action indirectly;

A colloquial expression to imply or suggest a conspiracy, manipulation or nefarious activity;

The title of the Joy Division song from the 1979 album *Unknown Pleasures;*

The title of the Joy Division song from the 1979 album *Unknown Pleasures* covered by the Killers on their 2007 album *Sawdust* and incorporated into the film *Control* about Joy Division; and

The title of the Joy Division song from the 1979 album *Unknown Pleasures* covered by Vampire Weekend during their live performance in Balboa Park for Earth Day 2017.

The band Shadowplay depicted themes of searching, loss, and futility in a world that was cold and always beyond control or comprehension, reflective of the band's experience in Manchester. Ironically, the lighting for many of the gigs for bands such as Joy Division, the Cure, Echo and the Bunnymen, Sad Lovers and Giants, and Bauhaus included lighting that cast shadows in dramatic fashion.

Shadowplay is a form of projection or insinuation used to cast or create a mood or alternate meaning, used by cinematic directors such Francis Ford Coppola in *Apocalypse Now, Dracula,* and *The Godfather,* and others. While the action in the foreground would guide the story, often there was a background in contrast or offering additional elements. Something that told more of the story or offered different information.

Shadowplay isn't necessarily a conspiracy or something underhanded. Nor is it something that is necessarily indirect. In fact, the organization of the light, the puppets, and the screen is all deliberate and organized, although these too are facets of conspiracy. The audience knowing the source of the light suggests a decided lack of conspiratorial intention, but aspects of obscuring remain. Is it in the knowing or the obscuring, that the conspiracy is formed?

Shadowplay was a state in which things were being controlled by means not understood or immediately visible. Such was the existence that I had, in which I felt things were beyond my control and being influenced from elsewhere.

5 – Girls

It's nothing new. Jonathan Richman talks about it, LL Cool J raps about it, and Kurt Cobain, Lloyd Cole, Lou Reed, David Bowie, Elvis Costello, Nico, Mike D, and the Beastie Boys sing about it. The topic is found in the book of Genesis. This is Radio KQRL FM 91.1, and I'm Sid. You know what? Let's set this up and listen to these songs and more. These are songs that would seem to indicate that everything in life involves women to some degree. Really, songs that should foreshadow or aid in my futile comprehension of dealing with matters concerning the opposite sex. Let's kick it off with the Beasties. Enjoy.

FCC transcript KQRL 91.1 FM 08.21.1999 0243
File as "Cobain"
Operators comment: Fail time check – Infringement

Girls. I mentioned that this was a story about a girl. And it is. Just a different kind of story. The story is different because Kenn and I didn't know which girl would become involved with us or even how for that matter. Would it be a story like in the songs "Veronica," "Angie," "Cynthia," or "Crazy Mary?" We had no way of knowing. But all the same, this story, like so many others, was about a girl, and I suppose more than one.

Unlike rock 'n' roll, girls were something that Kenn and I really didn't understand. But we tried, and we probably thought that we knew more than we did. Women easily confuse me, and I even become overwhelmed by confusion in their mere presence. Sometimes I get confused even when I think about women.

Kenn and I were never particularly adept with the fairer sex. We weren't lovers or *faggots,* as my father had suggested, or the bullies whose paths we'd periodically cross. Even at that, when

I would remind whoever was speaking such inaccuracies to me that "I was not a bundle of sticks and that that unit of measure had long since been considered archaic," the taunting would stop immediately. Unfortunately the taunting only stopped because it was displaced violence. A classic case of winning the battle but losing the war—a lesson that seemed difficult for me to really learn.

No, our predicament wasn't due to any gender bias. Again we found reflection of our lives in a Darren Hanlon song. This time it was "Electric Skeleton"—"*We're never lost for words; we just lack the wherewithal.*" For Kenn and me, our plight with girls wasn't a lack of interest; it was an inability to communicate with girls—a handicap that we carried from our youth that we never really rehabilitated. In fact, we knew so little about girls, what they wanted or how to interact with them, it could be said that we knew more about intergalactic travel than girls. I actually used to say that we knew more about time travel than girls, but that reference has been rendered confusing by Kenn's revelations.

Really, the examples of our failings with women were as plentiful and as varied as one's imagination. There was the time that Kenn and I had taken the bus down to San Francisco when we had tickets to see the former front man for Bauhaus, Peter Murphy, promoting his album *Deep*, at the Warfield Theater. The sheer overwhelming presence of Murphy on stage, with his haunting voice and pseudo-erotic antics left us in a state that could only be considered sexual arousal. There was simply something inherently sensual and forbidden about Peter Murphy that left one primed and hungry with an appetite for untold indulgences. In fact, Kenn and I found ourselves wandering around the city after the show.

Both Peter Murphy and the Warfield are worth seeing. Two birds with one stone? Well, you just thank your lucky stars and pay for your ticket. Peter Murphy is the consummate performer, and his time with Bauhaus merely solidified this fact. Then when you put Murphy into a venue like the Warfield, with its rich history dating to the 1920s, its restored gold, crimson interior, and a capacity that exceeds twenty-two hundred patrons, across upper and lower compartmented loge levels and sweeping upper and lower balconies? Magic. In fact, I think *The Muppet Show* appropriated the design used inside for the upper balcony, where the cantankerous critics aired their views. But the show was spectacular. Great sound. I mean Murphy's baritone voice would resonate without echo like a cello throughout the hall, leading your mind through various emotions. Lust. Forlorn. Bliss. Frustration. Everything that you would expect from a goth icon. Everything reflecting the human condition…at least this condition seen through Peter's eyes. Although Kenn and I could only afford cheap seats, the Warfield afforded good views of the stage from almost everywhere. If Kenn and I could see from a wing on the second balcony, without complaint, I suspect there wasn't a bad seat in the house. Sure, it was a bit of a drag that we couldn't mill about as we would otherwise. But damn fine. Really the gig couldn't help but be anything other than fantastic. Hallmark venue, memorable show, and topping it all off, we were in San Francisco. Peter Murphy was masterful and put together a legendary live show, and like all great shows, Peter Murphy left us wanting more.

But as always, once the house lights go on, our time as guests would end, and any unsatisfied desires would have to be fulfilled elsewhere. So without local accommodations, and in our awkward state of agitation, Kenn and I sought the only solution that we could consider with our limited knowledge of San Francisco. Even though this was the first time that we had been to the city, we knew instinctively where our appetites could be satisfied. So, like many young men before us—in fact, some merely hours before us—we headed to the Tenderloin district that was conveniently located in proximity to the Warfield Theater. Although we didn't know a lot about San Francisco, we knew that we'd find a sure thing in the Tenderloin. So leaving Peter Murphy and the Warfield, with the memory of the riffs from "Cuts You Up" resonating within our souls, the beat punctuating our gait, we turned up Jones Street, eventually passing O'Farrell, where we happily discovered a target-rich environment waiting for us and our base needs. Looking around, suddenly we saw that there was ample fruit for the picking. Had we looked closer, it would have been obvious that the fruit was bruised and more than a little worse for wear, but when you're hungry, fruit's fruit. So Kenn and I ambled up to the first of the available girls, full of optimism, appetite, and a lingering gothic eroticism stirred by an evening in Peter Murphy's proximity.

Naturally, Kenn started talking. I didn't really hear what he said, but the effect was instantaneous. She was a streetwalker. A professional. But in our rock 'n' roll-induced state of arousal, Kenn and I were not about to be restrained by taboo or stigma. In fact, a pro was as close as we were going to get to a sure thing, so we proceeded with gusto. I was drawn to her black micro mini skirt that stretched over her curves, but then of course there was also the short black boots that certainly weren't made for walking. But ultimately, although I've always had a thing for tight skirts, this one which showcased her long legs and curves, and the edgy boots, didn't hold a candle to the violet lace bra that was beckoning through her sheer blouse like a Midway game that announces "Every One's A Winner!" I looked past Violet's long bruised legs through her torn stockings and declared that she was an erotic treasure. Concluding, while I was transfixed on her breasts, that "Violet" seemed as good a name as any for someone that wouldn't tell you her real name anyway. Even through the fog of my hormonal distraction, I should have known enough to prevent Kenn from talking, but I didn't, or even if I did, I didn't do anything to stop him.

"Yo' money is no good here, baby," she said coyly as she turned back to her colleagues and away from Kenn and me.

"You hear that, dude? We're getting a pro for free!" Kenn exclaimed. I was still transfixed by Violet's form. The curves thinly covered by her skirt, her namesake bra concealing treasures that I sought to possess, even if only fleetingly.

"No, honey, I didn't say you wuz getting' it fo' free," Violet interjected. "I said I wasn't taking yo' money. So git lost." The words echoed in my head like a stone thrown into an abandoned warehouse, rattling around like the laughter coming from the other girls. Again, laughter at our expense, again Kenn and me on the outside. My experience with unrequited affections was ample, but this was different; this was the start of a denial that left me reeling at the discovery that the only thing that I would be receiving from a prostitute was rejection and humiliation. My arousal and esteem were now in a dead heat, freefalling into an abyss. What was it about Kenn and me that made us so universally repugnant to girls that we couldn't even pick up a pro? The street became an immediate swirling confluence of my dreams and problems.

Facing rejection from a prostitute wasn't unexpected given Kenn's ability to raise the ire of even the most tolerant and seemingly interested of women. Still I stood there, seemingly dumbstruck, but intent on discovering a solution, a passage into a harbor that I was seeking. A taste, just a taste of the fruit that I was yearning for. But if not from Violet, from where? Maybe her friend? How much money did we have? All of this occurred before we learned to cross, so the bulk of our budget had been dissipated on bus fare, Peter Murphy tickets, and a couple of beers. Was paradise always to be just out of reach? Why were Kenn and I always missing out, even if just by the slenderest of margins? Just past the circle of warmth cast by a fire?

My contemplation was shattered by a shrill voice, that caused Kenn and me to turn to discover that it came from a short figure in a full-length black leather jacket, with some sort of animal pelt slumped across the shoulders. Kenn was a full head taller than this peculiar-looking man, who appeared to be demonstrating the fireman's carry on the carcass of a large rodent. It was impossible to ascertain his weight because the bulk of the cloak draped over his shoulders seemed cumbersome and was juxtaposed by his lean face and boney hands that were laden with glittering rings and glossy scar tissue on his knuckles. His left hand was twitching and kneading the large glass spherical handle on his walking stick, giving the impression that he was nervous or high or simply lacking control over his emotions.

Still, although I looked at this animated little man, there was something that looked dangerous about him. The words that leapt to mind included *pariah, bully, abomination, repellant,* and *pimp*—all synonyms, perhaps.

"Yo! Gentlemen, yuse two lookin' or iz yuse buyin'? Cuz me and me'z ladies is runnin' a biz-nez here." I was confused. The pimp spoke some form of Ebonics, but looked Asian or from the South Pacific. I never was particularly good at determining nationality, maybe Thai or somewhere else in Southeast Asia.

"Well, hey, we were looking to buy or at least rent, but your laad-dies, so-called, were just telling us that they were closed for business."

"*Fuck,*" I thought as I saw Violet's expression change like seasonal transitions caught in a time-lapse photography sequence. Disdain and disinterest becoming concern and alarm, becoming fear and regret. Did Kenn really have to say *that*? Fuck, did he really not know better?

I looked to the sky thinking that I heard a clap of thunder and then turned back to see one of Violet's colleagues helping her up from the ground. Violet's short skirt, knocked astray from her fall, revealed stained and threadbare panties matching her bra, which drew my attention like a thousand suns, but then immediately brought me shame...and arousal. Shame for both my arousal and my inaction in the face of violence. Unsure of what else to do or where to look, I looked away and then back toward Violet only to see that her cheek was swelling and becoming crimson from where her pimp had struck her. Embarrassed by the violence and now with the fleeting arousal from the concert and Violet's violet bits, Kenn and I stood there looking as impotent and flaccid as we were behaving.

"Yuse said *what*?" The pimp hissed at Violet. I wanted to intervene, but any fire inside me was extinguished, doused from the ice water that flowed through the pimp's veins. Leaving me with nothing but cold embers in the hearth of righteousness. Without a sense of decency, I stood fixed in place. A failure. A coward. Nothing like the hero that I thought I had become that day with Kenn and McCloy. Nothing like who I wished to be. Why did I have to be threatened to be a hero, like I had with McCloy? Tonight I just wanted some action, and besides, why should I intervene in commerce between two strangers? This didn't really have anything to do with Kenn and me, did it?

Unlike when I had faced McCloy and felt courage rising around me like a bugle call, steeling my resolve and spurring me to action, this time the tide was retreating. The wind of courage had died in my sails leaving me to flounder in the doldrums of my emotions. Was this because I was in a strange town? Because Violet had caused me pain herself? Maybe it was just because courage ebbs and flows and I hadn't mastered my own emotions, but whatever the reason I was frozen and once again knew the stigma of shame.

I knew that ultimately, whatever may have justified my inaction, I had been a coward. Not only failing to act heroically or even decently, but failing to act all. Just like those who would stand at the margins, participating as bullies or those who would turn away leaving no one to witness Kenn or me being victimized, I refused to engage in what I knew to be right. Failing to be anything but part of the problem. I knew that there was no justification for my inaction and no label other than cowardice.

One of the other girls—probably named Ginger for her fake red hair—started to intervene, pleading, "Ronnie, she's just not feeling well. You know how it is." She was tall and busty, with a

Spanish or Mediterranean complexion, her seemingly smooth tanned legs, actually sporting bruises, scabs, and other marks like Violet's, but her complexion setting a stunning contrast to her white skirt. How had I not noticed Ginger before? I've always had a thing for redheads. Maybe because Ginger's hair color looked fake or it could have been a wig. But still, her ample breasts strained against her top, and when she stood under the streetlight just so, I could see the dark skin of her breasts, a vision that would easily offset the fake red hair.

With my arousal returning, I was oblivious and ambivalent to Ginger's nervous glances and rising concern. I could hear the audible anxiety, near panic, causing the words to rush from the girl to whose dark ample breasts I was transfixed.

"Come on, Ronnie, maybe you could give baby a little something to help her feel better and I could, you know, give you somethin' too. Something special, you know, like you like it. Whaddya say?" Continuing to stroke Ronnie's arm and along the chest of his dead critter jacket, with her long fingers, she trifled him again, her voice softly pleading now.

Ronnie didn't get a chance to respond to what I would have considered Ginger's very compelling offer, because suddenly a wave of shock washed across Ronnie's face at the same time that I noticed a steely grip around his arm. A man in a dark suit seemed to appear out of nowhere. There had been no warning, no threat or attention sought or given. The man in the suit must have stepped forward and calmly placed Ronnie's arm in a firm but nonthreatening grasp, the dynamic on the street changed yet again. Kenn and I should have never ventured onto the street awash with flickering neon signs of strip bars and the dusty awnings that promised massages or adult videos. I longed for the marquee with Peter Murphy's name on it, being early and listening to the sound check or heading back to the Greyhound depot on Folsom Street. Kenn and I could have been waiting for the bus; reliving the gig over greasy burgers and fries that would burn the roof of our mouths and then leave us feeling ill and spent during the ride home. What could have been, if I could go back in time or change decisions made. But we couldn't, and here we were in what was turning into a Mexican standoff over yet another girl who didn't want to have sex with either Kenn nor me. Not our finest hour.

I was obviously so preoccupied with our own situation, my debilitating cocktail of arousal and shame mixing like rotting fruit in a sangria that had been left out in the sun too long. Fruit rotting and becoming infused with alcohol but fermenting and spoiling the drink that was once sweet and refreshing, still leaving me intoxicated, immobile, and yet nauseous. That, and of course the ample breasts, thinly veiled, ensured that I hadn't even seen the figure in a dark suit arrive.

The entire scene struck me as out of place, so removed from what Kenn and I had been seeking. Confusing. The man was well dressed, but not flashy. Somber tones, comfortable, professional, but only casting a description of function or sensation. I couldn't remember what color his tie was, if his suit was black, navy, or gray. Brooks Brothers? Could have been, but I barely knew the difference between a Brooks Brothers suit and a snowsuit, but I called this guy Brook all the same.

If I had to pick Brook out of a police lineup, I would have failed. But there was *something* about this man. A power. A confidence. A resolve. A feeling of violence, without a threat. More of a promise or maybe just the potential. This man moved with a sense of calm and control that suggested that he didn't fully understand what he had interrupted.

The grip on Ronnie's arm was a grasp that appeared to offer no alternative but to yield. Brook was subjecting Ronnie's arm to absolute control, yet without a sense of the expected violence or domination. Where did this guy come from? Was he a Jedi, someone with a death wish, or perhaps he held an insurance policy that excluded suicide? Regardless, the sands of change were shifting too quickly beneath our feet, causing discomfort for Kenn and I, and from what I could see, also for the prostitutes and certainly Ronnie. My mind reeled with images of someone dousing a powder keg with rocket fuel. Something was going to explode, and I feared that Kenn and I would be collateral damage. Surveying the small collection of bodies around us, it was clear that I wasn't the only one who thought that way. The girls were seeking escape, but were too transfixed by the sudden turn of events and probably really had nowhere to flee to.

Just as Ronnie was raising his cane to strike this well dressed but seemingly nondescript interloper, and as the girls were flinching, the man leaned forward and looked into Ronnie's eyes. A transformation swept over the street, and while the man was saying something softly to Ronnie, inaudible from where Kenn and I stood, Ronnie's arm, raised in violence, slowly fell limp, and his back became rigid and straight. The tension in everyone washed away, leaving a palpable sense of relief and calm. Whatever we had all anticipated and even feared had passed without occurrence.

Releasing Ronnie, the man stepped back. "Ronnie, so we're agreed then?"

"Yeah, I gitz you," uttered a visibly shaken and considerably less menacing Ronnie. "Yo,' yuse ho's—"

"Ronnie," Brook interrupted, "I told you, be respectful. You told me that you understood."

"Yeah, yeah, right, ahhh, yuse girls git a night off." Then looking nervously at the suited man, as though he was seeking confirmation, Ronnie started dispensing twenty- and fifty-dollar bills to who I assumed were "his" girls. "Yo, take a couple o' nights off and gets some food or somethin'. Not none of dem drugs, but somethin' good, and ice fo' yo' face. I ain't gonna see you out here till next week, right? Ain't dat right, mister?"

It was just like in the movies with the cop holding the perimeter of a crime scene. There was nothing for Kenn and me to see. A stranger who was tall, dark, and handsome had averted the confrontation, and we were once again at a loss to understand girls or even ourselves. Without anything else to do, because we certainly weren't keen to look for another prostitute, Kenn and I just walked away. Even after returning to the bus station and home to Oregon, we never really understood what had happened that night, but we knew that it had been something profound.

Simply knowing that we had seen someone with courage, which we both lacked and couldn't understand, someone who took a stand for random people in a random situation, was enough. How was that even possible? I guess heroes do arrive at the right time.

Eventually, the stranger's heroics, the failed attempt at sexual liaisons, and the violent and near violent interventions that we had witnessed, all faded from our minds, but not the gig's details. In fact, by the time Kenn and I boarded the bus at Fulsom Street our talk had returned to the retelling of the Peter Murphy gig. The entire bus ride back to Oregon was spent either discussing rock 'n' roll or sleeping in ways that were guaranteed to cause discomfort later and perhaps arthritis in our older years. But there would always be a price to pay for rock 'n' roll, and we could settle that account later.

Obviously the confrontation with Violet, Ginger, Ronnie, and Brook (who was really the secret identity of Captain Corporate America) was a low watermark for our relations with girls, but our girl troubles went back even farther than that. It was like that song by the Violent Femmes, "Girl Trouble."

Listening to the lyrics, you'd think that the band had worse problems than Kenn and me, but you'd be wrong. As Kenn and I had discovered from our time at gigs, rock bands always had girls around. Girls, drugs, booze, and fast cars. Things that always seemed to surround rock 'n' roll. But maybe the Violent Femmes had it right. Maybe the band shared Kenn's views about the role of girls in the conspiracy against rock 'n' roll.

There were times were Kenn would exclaim with joyous satisfaction, "She totally talked to me, dude. She totally thinks I'm hot." Unfortunately, for both Kenn and me, there were no girls that thought we were hot. Only sad and different, or maybe indifferent, attributes which failed to make us cool or appealing. Although in this case, it was true. In fact, she had spoken to him. But unfortunately for Kenn, the part that he forgot to mention was that the girl of today's dreams was a cashier and had said, "That will be one dollar and fifteen cents," after Kenn had presented the bottle of Mountain Dew and bag of chips that he wanted to purchase. Polite? Perhaps. Engaging? Certainly. The expression of a romantic intent? No, not likely.

Managing Kenn's behavior and expectations was difficult for me at the best of times. With matters involving girls, the difficult suddenly became the untenable as Kenn's conversations would go from awkward to unconscionable, with me resident in my own personal Hell. I could all but hear Sisyphus say, "Dude, now that's a tough task," as he casually strolled up the hill with his boulder.

There were other times when Kenn was convinced of a girl's affections. Like the time he spoke to this girl Jenny, from school, at her workplace. Later, Kenn pronounced, "She is totally into me, man. Jenny gave me this wild look, like she didn't know what to do with herself. So I asked her out, and she was so stunned that she was speechless. I think I made her day!" Yes, Kenn, so stunned in fact that she neither confirmed nor rejected the invitation.

It was only later, through questioning and examining Kenn, that I managed to recreate a more complete picture of the events. As it turned out, the shock on the poor girl's face was due to her discomfort rather than any sense of being flattered. Kenn had omitted to tell me that Jenny was working as a dispensation clerk at her father's pharmacy and that Kenn had paid the pharmacy a visit to fill a large order for a broad-spectrum antibiotic. As if Kenn and I weren't unappealing enough to girls, providing a reason to think that either of us were contagious couldn't help. But Kenn wouldn't relent. I suppose I didn't help him as much as I could, though.

Like the dog that keeps running because there is always a car to be chased, neither Kenn nor I could claim to ever have had any serious or sustained contact with girls. So we turned to rock 'n' roll, as usual. Not only was rock 'n' roll the path of least resistance for us, but it was also intensely gratifying.

Rock 'n' roll was more than an outlet and an obsession for us. It represented more than merely a source of entertainment or a curiosity to be researched. Rock 'n' roll were the lenses through which we viewed the world. Kenn and I understood the world, because it was interpreted and expressed in music. It was our guidebook.

Therefore, girls were merely an extension of our understanding of the world. Kenn and I initially gained our understanding of girls through the songs that we listened to. Songs like "Jane Says," and "Classic Girl," by Jane's Addiction; "Alison," and "Veronica," by Elvis Costello; "And She Was," and "Girlfriend (Is Better)," by the Talking Heads; "Rena," "Cynthia," and "Andrea," by Blue Rodeo; "Blue Jean," or "Rosalyn," by David Bowie; or "Claire," by the Rheostatics. Clearly songs that were about girls, so by extension they could be applied or projected onto other girls. It seemed to make sense, and it worked for us.

But, strangely, this is where Kenn and I parted views. I followed the music into art, taking lead artists like Billy Bragg singing Woody Guthrie's words, as an example, the inherent importance of women, and following those words to reading "On the Sub-jection of Women," by John Stuart Mill. Marveling that suffrage sentiments existed longer than I had would have ever consid-ered, I then reflected upon the courage that it would take to make unpopular or contentious statements in the face of such cultural opposition. Mill was a hero, not only for his time, but in a way I had never realized; not for what he achieved, but what he attempted.

None of this information helped me understand girls as individu-als or how to interact with them, but I suppose it gave me a sense that they were complex. It also reinforced my understanding that rock 'n' roll was easier to comprehend than Mill's writings. But still, here was a hero who not only had a hand in writing our con-stitution, but also in standing up for women, because they weren't entitled to speak for themselves.

Kenn didn't care. But as I said, Kenn went in a different direction, but it was still a path led by rock 'n' roll. Or if not rock 'n' roll, a conspiracy, or better yet a conspiracy involving rock 'n' roll. The only thing better than a conspiracy involving rock 'n' roll is a con-spiracy of women against rock 'n' roll, and eventually I found a very common and recurring theme with Kenn.

Kenn identified theories, and he identified conspiracies. For Kenn it was never a "conspiracy theory" because that was the sole dominion of delusional paranoids. If really pressed, he would argue that he used his "theories" to *identify* "conspira-cies" or call them by name, because after all, the conspiracies Kenn *identified* were real.

Naturally, according to Kenn, our dilemma with girls had to be a conspiracy. How else could you explain the obvious fact that girls were only interested in guys who pursued the shallow in-terests of the day, such as school sports? Or guys who had good jobs or wealthy and liberal parents who lavished their children with cars and money or set them up with plush jobs, paving their course along a super highway of career advancement. Even in Kenn's case, his family had money, or at least his father did, but access to wealth and luxury was something they held over him to try to entice him away from rock 'n' roll and into some-thing more respectable. Something that would make his parents proud, like taking over the family business or being a lawyer. That was a different conspiracy that Kenn identified, a conspiracy involving rock 'n' roll but unrelated to girls.

The questions about girls remained. Why would they only be attracted to guys who were interested in clothes, who spent their money on cars and vacations, trips into the mountains? What could these guys possibly have over Kenn and me? We were making a real difference in the world. Kenn and I were providing an essential service for rock 'n' roll by providing research and increasing the knowledge base so selflessly, and really, was anything more important? But girls didn't seem to view this the same way that Kenn and I did, and growing up, even at college, we saw girls circle in a decaying orbit around guys who were nothing like us. It seemed that the common denominator was that girls just didn't like music. Or at least that was the conclusion that we reached.

The world was simple to Kenn; it was separated into things that were good and others that were Evil. Anything that didn't exist within a sphere that he understood and embraced, like rock 'n' roll, was Evil. Women were a natural extension of this concept for Kenn.

It had to be about the aversion that all girls held to rock 'n' roll. I mean, it could be that girls simply weren't interested in a couple of guys who were essentially reclusive, obsessed with rock 'n' roll, and lacked both motivation and interest for anything unrelated to music, and who were socially awkward.

But it was more than this. Kenn had a theory—the *Eve Theory*—named after the Garden of Eden incident. And this theory seemed to be valid. It even underscored the fundamental problem that we had with girls. I wasn't sure if Kenn's theories were correct, actually reflected our realities, or simply justified our observations. But I suppose that the difference between perception and reality is usually indistinguishable.

Girls have always caused unrest, distraction, and chaos. When I first heard Kenn's theory, it seemed farfetched, something devised to merely justify our patent failure with girls, but upon closer inspection, especially over time, it seemed viable. Throughout recorded history, women have been taking control over men's minds and willpower, like Eve from the book of Genesis. Rock 'n' roll has not been immune to these forces, and the result on rock 'n' roll has been disastrous. Nancy Spungen destroyed the Sex Pistols by luring Sid Vicious away with drugs. Yoko Ono distracted John Lennon from his wife, Cynthia, and the Beatles. Courtney Love wreaked havoc upon Kurt Cobain. The Killers' demise, or at least the initial hiatus, came at the hands of a young maiden who married Brandon Flowers, and then like a siren lured him into joining the Mormons. Flowers released an album without (the rest of) the Killers, but what do you remember about it? Right. Nothing.

You could make the argument that Sid was inherently self-destructive; Cobain struggled with his own demons, including the pressures of fame; or that Lennon and McCartney had been at odds for some time, but the fact remains that standing over the dying body, with a smoking gun in hand, there was a woman.

Genesis—the scripture, not the band—also claims that the exile from Eden occurred as a result of a meddlesome woman. This is a fact that the Evil learned early on and has since held onto so that this knowledge could be used against its enemies great and small. Napoleon managed to spy on his adversaries and allies alike with the aid of a compliant Josephine. Catwoman managed to undermine Batman's resolve. Jezebel tempted Jesus. Just because Kenn named his hypothesis the *Eve Theory* didn't make the premise any less viable. In fact, naming his theory not only legitimized it, but provided an ability to examine and test its accuracy. Presently, it seemed to float better than the RMS Titanic.

Eve, Jezebel, Josephine, Catwoman, Yoko Ono, Courtney Love, Nancy Spungen: a long line of women who sought to destroy men, and sometimes worse. Sometimes the target was rock 'n' roll. There was nothing more inhumane than plotting the death of rock 'n' roll, because if rock 'n' roll fell, so would humanity.

Kenn named all his conspiracies, although he would deny that they were *his* conspiracies. He would claim that he merely discovered *other* people's conspiracies. But I would argue that most things that are named are done so either by or after the discoverer. I would quote examples such as Newton's laws, the Hoover Dam, the Perseids Comet, and Faraday's law of induction, all bearing the name of the person instrumental to the knowledge of their existence. All though I would claim that the Hoover Dam was built; something else that Kenn would argue. The Hoover Dam was the source of another of Kenn's conspiracies, but that was something else. But Kenn wouldn't have any part of such a naming convention. I suppose it made sense; after all, Kenn only had four names and so, so many theories; if he kept to this convention he'd run out of names.

It quickly came to be that Kenn associated girls with evil. And not just evil as an act or adverb, but evil as a tangible thing. An object to be reviled and opposed at every turn. Actually, Kenn and I later learned that Evil was actually a pronoun and the nemesis of rock 'n' roll and the enemy of man. So once again, maybe this was one of Kenn's discoveries. Maybe he realized that the line between conspiracy theory and real conspiracy was blurred more than we would like. At the end of the debate, the result was always the same. Kenn's theories represented factual circumstances, and girls were the source of everything unholy. Their only purpose was to interfere with rock 'n' roll. I never found this conclusion particularly satisfying and often wondered if Kenn really believed it. Regardless of how long I remained friends with Kenn, how firmly he believed his various theories was a puzzle that I never solved.

In truth, everything we thought we knew about girls came from our understanding of rock 'n' roll. But maybe we had it wrong. Maybe there was more to falling in love than discovering a girl that giggles because you've said the perfect clever phrase. Maybe for Kenn and me, we just needed a girl who was rock 'n' roll enough for us, who could then teach us about girls. Perhaps if we could accept her for who she was and then teach her about rock 'n' roll we could overcome our failings. Maybe this way the *Eve Theory* could be solved.

This seemed like a valid approach, so we made lists of songs about girls and love. Unsurprisingly, Kenn and I had different lists. Kenn put his up on his blog site and sometimes Tweeted about it. Me? For some reason, I couldn't be bothered. But maybe I should have, maybe it would have somehow provided a deeper understanding of my romantic failings, but then maybe blogs and tweets aren't really the answer to everything.

Our lists might be considered interesting, something for psychologists to examine or riddle over while trying to unlock the answers of our great minds. For every point that I made with my list, Kenn had an equally valid counterpoint. Sitting up and listening to records, Kenn and I would move our lists around like chess pieces.

"OK, songs about girls or love," Kenn would offer.

I'd open with, "'Candy,' by Iggy Pop and Kate Pierson."

"'China Girl,' by Iggy Pop and David Bowie," Kenn would counter. Then he'd continue this attack later with, "Iggy Pop, 'I Wanna Be Your Dog.'"

"Iggy, 'Cry for Love.'"

Moving on from Iggy Pop, I'd say, "OK, Lloyd Cole, 'Perfect Skin.'"

"Whatever. 'Are You Ready to Be Heartbroken?'" Kenn was good, really hitting his stride, not only the same artist, but also the same album.

Kenn and I could do this all day. Often we did. I should have considered our lists as an indication of future conflicts on these issues, but we can't see the future, only the past and the present. I felt that there was home for romance and love, where Kenn only saw potential for ruination. Even signs that might have been obvious only seem so when reflected upon, so I suppose it was easy enough to overlook the signs of future discord. This was the fundamental problem with taking up positional views, regardless of whether such positions are taken among the best of friends. It still sows the seeds of discord. Positions that demand an adversary only ever lead to conflict.

It was easy to consider Kenn paranoid or a crank or delusional, easy but wrong, at least some of the time. Particularly regarding his *Eve Theory* about girls. As outlandish as it seemed, Kenn's *Eve Theory* was based upon an absolute truth, or at least the truth of our experiences. Unfortunately, this was a truth that Kenn and I had seen directly, more than just once: There is no living thing more capable of cruelty than a girl. Girls, the emotional equivalent of sharks, who needed neither appetite nor motivation to kill. Girls simply needed a target to direct their cruelty upon. Still we remained fixated upon women and like I said, this is a story about a girl.

Whatever the basis for our relative positions, be it conspiracy or observation, this was a topic upon which Kenn and I would ruminate with the predictability of a record on a turntable…something that we explored over and again.

6 – Over and Again

Over and again. Damn. I could sit and listen to that song all day, which is maybe what Brian Wright and the Waco Tragedies were thinking when they wrote it. Maybe that's why they called the song "Over and Again."

Good evening, I'm Sid, and this is KQOO, Radio Nowhere Oregon, located in a forgotten corner of the state and at 90.9 Frequency Modulation. The song gets me thinking, though, about all the things we do over and again. The things that we want to do; the things that we must do; and the things we can't help but do good, bad, or otherwise. It's eight fifteen; let's listen to Brian Wright "Over and Again," again.

FCC transcript KQOO 90.9 FM 03.02.2008 2015
Operator Comments: Cleared

Over and again Kenn and I would discuss matters integral to rock 'n' roll.

Over and again we would discuss various conspiracies, and who might be orchestrating them and even why.

Over and again Kenn and I would research the rock 'n' roll news of the day.

Over and again we would organize our music collections depending upon whatever whim or fancy lit upon us. Sometimes our stacks of vinyl would be ordered alphabetically, while at other times the same collection would be found by release date. Our collections could be ascending or descending; sometimes we kept regional influences together and sometimes subgenres would be collocated, so that we would have everything from the

UK together, but then subsets for ska, punk, acoustic, pop, and straight-edged rock. Such a pattern would then be repeated for Continental Europe, Canada, and America. Within the United States, we had sub regions for Pacific Northwest, California, East Coast, and everything else.

No organizational system would be complete without including notes to reflect important information, such as other art forms that bands, or band members, would engage in. So when Dave Bidini also published full-length books, outside of his role with the Rheostatics or later the Bidiniband, there was a note indicating this. Similarly, the project that Phil Collins embarked upon—where he had patrons in taxis perform karaoke versions of songs by the Smiths—was noted alongside the specific singles that were debased. Such notes would have been included in the subset if either Kenn or I had any Genesis or Phil Collins albums. We didn't. However, his sacrilege did end up on display at the San Francisco Museum of Modern Art, simultaneously proving that he would stoop to any depth at all and disproving that *The World Won't Listen*.

"Sure," I said, "Morrissey as a personality could be a bit much, but he's such an apt singer and lyricist that these shortcomings are easily overlooked."

"And perhaps rightfully so," Kenn concurred. "In fact the same treatment could be applied to Smiths guitarist Johnny Marr, who is awesome but also a tough nut to crack. Really, you'd think that the underlying talent that excused these two, these giants among men from their other indulgences is a nuance that Phil Collins should be cognizant of. I mean, really, this is the very same reason that he continues to fail."

Did the Smiths deserve some stick? Sure. A bit of a hard time? Absolutely, but come on…they were legendary and represent a great tragedy in how truly short-lived their reign was. That's my opinion at least, and Kenn would agree, though he'd usually go too far. "For my money, Phil Collins should have been locked in the trunk of a car and left in the desert with a bottle of water filled with glycol. His monkey business desecrating the Smiths in the name of art only confirms this. I'd like to see him try that shit if Jimmy Hoffa was involved in rock 'n' roll."

"Junior or senior?" I asked, genuinely interested.

"Doesn't matter," Kenn started, and then continued to mumble something about something, maybe related.

I actually did agree with Kenn more often, in fact, than I'd admit—sometimes because Kenn took things, especially his views, too far, and other times because I just didn't like the sound of it coming out of my mouth.

Sorry, am I off again? Yeah, well, fucking Phil Collins and Genesis will do that to a guy. Sorry, I was discussing the intrinsic worth of the organizational systems that we applied to our music collections. Yeah, that was a particularly bad tangent, but I suppose it does support the fact that what I had told DJ Scene could have worked. I mean, if Phil Collins's idea became an exhibit...but it was more than that; it was also an example of how art in all its forms is interrelated. I know, I haven't gotten there yet, but I will. Ok, first, back to the organization of our collections.

There was almost always a basis for the organization, and intrinsic logic that Kenn and I could and would follow and then build upon. We demanded systems that we could construct and know the function of, intuitively, without having to seek an explanation from each other.

"When you're done with the pizza, our exacting system this month is based alphabetically by the original act's name, then followed by subsequent recordings on a chronological basis with derivatives," Kenn announced.

"OK," I said, swallowing some 'Sink, "So the English Beat albums will be organized with *I Just Can't Stop It*, *Wha'Happen*, and *Special Beat Service* in order, and then albums by Fine Young Cannibals, General Public, Ranking Roger, and Roland Gift?"

"Precisely," Kenn confirmed, setting up for another set of music and another slice.

Again, it was just another way that we were genealogists of rock 'n' roll. Obviously certain bands made our efforts to build and maintain a structured organizational system more difficult. But it was OK, because the effort was worth it. In addition to being genealogists, this was also how we were preparing to become heroes; we just didn't know it yet.

Overly complicated? you might say. *Pedantic? Waste of time?* Well, now you're just sounding like one of our parents, especially Kenn's. But the reality was that the nurturing of our music collection was a labor of love, a passion, and unbeknownst to us, preparing us daily for the tasks that lay ahead. The hours that Kenn and I pored over our collections, liner notes, news items, and reviews allowed us to hone our craft just as athletes drill specific skills or the bands that we loved became better and better by touring, playing gigs, and rehearsing—no matter how small the venue or crowd.

To be fair, our collections were not always meticulously organized. Other times, our rigid pursuit of a systematic structure gave way to a more random assortment of records, which also held unknown benefits for us. Much like the discovery of time travel itself, and in particular this rationale, rather than a proper system, often led to some of the enjoyable sessions that Kenn and I would partake in. Usually it was the situation in which we were listening to something and then would go on a search for the next record, and while we would have an idea of what we wanted to listen to, we would come across something else, say Mazzy Star or the Temptations. Then, invariably, that would lead to spontaneous discussion or appreciation of some nuance that we perhaps hadn't previous discovered. Maybe we notice a riff from Curtis Mayfield that shows up in a Galliano song or how Jane's Addiction drew from an assortment of influences trying to pick up what was left behind by Led Zepplin, the Velvet Underground, and the 'Stones.

Kenn commented one evening, "You know, what we do; how we organize our music, people don't really get it. You know that some people actually call it lazy or unstructured."

"The world is just so cruel," I said with mock incredulity, "but seriously, who have you been discussing this with anyway? And why do you think that they would understand, much less even care? It's a good system, actually producing results through structure and serendipity." Although in reality, I suppose it could be both, or maybe even either. "Consider Joy Division's ominously titled debut album, *Unknown Pleasures*; what else could the title allude to but serendipity?" Sure, it could suggest something forbidden, but even that which was forbidden was often unknown. Isn't that what made the fruit from the Tree of Knowledge in the Garden of Eden all the more attractive? The fact that it was unknown, and also forbidden? Imagine, or even just remember, the spark, the eruption of your senses, the electricity running across your skin, when trying something for the first time that was pleasurable. A first kiss. A new food. The scent of an exotic flower. The first time I heard David Bowie. All such experiences were unknown pleasures, at least the first time. All unexpectedly gratifying precisely because they are unknown and unexpected. Sure, serendipity couldn't be considered an organizational methodology, but as a means for enhancing pleasure, could anything be better?

Intuitively, I knew that Kenn agreed, because we went back to discussing how we were organizing our music. We talked more and more about the variety with our musical organizational schemes, because it also was the same way that we planned our crossings.

If nothing else, leaving our collections in a random disarray from time to time prepared Kenn and me for the vagaries of time travel and experiences that we could have never predicted. Sometimes we crossed to satisfy a simple curiosity, like when we went to see the Pussycat Dolls or Madonna…you know, just to see what the fuss was about. This is something that we would have never indulged in before. We wouldn't. We couldn't. Both our time and our cash were too precious to be wasted on certain shows, even if they played somewhere nearby. Worse if we had to travel. San Fran. Seattle. Texas. LA. These places were relatively close to us and always hosted gigs we'd covet, but travel added to our time and cost, usually making these shows as accessible as if they had been on Pluto.

Fortunately, crossing toppled these barriers like tenpins, granting us instant and unfettered access to rock 'n' roll. All rock 'n' roll. Life couldn't get any better. We were no longer constrained or limited by a mere preference for certain acts, the price of admission, or the proximity of a gig. Kenn and I were elevating our game by voraciously devouring gig after gig. We were learning and experiencing music to an extent never dreamt by us. Really, time travel was better than even our wildest fantasies. This was rock 'n' roll nirvana.

I mean, could you imagine it? We're talking about recurring access to the Reading Festival, Glastonbury, Rock Against Racism, Vans Warped Tour; the Berlin Wall, CBGB's, The Roxy, Finsbury Park, U2's *Under A Blood Red Sky* at Sun Devil Stadium, Paris, Balboa Park, San Diego, Berlin, London; the Cramps recording

Rockinnreelinnaucklandnewzealand, in Auckland, Tokyo, Santiago, Nüremberg, SXSW, The Viper Room—just the tip of the rock 'n' roll juggernaut that Kenn and I were surveying. If there was a gig, Kenn and I went to it. Festivals, small intimate gigs, and massive stadium shows.

But it wasn't all about crossing or live shows. Kenn and I still listened to recorded music. As I've said, Kenn and I possessed voracious appetites, like junkies in search of the perfect high. Surfers looking for an endless summer. Or maybe we were somewhere in between the two. But recorded music would help us plan our crossings, or, for me, set my radio show program, or even just give us a chance to talk. There *was* such a thing as too much rock 'n' roll, and we had discovered that too many gigs simply wore us out.

Again, it was Kenn that took the first step. "Dude, this is important stuff. Being the righteous guardians of such an important cultural treasure, we need to foster a healthy disdain for music that doesn't make it across the line."

"Right, you mean like the glam rock garbage. REO Speedwagon, Flock of *Fucking* Seagulls, or other bands named after cities: Boston, Chicago, Chilliwack."

"Yup—the usual suspects. And what the fuck is with Chilliwack. *Chilliwack*, really? Fuck really, Chilliwack—a shit hole an hour away from Vancouver, and Vancouver Canada, not Washington. At least the others were decent cities. Bands like that, and others like Van Halen, Bon Jovi, Poison, RATT, and *NSYNC are a scourge. An abomination."

Sure, we passed judgment, but still, we didn't condescend to limit our intake. We weren't Armani suit-wearing automatons with MBAs who would only do cocaine and sushi served on naked call girls. Nor did we indiscriminately take on any music that came our way like some strung-out street junkie. But somewhere between the two, we found our place in the world. It was like the place that Social Distortion talked about, a place defined by their fourth studio album that Kenn and I found ourselves, *Somewhere Between Heaven and Hell.* Was it the medium of music or the message that Kenn and I loved? This was a question that I studied intently.

Communications theorist Marshall McLuhan said that "the medium is the message," but he might have been wrong. Maybe he had it right, but how could you really tell? I never understood how you could distinguish between which is the message and which is the medium.

McLuhan's argument claimed that the medium was the technology that transmitted the message, and that the information communicated by the technology was the message itself. What if McLuhan was right that the medium was the message, but was wrong that the technology conveying sound was the medium? It didn't really make sense that the message would be about equipment. No, it would seem that rock 'n' roll was the medium that conveyed the message. After all, wasn't it rock 'n' roll that the Evil was set on destroying? Not iPods. Not audio tapes. Not electronic media storage. Not radios. Rock 'n' roll.

The music itself was always the target, not the technology; shit, the Evil probably owned shares in the tech companies. Excuse me? The Evil? What do you mean, what is it? The enemy of rock 'n' roll. Come on, aren't you paying attention? You mean specifically? OK, we're getting there. Just hang on, you'll see.

Returning to McLuhan then, according to his view, the technology was the medium, but that couldn't actually be the case. It was the music and not the technology at all that was important. Put another way, the music was the information that was transmitted by the technology and consumed by the lucky listener. Sure, the technology played a part, but that part was the same as a person traveling. The importance was in getting to the destination in one piece, and it didn't matter if you rode in a rickshaw or a Concord.

Kenn and I proved over and again that the technology used wasn't so important, that rather it was the music we were after and not the transmission (notwithstanding Kenn's insistence on being a scientist). For us, there was always the source that we could access. Cassette tapes; iPods; mp3, mp4, and mp9; HiDAT cartridges; CDs; DVDs; podcasts and live streaming; even radio in forms of satellite, AM, and FM: all forms of conveyance that filled our need. Some better than others, and some with different functions.

Consider how we based our various positions:

Radio—remarkable average, but really driven by the station and the individual program. There simply were too many FM "driving shows" devoted to fart jokes, the local sports teams, and self-promoting interventions by "radio personalities" that deemed themselves to be interesting or expert, when in fact they were neither. However, there were a number of beautiful gems that glistened. Late night shows. Specialty programs that had narrow focuses and an even narrower collection of listeners, shows like mine. Of course it was great. Plus, radio always got a big nod from Kenn and me for nostalgia, especially since, in our experience, this is where rock 'n' roll all began. I've had a radio show now for years and can't imagine a life without.

iPods—iPods were great. Lots of data meant lots of songs, easy to update and small to carry. Apple should have gotten a Nobel Peace Prize for the invention. Their iPod invention became the AK-47 of portable music: capable of going anywhere, functioning under all conditions, and infinitely adaptable. However, they were still limited to the "bullets" that you loaded into them. But then so was the AK-47, and while I suppose that you didn't really load the iPod with bullets, you couldn't load the Clash into a Kalashnikov either. Yet both were revolutionary tools and always made me think of the *Sandinista*, Gil Scott-Heron and N.W.A.

Live streaming, file sharing and podcasts—great sources of new music. Unfortunately, until 2016 they were still limited in terms of availability and sufficient bandwidth to listen anywhere. Still, lots of potential there, and when it finally hit its stride, the remote access to live music was pretty good. It was still something that Kenn and I would always remember trying to listen to stream casts that would time out, or stall while the data was spooling. For most of our reflection, streaming was closer to running water through a frozen hose in the spring than really being at a live show, but I guess we could sit and eat pizza at Kenn's, which we couldn't ever do if we were really there. Sure, there was also significant legal and commercial issues relating to file sharing / hosting services such as Spotify or Grooveshark where arguments raged about balancing royalties against distribution, but I'll save that discussion for later.

CDs and cassettes—pretty good too, but dated. Really anything that was tied to a device with a short life span was. I don't know why you'd even go through the trouble of cassettes or CDs anymore. Certainly not cassettes; you were far better off going digital. I kept a running tally of the days that this device staved off the extinction that its predecessor, the eight track, faced. Some had predicted that December 20, 2012, was to be the end for cassettes and CDs, but somehow this form of media managed to limp past that date.

However, the *coup d'grace*, the *malliot jaune*, the *piece d'resistance*, the Holy Grail of audiophiles was, is, and will always be the turntable. If I were a great courtroom attorney like Clarence Darrow, I would present my case for the turntable like this:

"Your Honor, let me explain the obvious superiority of the near-perfect alliance between vinyl and the turntable, so as to dispel any of the myths that opposing counsel may wish to attempt to confuse this great court with.

Exhibit A: Superior audio quality. Sound is inherently an analog phenomenon, so converting it to a digital requires a degradation, a debasing if you will, a *manipulation* from the original. Manipulation is, again, one of the many agents used by the Evil to cast disparaging light against an enemy. This court should not stand for such adultery.

Exhibit B: Consider that you don't listen to a "track" or a "file," but a "*record.*" A record is permanent. Sure, it's the past tense of a "recording," but it also signifies an event, or memory, that requires preservation. Further, noting that "record" is the past tense of "recording" suggests the ultimate objective: to memorialize past events. And rock 'n' roll is always an event. A legacy for humanity.

Exhibit C: Not only is the "record" a significant means of marking an event, it provides a tangible experience. It can be held, collected, catalogued, coveted, and caressed. It forces the owner to address the question, "How should I organize the records? Alphabetically? By subgenre? Most recent addition? Favorites in rank order? Is it best to have no order at all? Pure rock 'n' roll. Stochastic. Random. Untamed.

Exhibit D: Vinyl has stood the test of time. Even now the young punks and hip-hop artists are releasing their works on "vintage vinyl" or using the wax itself as an instrument, as DJs do for "scratching" or "mixing." This form has not only stood the test of time, but also helped forge important innovations within music itself. This could go on, but this is the essence of the media. Versatile, robust, and timeless, like the principles of law.

And with that, Your Honor, and subject to any questions that you may have, I submit to you, that a *record* played from a turntable is the ultimate audio experience."

Obviously impressed, the judge would reply, "Thank you, Mr. Richardson, never have I before borne witness to such compelling advocacy. In fact, if I am lucky enough to serve this great state of Oregon for another thousand years, I may not again have the pleasure of such a lucid and finely crafted argument. Well done, fine sir, well done indeed.

"Of course you are quite right that any attorney taking up against your cause would have to be ill-advised, perhaps having allowed his commercial interests to eclipse his view of the law and justice. Shameful. May this infamy remind you to return to more noble pursuits. But back to you, Mr. Richardson, you have enlightened this court, and we are now indebted to you. However, you have also demonstrated that you are worthy of great responsibility, which you now have the obligation to shoulder as I render my judgment."

"But Your Honor, I have yet to make my submissions on this matter," my unworthy opponent, whose chronically poor judgment would allow him to interject, would say.

"Right, and I am saving you your ability to practice law in this great state. If you interrupt again, I will have the bai-liff remove you and charge you with contempt. *Am I under-stood?*" the judge roaring, with a falling inflection after the word "understood" suggesting that his question was more of a directive. The other attorney would nod meekly, know-ing, as everyone else in the room did, that the judge wasn't really asking and should be given a generous berth.

Without missing a beat, the judge would continue, "Mr. Richardson, you have given this court much to consider, and in order to do so, and in the event of an appeal or new trial of this matter," the judge said, leveling an icy stare at the other lawyer, "I will hereby remand all of the evidence and exhibits to this court and my personal supervision." Of course, I would think, the judge is no fool; he wants my re-cord collection. I would later curse myself for not seeing this coming, and then try to reorchestrate my fantasy sequence dialogue to prevent this from happening if the time actually came where I was called upon to advocate for vinyl. But that would be for a later time.

"Additionally," the judge would continue, "this court sees the danger posed by any opposition to vinyl or turntables and feels that immediate action must be taken in order to prevent anything untoward from occurring with this resource of historical and strategic importance. Therefore, I charge you with the responsibility of executing a death sentence against any and all who blaspheme, slander, libel, or otherwise denigrate this magical source of music. Mr. Richardson, you will also have the absolute right to deputize anyone that you should require to assist you in this endeavor. Sir, do you wish to advise the court at this time as to any of your deputies?"

"Thank you, Your Honor." I'd say. "may it please the court, I would request the immediate deputization of the following: my longtime friend Kenn Ramseyer, who has been instrumental in my defense of rock 'n' roll; Iggy Pop; Mikey from the Suicidal Tendencies; Joey Shithead from D.O.A.; Chuck Biscuits from Black Flag, Danzig, and now Social Distortion; Professor Griff from Public Enemy; and finally, Bob Mould."

I would retire from the courtroom victorious and with a reputation of legendary proportions. My car, some kind of vintage convertible Mercedes or Jaguar, would be waiting for me outside. Highlighting the impeccably maintained exterior and wood detailing and leather interior would be a tall, leggy blonde of stunning proportions. Following us would be Terminator X and the S1Ws from Public Enemy, in their high-gloss black-and-chrome Hummer, with "Fight the Power" playing through the external speakers as we convoy through the streets as a rock 'n' roll entourage.

"Right, let's meet at The Viper Room. We've got serious work to do," I would dictate into my hands-free Motorola, so that the entire retinue would be advised.

Amid the din of roaring engines and Public Enemy, Kenn and I would retire into a state of rock 'n' roll opulence hosted by The Viper Room. Drinks would flow, girls would dance, and all the music played would be vinyl, celebrating into the night our victories in saving rock 'n' roll. We would be honored for setting our mark upon history and would then assemble our deputies so that we could lead assault after assault on the Evil, until it was finally eradicated and rock 'n' roll was safe for all. Kenn and I would prevent the death of rock 'n' roll from coming.

Or at least that's how it would go in my mind, but that was really just how most of my afternoons were spent avoiding Eunice at Forestry. Time spent dreaming of something better. Of doing something important. Maybe even heroic. Strangely, these were the same goals that my parents had for me, which you would think would work out OK, but it didn't. In reality, my parents and I differed in the key definitions of "important" and "heroic," and that's where all similarities parted ways.

But reality was different, as it so often is. Not only was reality always different from my fantasies, but also my reality was different from nearly everyone else's, except Kenn's, I suppose. In reality Kenn and I spent time, over and again, immersed in rock 'n' roll.

Rock 'n' roll was great. It was simple, accessible, and timeless. It was straightforward for Kenn and me. Remarkable but uncomplicated. Not like girls or politics. For Kenn and me, repetition was everything. We were like Grand Master chess players repatterning and repatterning an opening attack. It reinforced our knowledge and allowed us to savor the tastes of the music that we so loved. Repetition was the sole purpose for recording music, to allow it to be played over and again.

Repetition was the key to excellence.

Over and again Kenn and I would discuss matters integral to rock 'n' roll; organize our music; discuss various conspiracies, or rather *theories*, and who might be orchestrating them and even why. Kenn and I would fastidiously research the rock 'n' roll news of the day; repetition was the key to being heroes, and repetition was how we enjoyed music.

So ultimately Kenn was right. He somehow unlocked the mysteries of time travel and, in doing so, put ourselves at the front of the stage of rock 'n' roll. These were heady days indeed, allowing us to cross continually. Repetition. Launching from *Louis Louis* into live gigs was simply astounding. Astounding. Time travel. Understatement. Yet that was the only way I could describe it.

Kenn's description of "fucking awesome" also was effective, but still seemed to fall short.

There we were, jumping from Kenn's house to gigs and coming back with barely any time passing; Kenn was right—this *was* fucking awesome. Not only did he discover a means for us to see all the shows we had missed, or that were too far to get to, but also he managed to do this without any impact on our other time.

As with most things, we started cautiously, but soon we were like teenagers who had just discovered sex or sailors who had been at sea for weeks without fresh fruit, and we satisfied our cravings, without fatigue or interruption. We were seeing live music, old live music, and recent gigs. With time the crossings became less disorientating for me, and I started using Kenn's trick of leaving the venue through a door at the end of the show, and then finding myself returned to his house. While crossing was still far from routine, it was becoming familiar and much less daunting than my first experiences.

The shows were electric, even when they were bad. The experience of crossing to see music itself was like being a part of something that you knew you weren't supposed to. Sharing in a secret with someone who extended you a confidence prematurely, like secretly growing drugs among your grandmother's tomatoes or being let into the zoo after hours...something safe but unexpected. An illicit participation isn't the precise phrase, but it conveys the thought.

Time is the ultimate force of change. Given sufficient passage of time, things that were once odd will become normal. Repetition helps. So even as odd as they were initially, things that Kenn and I had already experienced, such as the use of money and returning to Kenn's after crossing to find that our pizza was still warm, were soon so much a part of the experience that it seemed normal. Like an odor that you can't smell anymore. Kenn and I were traveling to where the rock 'n' roll wild things were, which is maybe why Kenn called this the *Where The Wild Things Are Theory*. Just like Max, he and I would travel to other worlds, through time, enjoy a wild rumpus with wild things, and return home with our dinner still warm. But even though we expected that time travel would be strange, as I'm sure you would too, there were certain things that we simply couldn't understand or process. Some things, like not really understanding how *Louis*

Louis worked, how we returned to Kenn's, and the lack of pre-dictability in our destinations for crossings, we took in stride. Other things we didn't.

What struck us as especially odd, and more than a little discon-certing, was that Kenn and I seemed to be aging. We'd come back from crossings tired and sore, just as you would from a normal gig. But this was different. Kenn and I both knew that you would normally get knocked and jostled around at a show, but it was more than this. Our discomfort and fatigue were as though we were losing energy through crossing, and that loss of energy was causing us to age.

Sure, even this made some sense, I suppose. After all, rock 'n' roll is hard on a guy, so it was only natural that traveling through time to see gigs was bound to take even more of a toll. Since we didn't know why, we just had to roll with it; after a while we de-cided that we had to slow the frequency of our crossings and be-come more selective with our gigs. If there was a toll to be paid, there would be time for it and we could settle our accounts later. Even in our nirvana, there was a limit to our rock 'n' roll intake.

Rather than returning from seeing the Ramones and then imme-diately crossing back to Rancid and Radiohead (if, for instance, we were in the *R* section of our collection) all in series, we needed rest between these gigs. Really it only made sense. It also solved the problem of our rapidly aging. Fortunately, slowing down the rate of our crossings enabled us to enjoy the gigs without feeling like a kid who had overindulged on chocolate Christmas morning and wound up vomiting orange juice by noon. We had the power to change the world, just as rock 'n' roll itself did. However as demonstrated by Icarus, Voltaire, Dr. Frankenstein, F.D.R., and Spider-Man, with great power comes great respon-sibility. What would we do with this responsibility, now that we had been given both the means and the opportunity? Well, Kenn and I agreed that we would be mere observers and would not participate or engage with history during our crossings. Simply put, we had seen too many movies where the slightest alteration resulted in unintended but dire consequences.

Changing the course of history? Not a chance. Kenn and I took the position that the past was the past and that's how it should stay. Maybe someone would be interested in fucking around with the fabric of history, but not Kenn and me. I mean, who knows could happen? It might seem like the right thing for us to try and keep Sid Vicious away from Nancy, but we simply couldn't be certain. There could be some unseen consequence of keeping Sid alive, like Afghanistan becoming a world economic power on the back of the heroin trade. OK, I suppose that was more likely to have happened if Sid hadn't died. But what about Earth destroying black holes or the creation of mechanized Godzilla monsters? These were the sorts of things that always happened when someone changed the past, at least in the movies and graphic novels we read. In my mind, avoiding a Godzilla rampage or Afghanistan's rising into a powerhouse seemed like pretty good reasons to resist changing history.

So the decision was made. Kenn and I resolved not to interfere with the past; we would remain passive observers and not directly interact. We would become voyeurs of rock 'n' roll. Time-traveling ninjas, passing in and out of gigs without being detected. We resolved that we were in this to rock, crossing only for fun, to observe and to research. Through this research, we would be better able to enjoy and impart rock 'n' roll knowledge to others, feeling the texture of history that you could only get by experiencing it.

How did we justify this beyond avoiding a mechanized Godzilla attack? Well, by using our ability to cross to make up for lost time. Simply attending the gigs that we wanted to see, but either hadn't or, for whatever reason, wanted to see again, was reward enough. But as earnestly as we made this pledge, it wasn't long before we were called upon to depart from it. Isn't that what heroes do? Break rules? Take chances, struggle with their consciences in order to make things right? Well, this is exactly what Kenn and I were called upon to do, forcing us again to acknowledge the changes we were required to make. Let me tell you how this came to be.

It happened for the first time in Fullerton, California, in the warm but setting sun of the early evening, changing the light to a soft, hazy aura and elongating our shadows. Having crossed to see another Black Flag show, Kenn and I found ourselves on a rather unremarkable street, a little run-down, but nothing scary. Well, not for LA— and certainly not LA circa late 1970s.

While not completely familiar with the area, by now Kenn and I had been to LA and its environs a considerable number of times.

However, it was often different for us when we crossed because we were arriving in different years or at different venues. So much changed during the time that we were crossing that Kenn and I would never really know until we arrived where we were going. Sure, certain places like London, New York, and LA were becoming familiar, but you couldn't let your guard down, especially by making comments about cultural events or politics. You'd look for indicators as to your time and place, things like buildings, fashion, and cars, but then Kenn and I weren't really interested in cars or clothes or architecture, so these hints often didn't provide a lot of help. A set list from the gig? Now that could have provided a road map, but still not always. Worst case we could have probably narrowed our arrival window to a six-month period. Unfortunately, these cues were often unreliable, and we usually had to catch up on news of the day from scattered newspapers.

Yeah, discussing politics was always complicated. But these things were just matters that we took in stride and tried to put out of our minds. Rather, we enjoyed our crossing, finding that we were embarking on a warm evening gig in LA. The sultry air was great, but so too was the knowledge that we were in LA and had fed *Louis Louis* a Black Flag album, which meant a promise of raw energy that they always delivered.

Being purists, Kenn and I didn't subscribe to the idea of "a favorite band," but for Kenn anything that Henry Rollins had been connected to, including Black Flag, was as close to a favorite as you could get. We'd cross to see Black Flag with or without Rollins; other Rollins gigs and *Rollins Band*; Henry's spoken word tours; all of it. Kenn couldn't get enough of Rollins, and fair enough, the dude was an icon and everything he touched was fantastic. Well, all of it except the television shows and some of the movies, like when he was some Moses-looking guy in that sci-fi flick with the dolphin. But all the same, given the significance of Rollins in Southern California, we had crossed a number of times and seen a number of questionable and very rough clubs, suitable, if not purposely built, for a Black Flag gig in the early days. Finding ourselves in Fullerton, Kenn and I certainly had nothing to worry about. Well, except that we didn't know precisely where we were, how to get to the gig, or even when it started, because unlike many of the other times we had crossed, Kenn and I found ourselves not in the bar, but along a street somewhere. I guess we still had a lot of work to do to refine *Louis Louis*, but like a rain tarp on a sunny day, it worked just fine for now. After all, time travel and rock 'n' roll required a certain flexibility and ability to adapt on the move.

Like most things that became initial challenges to us during our crossing, we had grown used to not knowing where we were, and had learned also how to easily find directions. A few shops down from where we had crossed, there was a flickering neon sign of a liquor store promising Pabst and Miller beer inside. More importantly, the lower half of the window was cluttered with the multicolored paper of various concert posters; we saw the Black Flag poster that we'd come for and entered the store with confidence and resolve.

"Hey, ya," Kenn greeted the bored-looking guy at the cash register. Joey, his name tag said. While I was fetching a beer each for us from the fridge in the cooler across from the counter, Kenn continued, "Two bags, please dude. How do we get to the Black Flag show?"

Joey was pleasant enough, even with that later-afternoon-bored demeanor that comes with being in the middle of an eight-hour shift in a cloistered shop. The shop was teeming full of every source of instant gratification you could want easy access to. Single cans of cold beer. An assortment of soda, chips, chocolate, and candy. A library of skin mags, emblazoned with massive-breasted women contorting themselves in improbable ways. And also tobacco and caffeine options because, after all, there was no limit to the sources of stimulation a person might desire. At the epicenter of this lowbrow consumption sat Joey.

"Sure, here to help," he said. Joey wore rockabilly sideburns, thick-rimmed glasses, and a half-assed attempt at a sneer, all giving the impression that he was bored. Bored with work, maybe bored with life, certainly bored of the options that his employment offered for sale. Passing the time, Joey was reading. Sort of. Reading as you could between customers and making sure that anyone who came in wasn't going to steal or hold you up. I would have pegged Joey as reading some pulp fiction rag off the wire rack located alongside the titty mags, but again proving that appearances can be deceiving, Joey was floating casually through *Moby Dick*. Right. Perhaps the only person I've met to actually read the book.

Although I wasn't doing a book report or a spot check on Joey's work practices, I found this discovery interesting all the same.

I was momentarily distracted from our assignment of getting to the gig. Having received our directions and our travel-ready beer stealthily concealed in their separate brown bags, we set off as directed and within a few blocks found the bar.

Why did we buy beer instead of waiting until we got to the gig? Excellent question. First of all, when you buy something, you're forced into an interaction with someone and into a certain familiarity that allows you some social latitude. Therefore you don't have to break the ice and can simply ask, "Hey, I saw the Black Flag poster on your window. How do I get to the bar?" without looking like an idiot or making people (us included) uncomfortable. Also, and perhaps more importantly, the receipt has the date printed on it. This trick allowed Kenn and me to know definitively where it was that we were presently. What do you think would happen if you simply asked, "Hey man, do you what day and year it is?" That's right—before you could turn and run, you'd have a clerk who's used to working alone on graveyard shifts either call the cops, pull a gun, or (since we were in LA) call his gang member buddies. Maybe even a combination of these things. Given that Kenn and I never really grew into the Oregon outdoorsman stereotypes, these were not acceptable outcomes for us; besides, it would interfere with seeing Black Flag, and if I'm going to get beaten and abused, better at a gig than behind some SoCal dumpster by a budding N.W.A fan.

Kenn and I looked for practical solutions to these problems, like keeping political discussions to general themes only. So, given that the federal tax guys provide a great deal of incentive to make sure that the bookkeeping functions are properly carried out, dates on receipts are the most reliable indicators to confirm a successful crossing that Kenn and I have discovered. It was because of the receipt for the beer that we knew it was late 1977 and we were in Fullerton.

As expected, the bar wasn't much. In fact, the façade could be aptly described as "beat to shit and left for dead." I anticipated the interior would be worse. It turned out I was right. Black Flag, even in their days prior to Henry Rollins becoming their lead singer, attracted some of the most volatile, unruly, and utterly destructive crowds in Southern California. While the band's reputation grew to reflect their epic live performances, unfortunately their reputation also preceded them to such a degree that it was difficult to get bookings. Consequently, bar owners who didn't care about their venues being trashed or who were well used to wanton destruction were the only ones who booked the band. I guess there were other situations that would work as well, like a tenant who was hours away from being evicted by the landlord, or who was carrying on something shady that needed a diversion; they would book Black Flag too. If you were going to see Black Flag during that time, you were going to a shit hole.

Drinking the beer from the bags, steeling ourselves for a show that was going to be loud, rough, and full throttle, we crossed a laneway and saw a couple of skinny teenagers drinking from a paper bag and passing it back and forth. Stupid stuff. Right, just like Kenn and I were doing, except that we each had our own beers. No matter for us to be involved with, except that when I looked at one of the kids, he seemed somehow familiar. Like déjà vu. Pausing for a second, I heard something caustic from one of the two, but the details didn't register. I turned and studied him more intently, and the kid who was talking to me started to shudder, then sort of glow, and I saw what appeared to be a hologram projected upon him. Kenn stopped as well, apparently having noticed this too. The hologram looked like an older version of this kid, but with rockabilly sideburns and covered in tattoos; one of the tattoos was a red-haired girl in front of crossed bones and the word *PAIN* below the knuckles of his right hand.

"Mike Ness?" I mouthed to Kenn. He nodded, confirming my observation.

"Whaaaatt?" Ness asked with more than a little aggression and contempt, especially considering that he looked to be four foot eight and 130 pounds, scrawny and wiry; more of a target for a beating than a threat of one.

"Hey, you going to the show?" I asked. "It's supposed to be good." I was trying to buy some time to understand yet another oddity of crossing.

"Nah, just drinking here," he replied. "Looking for work. No work, no cash, no shows, no big deal. Whatever, like I'm going to go see some pack of clowns that are sure to be around again, I'm sure. Why do you fucking care?" He showed no real interest in seeing Black Flag. Clearly while the kid had commerce figured out, he had lots to learn about music and where his life was going to end up.

"Looking really hard for that job, dude? Where? In the alley or in the bag?" Kenn asked.

As Kenn and I started heading off, I realized that we needed to act. Mike Ness required our intervention or his band, Social Distortion, wouldn't materialize. "Hey, we got to get him into the show," I told Kenn.

Kenn disagreed. "One of the rules we agreed to was that we wouldn't interact during our crossings."

"But Kenn, he glowed, you saw it. That's got to mean something. And after all, it's only one of *our* rules, not like something that you'd read in the *Trouser Press*," I said, making reference to a definitive source of rock 'n' roll material and guidance, "or the *Kenneth Ramseyer Rules To Time Travel And Rock 'n' roll.*"

"Yeah, I'm sure it means something, like the sun is getting to us or the beer has formaldehyde in it and it's making you stupid," he retorted, more interested in going the show than discussing it.

"Kenn, think about this. You're the science guy, with all your potential and infinite possibilities. You know the history just like I do. Mike Ness was just some dumb, teenaged kid drifting around until he saw Black Flag."

"So? He's right there, and like he said, there are plenty of Black Flag gigs to be had."

"Right, Kenn, but Ness only went to the gig because *someone convinced him to*. Kenn, it could be that this Black Flag is the defining moment for Social D. We've got to do it." I turned and headed back to where Mike was sitting amid the flickering holograph that was showing two versions of the same person.

"Hey, kid," I said, calling out to Ness, "you and your buddy should go in to the show. I'll give you the cover for the door, but I heard the owner shouting about being short bar help. It looks like you can pour beer can you clear tables too? Besides, if the cops catch you out here, you'd be due for a beating."

"Fuck yeah. You figure I'll get on," he said, his mood of social resentment yielding ever so slightly to the natural teenaged optimism.

"What the fuck," I suggested, "you're already not working, and you've really got nothing to lose. Worst case you see a show for free, unless you'd rather sit here and smack-talk people who walk by. You choose," I said, walking away, seemingly indifferent. Of course you know that Mike Ness followed me into the show. You also know that Mike went on to form Social Distortion and become a significant influence in punk and rockabilly music, helping to forge a connection between the two. Now you know how Kenn and I changed history for the better.

"Dude," Kenn said as we were walking towards the door with Ness and his buddy in tow, "I don't think that anyone knows what 'smack-talk' is at this time."

"Meh, they can figure it out with the context. Plus I don't hear these guys crying about a free gig."

As great as the Black Flag show was for Kenn and me, it was a bigger deal for Ness. Mike Ness didn't get the job at the bar because there wasn't one. I had lied. But it wasn't a bad lie, just a little one so that I could nudge Mike along the path he was supposed to be on, so it was more of an intervention than a lie. So I suppose it was OK. I mean everyone lies now and then to help people make the right choice, right?

I would later learn that Mike Ness never really trusted a stranger again, but the upside was that he and Dennis Danell formed the band that would leave a mark on rock 'n' roll that was more enduring than any of his tattoos. We actually didn't even see Ness during the show, except for once when he was trying to find his way through the seething throng of bodies thrashing around by the stage. Of course it was a good ol'-fashioned mosh pit that imprinted Ness with the inspiration to form a band. Kenn and I saved Social Distortion and, in so doing, ensured that the course of rock was kept true.

Returning to Kenn's after the gig, we fell on his floor giggling with delight. Barely able to finish a single slice of pizza without bursting into silly grins or retelling the story to each other, sharing perspectives of the same story that we had both just witnessed. Like children at our first sleepover party, our excitement felt like it was fueled by refined sugar and something safe but illicit.

We now understood that we were the custodians of something bigger, and that we had a duty to keep the great ship of rock 'n' roll running safely through waters fraught with peril. Our knowledge, our dedication, and our passion would be the navigation system that would keep our beloved music away from the reefs and shoals, the icebergs and storms that would otherwise interrupt our safe passage.

"How cool is this? Traveling through time *and* being required to change history." It wasn't like we were interfering in a capricious or self-indulgent manner. No, we were being called into action to use our knowledge and ability to travel through time and ensure that rock 'n' roll stayed on its proper course. Any lingering thought of remaining dispassionate about the history we were participating in dissipated faster than bar patrons after last call. Now there was no stopping us.

Kenn and I couldn't put time travel down. It was a power beyond our imagination and, in the most benign of crossings, meant a gig that we had coveted, and other times interactions with artists who needed our help. How could we resist the intoxication bestowed upon us by an ability to interact with history with complete impunity? Kenn and I had fallen into the Golden Age: time travel, all the gigs that we wanted to see, and the ability to shape the past. Or was it the future that we were shaping?

All I really knew was that crossing was changing Kenn and me and how we saw the world around us. I've heard people say that changing history is evil. Or that rock 'n' roll and punk rock are evil. Evil wasn't something that Kenn and I gave a lot of thought to ordinarily, but we did when it interfered with our passion for music. Evil, it seemed, despised rock 'n' roll. Why? I've never really been sure. But it seems to stem from some sort of morality-based argument—well, that and a lack of understanding of how important rock 'n' roll really was. Kenn and I had heard the arguments and claims before that "LA was evil" or "Black Flag was evil," and so on and so forth. As often as we heard all of this, intuitively we knew that it was rhetoric, and weak rhetoric at that.

But intuitive knowledge is one thing, and empirical knowledge is something else altogether—something tangible that you can hold and examine. Tangible experience with Evil only came through direct contact or observation, which is another thing that crossing provided us. More than once, Kenn and I crossed and saw where Evil grows.

7 – Where Evil Grows

That was D.O.A with "Where Evil Grows," and I'm Sid. Do these guys have it right? Is that what Evil is all about? Something within? Something inseparable from our souls, but merely managed like an appetite or whim? Maybe that's all Evil is, sort of the same as saying, "I feel like curry tonight," but malicious rather than delicious.

We hear people speak of things as Evil or an enemy as having Evil intentions, but is there a critical test for "what is Evil?" If there is no subjective criteria or definition, and if Evil grows within us, then we're all Evil, and it's just a matter of tolerance and preference. Is Eve part of Evil? Is there Evil in the Devil? What about weevils? Are they Evil? Are other beetles, and if so, what about the Beatles? This is Radio KQPL Portland FM 92.1. It's four thirty-five Monday morning. I hope you're enjoying the show. Let's listen to Evil all night. Changing speeds a bit, up next is something by Miles Davis from "LIVE EVIL."

FCC transcript KQPL 92.1 FM 04.09.1997 0435
Operator search: "Evil"

Where Evil grows? Is it somewhere specific? Kenn and I discovered the answer, and I can tell you that contrary to some beliefs, it didn't grow in rock 'n' roll. In fact, the Evil exists completely independently of art and is merely manifested in people's actions. People's motives and actions are the source of the Evil.

I can understand why you would be inclined to think that an examination of the human psyche would be precluded from Kenn's and my interests. But even though he wasn't a philosopher, this was an important question for Kenn. The Evil's source and indeed its motives was an important matter for us because of the role that the Evil played in disrupting music. Drugs, alcohol, censorship, lyric banning, noise bylaws, and girls were tools that the Evil used to interfere with rock 'n' roll, with varying degrees of success. All designed to destroy the freedom that rock 'n' roll represents.

In fact, almost everything I had explored and learned was related to music in some shape or form. My understanding of VHF, UHV, FM and AM radio frequencies and the physics they are based upon; socio-economic references to socialism, fascism, and various forms of economic imperialism; and cultural references, all derived from my interest in, or were sparked by, music. The examination of the Evil was no different.

Why? Specifically, I have no idea, but I suppose it didn't really matter why. The fact that the Evil represented a threat to rock 'n' roll was enough for Kenn and me. It could have been that the Evil had made a target of rock 'n' roll, because the Evil needed to control rock 'n' roll's longevity and popularity. Maybe just because the Evil is built on malice with a desire to tear the world apart when they find it disagreeable.

As you might have guessed, our initial conversations about the Evil started over pizza and rock 'n' roll. No, we weren't playing the Beatles's album *The Beatles* (commonly known as *the White Album*) backwards. The Evil that Kenn and I had previously discussed in a theoretical way was more benign. We would volley ideas and banter about various concepts or actions of Evil the way grad students savor discourse about Milton or Francis Bacon. Probably with the same arrogance and authority, all divorced from any sense of practical reality. The Evil we experienced was more insidious than anything that we had previously thought we understood or knew, and we engaged in it firsthand.

"I thought you were bringing pizza tonight?" Kenn asked with disdain, as I jostled through his front door with boxes in my arms, from our pizzeria of last resort.

"Yeah," I said, shrugging, "these guys were the only ones whose line wasn't busy."

"Because they make shitty pizza," Kenn replied. "It's the same reason you never eat in an empty restaurant. Haven't I told you my *Old Mother Hubbard Theory*?"

Kenn had. More times that I could count, in fact. Basically, you'd never let *Old Mother Hubbard* offer you something to eat, because her cupboard was bare, not because she was destitute, but because she was a terrible cook. Actually, I think that she was insane or at least suffering from delusions, but at the same time seemed to have been inspired by the Dubliners in penning "Seven Drunken Nights." But Kenn was essentially right. If a restaurant is open and empty, you should give it the same wide berth as the four hundred-pound monster that wants to offer you a short-term loan.

"But, dude," I pled, "you know it's the big game this weekend, and pizza is a hot commodity. Besides, it's better than nothing."

"Is it?" Kenn spat out his first bite and feigned choking. "This shit is evil."

Three pizzas, a case of beer, half a bottle of Frank's, and a few Mountain Dews later, all coupled with significant signs of indigestion, we determined that pizzas were incapable of being evil, although some were decidedly un-excellent. But in so discovering, we also discussed the genuine source of evil and how it would transform into *true* Evil.

The Evil's source has probably been sought after as frequently as the Holy Grail or the Fountain of Youth. But still there is a difference between the scholarly ruminations about the Evil and what Kenn and I had witnessed. The Evil was always found lurking around rock 'n' roll. On the periphery. Hiding in the shadows readying an attack or preparing to unleash drugs or hoards of girls upon innocent rock 'n' rollers who could fall victim to various distractions. The best that Kenn and I could hope for was to shore up some support and mitigate the overall damage.

Still, the source of the Evil wasn't a question that we could expect to find an answer to. Unfortunately, discovering the source of the Evil was sort of like finding trouble: It often found its own way to you, even when you weren't looking for it. The Evil was like that; it moved mysteriously.

Kenn used to opine, "Rock 'n' roll gives a voice to human experiences. This is what results in its massive popularity and why people identify with it."

I couldn't agree more, but Kenn always elaborated. "In fact," he'd say, "rock 'n' roll is the pizza of popular art, maybe not always to your taste, some better than others, but even in its worst form, satisfying to some degree. It's simply too bad that bands like Bon Jovi, Duran Duran, Wings, and Genesis as well as performers like Tone Loc, Roy Orbison, and Bryan Adams made pizza that resulted in food poisoning. Abominations."

Unfortunately, I have to admit that I also agreed with this view. I say "unfortunately" because I know that it sounds like an indefensible position, but it wasn't. Obviously, Kenn and I were loath to waste our precious resources on contracting food poisoning when there were so many better options available. After all, if you had the voracious appetite that Kenn and I possessed, you were better off eating well.

However, the profound impact that crossing had upon us even changed this theory. After our experiences with Mojo Nixon and Don Henley, we gave some of these otherwise substandard efforts a viewing. While they certainly weren't the first options in our queue, considering our duty as stewards for rock 'n' roll and the privilege we felt having discovered crossing, we sought these acts out, just to confirm our judgments about them. Going to the public library and signing out a Bryan Adams or Phil Collins album would result in the excruciating experience of remaining trapped in some show that occupied a place in rock 'n' roll's sordid past. But it was more than simply being trapped at a bad concert. I mean Kenn and I had been there before, but sometimes being at a bad gig was still OK, or at least good enough. Like the time with the Mountain Bends or the times that Kenn and I crossed to see Canadian legend Art Bergmann. As disappointed as we always were, Kenn and I continued to cross a number of times to see him. Actually, we thought that it would be OK, because John Cale produced his first album, but in the end he was so inebriated that if he had merely been a patron at the club, the bartender would have been legally obliged to refuse him service.

This was wholly different than having to be seen in public checking out of the library an album by Dio, Nickelback, Whitesnake, or Mariah Carey…conduct that Kenn and I rightfully found disgraceful. We would hide these records from public view, to avoid ridicule or having to discuss the music we were carrying with people that we might happen upon. Unfortunately, despite our efforts to conceal our activities, we still answered to it, more than once.

"Right on, man," slurred by one barely coherent high school stoner we once knew, catching us coming out of the library with borrowed albums. "That's like totally the best Van Halen album I've ever heard."

"Yeah," I would sheepishly agree, "me too. I won't listen to any of their other ones." Both statements were, in fact, true. The album that I had checked out of the library was the best Van Halen I had heard, and I wouldn't listen to anything else by them. Of course the fact that I hadn't listened to any of their other albums, with or without David Lee Roth, didn't detract from the accuracy of my response. Sure, the gig was a bit of a spectacle, but you could only go so far with the hair bands and watching Sammy Hagar wielding a machete and chopping the beer cans mid-flight that Eddie Van Halen was throwing across the stage, which seemed more like a trailer for a slasher movie than a gig. I secretly held hopes that some type of misadventure would occur, but these dreams could only sustain so many crossings, especially since the music couldn't. Still I preferred the passive-aggressive white lie to the unconstrained condescension required to correct the musical misguidance of the perpetually stoned.

Of course Kenn and I shirked the attention that accompanied the possession of these types of recordings because that was a natural state for us. He and I always dodged attention, regardless of the root cause. This was a practice that dated back to our dealings with McCloy and even our parents. This was a practice that provided continuity from our childhood through our teenage years and into the stalled adolescent existence of adulthood.

But it was more than merely our history of being repressed; Kenn and I felt that for our position, for our view of rock 'n' roll and the care used in building our collections that there was something inherently shameful about what we were doing. Taking music on loan from a public library was shameful enough, an act that amounted to an admission that our collection was somehow insufficient or wanting. Couple that shame with *what* we were borrowing and the act became almost intolerable. It was like having your mother or favorite aunt discover the pornography that you had assumed was safely stashed under your bed. It was one thing for Eliot Spitzer to have frequented top-dollar call girls, but if our record collections could talk, it would be the same as Mrs. Spitzer had really discovered that Eliot was with thirteen-year-old Thai boys.

It was in the bowels of rock 'n' roll that we saw acts that were more a function of promotion than of substance. Should we have been surprised? No, probably not. Kenn and I struggled with the justice of it all. How did Bryan Adams, Don Henley, and Phil Collins succeed when Bob Wiseman, Jonathan Richman, and Lloyd Cole remained in the shadow of relative obscurity? As painful as it was to witness such situations, it was even more torturous to see subpar live performances sold to teeming audiences by hype machines. These were acts that lacked any true rock 'n' roll substance, but Kenn and I went to see them anyway. It was just another thing that you take in stride when you're a hero. And sacrifice it was. I remember trying to implore an ambivalent God to cut off the Air Supply, to deport the Foreigner, to quarantine Boston, or to give the bloody Nickel back. Maybe I was trying to invoke the wrong God. Maybe I simply wasn't worthy enough to have a deity bother with me, even if my cause was worthy. Whatever the reason, my efforts failed to produce any result, and Air Supply still haunted me in shopping malls and while I was placed on hold, seemingly every time I called a government agency. So Kenn and I had to explore for ourselves what was going on with these bands.

While adventure and exploration were part of the attraction of crossing, getting trapped at a Loverboy show suddenly seemed like too high a price to pay. It was not as dramatic as being caught under a collapsing scaffold or stage like at the Radiohead gig in Toronto, or where our crossings required Kenn and me to influence history, but notable because we couldn't seem to leave a show until it was over. I know that I've indicated that sometimes Kenn and I stayed after gigs for reasons of "historical significance," but I'll get to that later. For us, our search for the Evil was the same as us looking for trouble…we often found it easily.

But back to Loverboy. We were not "Lovin' Every Minute of It"; we were hatin' every second of it, and the seconds seemed to drag for days. It may seem that Loverboy was an odd choice, but we were driven by the pursuit of knowledge. Also, there was a more obvious connection for us with Loverboy and parts of our collection. Actually it was Ron Obvious, the producer of Loverboy's hit "Lovin' Every Minute Of It."

Ron Obvious was on our radar, not for Loverboy, of course, but for his work with Canadian punk icons D.O.A., and the Subhumans, both great bands in their own rights, and even more so with Obvious at the production table. In fact, Ron Obvious was largely considered integral to their formation and early development. What seemed odd to Kenn and me was that Obvious would go on to design and build recording studios for Colin James, Bryan Adams, and K.D. Lang. Why would such a great contributor help such substandard acts? Maybe he needed the money; most of us do. Maybe that was his talent or form of expression. Maybe he didn't see rock 'n' roll in terms of black and white, as Kenn and I did, but rather on a continuum. A continuum like the radio frequencies, you have to keep adjusting late at night because their signal range changes with the cooling atmosphere. Maybe he was just doing his part to make something deficient sound that bit better.

That was the reason for this departure that Kenn and I attributed to him. Ron was obviously being a hero. Anyone associated with D.O.A., and the Spirit of the West, and then went onto Colin James had to be a hero. It was an act of greater kindness than you would expect from Mother Teresa. Kenn and I were certain that was the answer, but still felt disappointed that he didn't apply his talents to other acts south of our shared national borders. The question of "why" lingered, but unfortunately, we never crossed paths with him to ask Ron or Mother Teresa…at least not yet.

With the ability to cross at will and without time or expense passing us by, no show was left unseen, no band unexplored. Well maybe not *no* show, but we certainly witnessed most. What had originally started as a way of seeing what we *had* missed, crossings became about seeing if there was something we were *missing*, something from a particular time or period or something about a band itself. You know, like trying to see if there was at least a performance that you could give a nod to, something that would redeem a particular band or performer, but sadly this was often not the case. But even confirming that there was nothing redeeming about a live performance was OK. Kenn claimed that failures were every bit as important as successes, you know for the sake of the scientific process. It really became part of our collective existence. Pizza, beer, crossing, and rock 'n' roll. It just didn't seem like there was anything else for Kenn and me to do. So, crossing, and crossing again, is what we did.

Actually, to do any less would be to waste the opportunities that our discovery of time travel had facilitated. We once allowed ourselves to be consigned to a Celine Dion show in Vegas. Notwithstanding the plush booth-style seating and endless procession of alcohol, the show was a disaster for Kenn and me. We had suspected that it would be, but again, drawn like moths to a flame or free alcohol and opulent seating, we needed to see for ourselves. The verdict was self-evident, and as gamely as Kenn and I tried to overcome our prejudices, we just couldn't escape the inevitable conclusion, which Kenn committed to his whiteboard upon our return: No interesting lyrics + no real presence X monumental amount of hype = bad live show. Our verdict on Celine Dion was unchanged by her live performance. And while we tried to overcome our prejudices, I failed to overcome my lack of interest and fell asleep in the opulence of Vegas, with Dion caterwauling in the background.

I was shaken awake to a bouncer's angry voice. "You gotta get out. You can't get sleep off a drunk in here. It's disrespectful to Ms. Dion."

As my eyes fluttered open, I struggled to understand how hands the size of baseball gloves could grab me. I could hear Kenn saying something, but my eyes began to focus, witnessing the most splendid contrast of ebony skin, which glistened like oil, and ivory teeth, and eyes that pierced and offset the darkness that engulfed them. He was wearing some type of crimson tunic that all the lounge staff wore, and the gold lettering on his black nametag read "Joe."

"I'm…I'm enraptured by the music," I pled.

"You iz eider drunk or sleeping off a drunk. Ain't nobody enraptured by dis. You gotta leave," Joe demanded.

"Well, who's being disrespectful to *Ms. Dion* now?" Kenn was quick to add with his typically saturated condescension. "Why don't you go play George Foreman somewhere else and leave us in peace."

"Ah, you boys is fight fans, are yuz?" Joe said, with a hint of aggression seeping through his firm but polite demeanor. "Well, then you might 'preciate when I go Mohammad Ali on yuz."

"You mean Cassius Clay," Kenn persisted. "The fighter's name was Cassius Clay."

With that Joe grabbed us both by the collars and forced us into a jangle of legs stumbling and dragging toward the door. "No sleepin' drunk white boys gonna tell me that a black man ain't gots no right to change his name. It's one ting to disrespect some white woman singin', but it's som'din else to go at Ali."

Falling through the door, with Joe's intervention, Kenn and I retreated home in shame having confirmed our view that just because Celine has a powerful voice, it doesn't make it right to use it that way.

"Strange that the gig wasn't over, but we still crossed back," Kenn absently commented later.

"Kenn, you've got to watch your mouth. Joe's a certified monster. He could have killed us with his hands." I was serious... dramatic, but serious. The times that Kenn's mouth had put us in the breech were part of my past that I actively repressed, just like watching Celine live.

"Any beating we might have gotten couldn't have been any worse that staying at that gig. How do you think she got into this great country anyway?"

I suppose that Celine is probably only considered soft rock, but still. What was with the chest beating and the incessant playing up to her sugar daddy-turned husband? It was just so wrong, and in the end the show left us needing a shower and seeking to be deprogrammed by two hours of the Ramones and a case of beer. Fortunately, Kenn managed to produce *The Celibate Rifles Live at CBGB's*, and off we went again. Salvation at the hands of an Aussie rock powerhouse in NYC. Still to this day, the words that come to mind when I see that record sleeve are *rehabilitation, sanctuary,* and *therapeutic.* Maybe the Rifles wouldn't normally be considered therapeutic, but you should try seeing them shortly after enduring a Celine Dion show and nearly being throttled by a monster named Joe.

Crossing to cleanse ourselves with the Celibate Rifles re-opened our discussion about how it was possible that an otherwise wanting act could make it so huge just on the efforts of marketing and promotion.

Even beyond the terrible and among good acts, how was it that the Cure became a huge success while Echo and the Bunnymen enjoyed more modest rewards; the Mighty Lemon Drops even less so, and the Sad Lovers and Giants relegated to all but obscurity? All four bands were active around the same time, had similar styles and essentially the same influences and audience, but vastly different levels of exposure and success. In fact, I would go so far as to say that listening to the Sad Lovers and Giants is something that most people overlooked and are worse for it. I still get goose bumps when I hear the Cure's "A Forest." It floods me with memories of times, places, people, and experiences in which that song was a backdrop or on a mixed tape or college radio station. But the Sad Lovers and Giants have similarly haunting songs: "Cowboys," "The Best Film He Ever Made," and "Imagination." So, where were their just desserts?

How is it that Lloyd Cole, a brilliant lyricist, remains largely off the radar, but Bryan Adams is able not only to find a gig, but to parlay lyrics such as, "The only thing that looks good on you, is me" into a successful career? Was this further evidence that the Evil was afoot and operating behind the scenes, or was it merely the influence of commercialization and consumer indifference? Again, a subject that Kenn and I sought to explore with our access to the past, but not something that we would easily discover elucidation to.

"Look at this," Kenn said, handing me his iPad with an *All Music* article opened.

"Al Hirt?" I asked. "What about it?"

"How is that fair? Here you've got a jazz icon that gets a brick—like, a real brick—to the mouth during a riot in New Orleans. He's out of commission until he can heal and rehabilitate. Why is it that nothing like this ever happens to Jon Bon Jovi or Colin James? It's like they're protected by the umbrella of capitalism."

Kenn had two theories related to capitalism and in particular how capitalism protected its cash cows. The first was the *Adam Smith Theory*, named after the famed economist, and the other was the *Titanic Theory*.

"*Adam Smith* is a pretty straightforward theory," Kenn would postulate. "You simply observe that the consuming public is really largely an amorphous mass of collective consciousness only capable of demanding that which is supplied. Supply actually informs demand. In fact, if you really think about it, people are incapable of demanding something that doesn't already exist or is already in supply. Thus, we have the fundamental law of supply and demand operated in a way to feed an appetite that it created."

Between slices of pizza and changing a record, Mercury Rev to Radiohead, working a theme between *Deserter's Song* and *Hail to the Thief,* I added, "Sort of a perpetual sweatshop for the Emperor's new clothing?"

"Exactly," Kenn said, "but this was only one aspect of the problem."

Making up the other portion of the problem was the stimulus given to the *Adam Smith* model, and this manifested itself in many examples. For instance, Kenn and I had spent a lot of time discussing the horrible disappointment that was Bryan Adams and the harm he was causing the youth of the world, but still without discovering a solution.

Kenn continued to press this position. "How can any sense of right exist in a world that would reward the commercialization of a product, not on its own merits, but on the advanced publicity that instructed the masses that the Emperor's new wardrobe was better than anything else?"

As you might imagine, this gave rise to the articulation of what Kenn's viewed as another conspiracy. A conspiracy of how capitalism drove musical production and that true musical creativity was usurped by promotion, favors, and influence. I found it hard to argue, especially when one considers the various radio networks' payola scandals. After all, I had had a belly full of pizza, a beer in my hand, and a catalogue of music to select for our night's indulgence. There was always something (external and mendacious) with Kenn. For him, our relations with girls quickly became another such conspiracy, but so did the constant barrage that rock 'n' roll faced.

Of course the *Titanic Theory* was so named for the maritime colossus that the engineers claimed was invulnerable. Ironically, the *Titanic Theory* also encapsulated the immense marketing efforts that facilitated the success of both the James Cameron movie and Celine Dion's career. Look at the evidence: Dion was little more than some sort of wailing francophone banshee, and the story that James Cameron based his movie upon was as airtight as the inner ballast compartments of the *Titanic* itself...all failings that should have consigned Dion, the movie, and the ship to an icy grave at the bottom of the Atlantic. But while the ship sank, the others floated...in fact, soared. As sore as that made Kenn and me, it was the fact that marketing alone propelled something that should have, by rights, failed. In fact, I would say that failure should have been guaranteed but for the efforts of some marketing geniuses. As Kenn explained with *Adam Smith,* a market was manufactured and an insatiable audience consumed both without critical thought.

Sure, Dion has a powerful voice. The painstaking detail, effects, and technology that Cameron developed, even revolutionized, for the film, were enormous. Of course it was a conspiracy. What else could it be? Why didn't anyone ever point out that the Zeus-led Olympian gods ultimately defeated the Titans? Maybe there was a metaphor there, the Titanic destroyed at the foot of an aquatic Mt. Olympus.

The Evil is something that you hear about and think you understand or at least recognize in the world at large, but do you really? You hear songs about evil or band members that adopt "evil" into their moniker, like Evil Dick, which Kenn used to call me from time to time, but who is actually the front man for an Australian band named HITS. According to the band's press and even the comments from the bass player, Tamara Bell says, "He's more bark than bite." Even Miles Davis recorded an album called *Live – Evil.* But evil of this type never really held a candle to what evil really was when *evil* changes from an adverb to a pronoun. When evil no longer represents a description of an action but becomes the very personification of itself.

Once again rock 'n' roll reflected our reality, and the Evil was no different. It was just like a Forbidden Dimension song Kenn and I had discovered, called "Cold And Lonely Evil," like Offspring's "A Conspiracy of One." That "one" was the Evil. The sort of Evil that has marauded throughout history, capable of acts so heinous that victims and witnesses alike were so aghast that all they could do was stand silently by as the perpetuation of human misery continued unchecked. This was the Evil that sought to cause the death of rock 'n' roll for no reason other than it represented something different and divergent to other tastes. This Evil was the bully of culture and art. Only content when repressing humanity. Unsurprisingly, the Evil became our sworn enemy.

How did Kenn and I know when we were confronted with the Evil? Well, we had seen the Evil before. Although we suspected that Kenn was right, he and I crossed to confirm his theories.

"Dude," Kenn would implore, "it's the basis of the scientific method. We have to check. Verification is the only way to confirm the validity of an assumption."

It certainly justified a lot of crossings. As self-appointed protectors of rock 'n' roll, we needed to know firsthand, so we engaged our ability to travel through time to find out what the deal really was. It was during our crossings that we discovered how the Evil leveraged itself against rock 'n' roll to achieve their mandate of obedient morality.

Kenn and I had seen enough to know that not everything that was wrong with history was due to the Evil, but in their desire to destroy rock 'n' roll they were alpha predator in the open savannah of the arts. Their methods were as old and enduring as granite. Efforts designed to marginalize, to label music and all associated with it, were shameful and base. Wasn't that the way it was done with an enemy? Marginalize. Vilify. Debase. The tools of hatred that worked to victimize the subject who was targeted but also those bearing witness.

It's one thing to stand against the suppression of expression or the violation of rights, but if you make the victim ugly enough, the act of defending is also unpalatable. Consider a simple confrontation on the street, where a burly construction worker is screaming with unbridled rage at an older woman, who is struggling with a package in one arm and a walking cane in the other. Almost immediately other pedestrians intervene on the side of the woman, even without all the facts of the incident. But when the situation repeats itself between two construction workers or a kid on a skateboard or a homeless person, the reaction tends toward nuisance and ambivalence.

Now consider something rebellious and labeled as uncouth. And if nothing else, rock 'n' roll represented rebellion. That's why it has always been so important for society. Important enough for Kenn and me to stand up for. Important enough for the Evil to try to destroy it and ruin it for everyone.

How important is rock 'n' roll? Not only is rock 'n' roll an art form, but it is also an expression of freedom. Of individuality. It's usually one's first experience with rebellion. Rock 'n' roll represents accessible insurgence. That's how it was for Kenn and me, even in the beginning. We listened to music when no one else was around. Later, we hid under the covers of our respective beds listening to the radio in the dark, long after our parents had told us to go to bed. Hiding our actions. Hiding that we were listening to rock 'n' roll as though we were masturbating, worshipping Satan, feeding a drug addiction, organizing a coup, or joining a local socialist party. Imagining that our transistor radios were as important as those used by Radio Free Europe, Radio Essex, or the Mexican Radio. To Kenn and me, access to rock 'n' roll was as important as defying the Nazis.

We had once thought that *listening* to rock 'n' roll was what we were hiding. We were too young to understand that our parents were just sending us to bed because it was late. All the same it became a sense of rebellion for us. Something to stand up for. A cry to rally around. Rebellion in the key of "E," and now we realized that Gil Scott-Heron had been right, "the revolution would not be televised, the revolution would be live." We found revolution in live music and in living with music.

As we were working through a set of LA Punk, chronologically starting in the '80s, Kenn and I consumed our pizza and scoured the Internet for information that supported the bands and were derivative in nature. Chasing the story of the Dead Kennedys litigation regarding obscenity, then the distribution of royalties within the band, and then following Jello Biafra's conspiracy theories, our conversation returned to the role that rock 'n' roll plays in revolution.

"Rebellion is the act of taking a stand. An act that requires facing adversity while still finding a way to move forward." Kenn was right; rebellion was more than hiding under your bedding and listening to the radio after your parents sent you to your room for "lights out." Still it's an act within everyone's reach.

"Yeah," I agreed, "a chance to be heroic." Rebellion was taking a stand, making changes in the face of opposition. So it's natural to think of rebellion and rock 'n' roll in the same context.

"Rock 'n' roll has to be outrageous, brash, and arrogant in order to become the voice of change. Part of the attraction to rock 'n' roll is the sense of excitement and danger that comes from being a part of something that cuts across the grain. That's what people fail to see. That's why it's such a problem for the Evil."

"Kenn, it never ceases to surprise me how many times there's a backlash involving music. I mean it's becoming cliché now to try to cause a stir before a major album release; just another way of remaining current. Look at the unabashed use of Michael's funeral by Joe Jackson to promote himself. Or Miley Cyrus at the MTV VMA's, her Rolling Stone cover and Wrecking Ball video. Tell me that this is any different than Madonna kissing Britney at the same VMA's, some ten years earlier?"

"Same, same. And same as Madonna's industry of promotion." Kenn agreed, "but all the same, she should have called that song "Train Wrecking Ball", because while she can sing, she's a train wreck, I'd bet my "(White Man) In Hammersmith Palis" single with "The Prisoner" b-side, she's dating Lindsey Lohan inside of a year.

"Don't bet with Clash singles buddy; some things just can't be replaced. But yeah, promotion meets revolution, meets revolting."

The rebellion associated with rock 'n' roll was part of the enduring image and what made people hang onto the music later in their lives. It reminded people of their past adventures, of dreams and hopes. Standing up to The Man. Being counted. Lauded for making a difference. Stirring of one's being and awakening one's spirit. The ability to scream in a crowded nightclub, but as part of something alive. Freedom, and making a contribution to the world.

It was like when we had crossed to see Nirvana only finding ourselves instead with a despondent Dave Grohl in a rehearsal studio. Kenn and I didn't need to wait to see his shimmering and glowing holograph. Kenn simply walked over and gently put his hand on Grohl's shoulder and said, "Dude, this is rock 'n' roll. It's bigger than one band or even Kurt. You still have a voice that needs to be heard. Don't worry about sounding perfect. It's about what's going on inside your head and in your heart."

Grohl just looked at Kenn and sort of nodded. Years later you'd think that Kenn should have been given credit for inspiring the start of the Foo Fighters. In fact, Kenn should have been credited for Grohl's 2012 Grammy speech, when ostensibly he used the same words. Kenn never got the credit he thought he was owed. In fact, Dave seems to have no recollection of Kenn or me at all. Strange the things that heroes do, without getting due credit. But rock 'n' roll calls people to action, even if that action is nothing more than dancing or gathering in a club.

Sometimes the Evil claimed that their opposition to rock 'n' roll was based upon scripture or an immorality seemingly inherent in music. But how can that be? Words immoral? Nonsense. Words are just words. Of course words mean something, and their meanings are important. But people are the only ones who can give words life. It's people that can be immoral. Immoral in their intended use of words and their purpose. Acts can be immoral. Thoughts can be immoral. Motives and people can be immoral, but not words. Words merely assist in an expression, immoral or otherwise.

Sure, it doesn't help the Evil's view of rock 'n' roll, when Darren Hanlon proclaims, "If you want to be my savior, you'll have to learn to sing," in *Butterfly Bones*. Worse still when someone scrawls above a urinal in CBGB's, "I can't believe in a God that won't dance." But is this immoral or merely interpretation? Is Hanlon looking for a deity or having a conversation with a supreme being? Does it matter? Maybe it was a metaphor, but maybe it was a plea to a system of belief that was based on something other than judgment but rather acceptance and celebration.

Kenn and I had seen how organized religion had been leveraged by those at its helm to cause abuse and repression based on misguided justification, but concluded that it wasn't religion, but the organizations that facilitated abuse that was the problem. A religion in which people sang and danced freely couldn't be as bad as one that perpetuated exploitation or abuse. That was at least how Kenn and I processed our surroundings and also sidestepped any evaluation of religion, which was ultimately beyond our resources or interests anyway.

Unfortunately, this wasn't enough, as the Evil would breathe down our necks in the name of morality and try to besmirch music as a source of harm. Certainly music was misinterpreted and misused. Charles Manson used *The Beatles* album to lead his followers and color his actions. But strangely it was only *music* that was commonly singled out and vilified rather than other forms of art. While there was broad mention of Mark Chapman's claim of having been motivated by *Catcher in the Rye* to murder John Lennon, there was never any backlash towards the book or the author. Similarly, the murderers Christopher Wilder, Leonard Lake, and Charles Ng were all found with *The Collector* among their possessions and claiming inspiration from its text. People couldn't really say that a book or a painting or a song could spur an unmotivated mind into murder, but they never resisted the opportunity to denigrate music. Musicians like Frank Zappa, Ice-T, Public Enemy, the Butthole Surfers, Tool or the Dead Kennedys were the problem, not books, not paintings, not any of the myriad of social problems that could build a sociopath.

Perhaps this was just a distraction or an easy answer. What if Manson had been carrying a copy of *Moby Dick*, a Bible, or a baseball card instead of talking about *The Beatles*? The music was only an issue because the Evil had made it one.

We had crossed to see the Talking Heads, and as it turned out we were early. Not like during the opening act early, but like roadies unloading the gear and skeleton bar staff kind of early. Unfortunately, the crossing placed us in the bar, so it wasn't a case of grabbing a beer down the street or talking a walk. We were in a mostly empty bar with the house lights on.

"Hey," the bartender called out at us. "What are you guys doing? We're still closed."

Fortunately, this wasn't the first time that we had been early to a show. In fact, long before we discovered crossing, we would often arrange our evenings so that we were at the show for the sound checks or to help the roadies set up. It was a practice that I learned in conjunction with my radio show, when the Supersuckers came through town. Basically, the station manager was looking for all the help he could find to help the band set up in exchange for free admission to the show. As it worked out, we were moving gear around before and after the gig, and Eddie Spaghetti tossed us a couple of beers. Beer and free rock 'n' roll, just another way of saying heaven on earth, and all of this was ours, even before we discovered crossing.

The formula was actually pretty simple: (Rock 'n' roll + beer) x zero dollars = awesome. Did we enjoy free beer with the Talking Heads after the show? What do you think?

Kenn and I looked at each other and shrugged. "Dude, it's not like that. It's OK. We're with the band," I replied.

As it turns out, if you grab some gear and look like you belong, then everyone else thinks that you do. It's actually genius in its simplicity. Basically, the real roadies think you're with the bar, because they don't recognize you. The bar thinks you're a roadie because you're not bar staff and because you're moving gear around. Helping to set up, everyone lets it go. By the end of the night, you're drinking the band's beer, having seen the show for free. I guess nothing's for free; you've helped set up and load the vans, but then again you're also part of rock 'n' roll, so it's even better. It's like the proverbial free lunch, but without any downside. Although I originally came up with this rather creative work for our chronically deficient rock 'n' roll budget, it was Kenn who once again took it up as a theory and thus named it. Inspired by the *Little Red Hen* story, where it was only through cooperation that the work and the rewards would be shared, Kenn named volunteering for the band the *Red Hen Theory* even if it was more like *Little Red Hen* meets *High Plains Drifter*.

Since the *Red Hen Theory* worked before, Kenn and I knew that it would work again, we agreed to use it if necessary during our crossings. This time was going to be no different than any other. In fact, because it appeared that the gig was at a large venue, it would likely be easier. The Talking Heads had lots of gear, and because they were hitting their stride they had a good following. So there would be lots of guys like Kenn and me milling around getting ready for the gig, who would be hired casually or as part of the regular road show. There was really no telling who was who, at least not without some effort. Besides, it wasn't as though people would really think that a couple of guys were going to travel back in time to help the Talking Heads set up for a show all for a free gig and some beer. Even at that, what was the harm? What would the Little Red Hen say?

"Right," the bartender said, seeming ambivalent, "the rest of the guys are using the freight dock around back. Buds and Corona gonna be all right for the band's cooler?"

"Yeah, should be fine." Kenn fell right into the role. "Maybe some Pabst and Cokes would be good too." The trick was to sound like you fit in, while not offering too much information that might open up questions, dialogue, or complexities…you know, like ordering Fresca.

"Got it," the bartender called over his shoulder as he was filling the sinks with ice. "I'll have it sent around to the change rooms."

"We'll grab them for you if it's easier," I offered as Kenn and I introduced ourselves.

"Sure, won't be long," he said. "Good to meet you guys; I'm Joey. If you need anything let me know, that's what I'm here for. Should be a good show tonight, yeah? The band's good to go?"

"Yeah, they're always good," Kenn replied emphatically. "Never know wha' you'll get with David, but that's part of it."

"Yeah, part of the experience," agreed the accommodating bartender.

About fifteen minutes later, Kenn and I returned to the bar and retrieved the coolers full of ice and beer from Joey.

"Cokes are coming," Joey added as we hoisted our loads. "I figured the beers should be on ice first. Gimme another five or so."

"Thanks, we'll be back," I confirmed, glancing back over my shoulder at Joey. Laden with our cargo and acting the part, we started toward the changing room, which was at the back of the club.

At this time the lighting guy was getting the stage ready, and light was bouncing around in weird ways. Random flashing and pulsing of colored lights played throughout the bar, illuminating the walls and ceilings and passing through open doors, as he programmed, tested, and set the lighting. As a result Kenn and I were actually seeing spots, and everything had that same sort of shimmer and glow that Mike Ness and David Grohl had had when we crossed paths with them. The blur upon everything in the bar was as distracting as the prospect of meeting the Talking Heads either before or after the gig.

Noticing a door that I thought was the changing room that was slightly ajar, I gently nudged it open with my Doc Martens, so I didn't have to put my cooler down. Rather than witnessing the band getting ready, we saw a room that was being used for storage, but still had a folding table, a few chairs, and people in it. OK, it's not really mysterious to see people, but these were not the people we had expected to see.

Kenn and I would later discover that we had just come in direct contact with the Evil. We didn't know what it was at the time, but even then, it seemed like something was amiss. The band wasn't in the room, but there was a small group of three in the midst of a conversation that they abruptly truncated as soon as they noticed us. Three people huddled together as though they were telling an inappropriate joke in mixed company or hatching a nefarious plan, like perhaps something that would cause the Talking Heads to break up. But it seemed OK to Kenn and me, because no one was glowing or shimmering, and there wasn't a hologram to be seen. At least that's how it seemed when Kenn and I discussed things later. While things seemed odd, it was a back room in a bar, which was a pretty standard place for lots of shady things. Whatever was going on, it just didn't concern us… or so I thought.

Time travel was odd. I suppose this was an obvious conclusion. But even as veterans with a multitude of crossings under our belts, Kenn and I continued to face oddities that seemed un-predictable. Out of all the experiences we had had during our crossings, the greatest difficulty with time travel was trying to mentally relate to the events of which we were becoming a part. It should have been easy. But it wasn't. People like David Grohl pretending not to recognize us years later didn't help.

Traveling back to a time in history that Kenn and I knew so in-timately should have been more than familiar. It should have been like a weaver entering the fabric he had painstakingly built with his loom. But it wasn't. The fabric of history was different when Kenn and I looked at it from the present than it did when we were a part of it. Kenn explained this as "relating to percep-tion measurements, which are the basis of stellar observation."

"Look, dude," Kenn would explain with exasperation, "try to keep up because this is science. There is a 'perception shift' based upon where you observe things. Like the way you can block out an entire mountain with your thumb when you close one eye. In our case the distance happens to be temporal, and it is time that changes not only what we see but how we see it."

"You mean parallax," I corrected. "Parallax is a means of mea-suring distant objects, particularly the space between them."

"Sort of," Kenn snorted. "What you've heard of parallel uni-verses and what you think *parallax* is, well, that's only a part of it. But basically what you see from a distance is different than what you see up close. So your perception shifts in relation to your proximity to what you're seeing. Just like an earthquake on the other side of the world doesn't seem as bad as a large car crash on I-5, or how the atrocities of Afghanistan seem worse than those in Vietnam. It all relates to proximity and how that proximity changes your perspective. The activism of today becomes the institutions of tomorrow."

"Kenn, you're quoting lyrics from the Weakerthans's song 'Confessions of a Futon Revolutionist.' It was the band that said, 'The activism of today becomes the institutions of tomorrow. But it is an allusion to how things change over time.'"

Kenn was right. Well, maybe not with the details of his explanation but the gist of it. Imagine if you were a cultural historian and you could travel back to a time where African slaves toiled on tobacco plantations. How could you exist in that time without trying to impart your enlightened understanding of the world or tell Columbus that regardless of how cool it was that he survived a trip across the Atlantic Ocean, that he hadn't really discovered a route to India? The reason that you couldn't actually do these things is because it would be impossible to explain those facts in the context that you found yourself in. It would be impossible because you're as alien as if you had come from Mars, and you lack any ability to articulate your experiences with the people of past generations.

But it was more than that. If you look at measures of time, other than rock 'n' roll, using geological references or even in terms of American history, Kenn and I weren't really traveling that far back in time, but we traveled with such a frequency that certain details blurred or faded into one another, sort of like how fuzzy logic works. Kenn also tried to explain fuzzy logic and indiscrete boundaries to me but without any real success. After a while it wasn't just the logic that became fuzzy, it was also the people that we met or saw at gigs and even the musical references: songs that might be performed live without being recorded yet. You can only imagine the look either of us would get when we made a comment out of time. It's one thing to mix metaphors, but quite another to refer to something that won't happen for another decade. Now imagine how much worse it would be to talk about a tour or an album unknown to the time that Kenn and I presently occupied.

We had to be sharp with our general historic knowledge, a task that we attacked with mixed success. Our best defense in these situations was one that we had learned from years of being bullied at school and chastised by our parents for our choices. We kept to generalizations or remained silent. This also made our decision to interact as little as necessary with the fabric of history easy.

I suppose this blurriness or oddity had the potential to attach itself to all of our crossings, but here we saw three people who looked familiar. But familiar to what? Isn't what makes identifying people easy the fact that they seem familiar within a certain context? How many times do you see someone you know, but out of context, and struggle to unlock his or her name from your brain? So, now what was the context for Kenn and me? Did we know these three from the past? Our past? Past crossings? Our present or the future? Had we been to gigs before where these three had been? How could we know? Kenn and I didn't even know where we were until we had gone outside to grab gear from one of the vans.

But all the same, here in this room, now, there were three people. Two huge men and a girl. The girl seemed ordinary but pretty. Although she might have just been pretty, but in an ordinary way. I could only see her obliquely, a glance of her face from over her shoulder that was slightly toward the door, but she looked appealing from what I could see. I suppose that all women were considered appealing to us, but there was something else here. A sense of déjà vu, perhaps. But I couldn't tell if it was a déjà vu from our own past or the one that we had traveled into. Girls were confusing enough without introducing time/space paradoxes.

Adding to the confusion of it all was that I couldn't say what was attractive about her. The jeans and long-sleeved cotton T-shirt didn't reveal anything good, bad, or indifferent about her figure, so any sense of her being a beauty was indeterminable. In the end, the combination of rock 'n' roll and women is more intoxicating than alcohol, and the blend is always undeniably attractive. I suppose that she fit my main criteria for finding a woman attractive: I did not visibly repulse her (at least not yet), and she was alive.

Of the two large bald men, one was a muscle-bound gorilla who dwarfed the other man, made the girl appear disproportionately small and the room itself cramped, like perhaps the back of a small delivery truck. He had his back to us as he was hunched over the table, as though ducking under a low-hanging light. In fact, it appeared that his posture was a result of doing just that, a lifetime of trying to shoehorn himself in to a world built for the average. If you had painted this dude a metallic black and given him a voice synthesizer, he could have passed for the family robot from *Lost In Space*. He was wearing a black leather jacket, and his back looked like a school blackboard, but even under the jacket, you could see that he contained the power of a bulldozer. Rising from the base of his shoulders, without need for a neck, was a bald head, resembling one of those blunt Cold War missiles you'd see photographs of in school. I remember a feeling of embarrassment sweeping through me as my arms cried like hungry babies due to the weight of the fully laden cooler; I could imagine Frankensteinzilla carrying one under each arm like they were loaves of bread.

Nothing really looked particularly amiss about him. In addition to the black leather jacket, he wore dark jeans and ankle-high Docs. He looked like just a monster of a man talking to friends. He could have been a neo-Nazi or some form of fascist, but it was only his size and his shaved head that gave him that look. Otherwise, it was a standard rock 'n' roll uniform for attending gigs, and you just can't judge a skinhead's politics by his haircut. The only difference with what Kenn and I were wearing and this human moose was that we didn't own leather jackets, and even if we had, the jackets wouldn't have required the leather from two cows to make.

As the other man rose, Kenn and I understood the proper dimensions of the people whom we had inadvertently interrupted. The familiar-looking man rose and turned toward us, hurtling us back to memories of being face-to-face with McCloy. This man looked similar to the sinister bully from the schoolyard that I had so many years ago stood up to and blackmailed. They looked the same but couldn't be. It was impossible. This man was larger, older, and bald, but he looked as though Harv might have once he had aged.

It would stand to reason that Harv would grow up, but something still didn't add up. Even though I wasn't particularly apt at math, I didn't have to be a genius to understand that we were now in New York City, and Harv was still a young teen in Oregon. Science aside, my deductive logic kicked in. I actually did better in philosophy in college than Kenn had in high school science, so I immediately discounted the possibility of this man being Harv. I knew definitively that this couldn't be Harv, because when Harv had been tormenting us, the Talking Heads were just starting to fall apart, so Harv's older self couldn't be at a gig. There was no way that an adult version of Harv could be here, because we would have all still been teenagers. But I suppose that it could have been his uncle or some type of relative.

Which I suppose was why I called this guy "McCloy" anyway. It just seemed to make sense. Strangely, this made more sense than I knew, because it actually turned out to be his name.

McCloy was an imposing man. Although he appeared to be two hundred pounds, he looked like a miniature version of Tor Johnson, the Swedish actor/wrestler who became immortalized as the villain in classics like *Plan 9 From Outer Space*. His fair complexion and gleaming baldhead contrasted starkly with his dark suit, which covered an opened dress shirt. The only intrusion upon the vast unspoiled expanse of McCloy's suit was a small lapel pin of polished silver metal. It looked familiar…something we had seen perhaps? Something evocative, inspiring goodness or awe. It appeared to be a pair of stylized musical notes, actually a pair of triple note beams, but laid over each other to look like a pair of capital letter "M"s. The lapel pin had an expensive appearance, as though it were more than a mere decoration or a gaudy declaration of membership to a political party or community organization like the Rotary Club. No, what Tor was wearing looked like an award or commendation. A medal of distinction, perhaps.

Although I knew it wasn't Harvey, just seeing him was unsettling, and this feeling rippled through the room like a chain of dominos being turned over. Considering the size of this human monster, it was even more alarming. But for some reason, Kenn and I let it go.

It was only after the gig and upon reflection that we registered the part of the conversation that we had interrupted. Back at Kenn's, we replayed the events and tuned in to the words we'd heard earlier.

"Look, we need to strike at these guys hard and decisively," commanded the McCloy-looking character, who carried the assertion of someone who was in charge. The kind of man who was used to being in control and wielding it to get his way.

"Are you going to get him to fall for you or what?" he asked again, this time with the woman responding with an affirmative nod and a barely audible, "Yes, Lon."

"Good," he continued. "It's your job to get them infatuated with you, so that we can crush them when they become vulnerable. If not, then we'll need you to steal and destroy their equipment."

"But Mr. McCloy, why don't we just try to steal their music and then make it bad?" asked the human monolith.

It was the sort of question, if asked by this same monster in a movie that would have been met with scorn and ridicule, but here the atmosphere seemed insidious enough to welcome such stratagems. Something palpable, like the smell of decay from a source that can't be found. A sense or a feeling, like a fleeting déjà vu that you couldn't place which caused preoccupation. But there you had it. Without knowing it, Kenn and I were brushing alongside an Evil that would use its freedom to destroy that of others. We knew intuitively that this wasn't right, whatever it was that was happening. Unfortunately, we failed to recognize the threat that was present at the time and therefore couldn't intervene.

I felt a twinge that I knew this man, and the woman, too. But it was the woman who drew my attention. Like a faint aroma that you recognize but can't name or even find the source. There was something that felt comforting and familiar about the girl, but coupled with the rest of the group there was a dissonance that stirred within me like an addiction that had once been kicked.

"Hmmmm," contemplated McCloy, "you know, that could work...maybe we would have to..."

At that moment when the group noticed Kenn and me struggling through the door laboring with our coolers of beer and ice for the band, McCloy's thought interrupted mid-sentence.

"You guys with the band?" Kenn asked with what he assumed was a rhetorical question.

"Ah, no, we're ah...we're ah trying to manage them, but you're looking for the room across the hall," the girl said over her shoulder, seemingly holding McCloy's gaze. Silently they watched us leave, but we could hear them continue to murmur as they started to gather the various notes, papers and binders that were spread out on the table. Their demeanor was confident but slightly rushed and distracted as they collected whatever else that they had, stowing it in attaché cases and make their way to the exit at the rear of the building, where everyone else was busy setting up.

"That was sort of weird, hey Kenn?" I said.

"Maybe," he said, shrugging. "Management is always weird. Let's get this beer down and then go back for the Cokes. We should probably conduct some empirical testing on an appropriate sample. You know, to ensure that both were cold enough."

Strangely, Kenn and I never realized that we were in proximity to such heinousness. It was only later that we would fully understand who Lonnie McCloy was. And worse, what he was capable of doing in order to disrupt the rightful order of things.

We thought we were just going to gigs, collecting more information, satisfying our appetite for live music that had previously eluded us. At the time it seemed natural to work at smoothing a few wrinkles that time had forgotten along the way. Sort of mixing business and pleasure, I suppose. Really we just wanted to be the guys that helped anonymously from the edges of the scene. You know the type of person that you think of when some megastar is interviewed and admits, "Yeah, but you know if it weren't for the random guy that gave me a break..." or, "I met this guy after the show who told me..." that "none of this would have ever happened." Kenn and I were becoming *those* people that they were talking about.

But this didn't change the fact that at the time we were just crossing to see the Talking Heads, masquerading as roadies/bar help. As we found the changing room, finished our tasks, and settled in for a great gig, our thoughts of anything else, including McCloy, yielded to the escape that rock 'n' roll always provides.

I looked at Kenn as the Talking Heads took the stage and heard him say, "Here it goes again."

8 – Here It Goes Again

The best thing about rock 'n' roll is that it never stops. Neil Young said that Rust Never Sleeps, the Beastie Boys refuse to sleep until they hit Brooklyn, and Katie Herzig has an album about the waking sleep. This is KQOR 89.9 FM, it's three forty-five a.m., and I'm Sid, so obviously I'm not sleeping.

Rock 'n' roll inspires and is derivative. It both creates and replicates, which obscures its beginning and frustrates its end. Like a record or a new track or a radio show, rock 'n' roll keeps going around and around. So all this brings us to our next song; we could play "Do It Again" by Wall of Voodoo, but instead we'll hear "Here It Goes Again," with Ohio's OK Go.

FCC transcript KQOR 89.9 FM 05.31.2014 0345
Operator comments redacted

"Here it goes again," Kenn exclaimed. Once again, we were making plans to leave the sanctuary and satiety found in Kenn's basement, to pursue rock 'n' roll. With the taste of The Sink and Hawaiian pizzas and beer lingering on our palettes, Kenn and I would soon be crossing again to find another gig.

"What do you think we should cross for this time?" I asked.

"Dude, this time it should be something legendary. Something colossal. Something loud."

"What about rather than something, we find *everything* louder than everyone else?" I asked, working in the name of the 1999 live Motörhead album. Could there be any other option than Motörhead? No, of course not. Over a feast of beer and pizza drenched in Frank's sauce, Kenn and I discussed music and what the breadth of our crossings had taught us. We had discussed bands that we knew intimately and others that we weren't familiar with at all. Naturally, we decided that we should try to learn even more. Since discovering and refining crossing, we had been to so many gigs now, seen so many bands and different bars and clubs, which we would have never otherwise been able to do.

But what do you do when you've been to so many gigs and have learned to change history? You continue to do so. You repeatedly change history through your actions and decisions. Not history repeating, but repeatedly changing history. And not the same history multiple times, although I suppose we did that too, but different historical events Kenn and I were changing. If you're heroes like we are, you do it again, right, just like the Beach Boys or, in fact, Wall of Voodoo.

Why travel through time? Well, of course, to see gigs we'd missed. Why intervene with history while we're there? Well, who said we were intervening? Kenn and I were part of an adventure. The adventure of rock 'n' roll, which was replete with stories of gigs that never were, but almost were. Stories of guys who needed a chance or a nudge in the right direction, so why couldn't that be Kenn and me? Life is a matrix of choices, a series of crossroads. You can't really believe that mankind is the ultimate male driver who refuses to heed directions and is content to drive around for hours, lost, but within a mile of his ultimate destination. No, there must be influences that we can't explain that help direct our hands. Unseen, but still tangible. Kenn and I were the adventurers that guided the hands of rock 'n' roll. Not only was this our newfound responsibility, but it was also something we were loving.

But as much as Kenn and I loved being part of rock 'n' roll history, we only really ever sought to understand and learn more about rock 'n' roll. We never actively sought adventure; it was always just something that we stumbled upon, like the last temptation of Motörhead or the time with the Stranglers in Nice, France. Regardless of the adventure, the conspiracy, or the venue, for Kenn and me, it was always about rock 'n' roll. Adventures would come and go, some more ambitious than others, but we always returned to his place, ready for a new start.

I had an intervention during one of my radio shows that acted as a clever segue way into the Velvet Underground song "Rock and Roll."

"Good evening, this is KQRL, Redlands, California. I'm Sid, at eleven forty-five at night. It's a little earlier than I usually start, but I'm covering for Mandy who's double booked. We're all about the rock 'n' roll here. All about the learning and discovery. Because you know that it's "rock" and "roll." It's both. An object: a rock. Rock, as solid and unyielding as granite, capable of remaining resolute throughout time. It is a movement both primal and perfect. Cavemen realized that it was easier to roll something rather than carry it, and humanity has been doing so ever since. An ultimate movement that has not required further refinement. Not like swimming, where strokes have been improved or suits have been designed to allow humans to swim deeper or longer. Not even like walking, where sports shoes have been designed to convert energy to maximize efficiency. No, rolling has remained perfect since it was first discovered. Mobile and flexible enough to move with the ebb and flow of life, to move along with the tide of humanity and the vagaries of fortune. This is what rock 'n' roll is all about. Let's hear what Lou Reed and Sterling Morrison have to say about it."

Sure, the intervention itself was rather long and more self-indulgent that I'm usually up for, preferring to play music rather than blither, but it served a point. It introduced the song and conveyed how I feel about the importance of music. Actually, it kicked off a pretty good set, all with rock 'n' roll-themed titles or at least the word "roll," including Adele, Peter Murphy, and David Bowie.

According to a Wikipedia search, rock 'n' roll is defined as:

> Rock and roll (often written as "rock & roll" or "rock 'n' roll") is a genre of popular music that originated and evolved in the United States during the late 1940s and early 1950s, primarily from a combination of the blues, country music, jazz, and gospel music.

Blah, blah, blah...quotes Encyclopedia Britannica, blah, blah... initiate the "decline of rock 'n' roll" discussion. Really? The "decline" of rock 'n' roll? Yeah, really. I couldn't make this up if I tried.

The death or decline of rock 'n' roll discussion is predicated on the theory that an unstoppable force could be halted by the death of a few. Unthinkable. Just as unthinkable as saying that Christianity should have died at the feet of the crucified Jesus, or capitalism with the departure of John Keynes. On first impression, this may seem blasphemous and preposterous. I assure you it's neither.

Often it is the sacrifice or the loss of something that underscores its true importance. Martyrs for a cause; extinction of a species; clean water. Nothing accentuates an object's value or importance better than its disappearance. Sometimes it takes the death of a central figure to perpetuate the message. What would Christianity be without Jesus' crucifixion (and subsequent resurrection)? Cubism survived Picasso's death; pop art continued after Warhol passed away; and even by extension, the Velvet Underground relationship ran its course during Warhol's lifetime. John Cale, Lou Reed, and Sterling Morrison all went on to continue their contributions to music, and Cale's minimalist approach to music set off a chain reaction of exponential growth. This is perhaps the ultimate test of something's resilience, a test to see if it can stand on its own. Disco needed cocaine; the Branch Davidians needed David Koresh; televised poker tournaments needed the NHL hockey labor disputes; and stability in the Balkans needed Tito. Without relying upon these crutches, the organizations they assembled would crumble like pillars built of sand. Rock 'n' roll stands alone and stands strong. Rock 'n' roll is incapable of dying because of its ability to perpetuate inspiration. Again, this was a subject that often occupied the research that Kenn and I tirelessly pursued.

"Eno!" Kenn exclaimed randomly with a mouth half full of pizza. Naturally, I assumed that this was a suggestion to cue up some old Roxy Music as well as some Bowie and Coldplay that Brian Eno produced, to round out the set I was building of his solo works.

"Good one, pal," I confirmed as I pulled various albums from the collection.

"No," Kenn said, "I didn't mean to play Eno, although it's all good, but look at this." He finished handing me an article printed from some online news clearinghouse.

It was never enough for Kenn to let me read something myself, as though during the course of the my college degrees I had never mastered reading. No, Kenn had to prove that he committed the article to memory. "During a December 2009 Reuters interview, Brian Eno poignantly articulated the idea of rock 'n' roll being both derivative as well as inspirational. Like a Big Bang Theory fueling its own perpetuation. While discussing the contribution of the Warhol-managed Velvet Underground, Eno states, "The first Velvet Underground album only sold ten thousand copies, but everyone who bought it formed a band." Thankfully, people are still buying albums and forming bands. The irony of Brian Eno being quoted in reference to the Velvet Underground is interesting in itself.

Kenn was right. Eno is an artist, not the loosely defined term applied to some musicians like Sid Vicious or Jon Bon Jovi, but the genuine article. Someone whose influence on music can aptly be compared to Picasso's impact on cubism. Eno was an original member of Roxy Music, which is something in itself, but more importantly he later went on to contribute to the expansion of rock 'n' roll by developing a genre called *generative music,* a form in which the artist selects the base notes or ranges to be used, and then music is generated in a random manner. Wind chimes provide a natural example, where the design and dimension of the tubes fix the notes, but when randomly engaged by the wind, it creates music.

Of course wind chimes aren't new, nor did Brian Eno invent them. However, Eno took the theory behind wind chimes and introduced synthesizers and computers, making other variations possible. The result was the creation of a mysterious and often ethereal sound, something new. Unique and now occasionally termed *Enoesque* or a result of *Enofication.* In addition to his trailblazing, Eno was also involved in producing various artists such as U2, Coldplay, the Talking Heads, Ultravox, Icehouse, Depeche Mode, Devo, David Byrne, Grace Jones, Nico, David Bowie, and others who have left the music world a better place, as well as also having a variety of solo albums. Consider this: Think of the music the Talking Heads made, the young artists they inspired. Now move on to David Bowie, U2, and Coldplay, and you soon see a body of work as expansive as an ocean. Sure, Roxy Music may have been modest enough, but everything else that Eno did afterward? Staggering.

I blithely added, "Yeah, well, you know you've made it big when there's a Jazz Butcher song about you."

"Right, just what we need, to complicate the discussion of Brian Eno, with a discussion of feelings," Kenn dismissed, then started to ply the article into an argument. "You know it's interesting that in contrast to Eno's view, commentators have traditionally bemoaned the decline of rock 'n' roll in the late 1950s and early 1960s. Sure, by 1959 rock 'n' roll had witnessed the death of Buddy Holly, the Big Bopper, and Ritchie Valens in a plane crash, Elvis's departure for the army (should the return of Elvis from his military service been heralded as a second coming?), Little Richard's retirement to become a preacher, Jerry Lee Lewis and Chuck Berry's prosecutions, and later, the breaking of the payola radio scandal, implicating major figures in bribery and corruption in promoting individual acts or songs, giving the sense that the initial rock 'n' roll era had come, or at least was coming, to an end. So-called informed commentators stood on the street corner with a dilapidated sandwich board proclaiming, 'The End Is Nigh,' like some crazy unwashed vagrant."

I just listened. Kenn usually had a point. There was still warm pizza that he wouldn't be eating as long as he was opining, and we had lots of music still on tap for the night. Admittedly I also drifted in and out of the conversation a bit, keying in on different comments Kenn had made and taking a new direction with them. Like suggesting that we should cross to see Ritchie Valens or Little Richard. Otis Redding maybe? All of these were possibilities, but I think there was another possibility: Exploring the controversy that surrounded the different facets of rock 'n' roll, like Kenn was soap boxing about now.

"Bribery and corruption in rock 'n' roll. Shameful? Of course, End of days? Hardly. Symbolic of the inherent composition or nature of this form of music, it's fans, and creators? Of course. Or maybe this was just capitalism finding its way into music. But capitalism doesn't lure anyone into dishonesty and greed, does it? Just like the corruption found in politics, the International Olympic movement, university sports, or the various churches besmear only parts and not the whole. But could it be? Was this just another example of rock 'n' roll reflecting universal human conditions?"

"Yeah, Kenn, hardly the death of rock 'n' roll."

"I would have started wringing my hands and watching for the falling sky when disco became popular or when Elton John, Jim Croce, Wings, Pink Floyd, or the Jackson Five came onto the scene. But even this is wrong. To take such a view would be to allow my tastes to overshadow the facts, which is ultimately what we stand against. Still, Wings, Pink Floyd, and the Jackson Five represented a serious threat to rock 'n' roll. Thankfully, like the events preceding 1959 and many since, rock 'n' roll withstood it all."

Kenn was right, and even though we didn't listen to the Blasters anymore, they were right when they said that rock 'n' roll will stand.

Some music historians have pointed to important and innovative developments that built on rock 'n' roll over various periods, including multi-track recording; the electronic treatments and manipulation of sound originated by such innovators as Joe Meek, and the Wall of Sound productions of Phil Spector; continued desegregation of the charts; and the rise of surf music, garage rock, and the various dance crazes. This includes later infusions of punk, acid jazz, hip-hop, and other derivatives, all the while with an integration between the forms. I would agree, innovation was important to rock 'n' roll, and for all the trouble that Phil Spector attracted, ultimately his contribution to music would remain indisputable.

Rock 'n' roll is defined by innovation, and for my money, anything that built upon it, improved upon it, or incorporated it in an original or inspired way, was rock 'n' roll to me. The DJs who mixed classic Elvis and jazz tunes across updated beats, like the Propellerheads and Tom Holkenborg (aka JXL)? Check. Acts like Luna, the Rheostatics, the Ramones, D.O.A., and the Stiff Little Fingers that incorporated Glam Rock riffs or '60s anthems into their work? Check. Hip-hop and rap artists like Ice-T and Public Enemy, who sampled rock songs? Check. Innovators like Jello Biafra and Mojo Nixon, who tried to synthesize punk with country music? Check. Anything that was creative and tried to push the boundaries of the music, regardless of whether it was to my taste or not, including acts like Gorillaz, Galliano, the Datsuns, Sting, and Grace Jones, they always got our nod. It was all part of the innovation and all expressive. However, to say that rock 'n' roll was defined by a few discrete acts or events and was not a living, breathing entity just didn't make sense. Some of these same historians would say that without the innovation or a check in the development of this music, it was due for decline. Horse feathers.

The decline or death of rock 'n' roll? Please. Kenn would talk about conspiracy or scientific theories, but I saw things differently, more from a sociopolitical perspective. No more could rock 'n' roll die than nationalism could be extinguished, notwithstanding attempts to do so throughout Africa, the Balkans or Eastern Europe or even during the debate around the Treaty of Westphalia. The very fact that this is even a discussion that occurred in 1959 become hilarious when looked upon with the benefit of hindsight. But this is also part of the human condition, to repeat our past and our history, so in a sense it is also a part of rock 'n' roll.

In a similar fashion to the 1959 reports, the BBC claimed during its reporting of Sid Vicious's death on February 3, 1979, that the punk rock scene was on the wane and that its death was imminent. The BBC actually heralded this event as the beginning of the end. But was it? Consider that the Ramones played over 130 shows in the remaining 331 days that year and released no less than ten albums since Vicious's death. Acts like Rancid, Green Day, the Offspring, Agent Orange, Rollins Band, the Forgotten Rebels, D.O.A., Anti-Flag, X, Died Pretty, the Lime Spiders, Social Distortion, the Cramps, and many, many others all recorded music, toured, and contributed to the scene. Further, Bob Mould formed Hüsker Dü in 1979 and has been making music either as a solo artist or with Sugar, a subsequent band, ever since. But this shows a mere general trend, lacking specifics, but still supporting the fact that rock 'n' roll is incapable of dying.

In 1981 the Scottish punk band the Exploited released an album with the title track, "Punk's Not Dead," attempting to both address the question and comment on society, perhaps with little notice from the BBC or anyone else at the time. But, like punk rock itself, the Exploited were still at it twenty years later. Similarly, yet in a very different vein, Australian artist Darren Hanlon responded with his song "Punk's Not Dead" in 2002. It was not a cover of the Exploited's earlier anthem, as you might expect, but still enlivened the discussion, even if there was some concern as to whether Hanlon understood the original question or not. The important part was that punk, an extension of rock 'n' roll, not only survived the passing of Sid Vicious, Elvis Presley, and John Lennon but survived years of various incarnations, events, and challenges. Punk had become part of the social fabric and an experience that most people identified with, even if they didn't understand or participate in it. Ironically, the antisocial had become habituated. But this was really just like anything else. Given enough time, the peripheral becomes centralized; the strange, familiar; the alien, naturalized. Even in the middle of Kenn's rant about the perpetuation of rock 'n' roll, I tried to remind myself to research how often intolerance eventually gave way to what would become mainstream. Examples like Romans persecuting Christians, genocide in the name of imperialism, and isolationism becoming preferential trading. This was a pursuit that I could coattail off my time avoiding Eunice, rather than now when there was music to listen to.

"You know it's simply the misarticulation of or the perception of loss that causes the hue and cry that rock 'n' roll was dying." Kenn was still at it. "A way for one to express his loss and the depth of his grief, much like hearing a widow saying "I'll never love again." Of course for some widows it's true, but for others, I suppose it's just a nice thing to say."

"But come on, Kenn," I said, deciding to participate again, "some couples actually die within a few days of each other for reasons that can't be explained, like CBGB's and Hilly Kristal, Bonnie and Clyde, or Sydney Pollack and Anthony Minghella—couples that need each other."

"Sure, but rock 'n' roll is rather apart from such examples," Kenn retorted, reaching across for one of the remaining pizza slices, now room temperature, with Frank's congealing in small lava red pools. "Rock 'n' roll survives like JFK and Jackie Onassis, or Michael Todd and Elizabeth Taylor. It survives and endures. It changes form, it evolves, but it always continues to pound out the beat of human existence. Rock 'n' roll is as steady as stone and as mobile as a wheel."

Still, people muse over the decline or the failing of rock 'n' roll, either as a genuine belief or a rhetorical device. These musings seem to happen throughout time, such as in 1977 when Elvis died, and again when U2 broke up. Sure, there were derivative acts, but they would also become clear examples of why "well enough" should be left alone, these situations did not represent the demise of the form. In fact, we would come to learn just how resilient rock 'n' roll was and that it wasn't the mere absence of certain elements or bands that would cause the demise of music or even the abuse that it suffered at the hands of *NSYNC, Avril Lavigne, Billy Joel, or James Blunt.

This isn't to belie the invulnerability of rock 'n' roll, for patient drops of water have carved even the hardest granite valleys. But like the erosional forces of mountain waters, one has to take an active stand to degrade rock 'n' roll. It was these forces, the minds and energies that attempted to frustrate the human spirit. The actual threat to rock 'n' roll wasn't ever internal or caused by the vulnerabilities of human frailties, but rather by attacks from the Evil. Congressional hearings, censorship, and attempts to undermine its value as a form of art—these were the dangers that rock 'n' roll had to face.

As Kenn and I stood at the hub of rock 'n' roll watching the spokes of history flicker past, sometimes slowly so that we could count each wire, and others so quickly that they became a solid blur of silvery mass, we watched both the intentional and inadvertent consequences unfold. Fortunately, we were given the opportunity to intervene. Intervening is what makes us the heroes that we are, but someone had to take a stand. We always thought that someone had to stop the Evil. I just never knew that it was going to be Kenn and me. Why would we? What role could we play? Stopping the Evil was something that didn't concern us. A fight we didn't need to pick. After all, if rock 'n' roll couldn't die, then the actions of the Evil merely constituted a nuisance, but not a mortal threat that could foreclose a future.

So prevalent was punk and similar leaning rock 'n' roll, that punk bands covered acts like Tom Jones and Johnny Cash. Cash later reciprocated by covering the shock-punk Nine Inch Nails song "Hurt." Sid Vicious was lost, but punk kept on head-butting, kicking and screaming its way through our cities to remind us that we all needed an outlet for something primal, that there were issues to be questioned, and that rock 'n' roll was more than a one-trick pony. Kenn and I marched alongside, steadfast in our dedication and vigilant in its vanguard. And when I say vanguard I understood that to be running radio shows, crossing to gigs, and amassing collections.

You could argue that punk was merely an abomination of rock 'n' roll, but Kenn and I wouldn't agree. So you'd be wrong. But for argument's sake, examples attempting to define a purer version of rock 'n' roll, other than those represented by Wikipedia, also exist. Kenn's response to Wikipedia was as subtle as a sawed-off shotgun, "The Velvet Underground, Led Zeppelin, the Blasters, the Cramps, Lloyd Cole, Lou Reed, the Killers, Love & Rockets, AC/DC, and David Bowie, to name a few, have all attempted to convey what rock 'n' roll means, the impact it has had on the listener, or its fortitude, all through song. If these acts that have sweated, bled, and breathed rock 'n' roll in a perfected symbiotic relationship can't provide a definitive benchmark for the genre, how could a collaborative web-based resource? Simply put, the Internet failed. Wikipedia is fine but not definitive…well, unless you know," Kenn would say giving me a wink, "you know, unless we were the collaborators.

Looking for a more nuanced view of rock 'n' roll, one could turn to the online publisher AllMusic, which offers the following clarity:

> Rock & roll is often used as a generic term, but its sound is rarely predictable. From the outset, when the early rockers merged country and blues, rock has been defined by its energy, rebellion, and catchy hooks, but as the genre aged, it began to shed those very characteristics, placing equal emphasis on craftsmanship and pushing the boundaries of the music. As a result, everything from Chuck Berry's pounding, three-chord rockers and the sweet harmonies of the Beatles to the jarring, atonal white noise of Sonic Youth has been categorized as "rock." That's accurate—rock & roll had a specific sound and image for only a handful of years. For most of its life, rock has been fragmented, spinning off new styles and variations every few years, from Brill Building Pop and heavy metal to dance-pop and grunge. And that's only natural for a genre that began its life as a fusion of styles.[3]

As far as I was concerned, all of this was fine, including the Wikipedia nonsense, even when it felt somewhat sterile and clinical, or distilled for quick consumption. Ironically, both sterile and clinical are juxtaposed to rock 'n' roll, while quick consumption not necessarily so. Something for everyone, perhaps. But then if this isn't fitting as perfectly as Goldilocks, then what are we left with? We're left with derivative experiences.

Kenn sees rock 'n' roll as the seed from which everything of value grows. I see the situation differently. It was one of the points that I repeatedly rallied around despite Kenn's stand.

[3] http://www.allmusic.com/explore/genre/pop-rock-d20

"Come on, Kenn. If you really believe that there is nothing new or really original and that innovation is simply relegated to an assembly of existing pieces, then any discussion about the past or future of rock 'n' roll is irrelevant. But we know that this discussion is relevant. So then you find yourself in the midst of a swirling tempest of opinions and examples to support this position. Consider AC/DC as a source of lyrics that provide a self-definition and reflection of human experiences. We just need to point to "Who Made Who" and pull apart the lyrics."

Kenn started looking for the album of the same name and started singing under his breath, "Who made who, if you..."

"Right, Kenn," I interjected. "As I was saying, practically anyone who has ever turned on a radio and tuned it to a rock 'n' roll station would have heard of AC/DC and likely even the song "Who Made Who," from the album of the same name. Due to a familiarity that comes from having an album that sold over five million copies in the USA alone and having been released in 1986, the song "Who Made Who" lends itself well to interpretation and use in various other media. The most famous, perhaps, being in the adaptation of Steven King's short-story into the movie *Maximum Overdrive* and the updated release of his novel *The Stand*. Actually, you know, Kenn, this brings me back to the inspirational/derivative nature of rock 'n' roll discussion that we so often have."

"Not tonight, Dick," Kenn asserted. "Let's get some AC/DC on and consider where we're crossing to next."

"Sure, but back to the lyrics. Is this just a cute (supposing that anything AC/DC might do could be considered "cute") musing of a question of control or origin, or is this something more? Certainly the widespread use of the song in video games and popular culture gives some credence to such a theory, but then again, maybe it's just a catchy tune. However, it does explore the seemingly circular process of creation, be it human creation or artistic."

"Let's cross and get some weed?" Kenn asked. It was what he considered being subtle while telling me that he had lost interest.

"Andy Partridge, of XTC, alludes to the same question that very year on the track 'Dear God' on the American release of *Skylarking*, with the lyrics from an open letter to God: 'Did you make disease and the diamond blue? Did you make mankind after we made you?'" Obviously there is an inherent chicken and egg dilemma with the creation of something and the recognition of it." And so the conversation continued. In fact, it continued well past *Who Made Who* and was still in full swing at *Live at River Plate*, which Kenn and I crossed to see later, but after I finished my diatribe.

"Was rock 'n' roll self-perpetuating, or was it a construct of something else?" I knew that Kenn wasn't particularly interested, but to me this type of discussion mattered. "Did humanity create God, so that such a deity (either feminine or masculine) could then turn around and create humans in its own image? To say that God was only a human construct would be the same as saying that Isaac Newton created gravity or that Columbus created Cuba, when the fact is that they existed independent of discovery. However, this isn't enough to dispel the circular nature of the discussion, given the lack of empirical evidence of a higher being, compared to that of gravity. The existence of a god requires the acceptance of a fundamental premise rather than proof, but then if that premise is accepted, the discovery of such a god becomes like any other discovery, from science to geography. Dude, it's the fundamental belief, without the physical proof, that poses the problem for exercises of logic. But, again, we're getting away from the original discussion, that of rock 'n' roll and the themes that it represents. Even if no one ever heard a tree falling in a forest, they could still discover it lying on the ground."

"OK, can we cross yet?" Kenn implored. "I'm going to leave without you...either that, or I'll be lying on the ground myself like your philosophical silent tree."

Of course I let Kenn off the hook. Soon we crossed to see AC/DC, but my view of rock 'n' roll and philosophy still remained broader than Kenn's, as did my interest. This was a discussion that spilled into the creation and recycling of themes and materials in art as well. How many times has the H.C. Wells theme in *The Island of Doctor Moreau* been reused? Isn't that what the child "Sid" in Pixar's *Toy Story* had become? Fashioning his toys together in a macabre and sadistic manner in the same vein as Dr. Moreau's experiments? Or Dr. Frankenstein? Idi Amin? Pol Pot? The line between reality and fiction blurs as humanity's capacity for atrocities reaches new bounds. Are these simply themes, or are they reflecting human experience?

I remember asking Kenn, or my radio audience, more than once, "Can you honestly tell me that the first half of the novel *A Very Private Gentleman*, which later became the Clooney movie *The American*, doesn't remind the reader of Kafka's *The Burrow*? Was the *Hunger Games* trilogy anything more than an integration of themes from the *Survivor* reality television franchise? What about Steven King's/Richard Bachman's novel *Running Man* and the rash of movies made about men being hunted for sport? Didn't Richard Matheson's *Omega Man* and *I Am Legend*, Beckett's *Endgame*, Shakespeare's *Tempest*, Dante's *Inferno*, and Elliot's *The Waste Land* all cast the same apocalyptic and futile mood? What about Dali's paintings? If other forms of art inspired and cross-pollinated, why not music? Surely it must."

Regardless of our philosophies or my views on the derivative nature of art, when it came to disseminating rock 'n' roll, Kenn and I were of singular mind about the importance of our role and attacked it with vigor. Kenn preferred writing articles, reviews, and opinions that would be published locally or on his blog, *Not Noise Pollution*. Yes, an obvious nod to AC/DC. A worthy reference and a good outlet.

In fact, Kenn's writing was just like my radio show from years past. Actually, my radio show was probably all the things that I now complain about. It was self-indulgent, narrow, and unstructured, but it was something that I always managed to do regardless of where I was living. In retrospect it was only narrow in that it reflected my whims and fancies, which was OK, because the time spot started at midnight on Sunday. Actually, it was also my preferred spot for various reasons.

To satisfy the station requirements for my show, I had to put in at least two hours during my designated block, but didn't have to leave until the morning jazz guy rolled in at six a.m. Thus, I was left with a six-hour open canvas to weave magic and mix metaphors of one form or another. From time to time, I took up other spots to cover for other DJs, but mostly I ran late night slots. Regardless of when I was on the air, it was always a time that I enjoyed. A liberty of soul and mind that I didn't have anywhere else in my world. A freedom to program the show around my messages and themes, interventions that were certainly informed by research that Kenn and I had done together, but without his views shadowing mine. No boss. No parents. Nothing but airwaves and music, my voice, and the mic in the booth. At least that was I how I viewed radio in order to conquer my fear of speaking to whatever audience might be listening.

The music was very good and often outstanding. Not just for me, but for all the callers who dialed in. Before I started my show, I assumed that any callers I might receive would be trying to convince me to indulge requests for certain songs. Really, a hangover from my days of huddling over my small FM radio... you know, where the DJ always plays a "special request" from the cute-sounding girl who misses her friend, or some boy with a lost teddy bear. Since I hadn't had any direct experience, I assumed that what I had heard in those early days of rock 'n' roll exploration was a reflection of the world that I would find, once in the station booth. What I found was often quite different.

Strangely, most of the radio show callers didn't want to request their favorite bands or a particular song. They simply wanted to talk. I quickly learned that late night Sunday was a carnival of human loneliness. Even in a short two-hour show, I would anticipate a dozen callers. Well, at least a dozen calls—sometimes there were multiple calls from the same small set of listeners. So maybe it was just one listener and a dozen calls. Whatever, I didn't often listen to what the callers were yammering on about once they quit talking about music. If it wasn't a request for a song or a compliment about the show, I simply wasn't interested. Why would I be?

Calls would come in throughout the night, and usually I would find them tedious or distracting. Calls that would take my attention and energy away from the music that I was programming. But then it happened...something stranger than some lonely soul looking for someone to discuss T Rex with or to lament that Lollapalooza wasn't coming within an eight-hour drive from our town. A call that seemed like any other, except that it wasn't. This time it was from *her*. Someone unknown, but who sucked the air from my lungs, wrung the blood from my heart, and then breathed in a fresh breath of air while she administered adrenaline to restart my heart. But even that was later, but not much later.

It started in the way the calls usually started:

"Hey, man. Love the set. Really picking up your groove, this is great. It reminds me of when..." And then invariably, *"Hey, could you play*

[insert coveted song] *for me, it's just that…* [insert justification as to why I should indulge his or her request.]

It was always gratifying to hear that I was reaching people and getting the message out. So gratifying that I had merely assumed that listeners were fans, loyalists to the cause of rock 'n' roll. Even if the conversations quickly turned to a testimonial of heartache, desire, or other inane chatter, I still thought that all the listeners were music lovers. You know, just like Kenn and me, only not as dedicated, but certainly a rank of our number rather than the Evil.

I mean, why would I think that our enemies, the Evil, would be monitoring radio shows? Vinnie and Kenn always warned me that they were, but they're conspiracy theorists. What would the Evil expect to gain? It wasn't until much later that I learned that the Evil would stop at nothing to destroy me. That the Evil would tune in to radio shows across the county to listen, to learn, and assist in the construction of their plans, to plot the demise of rock 'n' roll. Abominable. It was only later that I learned that I was targeted and considered a threat, probably due to my importance and protector. It was as though the Evil had realized that Kenn and I were destined to be heroes before we realized it. And armed with this knowledge they sought to intervene before we struck their cause down; a pre-emptive strike, launched before we were even armed for battle. *I* was made the target… proof in my mind that my contribution to rock 'n' roll was greater than Kenn's. It was only later that I learned how I could become vulnerable.

But it was now when she called in. *"This is a great show. I've been listening for so long now, and it's becoming the highlight of my week."*

"Well, of course it is," I thought, absently recording the set in the song log and setting up the next tracks.

"I love your voice. What time does your show end tonight? All the way to six, or are you ending earlier? My name is Pyrah. I'd love to hear you play 'Sweet Jane,'". To this day, so many years later, I still remember the sound of her voice. How it made me feel—instantly curious, awake, powerful, central, like something primal was beginning to stir and come to life.

"Welllll, luckily for you, Pyrah, I already have that slotted in as first up, after the intervention. This must mean something," I replied suddenly, with unexpected attentiveness. "I like your name. It's different."

"Would you meet me after your show? I can wait outside of the station."

After how many years of evolution and still my answer was, "Sure. I'll see you at just after five." Logically, I knew the answer. With the endless battery of calls borne out of solitude and weirdness that I was subjected to during the course of my show, everything told me that the only connection that I wanted with any of my listeners was facilitated by fiber optics and that I should always maintain a Fairy Tale distance from. I knew instinctively the answer had to be "No, sorry, but..." But anything. An excuse of the late hour, of working in the morning, of being married, of being gay, of being on parole, of being married but with a gay lover, being impotent, late for my alien rendezvous with the mother ship from the Omega Quadrant, or being disfigured by burns received during a series of bad acid trips. Anything. An excuse of anything, but a "no" all the same. But something was stirring within me. My absent responses had given way to a focusing interest. My attention was being drawn across an entire horizon to rest upon a single peak. My interest was piqued, and I could hear myself saying, "You know, Pyrah, I'd love to." Really? Yes, really. I would love to meet a total stranger who was calling into a radio show at whatever late hour it was. I was hopeless.

As my show started coming to its triumphant end, building up to whet the listeners' appetite to tune in the following week, I started thinking about Pyrah and anticipating our meeting. Where did all of this come from? I was anticipating meeting a stranger? Sure, she sounded interesting, sexual, and...and what? A rock 'n' roll fan? Well, I suppose that was good enough for me.

It was tempting to start "Sweet Jane" again and set it to play all night, but I was afraid that too much Velvet Underground on a Monday morning could have undesirable effects on the remaining listeners. Or listener. So instead I opted for the extended version of the Stone Rose's "She Bangs the Drum," which would provide for a long introduction to Pyrah. It was actually a version of the song that I had pre-recorded, so that it would end with a final intervention where I would sign off for the night and effectively terminate the station's programming until the jazz guy arrived in the morning. With that and a delayed looped feed of station identification messages and public service announce-ments, I would conclude my show and have nothing left to do but meet my lady caller.

I left the station with my case of vinyl under my arm and a spring in my step, anticipating meeting Pyrah. A girl, or at least someone that sounded like a girl, who had asked me to meet her, *terra incognito*. Crossing the campus towards the parking lot that we had agreed to meet, my mind filled with possibilities. I advanced in a slightly cautious manner, but was also intrigued and aware of everything around me. I could feel the cool, fresh morning air that played on my skin like peppermint, heighten-ing my sense of excitement. A warming light streaked across the sky, invading the darkness: fiery reds attacking the blackness to produce yellowish blues. The morning sun was now dispelling the darkness that I had just before filled with great music. Night yielding to the promise of a new day. A new day full of new to-morrows.

Rock 'n' roll united people and was now bringing Pyrah to me. *Try denying that rock 'n' roll was powerful. Insignificant to the human existence*, I thought.

What a remarkable name, and she liked "Sweet Jane." That had to be a sign, because after all, *anyone who ever had a heart wouldn't turn around and break it*. Isn't that how the song went? My brain reordered the possible scenarios and changed the obvious ques-tion, *"How bad an idea could this be?"* into the obvious justifica-tion, *"How could this be a bad idea?"*

"Sid?" she asked.

Yeah, right, Sid. Let me explain. *Sid Itious* is my radio name. I don't often tell people about this, preferring instead to justify the secret as though it were a secret identity, but if I really thought about it, I would admit that I felt sort of silly about it all. Re-ally it was as much a part of local radio culture as the music I played. In order to have a show, you needed a program name that seemed cool and interesting, and hopefully I wasn't the only one who held this view. Then of course you'd want a *nom de plume* that reflected both your show and the image that you tried to fashion yourself after. Like *Mandacity With Mandy*, the urban man-hating lesbian and "womyn's rights" show, with a DJ who liked to rhyme. *Mandacity* was unfortunately sched-uled in the slot immediately ahead of mine, so there was always an awkward tension in the booth as Mandy's show ended and mine was starting. Kenn and I both maintain that Mandy hated all men and that I was simply collateral damage. Perhaps starting one of my earlier shows with the Cramps', "What's Inside A Girl" didn't help. But again, I digress from my meeting with Pyrah.

"Yeah, Pyrah?" I responded, "Hey, nice to meet you." I introduced myself and told her that Sid was actually never really my name, just what I used on air.

"Of course," Pyrah said, smiling. "I like it, but your real name is better. So...thanks for meeting me. I bet you have a lot of girls that call you. I sort of feel silly. You know, I've never done this before, so..."

"Hey, no," I assured Pyrah, noticing her discomfort. Was she shy? "Hey, look, I never do this either, and in fact the people that call in and ask to meet usually sound scary, have demo tapes they want played or want to convert me to a religion or buy life insurance or something. I avoid them like the plague."

"Ah, OK. I..." A suddenly nervous and seemingly self-conscious Pyrah trailed off.

"Pyrah, do you want to grab an early breakfast?" I asked, trying to restart the conversation that seemed to be stalling, or at least heading toward awkward grounds. "I haven't eaten since dinner, and there's this place a few blocks away that does twenty-four-hour breakfast..."

"You mean Pa's?" Pyrah asked, her eyes flashing and a smile dawning across her face again.

What a smile! To this day I always remember that first smile. It broke like the dawn behind her. Starting with a small sliver of a crescent moon and then opening to a slight part, showing pearly white teeth so straight, as though they had been cast. There was something else, something asymmetrical about her smile that drew your attention from one side of her lovely mouth and perfect lips to the other, in order to discern where the difference was. The asymmetrical tilt suggested something mischievous, playful, or curious, but maybe just shy. Something that stoked the fires of my interest and comforted me like warm broth and a wool blanket.

"Yeah, my treat," she offered. "The hot chocolate and waffles are my favorite there."

So it was decided, and not just because she was offering to pay. Pyrah and I agreed to meet at Pa's, both taking our respective cars.

All the way to Pa's, my heart was still pounding as it had when I first saw her leaning against her car. It felt like the kick drum on so many great songs, but the song that came to mind was "Like Wow – Wipe Out," by the Hoodoo Gurus. But there were others as well. Songs that tried to express my feelings of anticipation and excitement. Head over heels, like Tears For Fears. A longing look that Pyrah gave, enough to keep me fed all year, as spoken by XTC in "Harvest Festival." The world started to list away from me, and my knees got weak. There must have been an orchestra of angels playing with my heart, or perhaps just an Annie Lennox song in my ears. Both were pretty good, though.

You know the rest, don't you? Of course, we met at Pa's. The sun rose, day broke. Pyrah and I ordered hot chocolate and waffles, like she had suggested. Other patrons came and went, but we remained. We continued to order refills and shared a slice of pie—apple I think. We lingered, we giggled, we found the pause in conversation safe, rather than frightening. A pause offering depth and reflection rather than a void or chasm. Finally, as the shadows began lengthening again and the sun grew impatient waiting for us, Pyrah touched my arm. It was then I understood Darren Hanlon's song "Elbows." It was about human contact and filling gaps. She touched my arm, and I'll never forget it, even if one day I would wake to regret it. But even that…that fleeting departure from Hanlon's words, making them my own, I felt as though I were coming into my own. I was living a rock 'n' roll song. Actually, a multitude of songs.

At some point we went back to her place, but I don't know if it was that morning. We walked and talked and forgot about everything else. Forgot about the exhaustion that should have been setting in like hungry dogs. Forgot about the responsibilities that the morning usually ushered in. Forgot about everything except being together.

The days tumbled like dominos, each tripping the next in a sequence that only Pyrah and rock 'n' roll really connected. The days were full, but indiscrete, individually named and dated, but tied together by music and Pyrah. Details that would blur into a whole, separate points in space that formed constellations or an electronic image on a screen. What was a day without rock 'n' roll? What was a star outside of a constellation? Just a sun, I suppose, but that didn't make a lot of sense in my example. Maybe I would ask Kenn, as it seemed like sort of a science thing, but this was different. It was Love.

I had never felt love before then, and of course I had never fallen in love. Or Love. They were different, weren't they, *love* and *Love*? One was a verb and the other a pronoun, right? An action and a state of being, like enlightenment. This is how the two forms of love seemed to be, to me. Although the distinction was something that I had never understood then, and even now I don't. It was something that you could describe or experience, like physics, but I really didn't understand it.

If Love is also such a common experience, then why is it so elusive? People talk about looking for Love, finding Love, nurturing Love, just like some pet from the local pet store. So why didn't Love cross our paths more often? I had no idea that Love was such a difficult thing to discover, that it would be so intoxicating and so exhilarating. I had no idea that this girl and the discovery of love, or Love, would change my world forever. Obviously I should have, because it's always about a girl. It was just that this girl would turn my life into a ghost town.

9 – Ghost Town

This is KQOR 89.9 FM. It's twelve forty-five .a.m., and I'm Sid. It seems like the phone lines are dead tonight. Has there been a zombie apocalypse? An EMP detonation? Am I even on the air? Well, since it's like a ghost town out there anyway, I'll just keep my interventions short and queue up the next song. Here's "Ghost Town," by the Specials. If anyone is out there, enjoy.

FCC transcript KQOR 89.9 FM 11.03.1997 0045
Operator search: "sid*" or "sed*"

Ghost town. A ghost town is what Kenn and I would have seen had we walked the streets of London that night. But we didn't. Fortunately, Kenn and I arrived directly into the bar, having crossed to see the Specials. But outside was really a ghost town. Not a scene filled with haunts and torments from Poe's or Steven King's imagination, but something truly sinister, something from Orwell's *1984* or Kafka's nightmares, imposed upon an existing society rather than a future dystopia as one would have anticipated with the literary references. A world that was empty of human interaction and joy. A world that I now considered similar to mine...at least as I now understood it to have been before I had met Pyrah those few short weeks ago.

Pyrah and I were still in our early days, and I may not have even mentioned her to Kenn yet, given Kenn's views of girls. There was simply no real reason to introduce my world of Kenn to the world that was forming around Pyrah. At least not yet. So, I would still cross with Kenn, either before or after, or before and after my time with Pyrah. Kenn and I still had lots of gigs to see, and Pyrah had other things to attend to as well. It was healthy this way. Everyone had his or her own interests apart from the other. Something that was individual and could be called "my own" really was good for everyone.

So with that clean separation resolved in my mind, I showed up at Kenn's with a pizza and some Dew and suggested that we "roll two-tone" in reference to the ska scene of the '80s. Kenn was game, both of us being ska fans, and it suddenly dawned upon us that for all the crossings completed, we hadn't seen an ska gig yet. At least not the genuine article: A ska gig in England.

"Fuck, dude," Kenn said, applying generous amounts of Frank's on the pizza, "what are we waiting for? Let's do it." Before I had finished my second slice, *Louis Louis* was fired up to play "Dawning of a New Era" and sending us in search of the Specials. Why "New Era?" Well, it was a little cocky of us, because we thought that we were really onto something that we could control. While we were actually about to stumble onto something new, we had no idea what we were in for.

As I said, fortunately, Kenn and I did not arrive in the empty streets of London, but rather inside the bustling nightclub and could hear the band in the distance. I say that the band was "in the distance" because we found ourselves to be located near the fire exit at the back of the bar, past the toilets, so it was understandable that Kenn and I were oblivious to the world outside. Instead, the overwhelming stench of vomit, urine, and the yeast of stale spilt beer preoccupied us. But contrary to what one might think, this was good news for us. It meant that we were inside the gig. Thankfully, we didn't have to wait in line and negotiate with the bouncers, and most importantly, pay the cover charge. While ordinarily paying the cover wasn't an issue, this crossing was different as all we had was American money and no British currency, a problem that we wouldn't have solved until later.

Part of the fun of our crossings was that we never really knew where we were going, just that we were seeing a good band. Knowing that a good band was on the menu and that we were becoming a part of rock 'n' roll was enough. The rest was just detail that we could take in stride, so embracing the experience was all that Kenn and I had to do. As we made our way toward the stage, the experience was surreal. Although we were always learning to be better organized or prepared, we had not anticipated being in a British pub. Yeah, I know. It was stupid, especially after Nüremberg. Amateur mistake. I mean, really, where did we think we were going to see a London-based band? We knew that we had put the Specials through *Louis Louis,* so we could have easily anticipated where we'd end up. There were pretty good odds that Kenn and I weren't going to be at a gig in South Africa.

The oddly subdued crowd was properly described as a mixed lot. Black and white, a pattern of contrasts as obvious as a houndstooth. Guys in zoot suits, women in short skirts and foot-less tights, and everything in black-and-white two-tone. There were a few people dancing, but mostly the crowd was drinking and chatting. This was definitely the place to enjoy a good show. The Specials were onstage, and the pub wasn't crammed full, so you could enjoy a decent view of the stage without being jostled and stepped on. Grins rose across our faces like schoolboys with a new comic book.

"Dude, we're in the UK!" Kenn exclaimed. He was right, of course, but something seemed out of place. Like a door that wouldn't stay shut or pieces of broken glass that you couldn't sweep up off the floor. Something was close to being right, just not completely.

"Yeah, and at a Specials gig, but does this seem right?" I re-sponded, thinking that these were heady times indeed. Sure, Kenn and I had seen ska gigs before, in the States, but this was different. Why we had waited so long to see the Specials, I can't say. The bands that we had seen included Operation Ivy, the Mighty Mighty Bosstones, the Pie Tasters, the Bouncing Souls, No Doubt, and Fishbone. Great acts, but the watershed for this spring of talent was always the UK. Within that source there were three acts that were the bedrock of ska: the Selector, the English Beat (simply "the Beat" outside of North America, or "the Brit-ish Beat" in Australia) and the Specials. But here we were now, graced with being in the audience during a Specials show. It was always at moments of such realization that I had to admit that Kenn was a genius and that he and MC5 changed my life.

"Kenn," I continued, "does this seem as jubilant as you'd antici-pate a British ska gig to be?"

"Yeah, I don't know," Kenn answered, somewhat distracted. "Maybe it's just early in the set, or the Specials haven't devel-oped much of a following yet."

Kenn was right; crossing could result in anything. Anything was possible and besides, we could always see another gig later.

Maybe this was Monday night or there was a storm that made getting to the gig inconvenient. Did it really matter? I mean, seriously, was I listening to myself? We had traveled back through time and found a gig a little boring. It didn't really seem like a major complaint. "Probably right, Kenn," I managed. "Should I check if they take American cash, and grab beers?"

Pointing at the sign behind the bar, I said, "Look, Kenn, it's nine forty-five…auspicious indeed. We probably arrived at the start of the night, and the Specials should be just hitting their stride. Or maybe they were simply the warm-up act. Can you imagine who could be up next if the Specials were only the first act?" One of the really cool things about the British ska scene was that it was considered, in most instances, collaborative and close-knit. As a result, it wasn't uncommon that different bands would join in with other bands during their shows or provide additional sets on an impromptu basis. Perhaps this was our lucky night. Maybe the Beat, or Selector would show up or maybe the boys from Madness. Thoughts such as these reverberating through our minds, and with our spirits buoyed, we made our way toward the bar. Kenn ordered "a couple of pints of the house lager," confidently trying to sound "in the know"—something that he had seen in a movie once.

"Sorry, lads, last call was at nine; you know the rules," proclaimed the bartender, looking distracted, but still casting us a suspicious eye, while tidying the bar. Here was a pale, freckled man with a slight but athletic build who wasn't going to serve us beer? Surely he was putting us on. What was the saying the British used? Taking a pee or a piss? Pissing on Americans seemed like something that the Brits might engage in. He must have made us for Americans, unfamiliar and ignorant, thinking that he could play a trick. No beer in a pub after nine? Were we in Utah?

The bar itself was unremarkable except that the beer on tap wasn't anything that we recognized, and there were no small bowls of pretzels or peanuts out like we would see back home.

"Ah…wha? Dude, we're from the States and haven't been here very long," Kenn said, seeming confused, as did I. "Last call at nine? What are you talking about? We can pay; I'll even give you American cash."

Closing the small fridge behind him and wiping his hands on his apron, which bore the name "Joseph," our ambivalent bartender returned his attention to Kenn and me. "Morality measures, imposed by 10 Downing last year. Last call at nine and we close at ten. So, all the same lads, even if you don't know the rules… no drinks," the bartender stated flatly. "No cash. No choice. No deal. Sorry, lads."

"What's 10 Downing Street?" Kenn asked, showing his ignorance of British politics, notwithstanding being savvy enough to travel through time. It was a question that was left hanging in the air, a frozen scream across a tundra of ignorance as the bartender ignored us and returned his attentions to mopping the floor and folding bar towels.

Seemingly on cue, the band finished playing "Ghost Town," and the bar lights went on. Quietly and without any instruction, the patrons all but instantly spilled out of the club and started heading home, or at least elsewhere. Not knowing what else to do, Kenn and I thanked the bartender and left the rapidly emptying bar, through the door, and headed back to Kenn's.

"That was weird," Kenn said, trailing off and looking around.

"Is weird," I corrected. "This is weird, dude." I could feel the cold of the night air, and before us was an expanse of an empty street, dimly lit with streetlamps, but no cars or pedestrians. Just Kenn and me. Nothing was as it should be. We weren't in Kenn's house at all; we were on the streets of London and not in a Cat Stevens or Sinead O'Connor cover version, but the real thing. It was raining lightly, seemingly trailing off from a larger rainfall, considering the puddles on the street and the draining gutters. Confused and concerned about our predicament, we shivered, not wearing anything other than light sweaters and T-shirts. We would have to start planning our clothing better. But for now, we had bigger problems. Being trapped in the past again like Nüremburg didn't really appeal to me.

I suppose that to some degree we're all caught in the past, but that's different, and you could choose to do something about that. But here we were seemingly trapped in London, without proper currency or any idea what we were going to do. So we started walking along the street, toward a laneway that appeared as though it would run behind the bar that we had just left. Without a plan or a sense of direction, staying close to the nightclub seemed as good an option as any. Wordlessly, Kenn and I shuffled along, trying to contemplate what had happened and what we were going to do.

"At least with the Motörhead crossing, Lemmy was glowing," I commented, breaking our silence. "We could at least figure out what we were supposed to be up to."

"Yeah, well," Kenn confirmed, "Lemmy could always be counted on for being obvious. Maybe we should drop in on him and give him a scare."

I sort of chuckled, thinking about how we had left Lemmy in Nüremburg, and then said, "Before we get too fancy, let's see if we can sort ourselves out. What's that over there?"

Our attention was diverted from discussing the prospects of subjecting Lemmy to an eternity of time-lapsed torments to a figure of a crouching Jerry Dammers leaving the club with an armful of records. He was glowing and shimmering. His hologram showed an older Jerry Dammers wearing an updated suit and considerably more at ease than he currently appeared. A hologram again, showing a past and a present, just like when we saw Ness outside the Black Flag gig, Lemmy in Germany, and during various other adventures we'd had. A sign that Kenn and I were being called up. Rock 'n' roll needed us to do something. Something with Jerry Dammers. But what?

Keyboard player Jerry Dammers, of the Specials, was influential in forming the two-tone/ska genre in England, which largely took its cues from the Jamaican ska and steel drum rhythms, but coupled it with the energy and social discontent of London-based punk. Again, London was providing an example of musical innovation in its finest form and, of course, rock 'n' roll drawing from an abundance of influences. Full of energy, attitude, and dissent, but still you could dance to it. Well, as much as a bunch of Brits could dance, and honestly, Kenn and I were no better.

Dammers helped create the 2 Tone Records label and assisted a number of acts in songwriting and producing. In many cases, the reworking of classic ska songs turned the originals into hits again in the United Kingdom. Sometimes these efforts even reached the shores of America, at least when we were lucky enough. Unfortunately, Dammers's role with the Specials would later end unceremoniously as views regarding the direction of the band, both musically and politically, would differ internally. Dammers wanted to take more focused and informed political and social stances, whereas the rest of the band remained disinclined. As it happens in some relationships, people change, while others don't, and households become divided and incapable of standing. But both the Specials and Dammers continued on their separate ways. Fortunately, both acts continued to innovate and influence rock 'n' roll, with many laudable contributions.

But here in London in front of Kenn and me, crossing the street in the light mist of a cool night rain, Jerry Dammers looked haunted. He was scurrying across the street, looking suspiciously over his shoulder and around him like he was being pursued by something that possessed either an appetite or malice. The hologram flickered and faded out of focus, but the glow remained. We had seen this a few times now, although we never really knew how the hologram was supposed to act or what it really meant. Sometimes, the projected image was slightly offset from the person, like a 3D image viewed with the naked eye. Other times the image showed different clothing or an aged version. But it always showed something familiar to Kenn and me. Something that we recognized as the natural order of the world, as we understood it to be. Mike Ness with tattoos? That was obvious. But with others, like when we saw Lemmy, and here with Dammers, the difference between the hologram and the person wasn't clear. By this time we had seen the flickering and glowing a few times on a number of people, each time giving us the signal that we needed to intervene in some manner. Usually it was pretty straightforward. Even if it wasn't, it was something relatively minor that Kenn or I would catch from our knowledge of rock 'n' roll.

But what if this intervention required something more from Kenn and me? Suddenly, the disinterested bartender's comment about the "morality measures" issued from 10 Dow Corning Street, whatever that was, floated back to the front of my mind and became just as disconcerting as being trapped in London. Were we here to set that right? It seemed improbable. Kenn and I were about rock 'n' roll, not politics or moral guidance. Why the hologram on Dammers?

Unsure of what else to do, but knowing that I had to engage with Jerry, I offered a friendly wave and said, "Hey, good show tonight. We're just in from the States, and we are dying to say 'hi' and have to say we're surprised that it was over so early."

Kenn added, "Yeah, the bartender said something about 'morality measures?' What's the story?"

"Bloody Americans, ey?" Dammers replied in a typically unflattering British manner. "Wouldn't hurt you lads to learn a little about the rest of the world," he added. The slight hurt, but at least he was slowing down so that we could talk to him, even if we didn't have his full attention.

"Yeah, well, dude," I replied, "there is only so much time, and we would rather focus on the music than the politics, especially foreign politics. For us it's more interesting to know that Mick Jones left the Clash for General Public and that Phil Thornalley replaced Simon Gallup, than what the government is doing, but you know, maybe if you could indulge us..." I then provided a bit of a summary of the British music and in particular the ska subset that we were familiar with, just so that we could establish our credibility with him.

"Well, I see your point, lad," Dammers started, "but it's 10 Downing, the PM's residence, that's the Prime Minister—you know, the guy that took over for the king about a century ago, in case you don't know, that controls society and ultimately affects us all, even the songs that we sing. And actually to say 10 Downing is just a slang reference to the Prime Minister, because it's the Parliament that really controls Britain. To overlook politics in favour of any one thing is to be blind to your world. But I suppose we're just a little island a long, long way from dear ol' Uncle Sam," he concluded, leaving marks on me with his wit, sarcasm, and condescension. He did have a point, though, even if it was distracting and annoying to hear him enunciate the "ou" sound like they do in Canada and Britain, like in *favoouur*. What the fuck is with that anyway?

Satisfied that we might be "OK" after all, Dammers continued. "Listen, mate, rock 'n' roll in all forms is subjected to various controls and oversight in myriad ways. The charts control what's popular or how fast things will sell. Take the band the Smiths. Those poor bastards are being run absolutely ragged trying to keep up with the stream of singles demanded by the Rough Trade label." Shaking his head, he said, "Tsk, rough trade indeed those bastards. But would the Smiths be better off with full albums and tours? Sure, but only in terms of their sanity and cohesion as a band. That won't sell records. You can almost guarantee that band won't last past four or five albums."

Kenn and I looked at each other. How much did Jerry really know? I mean with the obvious advantage of hindsight or foresight or whatever you would consider what Kenn and I had gained through our ability to cross, we knew Dammers was actually right. The Smiths *would* break up after their fourth studio album, *Strangeways, Here We Come*. While they had other live albums and compilations, the band was disappointingly short-lived considering their prolific ability to produce new music. Maybe Kenn and I were unable to cross back home until we saved the Smiths from Rough Trade. While that would be awesome, it seemed like a stretch. But still, hope flickered in me.

Oblivious to my internal dialogue, Jerry continued, "In order to prevent the 'moral degradation of the populous,' rock 'n' roll is controlled by the Prime Minister's office through censorship and limits on the distribution of and possession of music and curfews."

Kenn and I stood there, stunned, flat-footed, and slack-jawed. This was the very result that the censorship opponents warned against during the American congressional hearings, but those hearings hadn't occurred yet in the time that we had traveled to. The concern was that censorship represented the thin edge of a wedge, so once governments or religious-based groups gained control over the content of music and the expression of artists, they would use this leverage to affect other changes. Changes that once started as seemingly modest or insignificant would then become more sweeping and profound. Once rock 'n' roll as an art form was marginalized, other art forms would follow, and the only expression allowed would be that of the state. This is what the Evil stood for. This was their battle cry and mandate. Kenn and I had heard this type of rhetoric before. We just hadn't known it to have been successful anywhere.

"OK, then," Kenn responded, soaking all of this information in, "where does Dow Corning fit into this? The bartender said something about them. Is it because of their corporate strength?"

"Wha' are you talkin' about, mate? Dow Corning? Do you mean 10 Downing? I thought that we just went through all that. Were you asleep?"

Kenn and I were both chagrined into acknowledging that was what he meant, but stammered on excuses to try to regain our footing. "Well, it was a tough trip over…you know, it was loud in the pub…" That sort of thing. But really our ignorance of British politics was laid bare in the abandoned street, and our embarrassment was more uncomfortable than the cold night's damp air.

"Jesus, you two." Jerry spat in shock and disgust. "Fuckin' Yanks, 10 Downing Street is the Prime Minister's residence. That's where Billy Bragg lives and dreams up all this shit."

"Billy Bragg is Prime Minister?" I exclaimed. "Fuck, you're right, we need to learn more about what's going on than simply Clash and General Public gigs. So could you give us more than just the penny briefing, please?"

All of the measures, as Dammers explained, came to be as a result of Billy Bragg's ascension to Prime Minister. To us, this was more confusing than time travel. Billy Bragg as a right-winged zealous Prime Minister? Political sure, but the Billy Bragg from our time was a socialist and moved by matters of social justice rather than that of a perceived morality. Passionate? Absolutely. Zealous? Not at all. To consider him such would be an abomination to all he stood for.

Certainly Billy Bragg, or at least the one we knew, wouldn't stand for imposed morality at the expense of individual freedom. But that was not the Billy Bragg who Dammers was talking about. This was a Billy Bragg who was now at the head of a political regime repressing artists and the youth. It was a reality that simply didn't accord with what Kenn and I had known.

Kenn and I looked at each other. "What the fuck?" Kenn mouthed to me. I was too stunned to even respond.

Somehow, when we crossed we found ourselves in a different version of history, in which Billy Bragg had been Margaret Thatcher's *aide-de-camp* during her tenure as Prime Minister. This wasn't as simple as catching Mike Ness at the right time to make sure he goes to a gig or passing along a mixed tape so that Dexter can go on to found Offspring. This was a world in which Thatcher passed away unexpectedly, and because of his intimate knowledge of policies as well as his charisma and drive, William (as he was known here) Bragg was tapped to step into the vacancy, which he did with a voracious appetite for change. Worse than his zeal and his purported close relationship with American President Ronald Reagan was the fact that Billy Bragg had an iron will and insatiable desire to reign with the sort of tight control that made Thatcher look like a pushover. Measures he personally enacted included curfews, limitations on gatherings to no more than four people at any one time, and constraints on the music industry, including levies, taxes, and fines for contravention of established Morality Codes. And of course no repressive regime could be complete without a police force, so Billy Bragg created a Morality Brigade.

"I'll tell you blokes what," concluded Dammers, "if Prime Minister Bragg keeps this up, it will be the death of rock 'n' roll. Rock 'n' roll will be displaced by Bragg's preferences, just like West Ham has risen to the top of the Premier League ladder at the expense of other teams, particularly Coventry..." He trailed off mumbling.

I coughed, while Kenn scoffed, "That's impossible. Rock 'n' roll can't die. It's bigger than that. People have claimed that before, but it's just a myth."

"Right, boyo. Right," Jerry said. "You lads look about young enough to take things for granted. Mind me and remember that everything can pass, especially things that you think will always be there. Although you never think it will happen, family members get sick, dogs run away, love fades, and even mountains crumble. If you think that there will always be a tomorrow, then rock 'n' roll is already in danger. Vigilance. Vigilance is the love that prospers, and rock 'n' roll survives only because we nurture it. There may always be a tomorrow, but it might not be the tomorrow you thought it was going to be. Mark my words, the Smiths will perish before their sixth album."

"Rock 'n' roll won't die," I said confirming Kenn's statement and fortifying my own resolve. Dammers was known for his activism, and perhaps it was these strange flights that he seemed to be taking with us that led to his eventual falling out with the Specials. "Look, we've heard this before, but it never happens. Not to worry, but still something needs to be done here today." It was the best that I could do to find a middle ground between agreeing and trying to tell him that he was wrong. Diplomacy in action. Kenn and I needed information from him, but couldn't concede that he was correct.

"Billy Bragg clamping down on music is so wrong," Kenn said.

Clearly this must be what Kenn and I were here to fix. The hologram on Jerry was a sign for us to get educated as to what was wrong. So, now we understood that Kenn and I needed to intervene somehow and get things back on track. We needed Billy Bragg to sell off his interests in 10 Downing Ware Street and become a musician, not a politician. How hard could that be?

Thinking about the details of our predicament, Kenn grabbed a newspaper from a garbage bin, with a headline announcing the second Premiership victory in as many years for the West Ham United FC, whatever that was. More importantly, for us, Kenn noted that the date was March 14, 1982.

Dammers interrupted my reflection on everything that we had just learnt. "Bollocks, here comes the MB. Here, take these!" Hurriedly, he started shoving records at Kenn and me while turning to head off in the other direction. Dammers had spun into action, but not quickly enough.

"The MB?" I asked, accepting the record that he was handing me, too perplexed to acknowledge how cool it was to have Dammers hand vinyl to me. "What's going on?"

"The Morality Brigade," he clarified, pointing to two lumbering hulks that were heading toward us, as Dammers fumbled with his vinyl. They looked like a cross between the British bobbies and National Front skinheads, but lacking the helmets worn by the police or bomber jackets of the National Front. But they still wore high-laced Dr. Martens boots and the knotted furrowed look on their foreheads that spoke of personal confusion, simplemindedness, or an intent to inflict physical violence upon someone. Maybe the look said all of those things. Although the hulks lumbered like oxen, with their heads slightly bowed in front of their expanse of muscular shoulders and broad necks, they couldn't be mistaken for mere thugs. Both men wore officious-looking leather jackets that had blue and white-checkered armbands with black "MB" embossed letters. These two looked ominous and imposing and were crossing the empty street on a direct path to interdict our little gathering, with the grace of dancing circus bears. Even without their short thick batons, it was an easy bet that they could crush our skulls with their bare bear hands.

On the collars of the uniforms appeared a set of stylized musical notes—actually a pair of triple note beams—but laid over each other to look like a set of the capital letter "M" in polished silver metal. They reminded me of something that I had seen before, yet couldn't place.

Just as I considered making a dash away, not really knowing where to go, but just away for now, they ordered "Halt!" It didn't seem like a good idea to comply, but taking Dammers's lead, we stood fast.

"Gotcha some records, do ya lads," they said, more of a statement than a question, Bear One managed to mix rhetoric with malice. "C'mon, fellas, you know the drill, no more than one record a person out in public. Plus," he added, checking a gray burnished military-looking pocket watch, "do you really think that you're going to be 'ome before curfew?" Again more of a statement than a question. Maybe even more of an indictment than a statement, but certainly not a question. Dammers was now glowing more intensely than ever, but this only seemed apparent to Kenn and me.

Bear Two was stepping back from Bear One to cut whatever angles down that might have provided us flight options and then started circling behind Kenn and me. Suddenly the damp and cold didn't matter to me as much as it had only moments before.

"Let's see what you lads ha' got," one of the state repression monsters demanded. Dammers was looking nervously around, shifting on his feet and avoiding eye contact, behaviour that seemed to cause as much concern to me, as it provided delight to the MBs.

Not sure what to make of all of this, I offered up the copy of *Keep Moving*, by Madness, to the MBs and stepped in front of Jerry. "Music, hey mate. Well, let's just see if you've got any more than the one you're allowed. You're not pulling a Joey, are you?" Again, Bear One demonstrating his command over rhetoric and now also irony, as I don't really think he considered me a "mate." I also thought better of asking what a "Joey" was or pointing out how impressive his observational prowess was to deduce that we were carrying music, in record sleeves of all things.

Bear One handed the record to Bear Two, who opened up the cardboard sleeve while a grin lit across his face. Not exactly the grin that either Kenn or I would have extracting vinyl from its sleeve. It was as though he and Bear One had found Goldilocks rummaging through their den, and she was covered in honey barbeque sauce. You know, the kind of sauce that was always "just right."

"Well, lad, it looks like we're in a spot of trouble, aren't we." I was quickly growing tired of Bear One's statements that sounded like a question. "You looked the type to pull a Joey. I bet you all are." He continued extracting a second piece of vinyl alongside the other. It dawned on me that pulling a "Joey" meant hiding something in a pouch, like a kangaroo. Sort of clever and entertaining, but in the present circumstances I lacked the capacity to appreciate the humor. As I strained to see what the record itself was, I realized that it was a relatively unimportant aspect of this confrontation and that my curiosity should be kerbed in favour of focusing on the peril that we were all in. Dammers was now glowing like the bottom of the space shuttle during re-entry.

"So you 'ake us for stupid d'ya, hey?" Bear Two added. Then he tapped one of his lapel pins, like the one Bear One also wore. "Morality in music. Dat's what 'ese represent. Bestowed upon d'ose of us who stand strong against immorality and the threat of rock 'n' roll. You see a man with these you know he's on the right path and has friends among dose who are united in the fight to irradiate the likes of you lot." We had seen this before, with the McCloy-looking version we walked in on at the Talking Heads gig.

As I was thinking, *yeah, you oafs are stupid,* I allowed my judgment to lapse. "Do you mean eradicate?" I asked aloud, but mostly to Kenn. "Because *irradiate* means to expose to or treat something with radiation or alternatively to illuminate by casting light upon something. I'm confused, sometimes *irradiate* is also used as a synonym for predicting something, but that isn't really what's meant. Is it?"

"Shush you," one of the MBs growled, glaring at me. With that, and obviously spurred by my ill-conceived quest for clarity, the MBs aggressively started closing ranks while clenching their fists.

Kenn spun into action. "Right you guys are, clever indeed. It's we who are stupid thinking that we could pass one by you. Look, we were at a show and it was all legit, but a couple of the boys caught up with some birds," he said, trying to use the local vernacular, "and had their hands full, if you know what I mean. You know, showing them a proper moral time and all." Fortunately, everything Kenn said with his American accent sounded like a wisecrack, but the MBs missed the sarcasm amid the forced jargon that Kenn was trying to adopt. "But I'll do you a deal," he offered, making both Jerry and me look even more uncomfortable than we already were. Kenn, always with an angle. But what now? I hoped to every god that I could think of, all my favorite albums, and any lucky charm I had ever heard of, that Kenn wasn't going to start on some conspiracy or be as obtuse as he was with girls. Drawing in a breath, I braced myself for the unknown. I held my breath, savouring it, concerned that it might be my last.

I had been here before. An empty street, a deserted playground, the school shower, the photocopier centre at work, anywhere, it was never a question of geography; bullies would always find Kenn or me, because we were always victims. Kenn and I, and now Jerry, were isolated, as victims always are. There would be no one to help us. Even if there was a witness to be found, this was the type of confrontation that people turn away from. Even in the stories, the Samaritan arrives to tend to the broken and not to intervene. No one watches bullies at their mean craft. Worse still is when the state sanctions the bullies. There would be no rescue, no due process, only repression. And Kenn, Jerry, and I were about to have a first-person view of repression at work.

"So, John Wayne speaks," the monstrous Bear Two said from slightly behind us and to the left. "What's on offer, lad?"

Kenn pointed at Dammers. "Let my friend here take all the albums now. He'll promise to go straight home, without any further delay, nor will he speak of this, shall we say *chance meeting*."

"Then you two come with us," he said, now pointing to himself and me, "and I'll show you an after-hours bar where not only are the Cramps playing, but drinks are still being poured and there are hotbox dancers. If we hurry maybe we'll see Congo Powers in her sequined bikini and Tommy gun prop." The glowing around Dammers started to fade, and I realized that Kenn's gambit could work.

The two morality Frankensteins looked at each other. "The Cramps? I thought that was just a rumour that they were in London. OK, lad, you've got a deal."

Bear Two readily gave Dammers his vinyl back and followed us, thinking of the commendations they would receive for arresting the Cramps in a London after-hours bar. With a strained concerned grin of appreciation, Jerry nodded his thanks to us, his glow completely lost now, and looking like a flurry of uncoordinated gangly limbs, made a running start down the street clutching at his records. He had bad form, but I bet that night he was as fast as any Olympian.

As Kenn and I rounded the corner and entered a laneway, with the two bears in tow, I doubled over in pain, involuntarily clenching my abdomen as though I had been hit in the kidney. My temples felt an incredible pressure, and one of the MBs grabbed my arm roughly and started to spin me toward him. I continued to spin, and sensing the absence of the grip on my arm that was both controlling and supporting me, I fell to the ground.

Was I afraid? Well, I was in London at night, facing my worst nightmare. Here I was with a bully, actually two, both of whom had the stature and disposition of an angry Kodiak bear. And the two bears also had authority and the state's endorsement. It was one thing to be subject to a beating or abuse by a rogue, but here Kenn and I were, alone in a country with strange and unknown laws and facing a state sanctioned beating. Things were getting worse by the moment as we were realizing that entering a laneway that was obscured from the main street was compounding the isolation and despair that we had felt on the empty street. There would be no white knight to ride by grabbing us by our shirts in order to whisk us to safety. In fact, there might not even be an ambulance to fish us out of the pool of blood and broken bones that we would soon be floundering in. The realization that no one knew who we were and the only source of authority was getting ready to exercise the might of the state in the end of deserted laneway was terrifying.

Kenn and I were going to be stuck in London until we could intervene with Billy Bragg, but it wasn't as though the two bears would take us there or that we would even know what to do in order to get Billy to take a more measured stance. Facing the cold of the night, chilling my bones, Dammers's revelations and now the two bears following us to a fictitious Cramps show, I felt my prospects sliding from dire, past calamitous, and accelerating toward fatal. Fear? This was a realization. A realization that Kenn and I were going to die in London. Soon.

Had my cold wet arm merely slipped from the bear's paw? Watching with detracted fascination through rapidly blurring vision, I could see that the hard wet stone pavement was rushing up to meet me and expecting some type of coarse treatment from our captors. A kick, a shove maybe. A firm booted foot forcing me to the pavement and then pinning me there while I became a meat-filled piñata for the bears to absolve any retained frustration upon? All of the options that I could contemplate only seemed to involve violence. I braced my hands and knees for impact upon the ground and what was sure to be a swift and brusque response from the bears, only to feel the soft carpet of Kenn's floor. I opened my eyes, feeling my body racked with pain as though I had been repeatedly struck by a multitude of hammers. As I laid there, looking over at Kenn I gasped between laboured breaths.

"Nice one, dude. That was some fast thinking. You are smarter than Einstein."

As my breathing returned to normal and resolve started displacing my body's discomfort, Kenn was already recovering from crossing back and was handing me a Dew and a slice of pizza that was still warm. "A little dicey, maybe," Kenn said. "There is a dry shirt and hoodie you can borrow. Fucking wash it when you bring it back, though. Not like last time." He continued with his classic best-friend grin.

"Yeah," I said, agreeing to the dicey bit, not the washing his sweater comment. Still laboring for breath, I said, "Yeah, Kenn, that was a little closer then I'd prefer. You know, just for next time."

"I wonder if crossing is like a dream," Kenn mused. "Is it possible for us to really die during a crossing?"

"Fuck, Kenn. Given the bruising and physical damage that we often have after we return, I'd rather not find out."

What had we achieved? What was the objective that let us return from the show? Did we need to save Dammers from apprehension? Did he have records that would have been confiscated or that would go on to make an impact? In the end it probably didn't matter if we knew or not. People are always affecting the outcome of history without knowing it. That's the power of action and consequence; it changes history. Only the change is made today, and what a day today had been for us.

Later, Kenn and I talked about the adventure, the show, and Kenn's clever diversion to allow Dammers to escape the MBs.

We explored the minutia of that crossing exhaustively, listening to ska and planning new crossings.

"So, what do you make of Billy Bragg being Prime Minister?" Kenn asked. "You're the politico."

"Yeah, I think that it's less about Billy Bragg being a political paragon and more about his zealous repression. I think that we need to understand what's going on better. I think that the chilling effect of his measures, or really anyone's for that matter, is the real problem. There is something that's just not right. Here, let's play a couple of sets from the Billy Bragg we know."

It was then that we discovered that while we had been discussing our "Dammers crossing," as it had come to be known, what we had failed to realize was that we no longer had a single piece of music in our collections from Billy Bragg. There were other glaring holes in the collection as well. No Beautiful South, no Darren Hanlon, no live Red Wedge recordings. In fact, anything that traced an influence back to Billy Bragg was lost.

It was then that we resolved to return to London to put an end to Billy's reign of imposed morality and set him back on the right path of socialism, human justice, and rock 'n' roll.

Once again I was excited, even inspired, by our crossings, especially the adventures that Kenn and I would face and the importance of rock 'n' roll, but now we had a crossing that required more planning and thought than before. Kenn and I finished the pizza while we savored the remaining Dews and beer from his fridge, and we talked about Billy Bragg. About his music, his importance, the fallout of him being Prime Minister and even the stupidity of the British system that would force the Prime Minister to keep his own house. Why didn't they get a White House like the President? I guess because they had to report to the Queen.

I had forgot that I was supposed to meet Pyrah, or else I would have called her. Well, probably I would have called anyway. But this was more important than a date. Once again, Kenn and I would be required to change a fractured history; humanity needed us to come through. So, again, Kenn and I took up the call to

save rock 'n' roll. The call to be heroes, true leaders of men.

Part III

Leaders of Men

Leaders of Men:

A title or description of a class of people who ascend, guiding humanity in one form or another;

A phrase of inspiration, but also of identification. The identification of the character or stature of a person, but also of the fact that humanity requires leadership;

The dreams of parents that their children will become leaders. Leaders in academics, athletics, arts, or affairs of state; and

A song by Joy Division from their compilation album *Substance*, released in 1988, eight years after the untimely demise of Ian Curtis.

Although leaders of men possess different skills, motivations, and talents, they all enjoy something unique that enables them to inspire others. An ability to excel in a field, which differentiates them from the others. But is the ability to excel the same as an ability to lead? Why is someone who is simply compelling assumed to be a leader in affairs of the state?

Made a promise for a new life...

Leaders of men are heroes. Heroes who make a difference by holding up an example of something better, something to strive for. Leaders of men make their rise for reasons as diverse as the talents that propel their ascent and may only be leaders of a modest group of followers, or masses that span nations. But what is the source of the power that these leaders of men wield? Is the power in their followers? From within the leaders themselves?

Made a victim out of your life...

What of the leaders who have risen to the apex of human hierarchy not for the greater good, not with benevolent intentions, but for malice? Leaders who simply lead to live out their goals, their dreams, to fulfill desires of wealth and power?

Thousand words are spoken loud,

What happens when the promises that they made in becoming leaders have been broken or turn into lies? Who is to blame the mark or the rogue? Then what? Do promises that provided a faulty ladder of hope leave one clinging to the bottom rung in despair?

Born out of your frustration.

Leaders of men define the period of their influence, but also reflect how society views itself. Is society the egg that needs the chicken to lead it, or is this merely the personification of symbiosis?

The leaders of men...

Leaders of men—these leaders in academics, athletics, arts, or affairs of state remain a rich source of entertainment, discussion, and fascination by those that they lead. But, why? What do we really know about them, and does what we know matter?

10 - Heroes

This is KQOO 90.9 FM. It's eleven seventeen p.m., Sep-tember 11, and I'm Sid. I don't really have any answers. I don't really know what is going on in the world or even with me for that matter, but I know we all have to do better.

I would expect that in the coming days there will be a great deal of discussion over being heroic. Of what he-roes do. How heroes strike at the wicked for the righ-teous. I don't know if this is right or not or if in the end it will make any difference, but I do know that being a hero takes strength. Strength to do what it right and what is difficult. Sometimes being a hero is an act of simple decency. But it's always taking a stand. So be he-roic in any way you can.

Since this is a time where we could use more heroes, up next is a hero of mine, someone that seems to think that everyday people can rise to become heroes. I hope he's right, the world needs more heroes. Here's David Bowie, with "Heroes."

FCC transcript KQOO 90.9 FM 09.11.2001 2317

Heroes. It always had a nice ring to it. It sounded officious and lofty. A title fitting of Kenn and me, telling the world that we were men of action but also of intellect; that we inspired others to be better. It sounded...well, it sounded heroic. That's how it was going to be for Kenn and me. Of course we were destined to become heroes—just look at what we had achieved already. We had traveled through time and space. We had found a way to access not only MC5 gigs, but also virtually any gig that we wanted. We had discovered that during our crossings, we could (and even had the responsibility to) correct things that were out of place. In effect we were being called upon to become heroes, to save rock 'n' roll, change history and right the wrongs of the world. The idea was so infectious that I could feel myself bursting with song.

"I'm not going to be the fucking queen, you fag," Kenn blurted out, seemingly from nowhere.

I was startled by my reverie. "Ah, was I singing out loud?"

"Yeah, Bowie's 'Heroes.' And you suck. I'm not going to be the queen to your king."

Right, I got that bit, but the singing Bowie part made sense. *The Rise and Fall of Ziggy Stardust and the Spiders From Mars* had been the first album that I really fell in love with. It changed everything for me and put Bowie on a pedestal above that of which any "Starman" could descend from. At one point I thought it was going to take me *five years* to listen to anything other than the first track. To this day, that song still gives me pause, but *Heroes*…well, that was great too, just a different album, and it was more apt for our circumstances. Although at that time I had never shared *Heroes* during the course of my radio shows, Bowie was a frequent part of the lineup.

"I was just thinking that we'll be heroes, dude. It'll be awesome. You have to admit that being a hero has a certain attraction. I mean, just think of the respect, the fact that we will make a difference, and then of course the rewards. Heroes have often changed history and are the central characters in adventures throughout the ages. Martin Luther King Jr., Captain Cook, the pilot Captain Sulley—or whatever his name was, Odysseus, and Spiderman. That is the direction that things are heading for us, man," I enthused.

I wondered what it would be like. I would expect that being a hero was different for everyone. For me it was about the rewards, the respect, the free gigs, being a part of rock 'n' roll…you know making a real difference in the world. Not like volunteering or recycling bottles, but something that we would do that would make the world better.

When I look back, I think that I always knew that Kenn wanted something else for his efforts. Something like proving that he was capable of greatness or simply just of achievement.

Demonstrating that he was right. The rewards would come as they always do for heroes, but maybe it's just that the rewards were different for each of us. Maybe because we all need something different or maybe because that's just how it works. If consequences for actions are different for each of us, doesn't it stand to reason that the rewards are different too? After all, rewards are consequences as well, just good ones.

It was good enough for me that heroes were rewarded. But even though I knew that Spiderman was a true hero, and even though the Ramones covered Spidey's theme song, I never thought about the line that claimed, "Action is his reward." So I suppose if I had, I might have looked at things differently and maybe had different expectations, but I did always expect to be rewarded.

"Yeah, well, I love you, man…just not like that," Kenn said, seeming to be heading for one of his theories or more loquacious episodes.

OK, but like what then? What did that really mean? While it always seemed a little disturbing, I wasn't sure if it was more or less disturbing because he hadn't been drinking or getting high.

"Hey, fag, you're supposed to say that you'd love me too…just not like that," Kenn said.

I'd love him? But not like what? Was it that I didn't love him enough or wasn't manly enough or articulate enough with my feelings? It was always something with Kenn. Not knowing what else to say, I replied, "Seriously? What are we fucking dating? OK, sure, I'd love you, too: I'd love you to shut the fuck up and put another record on."

It had been hours that Kenn and I had been sitting in his house listening to music and thinking about the possibilities that our crossings would now hold. Empty cans of Mountain Dew, bottles of beer, and the remnants of the pizza were providing the evidence that Kenn and I had been at this for a while. The pizza box, pop cans, and beer bottles weren't the only things that had been emptied, so too was any idea that we harbored that we wouldn't intervene with the past. How could we not? Not only did Billy Bragg deserve more, but also changing history represented our best chance to become heroes.

The idea of becoming heroes was invigorating. Not only because of the possibilities of the rewards, but also because of the crossings themselves and even what we might expect to find in the past. Feist, a Canadian singer, formerly with Broken Social Scene, would say, "So much past inside my present" in her aptly named song "Past In Present." This certainly applied for both Kenn and me, separately as well as collectively, and soon we found ourselves pursuing rock 'n' roll to become heroes, rather than as an end in itself.

Feist's comments really apply to everyone. Memory creates both power and burden to bear and utilize. In fact, even people who can't remember are burdened and liberated by the past. Liberated in that they have the ability to make decisions without a view to what their life may have been like before, but also burdened with having the history concealed from them.

But for most people, the past provides a powerful source of direction and education. A force that shapes the present and the future, the same way a course of a river is carved through mountains, a course not easily altered. However, people are also haunted by the past like a specter in the night or a memory that won't fade, leaving an indelible smear of regret or lament.

For Kenn and me, the past made us friends. It sowed the seeds that would later become a love of rock 'n' roll. The past educated us; it taught us about what people were really like, how the world was. Not only how Thomas Hobbes envisioned it, but also with flecks of beauty and inspiration as portrayed by Everything but the Girl. While there were a seemingly infinite number of possibilities laid out before us, all because of our capability to cross and reshape history, the reality was that not only did our past limit these possibilities at a real and finite level, it did so by narrowing our crossings even further to specific times. But even the past times that made us friends held memories of pain and sorrow that we carried with us into the future. That was a future that we couldn't change or escape. The best that we could do was find rock 'n' roll and understand it. All so that we could make it better.

Specifically, we spent a lot of time in the '80s, and going back even farther than that. Why? The answer lies in my view that art is derivative in nature.

Obviously, MC5 dictated our initial crossings. So, again, we were limited to the time and the bands that they played with. Later, with disco taking up so much of the '70s, that also limited where we could go.

Disco sterilized nearly a decade for crossings. A venerable wasteland of tragedy and misery dressed up in glitter and faux happiness, fueled by cocaine and self-indulgent excess. This is different from rock 'n' roll. OK, maybe not always the self-indulgent part or the drugs or the misguided self-destruction or the dubious wardrobes, but certainly the music. I mean, I'd have to do drugs to even go to a Village People show. Velvet Underground? Wall of Voodoo? The Rolling Stones? The Stone Roses? Talking Heads? Blondie? Sure, drugs might be a part of the scene or even the band itself, but the music was good. Disco, not so much.

Disco represented a desperate and desolate land that we never ventured into. Do you really think that disco held any *real* value to anyone? It was a musical abomination. Much to our disappointment, Europe was much the same with the invention of techno. In fact, when acts like Soundgarden, Nirvana, Pearl Jam, and Mudhoney were launching the grunge scene out of Seattle, bands such as Depeche Mode, Kraftwerk, Cabaret Voltaire, and Yello were saturating Europe. Regardless of why or how these aberrations occurred, these were the times and places that Kenn and I avoided at all costs. Places as hostile to our ears as fingernails dragged across chalkboards. A kind of music that assaulted our sensibilities like a SWAT team kicking in a meth lab door. But our interest in the '80s was more than a simple curiosity.

The '80s were important not only because of the music, notable for pushing the boundaries of music and society, but it was the acts of the '80s that sowed the seeds of inspiration for the bands of the '90s and into the twenty-first century. Consider that without Social Distortion there was no Green Day or Offspring, which obviously made the mission with Mike Ness so important. If the Red Hot Chili Peppers had not been active and willing to share and collaborate with others, there would have been no Pearl Jam or Soundgarden. Older influences such as David Bowie, Queen, Meatloaf, Kiss, and Buffalo Springfield led to Public Enemy, Radiohead, the Rheostatics, the Smiths, Blur: all interconnected through influences...yes, even Public Enemy.

Combing through the history of rock 'n' roll, making sure that everything stayed in place was vital, because if we failed to ensure the integrity of our musical history, then there would be no Pixies. No Galaxie 500. No Nirvana. No Jet. Consider what would happen if there had been no Velvet Underground, the result would have been devastating. If the Velvet Underground had actually been removed from rock 'n' roll history, the affect would be more complete than if the entire global nuclear arsenal had been deployed against humanity. Sure there would be some survival, but not much, and nothing pretty. Sort of like the world in the *Mad Max* movies, except with rock bands.

I suppose this seems dramatic, but consider that the list of musicians who have claimed to be influenced by the Velvet Underground includes: David Bowie, Patti Smith, New York Dolls, Television, the Talking Heads, Bauhaus, R.E.M., Sonic Youth, the Pixies, the Stooges, the Replacements, Galaxie 500, The The, XTC, Roxy Music, Joy Division, Spacemen 3, Henry Rollins, Black Flag, and this is just a start. Now trace what happened to these bands, what they became, who they influenced, and their contribution to rock 'n' roll, and you'd be left with the conclusion that the amplified guitar, the stack of speakers, and the Velvet Underground are such vital parts of the composition of the art form that to remove these elements would be to remove chlorophyll from plants.

It all made sense, plus the old guys always told us that the '80s was the place to be for rock 'n' roll. Turns out they were right. Old guys? Well, guys born in the late '60s and early '70s. Guys who, at the time, were ten years younger than I am now. That seems strange. But then that's the really strange part of strangeness. It's strange that there is always something that seems strange, no matter how used to the unusual you are. That Kenn and I would also take our turn becoming old guys should have been predictable, but somehow in our youth, while crossing and watching rock 'n' roll, it wasn't. Weren't we just going to stay as young as rock forever? Maybe not. I suppose that's strange too, but you could forgive us for failing to appreciate the ceaseless march of time now that we had discovered how to travel through it.

"How long do you think we can do this Kenn?"

"Do what? Eat pizza? Probably forever."

"Ok, but then answer Darren Hanlon's question: is *forever* a person's life or the time since we've been seventeen?"

"Nice one. I love that album *I Will Love You At All*. What do you mean, is this another one of your downer conversations?"

"I think that time travel is changing our appreciation of time and history."

"Likely. Pass me the Frank's"

"No, seriously buddy. Consider that with the access that we have to the past, we don't have to regret or lament the gigs that we missed, like we used to. The past is now closer and easier to manage than our future."

"Dew? I think I know what you're saying but I've always liked the past more than the present or the future for that matter. I like imagining what the past was like, I know what it's like now. Before I put on some Leonard Cohen and think about killing myself, can we change the subject?"

We just listened to music in silence, while I continued to ponder this. We didn't have the same appreciation for time that we once did, not like the old guys did. The old guys seemed to get music and time.

That's probably why it made sense that it was the old guys who first started teaching us about rock 'n' roll. I mean, after all, they had the music collections, hosted the radio shows, and had simply been around longer. It is always that way, with previous generations teaching the subsequent ones the virtue of their wealth of experience.

Just like when Sammy Hagar was addressing major social issues like traffic law enforcement with his song "I Can't Drive 55" and Nickelback's Chad Kroeger would be found later demonstrating his own lack of regard for motor vehicle laws, (with what could have been a song called "I Can't Drive Below Point 15," in reference to his impaired-driving conviction), Kenn and I focused on bands that made good music. This wasn't to say that we didn't enjoy songs that were silly, whimsical, or even trite, but if you're going to be ridiculous, then take it seriously, like Darren Hanlon singing about racquet sports, Jonathan Richman crawling onstage singing "I'm A Little Dinosaur," or the classic Jonathan Demme direction of *Stop Making Sense*, in which David Byrne of the Talking Heads walked the line between being zany and out of control. How could these guys be heroes? The answer was simple. *These artists inspired others to be more than they would have otherwise been.*

Through ridiculous antics, these acts forced people to re-evaluate perceptions of the world and furthermore to question those perceptions. This is the first step to making the world a better place. A step that requires us to understand what it is that surrounds us, so that we can decide if we like it or not. That was the place that people could rise above, if they were so inclined, like Kenn and I were. We would use our knowledge to be something more.

Arguably, being more than Sammy Hagar or Chad Kroeger wasn't a tall order, but to achieve more than they had, at least in the world of rock 'n' roll or Jonathan Richman or David Byrne? Well, that was something else. Were they heroes, or were they simply idols? Was there a difference between being a hero and an idol? Or was this just another line that time had eroded through neglect and lackadaisical use of language?

Certainly both heroes and idols were revered and worshiped, looked up to, and admired. But was it the same for both of those types? Didn't a hero have to face adversity and rise to an occasion? Lead some form of triumph over improbable odds? But not idols. They were blindly worshipped or represented a religious belief. Merriam-Webster defines "idol" as an object of extreme devotion, but a "hero" as not someone who attracts the devotion of an idol, but one who is admired for his achievements and noble qualities or who shows great courage.

So you could be an idol without doing anything or by simply being cool or talented. You could be worshipped without having saved children from a burning building or by remaining selfish or without changing history.

"What do you think it takes to really be a hero, Kenn?" I asked, taking advantage of the Strangler's album *No More Heroes* playing in the background to change the subject. "What's the difference between being a hero and an idol?"

"Yeah, I'm not really sure," Kenn conceded. "I mean, James Dean was an idol, and he could barely drive a car. Was he a hero? Was Bono, from U2? It seemed that being a hero was separate from being an idol, when considering the basic composition of the two. It took an act or event to make one a hero, whereas being an idol was more driven by charisma or something other than an active choice. I mean, didn't Bono try to change the world? Wasn't he being active in trying to improve the lot of those around him, the vulnerable? That was the motivation behind the ONE Campaign that he and Bob Geldof co-founded—to improve the conditions for people, by reducing poverty and funding the treatment of communicable diseases. But there you have it—Geldof and Bono, icons and heroes. Different aspects of their worlds converging, perhaps fittingly as *one*, to bring the attention to an issue that only an icon could demand, but with the social responsibility of a hero. What about Yves Chouinard? Here was the founder of Patagonia, a fashion mainstay of the Oregon outdoor enthusiast, who is arguably an environmental hero for initiating various environmental initiatives and supporting others, perhaps even the inspiration behind the ONE Campaign as Patagonia had long pledged the greater of one percent of profits or ten percent of worldwide sales to environmental causes. But greater even still was the lesson that Chouinard imparted that being a hero wasn't something that you could simply purchase like naming rights to a building. That making a difference required more than simply cash, so the company empowered their employees to participate in environmental work and improve their supplies and the manufacturing techniques in order to reduce impacts upon the environment."

Barely stopping for a breath or to seek my comment, Kenn carried on. Why I hadn't anticipated a rant is, I suppose was due to my own shortsightedness. But by now we were well into *The Raven* album, and Kenn showed no signs of slowing down.

"Billy Bragg states that, "Virtue never tested is no virtue at all", in "Must I Paint You a Picture?" This might be the same for bravery and heroism." This offered me the segue I needed.

"And this brings us back to the fact that Billy Bragg requires an intervention. So, Kenn, we're gonna be heroes or idols or legends. We're gonna be living out the Bleached song "Searching Through the Past," so that we can find a solution to what's causing Billy Bragg to be a tyrant.

We needed answers to what was different and what had gone astray. Were Kenn and I looking for something specific? Well, I suppose that we were, but even without knowing what we specifically needed, we were assembling a general inventory. The gigs, the influences, and the milestones, anything that could have been recorded...and the subsequently missed or interrupted. But suddenly this was different. It wasn't like the times that we simply nudged someone down the right path or gotten him or her into a gig or given that person a demo tape.

Just like our intervention with Lemmy, we needed a different way of looking at things. A new approach or clearer perspective.

Something like what was mentioned in the liner notes from Shriekback's album *Big Night Music* announcing: *"Shriekback has chosen to make a different kind of music—one which exalts human frailty and the harmonious mess of nature over the simplistic reductions of our crude computers."*

There were so many things that Kenn and I looked to become involved with during our crossings. Courses of history to be explored and charted, so much to learn, see, and do: We were starting to realize that history was different from the past. The past was merely something that had occurred, whereas history was that which was recorded.

Just like an unheard noise transmitted: If a tree fell in a forest and no one knew, it would still have occurred. It just wouldn't become history until someone told a story about it, regardless of how accurate that story may or may not be. For Kenn and me, now that we had saved Dammers from a beating and ensured that Mike Ness formed Social Distortion, we knew we had serious work to do, including the contributions that only heroes could make. There would be other interventions and courses of action, but for now, our immediate objective was to restore Billy Bragg to the singer/songwriter that he was, thwart his plans as Prime Minister, and restore things to the order that we understood them to be. We weren't really sure how we were going to rebuild this puzzle, but I was beginning to see the jigsaw falling into place.

11 – Jigsaw Falling into Place

Perspective is everything...in how we view ourselves, how we view others, and how we see the world around us. This is KQOR 89.9 FM. It's one eleven a.m., October 15, and I'm Sid, and before we get back to great rock 'n' roll, we're going to give some perspective to...perspective.

It's like the old saw about "half empty/half full." Which is it? What kind of person are you, and how do you see things? Does it matter? I think it does, and I think that it can change. Rock 'n' roll changed me. It changed my life and the world around me by providing inspiration and entertainment.

Perspective is everything. Sometimes you see things falling apart, and other times the same separate pieces all come together. Plans are sometimes like that. Things that seem hopeless can be like the Radiohead song we've got up next. Here's "Jigsaw Falling Into Place." Stay tuned and enjoy.

FCC transcript KQOR 89.9 FM 10.15.2008 0111
Operator search redacted

Jigsaw falling into place, just like the Radiohead song, was how I could see all the pieces coming together and forming a clear picture of what needed to be done. At first I was worried it was hopeless, a disaster. A solution that was too hard or a bridge too far, but it wasn't.

After all, Kenn and I knew what needed to be done. We could see the result—anyone could—but we also needed to flesh out the course to achieve our endgame. Which pawns we'd sacrifice at what time, so that Billy Bragg's defenses could be slipped and history righted.

It wasn't really like chess, though. Kenn and I weren't going to kill a king…just redirect one. Actually, as hard as Kenn and I tried to adopt the chess metaphors from songs, since we'd never really played chess, the metaphors were lost on us. Songs such as "Fortune Faded," by the Red Hot Chili Peppers, and "White Russians," by the Sad Lovers and Giants sounded cool but didn't really help. Maybe music didn't explain everything. But what I was really trying to convey was that Kenn and I had to develop a plan to rescue Billy Bragg, which was a puzzle of sorts.

There really isn't much to a puzzle when you know what the solution is. Realistically, if you know the solution there isn't a problem. At the same time, if you don't believe that a question is capable of being answered, you'll never crack it. So problems rely on the possession of a little knowledge. Too much understanding and there is no problem; too little and the matter is incomprehensible.

If you think about history, but from the only logical perspective, which of course is looking back, then, there is a fundamental lack of surprise as to how things work out. I mean, you already know the ending, don't you? Even as a kid in school, before the lesson even started, I knew who won the Civil War. I knew that the Second World War ended with Japan and Europe's devastation and that the Black Death was cured or contained or at least stopped being a major problem.

So you know how this story ends already. Or do you? You know that it's about a girl and about rock 'n' roll. You also know that Kenn and I saved rock 'n' roll, and you know that Billy Bragg didn't really end up being Prime Minister, but is that enough? Isn't history more that just an enumeration of facts, mere incidents of time, just like rock 'n' roll is more than a listing of bands? Of course it is. People don't study history as a means of learning how to memorize a shopping list of old details, but rather the reasons or conditions that led to events occurring.

History always intrigued me and I've always studied at history in a way that was more explanatory than mysterious, because of course, the mystery had been solved. But how? And why? What I never understood or appreciate was how difficult achieving a specific solution that colored history books could be. I mean, given what we now know, vaccinations make sense. So now imagine if you could travel through time, like Kenn and I could, and were charged with a specific responsibility, like building a particle accelerator. Sure, you could go back to the late 1800s and build something that hadn't even been the subject of science fiction at that time. All you would have to do is make sure that you remembered the drawings and that you could find materials once you finished crossing. Fixing history would be the same way, merely an exercise in keeping track of the parts that had been separated from the whole. All Kenn and I had to do was keep track of the history that we knew and make sure it sorted out again. Right?

We had seen that there were alternate outcomes that were worse, but what about ones that were better? What about variations that produced the same result? Did we really need to have the specific knowledge in order to cross, and repair what was wrong?

"How do we know that people will even listen to us, dude?" Kenn asked. "I mean it can't just be a case of lighting a path home for Billy Bragg. How do you take a zealot and make him reasonable?"

"Well, Kenn, you have to operate on the premise that knowledge is eternal."

Kenn responded with a distracted grunt that sounded sort of like "huh," only more ambivalent.

"You know it's not as complicated as science or anything, but while I was wasting my time at college, I learned a few things. Like for instance, in the discourse "Meno," Plato discusses how Socrates believed in the immortal soul, and that knowledge is eternal, being connected to the soul. For Socrates it wasn't ever a matter of learning, but of remembering. The heuristic support to this was that one of Meno's slaves was able, albeit through coaxing, to recite geometric truths. So in following Socrates' logic, we should just be able to cross and hand Billy Bragg some bad music and then some good music, and then all of this will be just a simply misunderstanding. Maybe there is a scientific theory about how opposite forces operate on a body to redirect a body onto a desired course."

"Yeah, it's a super-secret complicated science called 'calculus,' you dick." Then Kenn said snidely, "Don't say I told you."

Right, never to be upstaged or lectured, Kenn always had a comment and needed to front conversations. But still I was skeptical about how it might work.

Kenn made it sound so easy. "So we just have to roll into town, load up the good stuff on Billy Bragg, show him what he's missing, and then we're done. We're dropping beers with him and spinning vinyl, right?"

"Pints." I corrected, "Billy Bragg would say *pints.*"

Of course. Just like you could cross and find Robert Oppenheimer and say, "*Hey, Robbie, check this shit out! I can simply turn nuclear fission into a weapon of incomprehensible destruction by making this minor modification.*" Then you'd show him how to create atomic bombs for the first time and say, "*Pretty cool, right?*"

What would you expect the reaction to be? You know, if you were really honest about it. Would you really expect Oppenheimer to say, "*Hey, way cool. You guys are pretty clever, and I can tell you're from the future because you're wearing X-Files and Star Trek T-shirts?*" Well, two things are wrong with this scenario, and both relate to you not being honest about your expectations.

First of all, Kenn and I always wore black T-shirts and jeans for crossing, for the same reason that all lawyers wear dark navy suits: They just do. Black T-shirts and jeans are a pretty standard rock 'n' roll uniform because they are nondescript, un-placeable, and, most importantly, timeless. Can you imagine the embarrassment, or worse the fights that it could cause to cross to a gig with a concert or album from the future? How do you explain that? "*I'm from the future. It's OK. It'll turn out fine. You'll like it there. You can trust me. I'm not really a delusional sociopath...I just don't like people touching or looking at me so STOP!*" Yeah, I know. It sounds like I may have tried it once or twice, but I'd rather not talk about it.

The other reason is that even if Plato and Socrates weren't completely right, regardless of whether you're remembering something or learning something, you've got to start with a concept that you believe will work or a problem that needs a solution. Without belief in a solution, there *is* no solution. Consider the infamous Trojan horse. I mean it's not like a couple of soldiers were standing on the beach in stunned awe, asking, "*Hey, Odysseus, what the fuck is that?*"

"*What, this? Well, you know how I like thinking about things and riddles and whatnot. Well, I was sitting here trying to remember all my past knowledge pertaining to particle acceleration and nuclear fission. You know thinking that maybe we could just nuke Troy, since the rest of the battle is going on forever, but you know I just can't get there. Besides, where would we get the enriched uranium? So I decided that I needed something simpler. But then, just like that, I remembered that Trojans like horses and they're really easy to trick, so the idea just popped into my head that maybe we could build a massive wooden horse and hide in it, and when I say "we" I mean you boys in the army, and then we could sneak in and kick some real ass. You know, while the other part of "we" — the philosophers and strategists — sit on the beach eating figs and threading conch shells."*

Solider One would comment, as Soldier Two stands silently, shaking his head in disbelief, "*Wow. Good thinking, dude. You're a real force to be reckoned with.*"

While the other solider would stand there, asking, "*New-klee-ur or n-clear? Enriched uranium?*"

"*Thanks, buddy,*" Odysseus would graciously acknowledge. "*I figured the wood was easier to come by than the uranium, plus there is the whole workplace safety requirement and handling procedures that come with the nukes, not to mention a decided lack of plunder once Troy gets nuked.*"

Wouldn't that work? Wasn't the impetus for sacking Troy the same motivation that drove the Manhattan Project and the decisive attack on Japan in 1945? So why not Troy? I suppose it could have happened. I mean, aside from the problem of obtaining uranium. Well the uranium and the required triggering device.

All I'm saying is that maybe Socrates didn't have this one right. Maybe only some things can be remembered from a previous existence, like breathing, riding a bike, which is your dominate hand, or not to feed or pet mean-looking dogs. Whereas other things, like nuclear fission, how to talk to a girl, driving a manual transmission, and time travel have to be discovered or learned from scratch. Or maybe it's not so much remembering these things as it is learning through a series of intuitive steps, like perfecting nuclear fission and talking to girls...a way that the impossible can become possible. So, like I was proving with my budding relationship with Pyrah, everything was possible.

But, even if one could just hand a GPS receiver to Columbus and point him toward the New World, he would first have to believe that something lay beyond the horizon, which he could not see.

Intuitively, Kenn and I knew this to be the case; however, as we know, we didn't always follow our intuition.

But if you had discovered time travel, like Kenn and I had, you would expect to hold an advantage and be able to alter virtually all outcomes. I mean, imagine saying, *"Excuse me, General, the Sioux Indians know this terrain pretty well, and there is a better than even chance that if you elect to wage battle from the bottom of this valley, with an outnumbered force, that this may just be your last stand."* The possibilities are infinite, aren't they? Well, maybe not really endless, but certainly vast.

Of course Kenn and I held an advantage over the people we encountered during our journeys to the past. We had spent our lives collecting, assembling, and learning everything that we could about rock 'n' roll. So, when looking at the problem of fixing Billy Bragg, we were profoundly confident. We had all the background information. We knew how things were supposed to turn out, so how could we fail?

Well, some things were actually harder that you would think. Being heroes, we knew we had responsibilities, but we also knew that there would be rewards, so we had to make sure that we capitalized on both. I mean it's the hallmark of a poor houseguest that doesn't eat the meal served. It's the pinnacle of rudeness not to accept gifts. We figured that our rewards were in the same category. We had an obligation to accept them, and if the rewards weren't just sitting there gift wrapped for us, I suppose we had an obligation to seek them out. So we did, and this is how we discovered that time travel was actually really complicated.

OK, I mean really complicated, like it had rules that we didn't know or even comprehend, not complicated like crossing with MC5 or finding a way to see other bands. We had already mastered that, but we would learn that we couldn't master other elements of time travel, elements like consequence. Ultimately, it was these consequences that made traveling through time complicated. Well, that and also the bit about figuring out what the rewards were.

What is the first thing that comes to most people's mind when they think of rewards? That's right, cash. Kenn and I were going to be rich, and we deserved to be, didn't we? I mean, look at the riches that Jay Z and Beyonce, Coldplay, U2, and even fucking dead Elvis Presley pulled out of the economy. These people are all industries unto themselves. So, if Kenn and I were busy saving their industry, weren't we entitled to a little cash as well?

But the problem with that was that it wasn't like Bono or Chris Martin were calling us up and sending us a tithing. *"Yeah, Kenn, brother, it's Bono here. Have you got a minute? You do? Hey, great, thanks, man. Look, I just wanted to say it's so amazing that you two saved rock 'n' roll for all of us. It really means so much and makes the world so much better. You know, brother, we just wouldn't be here without you. We're gonna send you some cash…"* Yeah, right. Knowing Bono, rather than actually send cash, he'd probably make a donation or some shit in our name, which might be OK if we were getting cash from other sources, but neither seemed to be happening. The truth was, aside from the gigs, and Kenn's credit card trick, which was not a scam, but more of a system, we were getting nothing. So, again, being men of action, as heroes must be, we devised a plan.

It was a simple plan really, and one I'm sure you've already thought of. In fact, it's the same one that everyone thinks of when contemplating time travel…sports betting and lotto. It would be simple, right? Like the Love and Rockets said, *"It's as simple as a flower, that's a complicated thing…"* Interesting, that song is called "No New Tale to Tell," which also reinforces the idea that stories and themes get recycled. How is this true? Well, we've just talked about how everyone considers rewards to be cash and if given a chance they would travel through time to place bets. Not really *terra incognito,* is it? So, why didn't Kenn and I do the same? Well, as it turns out, Kenn and I actually did use time travel to place bets and play the lottery.

You can probably guess how this worked out, as I am not rich. The short version is that our plans for betting and lottery tickets simply didn't work at all. The plan should have worked, but it never did. When contemplating our crossings, we couldn't always predict where we were going or the time itself. We knew the band that was headlining, but that was it. The album roughly dictated the period that we mixed with the *Guitar Hero,* but a precise date or venue, the presence of other bands, not so much. In fact, nothing else could be guaranteed, except that we would end up at a gig that the band fed through *Louis Louis* had either played or would be playing, and even that was pretty limited.

There was some predictability, like if you were going to see the Ramones, you stood a pretty good chance of ending up in New

York City; the Cure, in Europe; or the Hunters & Collectors, in Australia, but with other bands, like the Hives or Radiohead, you could end up anywhere. Some live albums had a tendency to get you to specific times or certain venues, but it was merely a tendency. Of course Kenn and I insisted upon seeing some shows again and again, but that required a lot of trials to get us back to the show that we were looking for. Sort of a drag, but it was the sacrifices that heroes endured and wore like a badge of honor. Right? Yeah, right.

Well, that brings us back to the fact that Kenn and I thought we were entitled to rewards that didn't seem to be forthcoming, which, in turn led to the lottery tickets and sports betting. It did work initially, just not for us in any meaningful way. After all, history can't really be changed, but it's complicated.

The scenario was as you'd expect. Kenn and I would load up on winning lotto ticket numbers before we crossed. The task itself was relatively simple. Most state lotteries are required to publish the winning numbers in some manner. So, we would narrow down the states that we were most likely to cross into and then obtain the winning numbers. Easy.

Like we had learned early on, we often found that we would happen into a convenience store, make a notional purchase, and then carry on to the gig. So, we'd also pick our winning lotto ticket and then wait to reap our fortunes. Sure enough, the tickets that we would purchase would win. I mean it's not like we were changing that part of history, right? That would be stupid. So, we'd have a couple of beers (charged to Kenn's credit card), watch the gig, and then cross back with a winning lottery ticket. Genius in its simplicity.

I'm sure you could just imagine Kenn and me driving up to Portland, the nearest airport of any consequence, getting on an airplane, and flying to the Big Apple with a $47 million winning lottery ticket. We flew first class, drank free beer in the first class lounge, gorged ourselves on food we didn't recognize, all served on small crackers, and hired a sedan to pick us up from JFK and take us to the lottery office. We giggled like schoolgirls the entire way, even up to the time the clerk at the counter looked at our ticket and said, "Thank you, gentlemen, please come with me. The director of winnings will be with you shortly." Forty-seven million, even after taxes, was going to be pretty good and really just the start of the harvest. We could still go back in time whenever we liked. Then the director came in and explained to us that lottery tickets expire if not claimed within twelve months.

Then we stopped giggling, "Really?" Kenn asked.

"Really," said the director.

"You're joking," I said.

"I'm afraid boys, I'm not joking," the director said.

"Really?" Kenn asked.

"Really. I must also ask, how did you come to possess this winning ticket, by the way?"

"Really, really?" I asked.

"Really, really." The director repeated. "I'm really, really not joking."

I think he told us a few times; we did have a nice trip to New York, but unlike the crossings, Kenn couldn't explain his way out of the charges on his credit card. So the euphoria of certain successes and riches beyond imagination deflated and filled the pit of our stomachs like an angry snake on the morning of a hangover.

We tried a few times afterward to get the lotto tickets to work, but we never managed to get to a gig that was within twelve months that had large prizes. But that was OK, because we still had sports betting to make use of. The take would be smaller, but more repeatable, and what were we going to do with $47 million anyway, other than organize our own super tour, create a super-cool record label, and live on a beach. OK, we had plans for the money, but this could have worked too. So we thought.

In fact, it worked worse than the lottery tickets because we couldn't say that "we found the ticket in an old shoe box" or "in something we bought at a garage sale," like we had presenting the winning ticket to a state lottery corporation. As it turns out, bookies don't really care too much for people winning a lot, and like it even less if they wait awhile to reclaim the winnings. Worse, is that bookies aren't state regulated like the lottery boards, which allowed the bookies to hire goons...goons who are also not state regulated. As you can imagine, the way the goons explained limitation periods around the collection of winnings to us, we didn't ask a lot of questions.

Embarrassed, beaten, and broke (but unbowed!), we gave up on chasing our fortune during the crossings. It was frustrating, but the rewards that we'd be receiving would have to come later and from a different source. So, changing the fabric of history seemed like an easy thing to do, but even as prepared and well armed as we were, things just weren't that easy for us.

But these were not rock 'n' roll related, and our plan was formulating in my mind like jigsaw pieces falling into place. We knew that we were going to change Billy Bragg's life. Like so many before him, and even Kenn and me later, Billy Bragg's life was going to be changed by rock 'n' roll. It was just as simple as that. Kenn and I didn't need to plan anything. We just needed to get in front of Billy Bragg and show him some rock 'n' roll. We were certain that we knew everything we needed to make this intervention work. We knew how the levers worked. We had discovered it all. Well, we thought we had discovered it all. Unfortunately, we hadn't discovered that we were a just couple of American idiots.

12 – American Idiot

A new kind of tension? Tripping over ourselves to create more problems than we're solving?

I'm Sid Itious, and this is KQOR 89.9 FM. It's one oh-nine a.m., April 15. Are you tired of the American idiots at every turn? Tired of the world thinking we're all stupid? Is this a joke, or are we the joke? Here's Green Day giving us something to think about; are they being glib and comic, or simply offering a sardonic prediction of where we're heading? Oh, yeah, and by the way, these questions are all rhetorical, so don't call me with your answers, you idiots.

FCC transcript KQOR 89.9 FM 04.15.2005 0109
Operator comments redacted

American idiot? That was someone else. Something that unforgiving foreigners said in loud obnoxious voices to American tourists who were in Europe or Asia or wherever else. Words said in disgust to someone else; an insult. Not Kenn and me. While it was true that we had been subject to an exhaustive repertoire of insults, this was something entirely different. American idiot. It couldn't possibly be an expression used to describe Kenn and me, certainly not in reference to rock 'n' roll. But it was.

Kenn and I were so confident in our success that we didn't even consider having to plan or organize how this was going to happen; it just was. It was going to be just like finding Mike Ness or the interaction with Jerry Dammers, just something that we could adjust to as we went along. Weren't we smart enough? You'd think so. Kenn was a scientist, and while actually under-motivated, he was a really smart guy, and I had a quiver full of degrees to my name. English, philosophy, history, politics; surely they must count for something.

Didn't we know everything that we needed to? We thought that we did, but our intervention with Billy Bragg was anything but straightforward. Had studying the history of rock 'n' roll not completely prepared us for the future? Or even the present? Could the answer be that Meno was wrong, that we really didn't know everything that we needed?

Kenn and I were smart enough to know that we couldn't just jump into a taxi and say, "Take us to the Prime Minister's house," but we also knew that there had to be tours that would take us nearby and perhaps even inside the famed manor. Again, Kenn and I proved to be American idiots. We weren't going to get a tour of 10 Downing Street regardless of what we wanted. Unfortunately, the closest that we could get was some street called Whitehall Parliament Street, and even then we could only glimpse Billy Bragg's residence through the towering shiny, black iron gates. Gates erected and guarded to keep the unwashed masses of the governed away from government. Totally undemocratic. Any decent democracy…you know, one that is for the people and by the people, would allow access to the locus of a nation's political power. And while not completely comprehensive, the White House offered tours, but then again, maybe that's because an American President doesn't have to ask for permission from the Queen. Anyway, the Morality Brigade monsters controlled the regal iron gates that lined Whitehall and prevented access to Downing Street, and while this looked both picturesque and officious, all it really meant was that getting to Billy Bragg wasn't going to be as easy as perhaps Kenn and I had thought. That was OK, though, because heroes like us needed a challenge. Anything easily gained lacks value.

Our tour guide informed us, "Past that gate is Downing Street and our Prime Minister's famed residence," as he made a sweeping gesture with his arm toward a row of doors that we could only see obliquely from the vantage point our tour offered.

Kenn asked the obvious question, amid a sea of nodding faces, "So, which one is 10 Downing?" referring to the series of black doors set into a large, basalt, black brick building along the virtually empty Downing Street. From the limited view that we had, and the photos that were on our brochure, we had a slight sense of what the street looked like. We saw the windows framed in thin white trim that appeared to be manufactured or cut from the solid façade, all providing a fitting image of the great British neatness and elegance. Still, from what we could see, the block looked like an ordinary row of townhouses. Nicer perhaps than many that we had seen during the bus tour, but unremarkable all the same.

Our tour guide responded to Kenn's question in a stunning example of just how rude the British can be, saying in a derisive tone, "Probably the one with the number ten on it, sir."

"Yeah, but you can't see the numbers from here," Kenn decried.

"Probably?" I thought. If he didn't know for sure, what was he doing guiding tours and talking down to people? I mean, without tours like this he wouldn't have a job, would he? But ultimately, I let this rudeness pass and listened to the rest of the tour, trying to elicit some information that would assist us in crossing paths with the Prime Minister. Unfortunately, all I managed to learn was that access to "Number Ten," as our tour guide called it, was exceedingly difficult, and even the press and domestic staff had to be on a vetted roster in order to gain access.

We had walked past the gate to the residence a few times by now, just to make sure that we knew the lay of the land. A police guard wearing one of the funny hats that they wear in Britain seemed to be the only one on duty. Upon closer inspection, he wasn't a policeman, but another member of the Morality Brigade. This couldn't be that hard. There was only one guard. It's not like the White House with its high fence and expansive grounds, all under the perpetual vigilance of the Secret Service. It was too bad that Britain wasn't more like Canada, where the Prime Minister there regularly found people who had let themselves into his home, probably looking for maple syrup or a beer in those stubby little brown bottles.

It was just a door into what appeared like any other home that Kenn and I had walked by. Well, a gate in front of a road, leading to a door just like any other, but we could see the door. But the door wasn't that far from the gate. A stone's throw? Shouting distance, maybe? Probably, Kenn and I could shout loudly enough to be heard a good distance.

Kenn turned to me and said, "OK, I'll be right back. I've got an idea, meet me at that bench we passed a couple of blocks back. When I get back, we'll..." With that he flagged down one of the old school taxis that they have in London, that were all black, shiny, and rounded. A Bentley or Berkley or some English-looking manufacturer, cool and antiquated all at once.

Kenn left me with his incomplete sentence hanging in the warm air, got into the taxi, closed the door, and then disappeared down the street, leaving me alone with a partially articulated idea and to be suspiciously scrutinized by the sentry posted at the iron gate. I walked along the street thinking about being in London, the prospects of changing history, and all the rewards that we'd receive for being heroes. We'd probably be given access to Billy Bragg gigs for life. Autographed copies of his records. Invited out for pints with Billy. I was buoyed with excitement and couldn't wait to revel in our success and laugh over our cleverness back at Kenn's house.

My reverie lasted a couple of hours as I walked back and forth along the street. Rested on benches and generally frittered the remainder of the afternoon. Draining time out of a day was something that I was typically good at, thinking about nothing specifically and a lot in general. My mind drifted between Billy Bragg, rock 'n' roll, Pyrah, and what Kenn might be doing, but most of my thoughts flitted around as a butterfly without staying in any one place for more than a brief moment.

Generally, it was a pleasant way to spend time in London. It wasn't like going to a gig or having hot chips in a pub, but still agreeable. I don't know why they call them "hot chips," but maybe because the British hate the French and can't call their chips french fries, like the rest of the free world.

I was feeling good about our time in London, even without a gig to go to. It was more than the warming air, the parklands, and wide boulevards and historic landmarks. It was perhaps something like contentedness, thinking about Pyrah and knowing that Kenn and I were going to set things right with Billy Bragg. Although we crossed under the pretense of going to some random gig, Billy Idol or the Cult perhaps, Kenn and I left the show nearly as soon as we had arrived. This time the gig wasn't the priority, because I knew that we would be making it possible for more and better gigs. All of this because Kenn and I were restoring a future that had otherwise been foreclosed.

As the shadows started stretching, the light mild breeze was becoming cooler, and I started becoming impatient with Kenn. Fortunately, before too much longer, a similar-looking taxi rolled up to where I was starting to get chilled, and Kenn jumped out beaming with his conspiratorial grin I had so often seen.

"This is totally John Cusack," he said after he finished explaining his pending course of action. As we walked toward the gate that prevented access to the Prime Minister's address on Downing Street, I was concerned that this brilliant idea of Kenn's might be vulnerable. What if we had picked the wrong track? Clearly the idea worked for Cusack because he knew the music that would soften Ione Skye's resolve. Also, Cusack was Cusack. Who would really turn him down? I mean, he ended up with the girl, even as Lloyd Dobler, not even the real John Cusack. It turned out music selection should have been the least of my concerns.

As the first few bars of David Bowie's "Modern Love" started playing from the boom box raised above Kenn's head, I could see the Morality Brigade sentry leaving his post and starting toward us. Don't even get me started on the boom box, because it was something that Kenn insisted upon that I would have never even entertained.

As the sentry held the cuff of his jacket up to his face, I guessed that he was in communication with others. Maybe even Billy Bragg. I could just imagine him saying, *"You got to get out here, this is awesome."* Strangely, the reaction was more awesome than I imagined. People were rushing out of adjacent buildings to join us in the celebration of song. The look of zeal and excitement was flooding over the men who were now teeming out of the nearby buildings. All rushing toward us visibly excited. It was like the end of one of those street-dancing videos where everyone was dancing. Just like Bowie and Jagger's cover of "Dancing in the Street." Again, Kenn and I as heroes, changing the world one song at a time.

How easy was this going to be? It was like offering a drowning man a float or starving hoards bags of food. Here was a population that was starved of good rock 'n' roll and how fitting to have David Bowie help in ending their suffering by providing acoustic sustenance. "Kenn, this is awesome," I said. I was triumphant. "We might get knighted or castled or whatever they call that here!"

So complete was the euphoria, one of the Morality Brigadiers was leaping toward me to give me a hug! It was too late when I realized that the closest gentleman was flying through the air and that while David Bowie was certainly rock 'n' roll, and a great specimen thereof, he wasn't punk and didn't really inspire slam dancing. How could this be? The guard had it all wrong; while "Modern Love" could certainly be danced to, slam dancing? It just didn't make sense at all.

And it hit me. Actually, both the realization and the airborne monster hit me at about the same time. The Morality Brigade security service wasn't celebrating with us; Kenn and I were being arrested. "Kenn," I managed to gasp as the wind was being knocked out of me and I was crashing to the ground.

I was too late. Kenn also had company, but of three large men. The boom box careened across the street, where others from what Kenn and I now understood to be part of the security detail quarantined it and whisked it away, as though it had been a bomb. Fuck, good thing we hadn't picked something decidedly Irish like the Pogues, Stiff Little Fingers, or U2. "Fuck me," Kenn and I both took turns muttering, when our mouths weren't being filled with boots or fists or clubs or some combination of implements.

Additional security teams that we hadn't seen? Who would have thought? Fortunately, after we were incapacitated, we were dragged, literally, as in face against the pavement dragged, a few feet toward one of the adjacent buildings by where we had been standing. "Boyo, you two are in a great deal of peril," said one of the monsters that had held us fast from behind.

"Fuck, do ya think?" I responded, in my mind. Kenn and I may have missed some of the more obvious bits leading up to this point, but with our arms twisted behind our backs, multiple men treating us brusquely, and the abrasions that were starting to cover more and more of our faces from the asphalt, it was pretty clear they weren't going to ask us to build a mixed tape for them.

After being unceremoniously dragged to wherever, we were duly picked up, after a few kicks and punches to our backs, ribs, and abdomens, and then forced against a stone wall. As Kenn and I were standing there confused and contused, they aggressively searched us for weapons, drugs, and of course more music. Fortunately, we were "clean," as announced and confirmed by the supervising gorilla, who had large leathery looking ears, probably swollen from apprehending less compliant parties than Kenn and I represented.

"You lads will be coming in for questioning and will be held at Her Majesty the Queen's pleasure, for posing a potential threat to the Prime Minister," said one of the stern-sounding voices facing us.

I thought, "*Hmmm, the pleasure of the Queen.*" That can't be too bad, can it? It sounded like a nice time, with tea and those funny sandwiches without crusts but are full of cucumbers. There'd probably be some cookies, maybe even an espresso, you know, just as long as it's a pleasing time for the Queen.

I started contemplating the discussion that I would have with the Queen. I thought that was Margaret Thatcher? No, someone had said that she had died and that was whom Billy Bragg had replaced. Maybe if I had some change on me I, could see the Queen's picture first, so I could recognize her at tea. The Brits certainly have a confusing system. Who was really in charge, Billy Bragg, or the Queen? But the political nuances of Britain didn't really matter now. Changing Billy Bragg would still be easy now that Kenn and I were going to see the Queen. Even if Prime Minister Billy Bragg wasn't in attendance at tea, surely the Queen would be able to convince him, once Kenn and I convinced her.

We would be able to smooth talk the Queen and eventually sort this mess out. Then we'd concentrate on Billy Bragg, maybe even with the Queen's assistance, and all would be good. Sure, there was a bit of misunderstanding now with the Morality Brigade pulverizing our internal organs, but a little pain for heroes was all in a day's work. I was confident that our pain, like the blood in our urine, would pass.

While thinking about what kind of beer or flavor of tea I'd ask the queen for, I suddenly felt a hammer pound my kidney. As I felt the air being forced out of my lungs and my knees collapsing in weakness, I could hear something being shouted at me, but with my head spinning, it was something I couldn't discern. The force of the physical blow to my kidney was retreating, but it was replaced by a fiery sensation of blood rushing into the damaged area. My abdomen was certainly the source of where internal damage was occurring, leaving me faint and lightheaded, yet with areas on my torso that were increasing in temperature from warm to blisteringly hot.

Another member of the security force spun me around in a different direction from that which I was falling and through a sea of stern faces, course hands shoving me through the now open door of a large police van. The Morality Brigade's vanguard had closed ranks, and I lost sight of Kenn, leaving me with only their shouts of violence, directed at me. As I was being forced to the van my breathing accelerated, I tripped or got tangled on my feet or someone else's foot or something loose on the ground. I lost my balance and fell, unable to grab the door frame or an outstretched arm for balance. Flailing and panicked, I plummeted downward, closing my eyes as a fist was rushing toward me, bracing for another impact, only to discover that I had landed back in Kenn's house. Despite the pain that racked my body, I felt relief. Relief to see that Kenn was there, even though he was also doubled over in pain and appeared to be bleeding. Relief to be home. We were safe, but had failed to make contact with Billy Bragg.

"Maybe they weren't David Bowie fans," Kenn suggested wearily, spitting blood into an empty beer bottle.

Right, like there was anyone in Britain that didn't like David Bowie. "Yeah, or more likely maybe they thought we were a menace or a threat to Billy Bragg," I replied, getting to my feet and looking for ice put on my face so that I could try to extinguish the fire that had been set on it. As always, the only thing that I could find in Kenn's fridge that was cold was Mountain Dew, beer, and Frank's sauce, so I took three beers; threw one to Kenn, opened one for myself, and wrapped the third in a wet dish towel and held it to the side of my face. I hoped that once the fire on my face had abated that I could turn my attention to my ribs and stomach, which felt wet, as though they were bleeding through my shirt.

It was more likely that we were seen as a menace than that David Bowie was unpopular. Kenn and I were probably seen languishing around the gate to 10 Downing Street for the better part of the day. The black T-shirts and jeans probably didn't help, and then of course there was the issue of the boom box being held overhead, David Bowie or not.

"Yeah, well, it worked for Cusack," Kenn said, undeterred, despite his physically broken condition, "and I'll be dammed if I'm playing Peter Gabriel. As if that would work anyway."

When I considered Kenn's plan, the John Cusack theory seemed good, so we actually crossed and tried it a couple of other times, before we gave up outright on it. Probably just as well for our internal organs. But the principle was that if we were continuing to go back to the same time, we wouldn't be remembered by the security detail. That part actually seemed to work, but Lloyd Cole, the Jam, James Blunt, the Cure, Sting, Weddings, Parties, Anything, the Weather Prophets, the Sundays, Soundgarden, and the Smiths all failed to convince anyone that we were destined to change the Prime Minister's mind about rock 'n' roll. Sadly, these actions only proved that Kenn and I could take a beating, but even that didn't change anything. It was always the same, and it played out like the Surf Punks song "And Then the Cops Came." Failing to correct Billy Bragg's path with rock 'n' roll seemed like too good of an idea to fail, so to be sure, I built a list that I updated after every attempt to "John Cusack" Billy Bragg back. Here we were, acting out stanza after stanza of the Surf Punks, except we didn't seem to learn from our beatings. If we had been committed to recording our results, in keeping with the scientific method, it would have sounded like "And Then the Cops Came," with a list looking like this:

Artist	Song	Result
David Bowie	"Modern Love"	Mild beating and arrest
David Bowie and Mick Jagger	"Dancing in the Streets"	Mild beating and arrest
Lloyd Cole	"Rattlesnakes"	Light beating and arrest
the Cranberries	"No Need to Argue"	Significant beating and arrest
the Cure	"A Forest"	Indifferent beating and arrest
Soundgarden	"Black Hole Sun"	Gratuitous beating and arrest
James Blunt	"Beautiful"	Aggressive beating and arrest
the Talking Heads	"What a Day That Was"	Creative beating and arrest
the Surf Punks	"And Then the Cops Came"	Significant beating and arrest
Weddings, Parties Anything	"Scorn of the Women"	Mild beating and arrest
Led Zeppelin	"Immigration Song"	Harsh beating and arrest
MC5	"Future/Now"	Violent beating and arrest
Died Pretty	"Mirror Blues"	Prolonged beating and arrest
Joy Division	"Ceremony"	Depressing beating and arrest
New Order	"Ceremony"	Invigorating beating and arrest
Galaxie 500	"Ceremony"	Moderate beating and arrest
Jonathan Richman	"Pablo Picasso"	Sustained beating and arrest

Actually, this is only part of the list, but you get the idea. It was more than the cops coming as well, it was the secret police as well as the Morality Brigade, and they came with beatings.

We were beat over and over again. Fortunately for us, it seemed that none of the damage was ever long lived, perhaps another nuance of crossing. I guess that even this made sense because if we had received a beating in the past, then the injuries would have mostly healed by the time we returned to Kenn's. Not perfectly, but certainly better than you could hope for. Kenn and I noted that this process was never instantaneous, which I suppose was fair enough, but we also made note to make sure we didn't tempt fate too much. After all, not even time will cure permanent damage, and dead heroes don't get to enjoy rock 'n' roll.

We did finally admit, amid our discussions over the next few hours, while we coughed up and spit blood, applied ice bags, and consumed more cold beer, that we needed a different approach. A plan that was more forceful. And forceful without Kenn and me being on the receiving end of the force.

It seemed logical that since crossing to a period after our meeting with Jerry Dammers didn't work, we had to go back farther into rock 'n' roll history. So we did. Since we couldn't directly communicate with Billy Bragg simply by going to his home, Kenn and I reasoned that we would have to find him out among the people. That was the kind of thing that politicians did anyway. They interacted with the small people in order to seem responsive and approachable. *Connected to the electorate,* I think they call it.

Kenn and I decided that we would capitalize on one of these public appearances. Kenn had it all figured out. We'd just drive up alongside Billy and then roll down our windows and play him some great music. Then he'd have to listen. It would be like a drive-by Lloyd Dobler. Billy Bragg would hear the music, and we'd have a means of escape.

It was genius. Foolproof. Once Billy Bragg listened to what we were playing, he'd love it. Just like the people who tuned into my radio show. After all, it was a radio show that caused Pyrah to fall in love with me. This was a brilliant plan, plus it would allow us to get past the security force, most of whom, as we had proven unequivocally, were Special Forces in plainclothes. This time it would be easy. At least that's what Kenn had told me.

Again, I found myself going along with Kenn's idea, because it seemed reasonable. I should have known better. "Reasonable" and "Kenn" were two elements that could never exist together, like sodium and calcium. I should have also known that I didn't have the whole story either.

After crossing, Kenn and I rented a car, and I agreed to drive. Kenn could navigate and work the stereo. I was just a bit better driver, which was important since we had to drive on the wrong side of the street.

I found our way to an area along Cromwell Road, where we'd wait. Kenn had learned that Billy Bragg had a scheduled appearance in front of the Natural History Museum and that was going to be our opportunity to intervene. It seemed fitting. The natural course of history had been upset, so what better place for us to repair it?

While I was playing with the radio in the rented car, I managed to find BBC radio coverage of the address and was impressed at how Billy Bragg, the Prime Minister, sounded much like Billy Bragg the musician. He spoke with the same passion, the same energy and purpose. His use of rhetoric and imagery was both inspiration and engaging. Unfortunately, it was his message that seemed wrong, out of place, oppressive, rather than liberating. Rather than speaking about compassion, he was calling for strict measures. Rather than promoting understanding, he was being inflexible. He was directing a course of isolationism, rather than community. Although still compelling as an orator, this was the complete opposite of the Billy Bragg that Kenn and I knew from our love of his music. Billy Bragg the Prime Minister wasn't even a shade of the man that had inspired so many others. While it sounded like the same man, everything that he said summoned us to action, but rather than action as his musician self, Kenn and I were being called to *oppose* him. To intervene. To restore. To defy a man who had always been a hero to us.

That was a thought that we had to expel from our minds. How could Kenn and I consider intervening against a man who was a hero of ours? It was one thing to stand up to a bully, yet quite another to a hero. No, we had to view things differently. Marginalize the issues. Characterize the problem. Kenn and I had agreed that Billy Bragg wasn't himself. Sick, perhaps. That way our actions were *helping* him; not in opposition, but in aid. Billy Bragg needed our help. Kenn and I weren't acting against a hero, but intervening to save one. This was an intervention to save Billy Bragg. But it was even more than that; it was a stand for rock 'n' roll, which is where Kenn and I managed to draw our inspiration from.

We heard London calling for aid, and Kenn and I were answering. It was a sight to behold; I was at the wheel of the rented car, and Kenn was in the back, at the ready, with the boom box. This time we were planning on playing "We Are Not Deep," by the Housemartins. No one could resist the bands catchy hooks, plus they were political and appeared on the Go! Discs label that they shared with the healthy Billy Bragg.

The public address started to come to a close, and Kenn said, "OK, let's go, and remember we're just rollin' slow." That was the plan, so that's what I did. As we crossed Queen's Gate, still back from the entrance of the museum, we could see the beginning of the crowd dispersing and a police officer waving us onward. Then suddenly, Kenn hissed, "There he is, there's Billy! Slow down! Rollin' slow, rollin' slow."

Kenn was pointing to a man who was obviously Billy Bragg, but with a shimmering hologram projected upon him. Like before, the hologram was the sign that something had to change. It was the indication that this was the target with whom we had to intervene and return to the proper course of history. Fleetingly, I thought *"Hmmmm, how easy it is to change things that are pointed out for you."* For a distracted moment, I wished that the present was like that too.

As I slowed down, much to my surprise, Kenn threw the door open, grabbed the glowing and flickering Billy Bragg, and pulled him back into the car. "Go, go, go. Fuck, dude, go! Hit the fuckin' gravel!" Kenn screamed as he wrestled with a surprised and rather pissed off Billy Bragg. Kenn was imploring me to do something faster or turn some way or other, all of his yelling a blur of white noise without meaning. None of Kenn's words managed to penetrate my brain, which was filled to capacity with shock and disbelief. "What. The. Fuck?" my brain screamed. *"What had Kenn done now? It was always something with Kenn, but now kidnapping a Prime Minister as he walked along a street? I thought we were rolling slow in whatever dumb affectation Kenn was putting on. I thought we were just playing the Housemartins."*

Without thinking about anything else, I hit the gas, lurching the car forward with squealing tyres. Kenn turned on the music and tumbled over into the front seat beside me.

"Really, Kenn?" I shouted over the roar of the engine, the music, and a swearing Billy Bragg. "You thought playing "Gangsters" by the Specials was a good idea?" In the rearview mirror, I could see that Kenn had restrained Billy Bragg and was in the process of taping his mouth and putting a sack over his head. Fuck, we were really going to be in trouble this time.

"Change of plans," Kenn replied nonchalantly, as though he had decided to return with hamburgers rather than the pizza that he had gone out for.

"Change of plans!" I yelled with exasperation and a significant amount of mortal fear. "You said we were gonna play the Housemartins, not kidnap the Prime Minister." I had turned onto Exhibition Road, still accelerating, and was starting to plan a series of subsequent turns in order to evade anyone who might be following us.

"Yeah, and now we're playing the Specials," Kenn replied. "Take the A13 Trunk Road to the sea," Kenn ordered, leaving me unsure if he was giving me driving directions or requesting a song.

"Kenn, fuck off," I replied. "You know that this isn't about your music selection, but about kidnapping a head of state." I was turning erratically and continuing to check the rearview mirrors, concerned that I couldn't detect anyone following us. I knew that Kenn's reference was a Billy Bragg song; that really it was a British version of "Route 66," by Bobby Troup, which ordinarily I would have found funny, but now I was furious. Kidnapping? I hated Kenn for running off with his lukewarm ideas: I hated myself even more for going along blindly. Unquestioningly, as though he had a track record of inspired solutions. This was just another example of Kenn having something to prove, I just had no idea why or what was always so important to him.

As furious as I was, I focused on my driving, slowing down to match the flow of traffic and avoiding attention. After about twenty-five minutes of driving and still no sign of being followed, I turned the car into an industrial area known as Park Royal and found an abandoned warehouse. At least for now, this fortuitous discovery would provide us with a reprieve and somewhere that we could talk to Billy without fear of discovery or apprehension by his security detail. In the back of my mind, I was concerned. Where was the security detail? Could Kenn's plan have worked that well?

I noticed that the tape that Kenn had tried to apply must have failed, because I heard a calm voice from the sack. It was during this time that we heard the first of very few words uttered by Billy Bragg, a sign that he was vastly different from the Billy Bragg of our original time. "You lads are making a huge mistake here," he said with a sort of sigh and soft resignation.

"No way," Kenn countered. "This is important. We need to show you something."

"Look," Prime Minister Bragg continued, "this isn't just like taking a demo tape to Capitol Records; you've committed a major crime."

"What crime?" Kenn said incredulously. "We're just taking you for a drive."

"A drive?" Our captive was starting to show some of the emotion that polarized many a debate when he was a musician. "You call this a drive? I've got a fucking sack over my head, and you've taped my mouth shut. Or you've tried to. If you're not better with abduction than with gaffer's tape, you'll likely end up dead before long."

"Dead?" Kenn asked, confused. It was clear that once again Kenn hadn't thought this through completely. "What are you talking about *dead?*"

"Is your buddy an idiot?" The question was directed at me.

"No, a scientist actually." What else could I really say?

"Listen, you can't just go around kidnapping the Prime Minister of England," Bragg stated. "It's just not cricket."

Kenn fielded this one. "Of course not, but you say that like it's a bad thing." I could only imagine the quizzical look on Bragg's face. Especially now, as I had completed a series of turns and was slowing the car to a stop.

Kenn assisted Billy Bragg from the car, still bound and wearing a sack over his head. He led him over to a low crate and sat him down.

"Kenn," I started.

"Look, Billy," Kenn said, ignoring me and crouching down to speak gently into Billy's ear, "this is serious. You're in a lot of trouble."

"Billy Bragg was in trouble?" I thought. *"Fuck, how would we then describe the situation that we were in?"*

"Dude," Kenn ordered, "grab the boom box and set it up."

What was it with the boom box, I wondered? How was it that Kenn had no issue with a "boom box" but mention a mixing table and you're in league with the devil, but that's how it always was with Kenn. So I let the issue with the boom box go. I had bigger problems, so I returned to the car and retrieved the music, while Kenn took the bag off of Billy Bragg's head and offered him some bottled water. The hologram was still as strong as ever showing a man with a stern but compassionate disposition and eyes that housed kindness, wisdom, and understanding, rather than the vacant and puzzling eyes of the present Billy Bragg.

We started the music and played Roxy Music, Brian Eno, Lou Reed, the Hunters & Collectors, Tones on Tail, the Ramones, the Sneetches, Harvey Danger, the American Music Club, and the Cocteau Twins; we even played the Housemartins, so that Kenn could make me feel better that we were returning to the "original plan," still forgetting that the "original plan" hadn't mentioned kidnapping. During this entire time, Kenn and I tried to explain to Billy Bragg the errors of his ways and how he was destined to be a musician. How he had a better path to take, something more positive and inspirational than the repression and narrow-mindedness that his political regime was responsible for. How he could use the Prime Minister's office as a platform for better things. To make the world good and filled with rock 'n' roll.

For Billy's part, he didn't really say much, nor did he struggle. I thought that this was because he knew our assault had been such a surprise and that no one had been able to follow us or that maybe we were convincing him of our message. Perhaps he was just like me, a kindred spirit who was really yearning to discover rock 'n' roll. But maybe it was something else entirely.

Kenn and I tried various tactics to connect with Billy Bragg. To convince him of his wrongs, the error of his ways, how his path was leading to ruination. We would talk while the music was playing, contrasting the freedom of music to the repression that currently existed, explaining how morality is something that is discovered from within and couldn't be imposed by a government, and sometimes we didn't talk at all in favor of just letting the music play. The idea that we would succeed in altering Billy Bragg's view was absolute. I considered it ordained, especially since we now had unfettered access to Billy, but still the hologram persisted. It didn't fade like it did with Mike Ness, Dammers, or Lemmy. Kenn and I failed to discuss this, but perhaps we should have. After all, it's often the details that are missed that are the most important.

During the interludes where Kenn and I just left Billy Bragg to listen to the music, we discussed how good a spot we had found. With all the other industrial noises, we could stay here undetected for as long as we needed to. I was inclined to admit that Kenn's plan, as far-fetched as it was, seemed as though it was going to work, but then the industrial-based white noise started to sound more like a helicopter, although it was really hard to tell. As my resolve was abating and then starting to become a full-fledged retreat, a number of shadows began enlarging against the windows until a multitude of black-clad soldiers repelled through shattering glass.

As falling shards of glass broke on the concrete floor, machine gun fire filled the air, and Kenn and I both recoiled as plastic riot bullets rained upon us like a hailstorm of angry wasps. Smoke and flashing lights turned our happy little abandoned sanctuary into a chaotic cacophony of violence, with the acrid smell of the canister grenades that had tumbled along the floor amid the glass fragments. Before Kenn and I knew what had happened, we were restrained against the cold concrete floor, welts rising from being struck by riot bullets across our bodies. I say restrained, but really there wasn't a great deal of effort required to quell any resistance on our part at this time. We had initially been surprised and then overwhelmed by smoke grenades and the punishing force of the plastic bullets. Over and again, Kenn and I found that our certain failure resulted in detention by some police arm of the British government. We also discovered without fail that our captors had very little regard for either our choices in music or the Geneva Conventions. The beatings that we took spoke of both.

I heard Kenn ask, "So what do you think? Are you ready to step out of politics to be a musician yet?"

There was no reply from Billy Bragg, but further questions from Kenn were now being muffled.

Looking up I could see that Billy Bragg was unharmed and now secured by and within a tight circle of paramilitary saviors. Unfortunately, this also meant that Kenn and I had yet again failed to influence Billy Bragg or restore the future to its proper course. Of course, it was then that we really noticed that the hologram hadn't been banished at all, but in fact appeared clearer and stronger than before. Failure was not complete, and perhaps we had even made things worse by trying to intervene with force.

Later I realized that we likely weren't followed because the Prime Minister had some type of tracking device on him. Maybe something biometric that could monitor his safety as well as his location. Kenn was an idiot. Why had I let him do this again? Fuck. I was even more of an idiot for following an idiot. American idiots. Our only saving grace was that with our hands bound behind our backs, in handcuffs, we were being dragged toward the warehouse door. My mind filled with pleas that the door would function in a manner that others had in our past. The past…a concept forever changed for Kenn and me, but all the same I found myself clinging to the antiquated idea. What else would you try to grasp but something that you once thought was unshakable, something that you understood? Doesn't the past adhere to everyone in one shape or another? But for Kenn and me, this was a memory of a past where doors functioned to take us safely home to Kenn's. So we had little else to do but hope that our experiences with doors would remain unchanged and that passing through the threshold of the warehouse would again convey us to safety.

I clenched my eyes shut, both in response to the physical agony that I was in and the intense anticipation that I clung to. Fortunately, when I could no longer hold my eyes closed, I gasped in a breath, and through fluttering eyelids I could see that my captors were preparing to hoist me through the door. Even though my body was racked in pain from being buffeted by the plastic bullets, and my lungs ached from the smoke that smelt like burning metal that choked the air, I was relieved to feel the sensation of falling and then being caught, by Kenn's carpet.

As you could well imagine, Kenn and I argued when we got back. And as you might also imagine, Kenn and I ultimately didn't resolve anything except for discovering the curative qualities of Frank's sauce. Yeah, it turned out that Frank's on pizza distracted us from the throbbing sensation emanating from the bruised ribs caused by the plastic bullets. But we also realized that the inside of our mouths were raw from being beaten and that the hot sauce merely drew our attention to our other injuries. The overall effect was to displace one source of pain with another. Curative effects and time travel do indeed move in mysterious ways.

But again, it is often the most unlikely of places where inspiration is found. It was while we were now forced to finish the Hawaiian pizza without Frank's RedHot, and while we continued to muse over the difficult task of kidnapping and reprogramming the British Prime Minister in order to save rock 'n' roll that the ultimate solution came to us.

"Wow, it's like we've lost a war or something," Kenn said despondently, regarding his "naked" piece of pizza. "Hawaiian without Frank's...we're really getting back to the basics, aren't we?"

Unfortunately, I was in my own malaise, reflecting on what seemed to be an endless cycle of immolation, so I was only partially listening to Kenn, but something resonated with me. "Huh? What did you just say, Kenn?" I asked, trying to shake the fog of my current physical pain and mental anguish off. "Say that again."

"It's nothing, Dick," he replied, using my least favorite moniker. "I just said that Hawaiian pizza is really basic without Frank's, almost naked and boring."

Interesting how "naked" can be "boring" sometimes, like with hot sauce and pizza, while at other times, like with Pyrah, "naked" always meant "sexual" and "exciting."

"No, what was the phrase you said? Did you say that we were *getting back to the basics*?"

"Yeah, so?"

As though a code had just been solved, Kenn and I looked at each other and started to nod. "Of course," I continued. "That's what we have to do, Kenn. We have to get back to the basics!" Not only was *Back to the Basics* the name of the compilation that brought the first three Billy Bragg EPs under one title, but it represented a simple way of looking at things. "Kenn, we've been thinking about this problem all wrong. You can't show someone the error of his ways if he doesn't have the same values. It's the values that people hold that govern their decisions and actions. Billy Bragg as Prime Minister has led government policies against music, because he doesn't like music." We're trying to show a rainbow to someone who's color-blind, or I guess colour-blind, since he was English, after all."

"Yeah, dude," Kenn said, picking up my line of thought, "it's not that Billy Bragg likes *bad* music, he doesn't like music at all, so we have to change that." Before anything else, Billy Bragg was a rock 'n' roll fan. He loved music and was a voracious collector and consumer, from the Clash and the Jam, who were contemporaries of his youth, to Motown acts that provided influence and inspiration to his songwriting. Somewhere along the way, Billy Bragg the Prime Minister had missed this experience and had fallen into the limbo world of people who find music "fine" or "just all right," but "no big deal." These were people that you would never convince of the value of music. How could you? It was like teaching the value of education to a star athlete who was merely at college waiting to be drafted by a professional team, or the super-hot knockout cheerleader from high school who was merely pursuing her education as a means to marry a doctor.

"Right, Kenn, so going back to basics, we have to find a time to interact with Billy in which he's still impressionable," I added. "You know, a time where he interacted with music and it changed his life."

After a few more beers, some Dew, and cold pizza, Kenn and I agreed that the time that we needed to target for Billy Bragg was immediately prior to Rock Against Racism, where he saw the Clash for the very first time. We needed to get him to a rock 'n' roll show that would provide and harness the same energy used by Dr. Frankenstein to reanimate corpses. Energy that would provide the spark of life, a source of inspiration; something that would leave him thunderstruck.

13 – Thunderstruck

I've always lived close to the West Coast, and as such have been at home with storms.

This is KQRL 91.1 FM, and you're tuned in at twelve twenty Monday morning, with Sid Itious. Storms are fraught with tension, but also contrasts. People say, "I love the lightening and thunder" or, "I hate the rainstorms. But aren't storms beyond all that? Wasn't King Lear considered insane for raging against the storms and boiling sea? Maybe he was just frustrated. At any rate, and back to the music, storms get our attention; they inspire comment or rally emotion. Storms define people. We name storms, and for all of that, I can't imagine a world without them. Here's the Young brothers, co-founders of AC/DC, sharing their views on the thunder.

FCC transcript KQRL 91.1 FM 03.21.2001 0020
Operator comments redacted

Thunderstruck. The look on Billy Bragg's face was clear. Thunderstruck. Gobsmacked. Awed. It was as though Saint Paul had just pulled up on a custom Harley Davidson Fat Boy with Martin Luther riding bitch and handed Billy Bragg enlightenment in the form of music. Billy was nodding, knowingly. Enlightened.

"Kenn, untie his hands," I directed. We had made our breakthrough with Billy. After hours of listening to the good and the bad that music had to offer, there was no way that anyone reasonable could withstand the message we needed to get across to him. I knew this intuitively, but it also helped that the glowing aura was fading like an old sun-bleached flag.

After all the beatings, arrests, and failed interventions, Kenn and I had finally gotten it right. Having crossed on the back of All Mod Cons, to see the Jam, instead we sought out and found Billy Bragg in the Spring of 1978 when more than anything, he needed to find the power of rock 'n' roll. Having gone back to the basics, we had found Billy Bragg, a youth, floundering as most of us do at a certain awkward age. The same age that justifies a gap year, backpacking throughout Asia, joining the Peace Corps, dating the wrong girl, buying a motorbike, trying weed, or worse for Kenn's and my parents, being drawn further into rock 'n' roll. We had found Billy Bragg spinning his wheels in a dead-end office job with a repressive and harassment-fueled culture that could only be fully described by Kafka or Coretta Scott King. At this pensive juncture of Billy's life, he was foundering without a keel in a sea of decisions. Worse than being at a crossroads without a map, Billy didn't even know where it was that he wanted to go.

"Really? This shit makes the Top of the Pops?" Billy was incredulous. "How is it possible and how do you know?" We had just finished playing "Chant No. 1 (We Don't Need This Pressure On)" by Spandau Ballet, so that we could make our point. Unfortunately, and three years later, "Chant No. 1" managed to find its way to become a top-three hit with the BBC in 1981, the same year that New Order's version of "Ceremony" only managed to crawl to thirty-fourth, a fact that proved that Denmark wasn't the only place where things were rotten.

Yes, it was brutal to subject anyone to Spandau Ballet, but desperate times called for desperate measures, and heroic as Kenn and I were, the parade of beatings that had followed us only demonstrated that we were out of options. Billy Bragg needed to see that the future could be devoid of music unless someone managed to take a stand and bring something interesting and intelligent to the art form. Simply put, we needed to do whatever we could to get Billy Bragg back on track. The ends would have to justify the means. Kenn and I knew that rock 'n' roll could change the world; we were now on the cusp of showing Billy that it was he *and* music that was capable of making the world a better place.

Fortunately, the effect of playing "Chant No. 1" was both instantaneous and obvious. Billy Bragg knew that he was listening to garbage. More importantly, he also understood that music like this was insipid and lacking originality (sounding like a weak copy of Life During Wartime, from a Talking Heads album released three years earlier) or any real sense of life; someone was required to take a stand. While it was astounding that this miserable track had found its way to become a top-ten hit, it was also a key example of how far popular music had fallen. Not only a true warning for the period, but it was the sort of information that Kenn and I could impart to reinforce our credibility with Billy.

Now more than ever rock 'n' roll was in need of aid. We needed Billy Bragg to answer the call, not even so much for his immediate contributions to the art, but for his long-term impact and the consequences of what would happen if he chose a different path. Looking back we should have tried this first. Billy Bragg would later go on to say that "Chant No. 1" had provided all the motivation that he needed to become a musician. Sometimes it's the most obvious that you can't see. In fact, Billy Bragg would later mock the song (and President Reagan simultaneously) with, "I Don't Need This Pressure Ron." Good times indeed.

"It's worse than that. They will go on to have ten singles in the top ten. You can't allow this type of thing to go on unchecked," I said.

"This journey has to start now," Kenn agreed. "It's gonna be a few years before this actually happens, but it is always the actions of today that decide the landscape of tomorrow. So, while you may not prevent Spandau Ballet from succeeding, you can give people an alternative. Don't you think the world deserves something better than Spandau Ballet?"

"Right, but as Prime Minister—" Billy started.

I cut him off with, "Billy, it's not just about Britain. This is a global problem. Canada has Celine Dion, Bryan Adams, Nickelback, Tom Cochrane, and Avril Lavigne, to name a few; in America we have REO Speedwagon, Huey Lewis and the News, the Backstreet Boys, and Hootie and the Blowfish. Farther afield things just keep getting worse. Don't even get me heading to South Korea and Psy. It's about the music, not government. Art, not politics. Humanity, not people. It's rock 'n' roll that matters, Billy. Music can change the world. Music can inspire and motivate people; we need you to understand this. You have to understand that it is human expression that has to be encouraged and given the freedom to discover experiences and find its own breadth and scope that is important."

"Listen," Kenn cut in softly, as he and I worked like any great song, with a contrast of volumes, tempos, and layered sounds, "we know that this is difficult, but it's also important. Sometimes it takes a grown man longer to learn what a child might learn in an evening." Kenn was back to planting lyrics again, to what Billy Bragg would later record as "The Passion." It was impressive to watch Kenn engage in this, even though it was ultimately simply a message to which Billy Bragg added grace. But I can't imagine anyone doing any better at suggestion; it was so seamless.

After allowing the future lyric to soak in a bit, Kenn continued and revealed the critical portion of our plan to Billy. "You need to go see the Clash tonight in East London at the Rock Against Racism gig. You're not gonna be Prime Minister. You may think that it's a life goal of yours to ascend to the Office of the Prime Minister, but really this is because you're still searching. You know that if you're honest with yourself that you don't really know what you want to do. Billy, you need to understand that you've got more important work to do."

"But how do you know?" he asked, still unconvinced. "If I can speak in confidence, being the Prime Minister of England is a lifetime goal. How else am I going to be able to bring about important social changes, bolster support for my local football team so that they can achieve the championship status that they so aptly deserve, all while marrying some local heartthrob?"

And so the penny dropped. The other shoe hit the floor. What we had anticipated and always knew as an absolute came to be.

You see? It's always about a girl, isn't it? But did this sound like a lifetime ambition, or merely ramblings from someone who had not really discovered what it was that he wanted to do? Presently, Billy Bragg was still a lost soul, like many of us are at that age.

Of course if you have something in your life that is actually important that can tether you, like rock 'n' roll, things will become just that much clearer. This is what we needed Billy to see. Repeating Kenn's stanza, I offered, "Look, Billy, this will be difficult to understand, but," I paused, still formulating my plan as I was talking, "we're angels," I said with some finality and confidence. Right, my plan consisted of now convincing Billy Bragg that Kenn and I were angels. "We've been sent to make this happen. It's part of the greater plan."

"Angels?" Kenn looked at me, astonished. I just shrugged. Being angels seemed every bit as believable as time travel, even more believable to some people.

"But, I'm not religious. Why of all people would an angel be sent to me?" he asked, his confusion rising steadily like a tide.

"What did you *expect*," Kenn countered, "your own personal Jesus? A song to be written about you? Are you really so vain?" Kenn was on fire, referring to the Depeche Mode song "Personal Jesus" that would be released ten years into the future, while referring to Carly Simon's effort from six years prior.

"I know. It's difficult to fathom, and for you of all people," I started, thinking that while I was manipulating him into seeing Rock Against Racism, that I might as well also plant future lyrics into his subconscious like Kenn had, "but you've got a socialism of the heart. You're a humanist, Billy. Come on, let's go to the gig, it will be good. Plus there will be hot girls there. Maybe even someone you'd fancy enough to marry." If there was nothing else for me to rely on, there was always girls and evolution. Ignoring Kenn's dirty look, we started getting ready to leave.

Kenn had his theory about girls and rock 'n' roll and how it always led to disaster, but the mechanism worked. There was an irresistible attraction that underlined women's ability to infiltrate men's imaginations and captivate their interest. Was it just the female form, or was it the prospect of love? Maybe Kenn's theory was just predicated on Lloyd Cole's lyrics in "Love Ruins Everything." Maybe it was just Kenn's own justification of his romantic, or at least lustful, failings, but whatever it was, I didn't completely agree that such a conspiracy existed. Certainly not now after having met Pyrah.

It had been a while since Pyrah and I had spent time together. With the litany of missions to save Billy Bragg and rock 'n' roll occupying so much of the time that Kenn and I had, it was simply a case of being distracted away from her. There was never enough time to do everything that I wanted. It was surreal to consider that my life was still so managed by the concept of time, even though Kenn and I could travel through time, virtually at will. Maybe I would be able to use this gift to make it up to Pyrah, or if she was mad, to go back to a time when she wasn't and smooth things out in advance. You know, change the past to change to future, like what we had done with "Chant No. 1." But those discussions would have to wait; Kenn and I had a mission at hand, and we were going to see the Clash!

I knew that Kenn would ultimately approve, although he hated the idea that I had to resort to luring Billy Bragg to a Clash gig with the bait of girls, but what could I do? While I could change some things in history, and others I could nudge along, there were things that were unalterable and man's attraction to girls was one such thing.

The fact remained that we needed to get Billy Bragg to Rock Against Racism through any means necessary. The presence of girls at the concert was just another tool at our disposal to assist us. Guys have been attracted to and falling for girls since Eden. They have been rendered incapable of making good decisions in the presence of girls and when lured by the potential of anything that didn't find humour (yeah, "ou"; still in London) in bodily functions and sports. Not very complicated, but seemingly something that evolution had overlooked among males and something that women were able to capitalize upon.

"Yeah? And girls too," said Billy Bragg seemed at least to be acting convinced. "We should stop and get Wiggy too."

"Of course, but let's get going then," Kenn said in a palpable state of contemplation, "Victoria Park is a spell from here, isn't it?"

"You were joking about the band with the blowfish name, right?" Billy said, still trying to put all the pieces together in his mind.

"We only wish, Billy, we only wish," Kenn said, shaking his head and wearing embarrassment for all of humanity. Me? I was embarrassed that we had to rely upon Billy Bragg thinking that he could hook up at the Rock Against Racism show rather than any sense of duty to save the world from bands like Spandau Ballet and Hootie and the Blowfish, but I suppose the result was the same, and changing history is onerous enough without nitpicking.

"But who would name a band *that*?" Billy asked.

"You think the name sucks? You should hear those monkeys. Dreadful. Truly a shortcoming of our boss's predilection for allowing free choice in humans, if you ask me. An absolute abomination." Kenn was still trying to keep the angelic appearance up, but perhaps losing some credibility with his word choice. I'd like to say I was convincing or that the angel bit gave him pause, but really it's always about a girl, isn't it?

Pulling me aside, Kenn asked, "So, is it the gig or the chicks that's getting him to the show?"

"Fuck if I know, Kenn. Maybe he thinks that we're angels or maybe that we won't let him go until he turns up at the gig. Bottom line is that we need him there, because that's when his inspiration starts to get traction," I whispered, knowing that if I was overheard now that any illusion of being an angel would be shattered like cold glass on granite tile.

After venturing across town, during which Billy mooched two pies, hot chips, and three pints off of us (saving rock 'n' roll had to come at *some* cost), we arrived at Rock Against Racism with Billy Bragg's longtime friend, Wiggy, now also in tow. Fortunately, we picked up Wiggy after Billy displayed the "receiving side" of socialism during our trek.

"Man, that dude was gonna eat us out of house and home if the park was much further away," I complained, forgetting how our consumption of cash was only a temporary situation during our crossings and perhaps being more annoyed with the seemingly endless distractions which seemed to have imperiled our mission. It was tempting to feel confident about being on track to succeed, but until Billy Bragg had experienced the Clash, anything was possible, and I was extraordinarily tired of having the shit kicked out of me for this objective.

"Right, because this is supposed to be easy. We're making a fucking difference here. You don't think that there is gonna be a cost? Do you know the price of wars?" Kenn was starting again. "The costs are huge! And I'm talking both in terms of human sacrifice and economic resources." I knew that I was going to be riding shotgun on a rant, and changed the subject.

"Who else is on the bill tonight with the Clash?" I desperately asked. It was always a good ploy to sidetrack Kenn with rock 'n' roll-based queries. My gambit worked, as Kenn responded with disdain and exasperation, but gave up his "cost of wars" monologue. Listing off the acts, while admonishing me for not remembering, Kenn was as predictable as he was pliable. However tedious it was enduring Kenn's barrage, it was infinitely better than whatever rant he was going to run off on about wars, human sacrifice, and the importance of our role for humanity. None of his rant was relevant or would change the fact that I was out of cash and now couldn't get chips at the show. I had always wanted to eat chips and drink beer at a Clash gig. I suppose we'd have to cross again just for that, because as it turned out, Rock Against Racism wasn't really that opportunity. But even if we didn't, I suppose it was just another cost of being heroes.

Looking over at Billy Bragg and Wiggy, the last of the glowing aura around Bragg had disappeared. We were on the right course, and success finally seemed to be at hand. Kenn and I were going to see the Clash with Billy Bragg, and as conquering heroes. Did it get any better than that?

Having made it to Victoria Park with a well fed Billy Bragg, his mate Wiggy joining us, we gained entrance to the concert and instantly started getting jostled around as the crowd began to increase. The Clash was full of energy and raw excitement, pounding through songs, stopping only to provide the occasional dialogue denouncing racism, repressive politics, and associated ills. After having bleated on incessantly about finding girls, Billy Bragg was now speechless, mesmerized by Joe Strummer and Mick Jones, as one usually was at their live performances.

As for the gig, it was one of the shows that Kenn and I soaked in like summer rains on parched soil. By this time Kenn and I had been to London a fair bit, but hadn't really spent any time in the parks, which is a shame, especially because London parks are magnificent. Inspired by Roman planning and a sense of leisure, Victoria Park is no exception to the spacious London parks that offer a festival of walkways, alcoves, large lakes, expansive lawns, and bordering canals, making them perfect for all manner of social gatherings, and the ideal venue for anti-fascism or anti-racism festivals.

The day itself was coolish, as it often is in London in April, with the trees bereft of their leaves from a long winter, but the skies were struggling valiantly to banish the grey clouds. But just as the sky was trying to drive out the last chill of winter, the warming spirits of the gathering music fans were uniting to exile the icy specter of racism. Victoria Park was magnificent, but it paled in comparison to the energy and enthusiasm of a major music festival headlined by the Clash and its ability to denounce acts and attitudes of domination. Kenn and I longed for a world without bullies, and racists were merely a subset that abomination, so understandably we were enthralled.

The effect on Billy was also obvious. He went from as being distracted as a cat afflicted with an attention deficit disorder in a room full of mice, to having the focus of an experienced surgeon that was cultivating a new cocaine habit. This wasn't the mere fascination of a newly converted fan, although he was, but rather a greater stirring from within. An awakening of something that he now wanted to be a part of, the understanding that music could change the world. Wiggy was totally locked into the music, like the opening scene in *Star Wars* when the Imperial battleship was reeling in the rebel craft, but Billy Bragg was absorbed by the bigger picture of the evening.

As the concert ended and people began to empty out of Victoria Park, Billy Bragg said, "These, these people," he stammered in awe, "are all here showing solidarity. Standing shoulder to shoulder against racism. A union of consciousness."

"Absolutely, Billy," I added. "Some gigs like this are about the music, and others about the underlying message, but they're all here, and that alone can make a difference. This is what you needed to see. Your future makes you a part of all of this. This is how you'll make a difference. Remember this solidarity. Remember there's power in a union of wills," I said, taking the opportunity to plant more lyrics. I had come this far already, and Kenn was way ahead of my scoring points on that basis, so what the Hell?

"So, you're all right then, Billy?" Kenn asked, knowing that he was, as he had stopped glowing and was taking it all in.

"Mate, that was incredible," he said, visibly thunderstruck. He sat down on the kerb exhausted and overwhelmed by the realization of it all. Wiggy begged off for some hot chips and a pint, and I was grateful that Billy's black hole of a stomach didn't need to be filled again. Clearly he was absorbed in what he had just witnessed. The first really good rock show is always like that. I suppose this is even truer for those who actually go on to become musicians.

"Kenn, give him the single." Kenn handed him a small seven-inch single wrapped in plain protective cardboard casing.

"It's by the Clash," I said, as he was inspecting the gift. "Billy, I know that you'll struggle to grasp all of this, but it's important that you understand you need to be in this fight. We need you. Humanity needs you to do this. And also you need to understand that we're not from this world. This will help make it clear to you in the days ahead."

"OK, thanks," not really appreciating what he had been given. "What do I call you, you know, if you're really angels and such?" Fair question I suppose. I hadn't really thought that far ahead. I had thought to tell him to just call us by name, just to be easy, and besides, we had lured him halfway across London with chips, pies, and pints, the promise of a gig, and the distraction of the female persuasion. We weren't even close to being angels. At least not in the traditional sense, but then again, Kenn and I were complicated. We were heroes.

"Sometimes we need something to hang onto, something that helps us remember an experience or a friendship," Kenn commented, leaving Billy's query unanswered. "You and Wiggy have been through a lot, and there's more to come. Remember how you feel tonight. Remember the crowd and the energy. The bands tonight won't last your lifetime, Billy, but this feeling and their effect can."

The single was "(White Man) In Hammersmith Palis" (with "The Prisoner" as the b-side), released as a single in the UK but released in America as a track on *The Clash*, the band's debut album. Billy didn't know it yet, but that single wasn't to be released for a few months still. He didn't have an original pressing, a signed copy, or colored wax, like a number of the other "collector's items" would later become, but he had something that didn't yet exist in London. Perhaps that would be enough to convince him that Kenn and I were serious. It was certainly going to be enough to make Billy Bragg a Clash fan, and the world could always use another. It might also be a reminder to Billy that there are things other than girls that could catch one's interest. Maybe this story wasn't as much about girls as I had thought.

Kenn and I had singularly changed the direction of music for generations. If nothing else, this would be the dawning of a new era.

14 – Dawning of a New Era

So, call me a cynic. Maybe I'm tired. Tired of everything being labeled as new, as though simply calling something new makes it so. Everything from a new enlightenment to New Coke. It's not new, it's modified. A derivative. Like everything else. Sure, Coke was new when it was actually new. But so was the enlightenment. However, since that time, it's been a derivative, a modification, or a revitalization of whatever former subject is now being claimed to be new again.

This is not a new show, nor is it a newly branded station. This is college radio at KQOO Oregon 90.9 FM. I'm Sid, and a touch surly tonight. It's nearly three a.m., but that's not the issue. The music is good, and I'm gonna keep it rolling.

Ironically, up next is the Specials with "(Dawning of) a New Era." I also like irony. I'll let you decide if it's cliché or simply sardonic. Enjoy or don't; I'll be here either way. It's what I do.

FCC transcript KQOO 90.9 FM 08.21.1998 0258
Operator comments – transcript provided upon request

A dawning of a new era was breaking. Kenn and I were there to meet this new heralded age with the morning sunrise, and we were electric with excitement. "OK, Kenn, let's try this again. Off to the Specials gig, fire up *Louis Louis,* and let's get ready to cross," I said. "Let's make sure you queue up New Era like last time we crossed and met with Dammers." We had discovered that if we played different tracks it would virtually guarantee that we would end up at a different gig.

So in order to make sure we got to the same gig, which we had to do to see if our intervention had worked, we had to play the same track. Even this didn't guarantee that we would cross to the same show. After all, time travel isn't an exact science. We had done pretty well, but still had some work to do. Even playing New Era didn't work for the first dozen or so times, but depending on whom I'm telling this story to, I tend to gloss over that bit. Kenn wanted to try Gangsters, but after the kidnapping Billy Bragg debacle when he played it, I absolutely refused to hear the song again.

There were other ways that we could have confirmed our success. Pretty obvious ones at that. Even the most cursory of research, even to this day, shows that Billy Bragg has had a prolific musical career, has been broadly influential both in developing other artists as well as promoting social causes, and has never ascended to the Prime Minister's Office in Britain. Still, it didn't hurt to be sure, and especially if it meant seeing live music in London. What would you do? Leave it to BBC One and the news of the day, or check it out yourself and be sure?

Once readied for the task, Kenn counted us in and struck the "E" chord. The room began to pull apart, as it always did. Despite our anticipation of the sensations, crossing always grabbed and shook me like an angry parent, leaving me disorientated and a little dazed. I was used to the crossing, although I had never been shook by an angry parent. But even though it was familiar, I would never be at ease with crossing. Familiarity didn't always equate to comfort for me, but other things did. Rock 'n' roll was one of the things that was both comforting and familiar.

Again, Kenn and I arrived at the nightclub and could hear the band in the distance. However, this time we were not at the fire exit located past the toilets with the stench of vomit, urine, and stale spilt beer. Somehow the stench of human waste was much stronger than I had remembered it being last time. Maybe it was the additional time that I had been spending with Pyrah. Perhaps rather than the acrid, stale odours of rock 'n' roll and the halls that they inhabited, I was becoming habituated to the soft fragrance of Pyrah's hair. Her perfume. The scent of the fabric softeners she used in her laundry. Was I getting distracted or soft?

Looking down I realized that the answer was simpler than that. In fact, Kenn and I were both standing in a concoction of vomit, urine, and spilt beer, both stale and fresh. "Still think the Chuck

Taylors were a good idea, Einstein?" Me? I was grateful to be wearing my Doc Martens, but secretly wishing to have the massive rubber boots that you see people wearing in abattoirs or at the Centers for Disease Control.

"Cut the shit, and let's go see if this worked," Kenn barked, ever the consummate professional, not allowing a little offal to put him off, as unpleasant as it was. These thoughts crossed my mind as comments or questions to ask him, but I decided that he was probably right and we should see if our intervention with Billy Bragg had produced the desired result.

"Cut the shit?" I teased. "It's you who's standing in it; you cut it if you want to. I'm not touching that shit." Kenn playfully shoved me, as I deserved.

Carefully we retraced our steps, heading back to the bar. Reenacting a sort of *déjà vu* sequence, we recognized the zoot suits, the various patrons, the girls in short skirts and footless tights and, of course, the music, but this time there was something different. Something palpable yet intangible and not immediately obvious. It was the vibe in the nightclub. There seemed to be more energy in the air, more spirit, more life. Everyone seemed more at ease and less guarded. As before the clock read nine forty-five, so we had managed to return to ostensibly the same time.

"Look," Kenn said with blatant excitement, "Dammers isn't glowing." We looked around and saw that nothing was glowing. Everything was as it should be, and for once the smoke hanging in the nightclub, trapped by the low ceiling, was enjoyable rather than being a nuisance that stung our eyes and made us feel lousy in the morning. Things were looking up. Was it simply our optimism, or was the music a quarter beat quicker and lighter? The band certainly seemed more animated, dancing and gesturing to each other, seemingly pleased with and enjoying their performance. Was the laughter in the bar more effervescent and the conversation more casual? It seemed like more people were dancing. All of these things created a sense of right. Like the universe was aligned, things were in their proper place.

Unlike the previous crossing, when the gig that Kenn and I caught was nearing its end, this was different. The first time, Kenn and I found a subdued affair with the band. While not mechanical, it certainly lacked the unbridled enthusiasm that was an integral part of the ska scene, and now on display.

Even Joseph was different. He was pouring beer like his life depended on it, all the while laughing with the patrons. From what I could hear, I wouldn't say that they were telling jokes, but I suppose you can never really tell in England. Regardless, everyone was having a good time. That was what I noticed, a levity that hadn't been present the first time that Kenn and I had crossed.

"Boyo!" Joseph called out to Kenn and me. "What's your pleasure, lads? Can I pull you a pint?"

Kenn and I were caught staring at each other. At the same time, we realized that history really can repeat, even when it doesn't. We had forgotten to bring the proper currency and only had American cash. As I was staring at a handful of bills, shocked and chagrined, Joseph continued.

"We're having a good night. This round is on me, lads. It's not that I know you, but you look like a good lot. Like there's something familiar about 'cha. C'mon, boyo. Drink up, enjoy the show. This is rock 'n' roll how it should be, and we only come by this way but once."

Well, auspices of auspices. Kenn and I weren't exactly going to say no to free beer or a warm welcome. So with a subtle "cheers" and the raising of our pint glasses, Kenn and I moved from the bar to the stage to watch the band.

The bar was thick with people: dancing, singing along, drinking, and carrying on. Soon enough, nine forty-five became ten thirty, which became midnight, and rather than turning into pumpkins, Kenn and I ate pies, drank pints (after Joseph agreed to take our American cash), and danced with any stranger that cared to. At one point Suggs and Chas Smash, from the band Madness, joined the Specials on stage and things kicked up a notch. Among the crowd, Kenn spotted Roland Gift, from the Beat, and I pointed out Elvis Costello. British rock 'n' roll royalty. How good was this?

Best of all, Jerry Dammers wasn't glowing. The hologram's ghostlike apparition didn't linger. It seemed like Kenn and I had gotten it right and returned rock 'n' roll to its intended course. This was massive for us. The intervention with Mike Ness was a start, but merely something we had stumbled upon, just like with our interaction with Lemmy. But with Billy Bragg, our role was so much more. We had to seek him out and directly influence him in order to restore rock 'n' roll to its proper course. We changed the course of British politics and let rock 'n' roll change the world. Kenn and I had a right to be proud of ourselves, and we carried this pride as an honour.

Elated, Kenn and I left the gig. The band had long since finished up but had started mixing with the crowd. The drinks were flowing and the girls were batting their eyes at everyone involved with the band, from Terry Hall, the lead singer, to some helper guy who was rolling up various cables. The girls were always there, and for a fleeting moment, I wondered why. Why did the girls seem to be drawn to the band and anything ancillary to it? It was like they had a mission assigned to them to couple with rock 'n' roll. It was always such a part of the scene that it was at once reassuring and disconcerting. Maybe Kenn was right about his conspiracy after all. But the night was running on high octane, and such thoughts disappeared like a butterfly on a rising thermal.

Obviously this was a night that was going to continue long into the morning. Perhaps it was the inspiration for the song "Friday Night, Saturday Morning," As we know, music reflects human experience, and rock 'n' roll doesn't come home early. Life imitates art.

As for Kenn and me, we were giggling like schoolgirls who had just discovered that "the boy" liked one of us. Not only was this a massive gig, but we had also restored the music scene to what it was supposed to be like. We were heroes—unknown—but heroes all the same. Our emotions and moods swelled like hot balloons. I wondered what our parents would say now?

We were like the vigilantes that moved among the shadows that no one knew about, but you would overhear the mothers saying, "It's such a nice, peaceful town," knowing that this was true only because you were taking care of business. We were getting our hands bloody so that these guys could dance all night, and I loved it. It was a great thing to be a part of changing history and making the world safe for rock 'n' roll.

It was a generic vigilante analogy that Kenn and I often used. If only because if we used Batman, then one of us had to be Robin, or if we used other superheroes, then one had better powers than the other, and if we fought, then Kenn would win and I would be vanquished or...what? We could be like members of the Bat Army from Frank Miller's *Dark Knight* series, but actually Kenn and I had discussed that too. The result? A debate over who would be the original, or if the original Batman, then how old and...right...we went on and on.

We kept our euphoria in check (barely) by realizing that as we were walking down the street with our fish and chips from a vendor who graciously accepted American cash as equivalent to British pounds; it was then that we noticed that we hadn't been returned to Kenn's home yet. Usually once the gig was over we would find ourselves back at Kenn's with the *Guitar Hero* and MC5 tracks. This was strange, but we were getting accustomed to the peculiar, so we just kept walking with our snacks until we approached a large park or exhibition ground of some sort. Across the street from us, there was some type of pavilion that was emptying out and spilling a jovial crowd into the street. It was glowing in a manner that could have been our indication of something amiss, or simply due to the light being cast from inside. As Kenn and I discussed this and the likelihood of it being one or the other, I commented that it was like *Ockham's razor.*

"You mean that Turkish kid that we did hash with on my parent's stove?" Kenn asked. "How does hot knifing—"

"Fuck, Kenn, you're the man of science." I interrupted him. "No, *Ockham's razor* is the theory that presupposed that the most likely outcome was the simplest. But something else that seems to be both relevant and obvious now is that we have fixed the lost time I had dissipated by missing gigs. My post-secondary education is now more useful than ever."

"We fixed time travel?" replied an incredulous Kenn. "We? I thought that *I* discovered it and you brought along your little Satanic wish box and helped out a bit."

I was never going to make up any ground in this discussion, so I ignored Kenn's comments. After more grousing it was decided that we would simply investigate what was going on in the pavilion. If nothing else there was an entrance, which held the potential to provide another easy opportunity to cross back, if we were now done in London.

Heading past the exiting patrons, we could see that there were a few guys stacking chairs and mopping up spilt beer. Beyond that, off to the end of a long serving table, there was a small gathering that had the look of a press scrum.

"Hey," Kenn asked, "is that—?"

"Yeah," I tentatively replied, slapping Kenn on the arm with the back of my hand, "it's Billy Bragg. Shit. I wonder, was this a gig tonight or a political rally?" With the Billy Bragg that we knew from the correct future, it could be one and the same, which was great, just as long it didn't involve him as Prime Minister. I half asked, half commented to Kenn, "Why are we still here? He's not glowing."

"Yeah. Don't know. I don't see anything glowing," Kenn replied, with a pensive confusion rolling across our elation like an evening fog.

As we grew closer to conducting our newly initiated reconnaissance mission, curiosity washed away our apprehension and pensiveness. Then we saw it. A glimmer. A slight glow, more of a flicker even, ever so slightly being emitted from Billy Bragg, similar to before but far less intense. Almost like an amber light, rather than the urgent beacon that we were used to. The holograph overlain upon Billy was ostensibly the same, suggesting that nothing really had to be changed. But yet we were still there, somehow anchored in London and tethered to Billy Bragg; missing the hologram that was always our sign of where change was required.

"Billy, do you really think that music makes a difference at all?" one of the gathering queried.

"A difference in what sense, mate?" Billy wearily replied.

"You know, socialism is on its knees, and if not on its knees certainly not making the gains it was in the sixties, throughout the world, and do you think songs about fascism or the ills of capitalism will change people's behavior?" the journalist clarified.

"Well, mate, of course. Of course history can be changed and directed by singing a few songs. In fact, some of the leading historians have suggested that had Churchill sung a few melodies to Hitler, the entire Second World War would have been avoided. Maybe even "Kumbaya." Do you disagree? Maybe you'd prefer "Fever" or "Que Sera Sera" Billy had turned on him and was gathering speed.

After allowing a moment's pause, a fermata in the song of dissent, Billy Bragg charged ahead. "Of course you can't stop racism by singing about it, but it doesn't stop you from trying. You're not going to change the world by hosting Billy Bragg gigs. But you have to bloody well take a stand. That's what I'm doing, and I'll love seeing other people try too." Indeed, this was the Billy Bragg of old, the Bard of Barking and not of 10 Downing Street. Kenn and I let out a quiet sigh of relief.

"Excuse me, Mr. Bragg," Kenn interjected, "there's no rush, sir, but I was asked to tell you that the van's ready to go. At your leisure, of course, sir. Shall I get you some tea or maybe some hot chips?"

"Thanks, mate. Tell them I'll be right there. Why don't you come back, though, and I'll walk you down. We can get chips together," Billy replied, turning back to finish his vivisection of the interviewers.

Billy Bragg continued with, "But you do know that while my messages to the audience at a gig is much like preaching to the converted, music can change people. The two largest musical influences in my life were the Clash and Spandau Ballet. I bet you never thought you'd hear those two bands in the same sentence, did you? Perhaps it's only a Bill Bragg thing." Kenn and I began boasting the sort of smile that comes when you know the story you're about to hear, even though you've never been told it.

"Seriously, the Clash and Spandau Ballet?" interjected one of the fanzine writers. "How do you expect anyone to buy this?"

"Well, mate, selling this is your problem, and really if you think that capitalisms is killing music, wait and see what it's going to do to journalism. But hey, that's the point, mate, I'm not selling this to anyone. A couple blokes took me to my first Clash show, and that was that. The Clash's power and raw energy and their call to unite people to make a difference hooked me. Isn't that what the world should be about? Making the world better than how we found it? So what do you think? Should I stop trying? Is it good enough, or is it just too hard, mate? Without bands like the Clash, the Smiths, the Housemartins or the Dead Kennedys, you'd only be left with acts like Spandau Ballet running rampant, and you know the state that the *Top of the Pops* is in already."

Aside from some chuckles made at the expense of the original question, the media crows were silent. "Right, then, so like these blokes said, I've got a van waiting. I'm off for a spot of tea and maybe some chips."

"Hey, lads," Billy called out to Kenn and me, "thank you."

"For what?" I asked in a cagey manner. By now, we were well used to the idea that people often forgot that we had interacted with them previously. Time travel is like that. Well, actually, people often forgot Kenn and me, even before we started interacting with them out of time.

"Well, for starts, getting me out of the mob. I tell you, it's part of the life, but they can really get on my tits with all their inane questions," Billy replied in an easy, comfortable tone. "Also, lads, just so you know, I drove myself tonight; I know that there isn't anyone in the van asking you two to fetch me."

Kenn and I glanced at each other. "Well, you know," Kenn started, "one can only take so much pop and politics..." Kenn, always vigilant for opportunities to plant lyrics.

"But that's not all" the musician continued. "I was being serious back there about music changing people's lives. I can't imagine what I would be doing now if I hadn't seen the Clash that April." Then he started to smile. "And that single you both gave me, you two really are angels. While I can't say that it's my favorite Clash single, it's certainly the most meaningful."

Kenn stammered, so I interjected. "Well, of course the Clash is a big deal. They have cast their light far and wide. Kenn and I have seen them, you know, a few times now. We own some of their vinyl." I continued, trying to maintain my cool affectation. "Their influence just can't be denied." Yeah, it was clear that I was so cool. Too bad it was just as clear that no one was buying my story.

"Mate, you both know that's not what I'm talking about. If you two had not taken Wiggy and me to Victoria Park on *that* night, I fear things would have been very different. I'm indebted to you. If there is ever anything—"

Kenn, who had since regained his composure and was lurching to strike at this opportunity like an angry cobra at a sleeping mongoose, interrupted Billy Bragg's offer.

"Well, there is a question," Kenn blurted out. "Who do you think is better, PiL or Style Council?" My eyes burned a glare at Kenn. If all the collective hatred that had trampled the earth had now been reduced to a single look, it would have only contained half the venom that I was projecting at Kenn at that moment.

This was a long-standing saw between us. At issue of course was, which band sucked worse—Public Image Ltd, known on the scene simply as "PiL," or the Style Council. It was a perennial topic of debate and one that we often attempted to lure others into. However, this time Kenn was far offside and knew it.

The debate itself wasn't that big of a deal, and the two bands themselves weren't terribly important, but their predecessors were. This was a rare case in which the debate wasn't about the music as much as it was a part of our relationship…you know, like the story the uncle tells at weddings, who's a messy drunk. It's the wedding that we've all been to, where the barely coherent and marginally lucid drunk blurts out a story that's supposed to represent advice. Like the story of the couple that had been married for forty years but still couldn't agree on the proper way to squeeze the toothpaste.

It's about the details, isn't it? Should the couple's preferences for managing dentifrice be randomly blurted out like a joke from an embarrassingly drunken uncle at a wedding? Maybe not. OK, certainly not. In fact, while entertaining, drunken uncles shouldn't be allowed to attend weddings, and some arguments, regardless of how trivial or significant, should remain behind closed doors. So Billy Bragg should have been left our of this, and Kenn knew that, but yet here we were airing out personal debate. It was just another example of the changes that had been occurring with Kenn.

The backstory is as follows: Johnny Lydon formed PiL (performing as "Johnny Rotten") after the implosion of the Sex Pistols. I always had a penchant for the Sex Pistols and slavishly chased anything that either Malcolm McLaren or John Lydon became involved with, and PiL was Lydon's departure from McLaren, replete with insults and scathing comments. Fair enough. But there should have also been some recognition that without McLaren, the Sex Pistols would have never found any traction. As it was the band had a functional life span of a lit magnesium strip.

Hating McLaren was the same as resenting a departed colonial government. You may not have liked them and are probably glad that they've been disposed of, but by the same token, now the country has running potable water and functional railways that hadn't existed before colonization. Never before and not since has a band left such a mark on history with only one album as that of the Sex Pistols.

Never Mind the Bollocks, Here's the Sex Pistols was that album. I suppose that there were also so many individual histories of the band members where marks were left, some more indelible than others, but in terms of the music, it was as much a watershed moment as the parting of the Red Sea or commandments being delivered from Mt Zion.

"Kenn," I started, "you know, Billy really doesn't need to get involved with this, and if he's gracious enough about offering a favour, do you really want to use it on this?"

Kenn's side of the argument was that the horse that he backed was more successful and prolific. Paul Weller had formed the relatively substandard Style Council after the Jam had run its course. Paul Weller's influence could not be argued; it was he who had previously inspired and propelled the Jam to become a band for the ages. It is also true that Style Council enjoyed more commercial success than PiL.

But for Kenn and me, the question wasn't about influence, but rather disappointment. Both the Sex Pistols and the Jam held so much promise and sense of possibility, which neither PiL nor the Style Council ever did. Perhaps it's like the expectations that parents have of their children, or the trouble with comparing siblings to each other. Each entity is a singular effort, just like siblings, and maybe comparisons among them was just a new way to fail and frustrate. Frustration that Kenn and I lived under constantly from our parents. Even with Kenn's parent's departure, he still couldn't escape it. Maybe this is why Kenn and I have a fascination with PiL and Style Council; they both represent the relationship we had with our parents. We could witness the disappointment that we caused. This of course was a realization that he and I arrived at much later. For now, and with Billy Bragg, it was still about the music, at least notionally.

If you were to suggest that the score might tip my way because of guitarist Keith Levene's involvement with PiL, I would commend you for paying attention, but would also provide the caution that you must mind the details. Levene was indeed an early player for the Clash, which would ordinarily make PiL an easy pick, especially for Bragg. However, this doesn't change the fact that in Billy's eyes, the Sex Pistols "were a bunch yobs."

I suppose that you can only go around with assumed names like "Rotten" and "Vicious" for so long before your image consumes your character. Ziggy Stardust becomes real. You become transformed from acting like something, to actually becoming that same thing. Maybe being a punk rocker is like any other station in life. Rather than you choosing it, it chooses you. Maybe this explains why lawyers look at things a certain way, yet doctors and accountants look at that same thing differently. Rock 'n' rollers look at life a certain way. They process the world and articulate what they experience. Music picks them just as much as they pick it. Iggy Pop would never be a lawyer, and Alan Dershowitz would never play at CBGB's. I suppose that there must be an exception given the success of Peter Garrett as a rock 'n' roll icon, but as far as I know he never practiced law, although he did become an elected member of the Australian government.

Billy Bragg was also a Jam fan and would become Paul Weller's personal friend. In fact, as Kenn well knew, history would bear witness (at least the history that Kenn and I were familiar with) to the fact that Weller and Bragg would collaborate in the formation of Red Wedge, a collective of like-minded musicians who supported and promoted egalitarian left-wing politics, and that would only serve to strengthen their bond. However, even without the friendship and mutual adoration between the two, Billy Bragg's style was more closely compared to that of Weller's than of Rotten's.

Undoubtedly, Bragg demonstrates Lydon/Rotten's passion and energy, although, Weller was no slouch in the category; he merely lacked Bragg's tenacity and longevity. It is Billy Bragg's lyrical strength and literary force that makes him easier to compare with Weller and his assorted projects rather than the incarnations of the Sex Pistols.

Consider the lyrics written by the artists. For example, Billy Bragg's "Brickbat," and Weller's, "Carnation." Both sets of lyrics convey a sense of human drama, self-exploration, and introspection, but they are also set into a broader social context. The lyrics themselves reflect a careful construction of metaphors and symbols showing the writer's care and attention to his language.

By contrast, if you examine the Sex Pistols's impassioned screaming in "Anarchy in the UK," it is clear that the acts operate in different worlds on the same planet. Now add Rotten's live performance antics of spitting on the crowd, and Vicious doing so much worse. Both were commonplace, which in some way was another action that left a mark (a very real, and very different type of mark) on society.

Did the Sex Pistols represent energy and passion? Sure. Nuanced language? Not really. Political? Maybe Lydon is making reference to the IRA (Irish Republican Army), the UDA (Ulster Defense Association—the large loyalist paramilitary group organized to thwart Irish Republicanism) and the MPLA (Movimento Popular de Libertação de Angola—the Portuguese name of the Angolan Labour Party that fought a forty-plus year civil war for independence in his lyrics, but stops there. There was no discussion, no identification, and no comment. In fact, he could have simply been reading the newsreel from the BBC, an eye test chart at his optometrist, or auditioning for a *Sesame Street* episode, for what he brought lyrically into the music. Not exactly the subtle jabs that Bragg would take in songs like "Waiting for the Great Leap Forward," "Between the Wars," or "Thatcherites." In my mind, there was really no contest as to where Billy Bragg's preferences would lie. Still, it was unfair for Kenn to ask him, given the circumstances.

The debate was never about which act was the best, but rather how badly each act compared to the one that came before. The impact the Sex Pistols, and the Jam, had upon rock 'n' roll is undeniable. However, so is the contribution that Billy Bragg made and continues to make. Kenn knew this, and of course he knew Billy Bragg's preference, and while this was not a bet as such and certainly not something that would change the outcome of history, he couldn't resist taking the inside track in this one.

What was going on with Kenn now? I just couldn't understand. Oddly, this would have ordinarily been part of the continuous dialogue between us, and nothing more. Involving someone else could usually been seen as an extension of the joke, but not this time. It marked a strange competitiveness that I had noticed developing in Kenn. Sure, we always had our silly games and contests, but this was more. It was as though he had to prove something in his conversations. He knew more detail about something, knew more bands, and was better at whatever the topic was. Was it something to prove to me,? I couldn't tell. For the first time in years, if not decades, I was struggling to understand what Kenn was thinking.

Billy, to his credit, perhaps sensing something was afoot between Kenn and me, attempted to dispel the situation. "You know, Kenn, it's a really good question, mate. A great question, really. Wiggy and I have often debated it as well, and we've come to the conclusion that both have been a terrible disappointment, although not as bad as the Pet Shop Boys, but all the same..." he trailed off, paused, and then continued. "You know, lads, the important thing is how the music makes us feel and how it brings us together. Perhaps that's what you two blokes should focus on. This is hardly the stuff for angels to be preoccupied with. Wiggy and I have been mates for a long time, digging through record collections and fanzines for countless hours. Sure, both PiL and Style Council could have been so much more, but that's OK too. Who are we to judge? Hey, by the way, if you two are really angels, why is this so important?"

"Well, Billy," I replied, placing my hand on Kenn's shoulder, "it's like the PiL/Style Council matter...some things don't really need to be answered, do they? Besides, we should be going." I was referring to both Kenn's attempt to embroil Billy Bragg in our debate as well as Billy's question. It was true that some things just were; the rationale behind the object was often less important than the fact of its existence.

Making sure that Billy Bragg's hologram had remained vanished, we closed the van door and then headed for the venue's door, which was closing for the night. It was always easier to cross through a door, and it seemed that everything that we needed to do was completed and we would be crossing back soon. "Good one, hey, buddy?" I asked Kenn. "Angels. Billy Bragg thinks we're angels. No wonder he claims to be a pagan."

I asked Kenn what he thought the next adventure should be. Shaking his head, he muttered, "Angels and pagans. What a mix." It was true. I suppose that I didn't really know what we were, other than true believers.

15 – True Believers

That was "True Believers," by Australia's Hunters & Collectors. This is not a new show. I'm here most weeks between Sunday at midnight and sometime Monday morning, and mostly I play music with little intervention. Sometimes I take other shows too.

However, the FCC requires basic interventions at maximum, or minimum, depending upon your perspective, time intervals. A sort of name, rank, serial number sort of thing. The Geneva Conventions of radio transmission.

This is 90.0 FM KQOO Oregon, at one twenty-five a.m. on the seventh of May, I'm Sid Itious. Station identified, back to music.

True Believers. Hunters & Collectors. Interesting on their own, but even more so when you consider that as a civilization we started off as hunters and collectors and evolved into what we're supposed to be now. So often we either aspire to be true believers or are led by them, even if the belief may be wrong.

But even if a belief is wrongly held, it's still held and often difficult to unseat. How is that evolution? Why did I keep talking after my mandatory station identification? Well, I suppose because you can never really silence a true believer.

FCC transcript KQOO 90.0 FM 07.05.1997 0125
Operator search: - redacted -

True Believers. That's what Kenn and I are. We have been ever since we learned to love rock 'n' roll. We're heroes too now, I suppose, but also true believers. We believe in the truth, a truth told through rock 'n' roll. In fact, even the lies and the tall tales that are told in the industry or through songs, carry a certain truth for Kenn and me. These are the truths of our lives, of the world we live in and of various experiences. Rock 'n' roll is a true art, and for many of us, a way of life.

Taking a cue from Mark Seymour, rock 'n' roll was the pleasure that we lived for. Being true believers of the art of music. Music was never the problem for us that it seemed to be for others. Unfortunately, facing the convictions of others was always a problem for us. Others who were ambivalent to music or thought that we should focus on things like relationships or responsibilities at work. Or even others like the Morality in Music organization that sought to control music. Evil incarnate

"Look at this garbage being spread by the Evil: 'Rock 'n' roll is immoral, evil, or worse, an abomination.' How can they even say that?"

"Yeah, I don't know, Kenn. These people who represent the antithesis of rock 'n' roll also undermine basic rights of free expression. It's just wrong and heavy-handed. It's like they're hating rock 'n' roll because they didn't understand it or thought that they were better than everyone else."

It seemed like finally it was my turn to take a rant, so off I went. "When the Evil proclaims that rock 'n' roll is bad for society or that it introduces moral corruption, they simply illustrate that they don't understand that societies need dissent. This showcases their ignorance. Moreover, dissent is an essential element of rock 'n' roll. Rock 'n' roll provides conflict, the desire for change, the energy required to dissent. The freedom to express such dissent and a safe outlet for it to be done. Would you rather have a noisy bunch of rock 'n' rollers at a show with a band that was smashing (their own) instruments, or riots in the street? There's no argument that this energy and frustration has to be let out somewhere."

"Rock 'n' rollers," confirmed Kenn. "Riots suck. They just bring the cops out and then make the pizza guys cancel deliveries."

Yes, how quickly the very fiber of society unravels during civil unrest; leave it to Kenn to elucidate the example that brought it all home, pizza deliveries cancelled for the riots. But I suppose our own experience was the premise that our true belief was founded upon. Riots in the Middle East or civil war in Syria never seem to matter as much as what's happening down the street from where we lived.

What we didn't realize is that the Evil was also comprised of true believers. We didn't think that it mattered, because they were believers of the incorrect faith. Unfortunately, we would learn that their resolve, however misguided, could be just as strong as ours.

All the conversations that Kenn and I had were always based upon our true belief. It was part of our constant preparation for being heroes. Honing our skills and building our strength. It justified our understanding of the world.

"It's like that movie *American Psycho*," Kenn stated with his usual authority while absently sorting through a stack of records.

"You mean the book?" I asked.

"No, it was a movie," Kenn said.

"It was a book first," I replied.

"It was a movie." Unmoved, as Kenn so often was, he found a piece of vinyl to play. "Everything But the Girl," I think it was. Right. Everything with Kenn is a movie because the dude doesn't read books, except the occasional graphic novel or comic. Maybe not even then, as some of those have become movies too.

"How obvious did it have to be to see that guy was crazy?" Kenn stated incredulously, gathering steam for one of his rants. I had to admit, I was curious, even if only cautiously so. Where was Kenn going with this?

"I mean seriously, the first time, I mean the very first time that he even favorably mentioned Huey Lewis and the News, that should have been it. *Wham!*" Kenn punctuated his point by slapping the back of his right hand into his left palm. "I mean, come on, the detail that he discusses the albums in? Clearly a sick individual."

What could I say? I just nodded silently, knowing he's right but also expecting that whatever comes next is going to reveal more about my friend than I likely want to know. This has happened so many times before. Usually he at least has an interesting perspective on things. "Kenn," I asked, with mixed trepidation and curiosity, "What do you mean, *that should have be it?*"

"I mean you just have to put guys like that down. If I were president...," Kenn started. *Fuck, here we go,* I said in my head, knowing that this isn't just a tangent. "I'd have a list," Kenn continued, now pacing around his basement, "you know, like they do already for guys that buy certain books like that Dante one, you know, not the volcano movie but the other one; *Catcher in the Rye*; *Mein Kampf*; *Satanic Verses*; or *Harry Potter*. Well, maybe that volcano movie too, but for music. Then when some twit buys a Michael Jackson album or downloads a song from Wham! or the Bee Gees, we would just deploy our police and round them up."

And just like that, amid the awe of hearing *Harry Potter*, *Mein Kampf*, and *Dante's Peak* in the same sentence, I realized that without knowing why I had never considered my friend for public office, there was a very good reason, maybe many. I didn't even consider correcting him or even asking about what he was talking about with the *Harry Potter* books. I just let him run. I suppose that something inside me just said it wasn't right, but without knowing what exactly was wrong. Was it the fact that when he had said "our police," he was implying that I was a part of this scheme, or was it the idea of rounding up people without due process that was wrong with Kenn's utopian fantasy? You might try to argue that it was really some sort of fictional dystopia, but can you imagine a place where art shone freely? Even under a tyrannical rule like Kenn was articulating, there was something clearly utopian about it. Just like Oz, perhaps, but maybe more like Australia. Whatever it was, utopian or something sinister, I was inextricably drawn in.

Sadly, I also secretly wished for the existence of a secret police force with a mandate that would allow them, in the night, to round up anyone involved with bad music and whisk them away like the *Disappeared* in Argentina. The truth was that I already had such a list that I was working on. So did Kenn. Abominations who deserved to be whisked away, making the world a better place.

Maybe in Kenn's America, these bands could be restricted to traveling only on helicopters. "Jon, it's so cool. Think about what the prop wash does to your hair, making you look all super-sexy badass, and shit. You guys totally need a Bon Jovi Sikorsky Sea King for the tour. We can totally get a deal on them from the Canadian Coast Guard. I mean these helicopters are legendary, aren't they!" Yeah, legendary for falling out of the sky during storms, over frigid waters, and killing all those on board. Perfect. But I guess this was where my daydream fantasy dovetailed with Kenn's rant.

Kenn was right, it was probably OK to dispose of bad musicians. His rant reminded me of this old guy that Kenn and I knew, Vincent—we called him Vinnie—who claimed that, "*There is no such thing as bad music, just bad artists.*" Vinnie was about twenty-five when we met him, about ten years older than Kenn and me, and hosted a local radio show and was a regular contributor to various musical publications. He also had a coffee shop.

Other than where to find him and his musical views, Kenn and I didn't really know anything about him. To us, he looked like any aging college student, sort of. Vinnie was always wearing jeans and canvas shoes, eyeglasses that matched the year, not particularly well kept, but always with an assortment of music and interesting information at hand. In support of his theory, Vinnie provided copies of the Sean MacGowan version of "Cracklin' Rose" and the Pogues's cover of "London Calling," the eponymous track from the Clash's first album. While "Cracklin' Rose" was inspired, London Calling was so bad that it was only saved by the fact that Joe Strummer was involved. Otherwise, it should have lead to the death of the entire band. Aerosmith desecrating the theme from *Spider-Man* (the cartoon, not the book), Motley Crew debasing "Anarchy In the UK"—further proof of what Vinnie had meant. It was later when I read that Theognis of Megara had written "*Fairly examined, truly understood, no man is wholly bad, nor wholly good*" that I decided that maybe Vinnie should have been a philosopher or that maybe his idea had been around longer than his own years.

Philosopher or not, Vinnie was aptly described as "off center" and certainly not someone whom our parents would have been happy to know we were consorting with. For us it was natural, probably perfect. Vinnie ran a coffee shop that played great music, so across the coffee bar our education in rock 'n' roll and espresso-based caffeinated beverages started to develop. There was little that Vinnie didn't seem to know about the green bean and the rock scene. As it turned out, he was also aligned with Kenn in other regards.

It should have actually been obvious the first time Kenn and I stopped at the coffee shop. We had heard Vinnie's radio show a few times and had chased and followed the few rumors that existed in our small town about Vinnie's day job, until we found his little coffee shop. It wasn't much, but it had been inspected and properly licensed, as both documents were prominently displayed.

"Kenn," I said, as we were approaching the storefront, "this place is a fucking dump."

"So what? Listen…I can hear the Pixies coming from inside."

And so with that, we entered Ka'Fiend and met Vinnie for the first of what was to become many times.

Later Vinnie would admit, "Yeah, I've always liked the name. It was easy to license and it suits me." That wasn't all, though. Over the cash register, Vinnie's menu read:

Fair trade coffee from fair trade beans. As it should be.

Cash Only (no $20s, $50s, or $100s, or other traceable bills)

No tea – due to the exploitation of tea farmers and their environment in developing countries;
No sodas – due to the behavior-altering effects of sweeteners and artificial flavors;
No bottled water – due to the mind-altering effects of plastic bottling;
No decaf – due to the water processes placing undue demands on our fresh water resources;
No corporate discounts – no reason required, but because they've never done a damn thing for me or anyone else

Beverages:
JFK – a single shot, light steamed foam, two other shots from out of nowhere, that I'll deny have been added;
Hinckley – two weak shots;
Americano – espresso as pure and bold, as the democratic ideals that founded this great country; just as watered down to fit the tastes of the masses of today;
Others by request and personal indulgence.

Over the years I shed my naïveté and became less obtuse to the world around me, but I don't recall when I realized that Vinnie was a conspiracy theorist. I suppose that alongside Kenn, Vinnie seemed sort of normal. Besides, there wasn't anywhere else to go to listen to rock 'n' roll and drink coffee.

Being around Vinnie was like listening to Rollins or Jello Biafra's spoken word albums, with explanations and views that would sound paranoid if not so reasonable. Things that had a different context or were considered dramatic to make a point. Biafra's views on the war on drugs being ineffective because of a lack of political will sort of seems like Kenn's views on...well, anything really. It seems unreasonable or simply ludicrous, but when you draw through the argument and premise of it all, suddenly the explanation seems viable to the point of compelling. Subsequently, compelling becomes true belief, and there you are, not only convinced but standing in defense of a position you once thought was peripheral.

Vinnie was right—there was no bad music, just bad musicians. It was an absolute that was obvious.

Picking up on Vinnie's teachings, Kenn and I always maintained that cover versions should be approached with care. Most local bands start with a collection of covers that generally yield to more original work, but unfortunately, this isn't always the case. Bands cutting their teeth in live performances is one thing, but established artists trying their hand at someone else's songs is quite another. Like any creative work, the artist has an emotional investment in his work that is intensely guarded, even zealously so.

It was as true believers that Kenn and I could understand this, especially as the artist and his work are often viewed as inseparable. The tension between the artist and the art played out in live action when Bruce Springsteen met David Bowie at Sigma Sound Studios in Philadelphia on the eve of Bowie recording a cover of "It's Hard to Be a Saint in the City." Not only was Bowie taking license with one of the songs on Springsteen's first album, but also the two singers must have seemed to be worlds apart. Late Springsteen embodied an ideal of Americana, but then he was awkwardly shy. Having just completed his first album, the future Boss was then channeling a Dylan-inspired look, complete with disheveled hair and beard, soiled leather jacket, coarse denim jeans, and road weary boots. Springsteen was traveling around either by hitching rides or taking public transit, living out a bohemian fantasy, only to meet a David Bowie who could only be described as his polar opposite. Bowie...the very pinup image of an androgynous space alien consuming any number of illicit substances, who was anything but shy, with over ten albums under his alien transponder device or belt or whatever. Worlds colliding with what must have felt like a shattering force and inescapable velocity.

What is the right answer, though, when it comes to art? If it's understandable that Springsteen or anyone else really, is protective of the creations that he gave birth to, nurtured, and raised as though the works were children, should these works be protected? Don't children grow up? Isn't that the responsibility or really the role of a parent? To prepare children for entry into the world as independent people? Maybe Brian Wright articulates it best in the song "Central Park." He says, *Art is only yours until the second you create it.* Maybe the Springsteen/Bowie interaction was merely a metaphor for the conflict that I experienced with my parents. Or Kenn with his. Or you with yours.

If I were a parent or creative enough to produce meaningful art, I might have a different understanding of all of this. Children and art should be loved, but they also need to be set free. Free to find their own way and to couple up with others, leaving their own mark upon the world. The only hope would be that every interaction, be it with children or cover versions, would lead to something better, interesting, or richer. Children who can't or aren't allowed to make their own decisions is the same as a painting left beneath the covers in the painter's studio. But then what of cover versions?

Art is full of examples where people have attempted to cover the same ground as other artists. How many nude sketches do we really need? Paintings of bowls of fruit or lilies on a pond? Sculptures of the same heroes, saints, or gods? Plays about the battle between good and evil? It's not as though someone could repaint the frescos of the Sistine Chapel without ridicule, but novels, plays, and operas all get made into movies, but are modified by the producer's individual touch or vision. These aren't copies; they are merely inspired by the originals. Interpretations. Iterations if anything, but not mechanical reproductions. Just look at the *Thor* or *Batman* movies. If you are going to copy art, which is essentially what a cover version is, then you had better honor it and somehow show it in a different light.

The Ramones's *Acid Eaters* is an example of both. Not everything that they covered on the album was great, but the 'Mones were.

Actually the Ramones were always great. More importantly, their cover versions brought something new to the illicit drug-inspired originals of the '60s, by acts like the Who, CCR, the Animals, Jefferson Airplane, and Ted Nugget's first band, the Amboy Dukes, laying down the standard for other acts to follow. Billy Bragg would later describe the artistic process, or perhaps lack of artistic process, as "running a song through the Ramones's buzz saw." Apt as always, Billy Bragg was right. Listening to the Ramones cover a song often mimicked the feeling of going to a museum with my father. A sense of speeding through every collection and exhibit so that you could get home and watch sports. Is the buzz saw analogy fair? Thirteen tracks played in less than thirty-one minutes—the total duration of the album. What do you think? But with the Ramones and their musical buzz saw, it was more than that. It was the band's attitude as well, and it was this attitude that embodied rock 'n' roll and made this collection of covers notable. Live fast, something better was on the way.

Certainly, the Ramones overcame an inauspicious start when the now legendary CBGB's allowed them to audition for a show. According to accounts, this motley assortment of kids, unrelated yet claiming to all possess the same surname, presented themselves fully equipped and asked for a tryout. The bar owner, Hilly Kristal, wasn't convinced that they weren't there to simply fence stolen instruments, but allowed them to play because the bar was slow that week and needed to book live acts. Apparently, the story goes that the manager, years later, was never really sure, notwithstanding how many gigs the Ramones ultimately played, if they were serious or not and if they were, whether they were serious about being a band or merely trafficking in stolen equipment. This is part of the charm of rock 'n' roll. After all, even the fabled Ziggy Stardust played a stolen guitar.

The Ramones prove decisively that rock 'n' roll is about expression, an expression of energy, of choice, and of dissent. Creative and artistic freedoms are the foundation of rock 'n' roll, like all art. Equally important is the fact that rock 'n' roll is, or at least can be, an iterative process. Also, like other forms of art, music must be permitted a certain degree of latitude to allow for the full expression of the human condition. Therefore, anything that seeks to control or limit this freedom or this choice or this expression, limits the human condition.

This expression was important enough that the First Amendment protected it in 1789. A right that is properly considered inalienable, but this was precisely the limitation that the Evil sought to impose. The control of expression. So that *their* message could be transmitted, but to interfere with the transmission of freedom. Actions that were calling on Kenn and me to man the vanguard for liberty, for justice, for humanity, and for rock 'n' roll. To make lists and cull bad bands like parts of an infected herd. Kenn was onto something.

"But Kenn, you realize that the guy wasn't really a psycho, right? Just consumed by self-loathing and bored in his yuppie rut." Unlike Kenn, I *had* read the book, but admittedly, after seeing the movie. The book disturbed me more.

Undeterred, Kenn replied, "Yeah, well, you would be self-loathing too, if you were a Genesis fan. Tell me one good thing that Genesis has contributed to society or the arts."

"The Mike Tyson scene in *The Hangover,*" I asserted without a second's hesitation, having to play to Kenn's forehand of watching movies.

"Touché," Kenn conceded, graciously.

But Kenn was right. This was a band that was as lacking as it was overrated. Genesis. I've never been a big follower of organized religion, but as far Kenn and I were concerned, the title "Genesis" was best left to the Old Testament and not for rock bands. But since there was, in fact, a band named after one of the most fundamental stories of the Bible, we created a natural argument to keep the band together. The fact that the band broke up, to me, said a few things about the human condition and the music industry, but unfortunately, less about mercy than one might hope. Perhaps, like Lance Armstrong, Icarus, or the Tower of Babel, shit happens to those who tempt fate.

"But thankfully, Kenn, they got what was coming to them, and the band ultimately broke up."

"Yeah, but it was a disastrous breakup. Horrible for music." Kenn paused, giving thought. "First, the breakup speaks to the fact that people like Phil Collins and Peter Gabriel were deluded by the belief that they were bigger than the music they were creating or even the band itself. That the music was about them and that they could do more individually than collectively. That they were better on their own. The band was just holding them back."

I actually knew where Kenn was going with this, not necessarily because I had heard it before, but some things with Kenn are simply intuitive. Still, I made myself comfortable; this was a ride to enjoy.

"But more than anything was the fact that people pursued their own success rather than something collective, regardless of how important they were trying to make themselves sound, disregarding friendship or loyalties. Genesis. The story of creation from the Old Testament. Genesis, a band characterized not by creation but disintegration. Where was the Old Testament god now, with his anger and vengeance striking down false idols?"

Sure, it could be considered a self-declaration that the band was as fundamental as the story of creation, as self-indulgent and egocentric as any other act had ever been, either before or since. People talk about the excess of Kanye West or the false bravado of rap artists, but compared to Genesis, these guys couldn't hold a candle. I knew that this wasn't where Kenn was going with his circuitous path, because it was more than that for Kenn. In fact, it wasn't even that the band didn't try harder to stay together that was the worst of it. I knew for a fact had he been capable, he would have given anything to keep those boys together. Because for every reaction there was a corresponding action; possibly better but potentially worse reactions. Like atomic energy, action: splitting an atom; reaction one (the good one): an abundance of energy to heat homes; reaction two (the bad one): nuclear war. The breakup of bands was a little different because really what was the harm of breaking an atom that you weren't doing anything with anyway? Bands by their very nature were already making music, so splitting them up, could upset this function. In this context, splitting atoms made sense to me, bands not so much.

Whereas when some bands broke up the result was good, like the Beatles or Bauhaus, the disintegration of Genesis was a musical nightmare. When a band breaks up, two things can happen. One is that all the constituent parts continue to make music at the same rate or even start to compete with each other, which creates more music. Basically, the sum of the parts become greater than the whole. Alternatively, the other potential outcome is that less music is made as a result of the constituent members simply calling it a day. The sum of the whole is equal to that of its parts. And falling apart results in useless parts.

Back in 2011 when R.E.M. called it quits, that was the end of the road. The guys stayed involved with rock 'n' roll, but their voices became silent, at least until Pete Buck had to come out with his Stooges-inspired work. By contrast, the Bauhaus break-up was a musical bonanza whereby Peter Murphy ventured out into a solo career leaving David J, Daniel Ash, and Kevin Haskins to continue as they had before Murphy joined them, with a series of bands such as Tones on Tail, the Bubblemen, and most notably Love and Rockets. The various members also contributed to Dali's Car and the Jazz Butcher. So, in the end, more great music was made than could have been made by one cohesive Bauhaus band. The same thing applied to the Beatles, with everyone making more and more music, with the exception of poor Ringo. Even our various interventions failed to help him. We tried to help him found Apple, start a successful solo album, and we even tried to have him displace Phil Collins in Genesis just to demonstrate how desperate we all were, but now we're on a tangent.

Unfortunately, rather than following Art Garfunkel or showing the dignity and class of R.E.M., when Genesis broke up, they ended up spreading their garbage around farther than they would have otherwise. I never forgave Phil Collins for not keeping that band together. I suppose, though, the Mike Tyson public service announcement played in *The Hangover* movie makes more sense in this light. Kenn and I might have to try to plan a crossing-based intervention to see if something can be done to correct Phil since Genesis is obviously beyond our reach.

Of course the Mike Tyson PSA was about the dangers of concussions in sport. How else do you explain someone being so enamored by Phil Collins without having suffered major head trauma? It's the only explanation.

Despite my reverie, I continued addressing Kenn's points about *American Psycho*. "Yeah, that's not really enough to classify the guy a psycho, is it? You have to admit that Bateman got it right about Springsteen."

"Who?" Kenn asked, as though the conversation had been paused somehow.

"Patrick Bateman. The character Christian Bale played in the *American Psycho* movie."

"You mean Marcus. I thought that main character's name was Marcus Halberstam, not Bateman." Kenn was rounding the corner on an argument that could spend hours circling the blocking in search of a parking spot, a search for which I didn't always have the fortitude.

"Pretty sure it was Bateman, but that could very well have been the point," I replied, rapidly becoming weary of this conversation.

"Oh. Yeah, totally. Springsteen," he admitted, shaking his head. Bateman was a psycho because Kenn believed that he was. Another example of how important belief can be. In fact, I think that the entire field of psychiatry in the '30s was based on this premise.

Belief is the foundation of all systems and every achievement. But belief can also be equally powerful in destroying things, especially when based on the idea that something is wrong or immoral. Belief has led to wars and injustice in the name of anything Holy, and rock 'n' roll has merely been one of many victims trampled underfoot.

Resolute in our belief in rock 'n' roll, if you will, we hadn't wasted any of our time on the devil or God, religion or politics, current events, or matters of which celebrities were found without underwear in public. Such things were a waste of our time, and even with our considerable mastery over time, we still considered our time with rock 'n' roll valuable. Too valuable to dissipate on other lesser things.

But strangely, now that wasn't going to be enough. It wasn't even as though we hadn't turned our minds to issues beyond rock 'n' roll, but we actually didn't believe in them or care about them.

Our experiences had shown us that the discussion of God didn't factor into what we needed out of rock 'n' roll and was just something that was used by people like McCloy to justify ruining our fun. To articulate their agendas or preferences as though they were merely following in the footsteps of the divine along the pathway to salvation.

Kenn and I didn't believe that these sorts of discussions added anything to our life and that if we didn't believe in God or religion that we would be insulated from all of its influence and power. This wasn't to be. As it turned out, mere disbelief wasn't enough.

Disbelief isn't enough to overcome or vanquish something. In fact, you first need to believe in its existence to then overcome it. Gravity. Force. Truth. Evil. Good. Music. Hate. Fear. Mortality. Forgiveness. Memory. Love. It was all there, and like a sunset or a snowfall, it happened whether you believed or not. If you thought that a sunset was a miracle or the result of Aries or some other god riding a chariot or merely the expected result of Earth completing a daily spin on its axis, it would still occur, and not believing wasn't going to stop it.

For all of the great things that the human mind is capable of, the first step to achieving anything is belief. Victims can't be assisted if they don't believe they have suffered at the hands of others. Racism can't be addressed if it isn't believed to exist. Illnesses that are not known can't be diagnosed or treated.

In the end it wasn't that religion or God was the problem, it was the people who claimed legitimacy though it. Maybe I should get the famous gun control shirt and strike out "Guns." "Gods don't kill people…people kill people for gods." The truth is, like guns, it's the malice that people possess that kills people. I suppose that it's always the way. People merely look for a means to justify their actions or allay responsibility. Religion is just as much a scapegoat as rock 'n' roll. This is the result of true belief being left with those who are unworthy, not heroes like Kenn and me. Not those dedicated to the pure pursuit.

Was this the legacy that the Jam warned against in their song "Town Called Malice," about a world of poor choices where control and influence was always something that others would wield? But for now it was enough that I believed in rock 'n' roll and that I could have a relationship with Pyrah. It was this belief that inspired me and was a source of both power and control. A power and control, like when she bangs the drums.

16 – She Bangs the Drums

This is CiTR 101.9 FM, and I am happy to be here at the University of British Columbia, as a guest, covering the regular spot for my friend Otto M'ton. You can also listen to the broadcast through real streaming at www.citr.ca. If you are listening live the time is three before noon November ninth; if you're listening to this as a recording, then it is some other time.

How I came to be in Vancouver or even Canada is an adventure, but one I won't indulge myself with and force you to suffer through. Rather we'll get back to music, but let's just say that life is an adventure, or a series of adventures, that move to a soundtrack or the beat of a drum. Find out what causes your drum to beat. We're gonna listen to "Just Can't Stop It," by the English Beat, but first, here's the Stone Roses.

FCC transcript webcast citr.ca 11.09.2013 1157
Operator search: "Canada"
File as "Suspect 25710"

"She bangs the drums, dude," Kenn said to me in disbelief. "I mean literally or figuratively or whatever 'not actually' is."

Of course she banged the drums. She was divine. I mean if you believe in divinity and that sort of thing. A fierce beauty—the personification of rock 'n' roll in a female form. And while we had discussed the fact that Kenn and I were true believers, by now it should be clear enough as to where Kenn stood with his opinion on women and divinity.

I still remember how this started. It was unbridled stupidity, as it usually was with Kenn. We had crossed to see Tracy Chapman and had found ourselves in San Francisco at the Mabuhay Gardens. The locals called it the "Fab Mab," but we only knew it by the name on the sign. The show was good, and Tracy was enjoying a good year with her hit "Fast Car." It was 1988.

Once again, after the show we discovered that we hadn't returned to Kenn's, so we decided to find a place for a drink and start looking for our hint as to what needed to be changed. Nothing at the gig glowed. We didn't meet anyone or see anything that shimmered or glowed. I suppose that as strange things were becoming familiar to us, now, after the Billy Bragg interventions, Kenn and I understood that we could be here for a while and should at least take a stab at coming up with a plan. There were worse places to be than San Francisco.

We had been to San Fran a few times by now, so we were feeling comfortable and even familiar. Familiarity may be the best sensation. You could see, or at least imagine, the promise that the city held in its boom years. Understand how natural disasters and siege failed to deter its citizens and those who sought their fortunes there. There was a history that was rich with story, connecting the past with a vision of the future that resonated through the designs of the streets, the architecture of the buildings, and even the failure that was worn by the slums. I loved the feeling that people came to San Francisco to start a new life in, say, Chinatown or Russian Hill, as a beatnik or a banker or a gold miner or entrepreneur.

There were bridges everywhere. Of course the Golden Gate Bridge and Bay Bridge are the two obvious ones, but there are metaphoric bridges as well. Bridges connecting people, cultures, and socioeconomic classes. Bridges that span time and space. Just like the crossings that Kenn and I had frequented. No wonder I've always loved the area.

For us, the Bay Area meant gigs, it always had and always will. We had seen Soundgarden, the Pixies, Hunters & Collectors, and even MC Hammer. While most of our choices were obvious, there were a few reasons we went to see Hammer. There was something mesmerizing about the way such a big man could move so famously. He was all the rage at the time. His backstory of him being a minister with an Oakland-based street ministry was compelling to us, as was his rise from poverty through adroit borrowing, his business acumen, and effective leverage of his contacts and talents. As we came to understand our role with more frequent crossing, and the power of the information that it would bestow upon us, it was our responsibility to check out the shows of the day. MC Hammer was simply just another stop along the way. A duty we had to honor, an obligation to fulfill.

I'm not a big MC Hammer fan, but he's right: "You just can't touch this." Hammer's showmanship and elaborate stage choreography, at the time, were unparalleled. Although he'll never be the loss that Lou Reed was; his show was an absolute triumph. Imagine P!nk's 2010 Grammy performance, and now turn the clock back over twenty years. It was that good.

While I can't even believe that I would say such a thing, the fact is that Hammer's act, involving a multitude of dancers, backup singers, other live musicians, and disc jockeys, was so well-organized there was always a blur of activity onstage, and yet never a distraction. Not only did such a presence give him a powerful visual appeal, it made him a major employer in the area. Sure Bowie, Queen, and Motown acts would have massive stages and intricate shows, and Britney Spears, Madonna, P!nk, Lady Gaga, and Justin Timberlake would have piles of bodies dancing in perfected unison or in theatric excellence to rival the Cirque du Soleil troupe, but it wasn't until the clock struck *Hammer Time*, that anything like this had been done.

I'd go again, but I think I'd listen to Public Enemy on my iPod during the show. Not just because of the music; there is something strangely appealing about imagining Hammer sliding across the stage with his billowing pants flowing behind him and hearing Chuck D bellowing out the lyrics to "Welcome to the Terrordome." Come to think of it, the Hammer gig had the same sort of raw energy that Public Emily generated; it would be a good fit. Maybe I'll put that down on a list of things to do later, like watching the Clash and drinking beer.

But we had left the Tracy Chapman gig feeling introspective, socially responsible, and refreshed, as you do from one of her shows, yet we were also acutely aware that we had failed to "cross back." Kenn and I walked out of the show into the warm night air, randomly headed down Broadway until we realized that while the street lacked the preponderance of strip clubs and massage parlors, which surrounded the Warfield, that such establishments still existed alongside the affluent financial district. More importantly, and just as distracting, Kenn and I saw an abundance of bars and eateries. Just as well I suppose, as girls would only serve to further detract us from the important task at hand. After all, the Evil had used the power of women against rock 'n' roll, and us, before.

Even if girls *hadn't* really been used, we didn't want to repeat the Peter Murphy gig drama. So, Kenn and I were still walking along the dark streets of North Beach when we came to a congregation of people handing out leaflets. None of these people or pamphlets glowed or shimmered or had musical instruments, so I ignored them. Kenn, however, took some of their materials, turned to talk to them, and then stopped outright.

While Kenn was talking to the pamphlet-wielding time vampires, I looked across the street at the Transamerica Building. The iconic pyramid was lit, showing the spectacular profile and capturing my imagination. I say capturing, because it held me fast without any real reason or provocation. Maybe it was less my imagination that was captured and more that I was impressed. It is an impressive building, but then so are many others in San Francisco. Perhaps one of my favorite things about San Fran is that there is something visual that can instantly engage your interest at the end of virtually every street. The Golden Gate Bridge rising in the distance above a bank of rolling fog; a solitary lighthouse beacon swiping across your line of sight from Alcatraz or Treasure Island like a nocturnal light saber.

Coit Tower, The Transamerica Building (the former building), The Transamerica Pyramid (the current one), Union Square, Lombard Street, the Piers, the parks, the Battery, the list goes on. Even when there wasn't a specific example of architecture to marvel at where you happened to be looking, perhaps there was a cable car or trolley that would pass by. But you're right, this isn't a tour of San Francisco or an enumeration of landmarks. We were on a rock 'n' roll mission but with an uncertain objective.

"C'mon, Kenn," I said, tired of Kenn lingering with the pamphleteers. "We haven't got all night, we've got a mission." Actually, we might have had all night, and maybe even weeks, but I was also worried that Kenn could spend that long railing against or for something. Kenn didn't even need to have a particular position sometimes; for him, it was often enough just to take a stand, something about "Dante threatening to save the hottest spots in Hell for those who don't pick fights" is how I remember him quoting it to me.

"What? You mean a mission to find a mission?" he goaded me.

"Yeah, something like that."

"Like a secret mission, maybe," he added, not letting it go.

"Ah-huh."

"Top secret, maybe? Maybe one of these pamphleteers is supposed to form a band?"

"Like the Weakerthans?"

"Maybe."

I don't know how long this carried on for, so you understand why I would be looking around taking in the splendor of the city. But despite my surveillance, nothing before me was glowing. "Let's find a beer. My treat."

"OK, big spender, let's get going." Kenn surrendered to beer and let whomever he was holding in captive conversation go. "Let's check that place out." Kenn nudged my arm, and I turned around and spotted a little bar.

"Good. Sure." It seemed like as good a spot as any to have a drink and sort things out, especially since it was across the street. The doors and windows were open, and the evening breeze was allowing the curtains to billow out, and the soft, but animated and energized sound of jazz was coming from inside. It wasn't rock 'n' roll, but it was music that expressed freedom, energy, and creativity, so it would do.

Heading into the bar, our eyes struggled to penetrate the softly lit darkness and noticed comfortable seating in booths and small tables, arranged as you would a proper living room. Not like Kenn's place, but something classy, like you'd see in an IKEA catalogue.

Finding our bearings and assessing the jazz band, Kenn and I saw ourselves to a modest booth and noticed that the half-full bar was mostly drinking martinis of some form or other, or wine. Since we didn't really know anything about wine, or even cared to, we ordered martinis. It seemed cool. Not really rock 'n' roll like bourbon, whiskey or beer, but cool all the same. Actually, why wasn't the martini considered rock 'n' roll? Wasn't that the drink the Social Distortion skeleton held in its hand? I figured if it was good enough for Mike Ness, or at least his "undead familiar," it should be good enough for Kenn and me. This was also before the time that martinis enjoyed their resurgence or well after the time they enjoyed a certain cache, but that was also part of being cool and about being in San Francisco.

Things in San Fran just seemed to march on without regard for time. Interested in owning a martini bar, a massage parlor, or a bathhouse? Someone would be sure to patronize your establishment and without trying to figure out if you are ahead of or behind the times. Kenn and I found this strangely comforting and actually a reasonable way of looking at things, especially in light of the crossings we were now mastering. Given all the time traveling that we had done, time itself was becoming less relevant to us, and the idea of fads or time-stamping things made less and less sense. In fact, time actually seemed more confusing to us now that we could travel through it, but yet it still seemed to control so much of our lives. But why should it matter at all? Isn't the very notion of fashion or fads a hallmark of intolerance? An industry built around bullies who impose their views on what people should wear, eat, or look like? Would eating disorders exist but for the torments of bullies in advertising? But this was one of many virtual dictators that ruled our existence.

"So, genius," I said, as we sat down waiting for our martinis to arrive, "looks like we're stuck in time. What do you think is going on?"

"Time is a merciless tyrant," Kenn started, strangely philosophical. "We are all forced to march toward the end of our days passing silently over the bones and the ghosts of others. It's not that time forgets those it has vanquished, time is simply a cosmic cat that plainly doesn't care about anything but its own whims."

"Soooo, you're saying that time forgot us at a Tracy Chapman gig? That seems like a bit of a stretch and more than a little dramatic, even for you."

Time may ultimately measure something's longevity, but even that is a *post mortem* analysis that is only possible because time has endured while all else has not. Like a measure of the rate of erosion. How long did it take for time to erode Elvis's influence?

The Beatles? The Offspring? Picasso? Shakespeare? Milton? Andy Warhol? Lou Reed? Isn't that the measure of influence, or is it about the message passed along?

Ultimately, once something is recorded, time stops for it. Wasn't that the idea of recording things? Sure, Elvis may not be considered timeless. Very few acts or pieces of art are, but most acts are capable of telling the story of the period or at least of their experience at a point in time. Do we not have the same degree of insight into the moods and mores of the artist's time period? We learn about society during the time in which the art is created, through the art and the reaction it caused. Consider the fervor that Elvis's gyrations and stage antics created, the brooding feeling of desperation in Charles Dickens's *Tale of Two Cities,* or Dumas's *Man in the Iron Mask,* or Edvard Munch's anguished painting *Scream.* Through these, don't we learn what society was like then? Can't you feel the pulling against the restraints of society with each shake of the Big E's hips? Can't you feel the desperation and futility of the self or the frustration of the social economics and societal structure from Dickens and Munch? Don't these themes still exist today? What would Kafka have to say about corporations that were too big to fail? How would today's landscape look to Dali? To van Gogh? Isn't the backlash against Katy Perry or Marilyn Manson similar to that which the Beatles or Elvis faced, or even the puritans disfiguring nude Grecian sculptures to prevent offense? What about Michelangelo? Strange that time marches on, but outrage lingers even if it simply becomes refocused. That intolerance seeks to mask or obscure rather than teach.

Maybe it was because of our partial command over time that I liked the timelessness of San Francisco. Everywhere one looked in the city, it seemed that time was less relevant than in other places that Kenn and I had been to—its bars and buildings, its denizens and transients alike. Which was why, we were here now ordering martinis from some tall, pale, wispy waiter. This was the image that sight I grew up associating with San Francisco; the waiter was wearing a pink (or was it mauve?) button-down polo shirt and straight-cut jeans and leather loafers, without socks. He was the very picture of proper manners.

I'm Joseph and I'll tell you about my *favorite* martini in the *whole of the world,*" he recited.

The martini was something with Tanqueray No. 10, espresso, and chocolate liquor, which was fine with us. As Joey skipped away with our order we turned our attention to the jazz band that was playing near the back of the bar.

It appeared that the small jazz ensemble was just finishing up its set, perhaps for drinks and a smoke or something truly illicit. Actually, only the girl playing the bass seemed to be stopping. Moving away from the riser with a purposive stride, with a touch of a skip, she left her crew behind, seemingly without a second thought. She left the graying man hunched over the keyboards playing with labored focus, the petite skinhead at the small percussion set continuing with his sharp snapping of the snare and hi-hat cymbals, the wiry and nervous-looking dude who would switch between a trumpet and alto sax that was always blurting out indulgent and rambling riffs, and the bearded guitar player, who continued doing whatever he was doing, all to carry on without a bass line. No wonder jazz never made any sense to Kenn and me.

Although only a casual observer, it seemed odd to me that a band member would just hop out of a song mid-stride, but then I suppose jazz was like that and perhaps maybe why I never really gravitated toward it. It wasn't because of the reasons my father had—being structured around race or Parisian popularity—but more because of a lack of personal enjoyment. But notwithstanding my own preferences, it seemed, even by jazz standards, this was odd behavior. Kenn was mesmerized.

"That's a little odd, don't you think?" I offered.

"Huh?"

"A band member just leaving during a set. A little strange, yeah?"

"I don't know." Of course Kenn would disagree. "We've seen it before and even so much more so with jazz. I mean, remember the stories of musicians hawking their instruments in order to buy drugs or the famous photo of Charlie Parker playing a plastic saxophone during a Canadian tour? Not that the tone-deaf and backward Canadians would have even noticed. They would probably be too busy mispronouncing things and spelling words with superfluous letters. There was the height of Parker's infamy, when a cymbal being thrown across the room and onto the floor interrupted the recording session, to both regain his attention and admonish him for his lack of time and playing off-key."

Kenn was right, probably even about the Canadians being too distracted to notice. Jazz was replete with such stories, especially involving Charlie Parker and illicit substances. In the end it spoke of Parker's talent, as he became a legend in spite of his many human frailties.

Jazz, despite our tacit tolerance of it, shared an essence with rock 'n' roll but spoke a different dialect. Sort of like Latin and Mexican. Basically, it was the same language, but just with different nuances.

The delivery of jazz was different from rock, but they both shared the same disdain for rules and the *status quo*. Some, like Wynton Marsalis, said that the two forms of music were mutually exclusive and shouldn't be combined, while others, like Wynton's brother, Branford, said that the two could be combined as a natural extension of themselves. Unfortunately, this seemingly minor difference in views between the brothers led to a more significant difference in views. More specifically, the fact that although the two brothers had previously performed together on numerous occasions, they were never seen together after Branford contributed on Sting's "Dream of the Blue Turtles." Ironically, Sting was originally a jazz musician, but turned to the Police as a more viable vehicle for his musical pursuits (as in he was a more successful rock 'n' roller than a jazz player). Again, an example of how intolerance contributed to turmoil and conflict, resulting in the end of a relationship between siblings.

I still maintain that this was one of the few instances where the Evil infiltrated rock 'n' roll without using girls. Maybe that's how things worked for jazz. Fortunately, it affected the jazz scene more than rock 'n' roll, and while it was an attack on art, that ultimately caused everyone to suffer, some assaults strike closer to home than others. I often wondered how many wars started over such modest issues…although, the rift between the Marsalis brothers, as great as they were, was not my gravest concern. Tonight, I still had pressing matters, such as how Kenn and I were getting home, and what we were going to eat at this bar.

But here we were, in what seemed to be a jazz bar, watching a small band, whose bass player seemed to suddenly remember that she had something else to do and abruptly left the small riser on which she was playing. She moved with purpose and a sense of lightness, but a resilient lightness not with a skip or a swagger, but something else, perhaps an internal beat. But in any event, she left the band she was with and walked around the bar and leaned forward to the waiter as he spoke into her ear.

There wasn't any sort of affection between the two, just a familiarity. It seemed obvious moments later that she was the bartender. Well, of course! It's like I should have known, but how? Actually, Kenn and I arrived at the conclusion the same time I raised the statement as a question. Was she glowing or was it the light? Were the bar lights glimmering on her moist skin, skin that was wet from commanding her bass, if it was in fact her bass?

It is amazing when I think back on it. I noticed that she was treating her bass, a Hofner, in fact, rather brusquely. I recalled her gait and her confidence, but initially that was all I noticed. Almost immediately afterward, I would notice that she wore a fitted black dress that was as smooth and flawless against her body as the very essence of the lacquer on the bass she was playing. Both were beautiful, but in a foreboding way, and I could imagine that if anyone was as rough with her as she was with the bass, there would be Hell to pay, and she'd keep the change.

Only now can I describe her as vividly as she was, having seen her so many times since. Again, the strange effects of time casting a pall over everything, because I am confused with whom it is that I now see—the girl I first saw that night or who she has now become. Even though she is no longer how she was then, knowing her for all these years reminds me of how she first seemed and looked. Although familiarity can breed complacency, this isn't the case with her; I can assure you, with this girl there's always Hell to pay. It's just that she's running a tab. But really, a girl? Yeah, it was always about a girl, even in a jazz bar after a Tracy Chapman gig in San Francisco.

The girl of our immediate attention had chestnut brown hair that she wore in a short bob just above the nape of her neck. But instead of a razor-sharp edge, as you'd expect, the ends were tattered, as though they had been torn like warm bread, producing a look that was at once disheveled, edgy, and low maintenance. Perhaps she had cut it herself. Maybe with a straight razor and broken mirror. Hell, maybe she broke the mirror in two, so that she would have a piece to see with and another to cut with. One had an immediate sense looking at this girl that any explanation was possible. Even now, having known her for years, I continue to be confused by her, and even my feelings toward her. But it was Kenn who always held the strongest feelings for her.

Her hair would attract your attention and draw your eyes as the roughly-hewn ends played against the nape of her neck, except where the hair was longer and would stick to the moisture from her exertion and the warmth of the evening. But you couldn't free your attention from her, and the nape of her neck forced you to make a decision. Should you continue to follow its graceful elongated curve to her muscular, tanned shoulders or gaze elsewhere? One of her shoulders, which was covered by the single sling arm of her black dress and the other by a multi-colored sleeve tattoo. Remarkable.

Why was it remarkable? Because it was 1988 and girls typically had discreetly placed tattoos of butterflies, unicorns, fairies, flowers, maybe a little braid of ivy, or crucifixes. Sure, *now* tattoos are more prevalent than graffiti in an abandoned rail yard, but not in 1988. What was the tattoo? Even now, I'm not really sure. The tattoo was ablaze with color and detail, intricate with details that could stand apart as singular pieces of art, but somehow wrapped into a larger whole montage. The sort of tattoo that immediately drew your eye, but then required careful study to discern. Kenn and I found ourselves in enough trouble with women, without staring, so we tried to avoid it. And staring at girls with tattoos just seemed like an easy way to find trouble. Of course, we could have avoided more trouble if we had avoided other more questionable conduct during the course of our adventures, but you could only ask so much of us, heroes or not.

But if not her neck and shoulders, then where? Well, rather than following her neck down toward her shoulders, if you chose the path that her hairline directed, you would be rewarded with a firmly set, but rounded jaw that gave way to a distinctive egg-shaped chin. Her face wasn't perfect or symmetrical, but rather nature's attempt at an ellipse, where the start of her chin was indistinguishable from her jaw line. Like an M.C. Escher drawing—you could see one side or the other, but not both at the same time. When you finally realize that you had stalled while exploring the perimeter of her face, you would see her bright-red lipstick upon her firm, small mouth; high soft cheek bones, also with bits of hair stuck to them; a well-proportioned nose with a rigidly straight edge and slightly turned up at the end. It was difficult to see if she was wearing makeup, especially from across the bar, or if the color was a result of the bar's lighting and having finished her set with the jazz band.

After absorbing the details of the lower hemisphere of her face, her eyes would captivate you. Even today, her eyes hold my attention as though they were headlights and I was a deer on the highway. Like her hair, her eyes are brown, except when she wears colored contacts for different effects, but the brown still shows through if you know it's there. But color is color, and some are blind to it, or it can be difficult to discern in various conditions. However, you would have to be completely blind to fail to see the expression that her eyes hold. She is at once curious and ambivalent; gentle and rough; caring and ruthless. Simply said, I just didn't know what to make of this girl. I actually still don't. But Kenn did and still does today.

As I was watching her take our order from our waiter, I could hear Kenn saying something, but honestly with the band, and the girl, it all sort of became background noise. The jazz-playing bartender turned to mix our drinks, and after careful measuring produced a large martini shaker and began agitating its contents. Watching this vision of a girl bartender at work, I can assure you that the ice, espresso, and alcohol weren't the only things in the bar being agitated. As if she weren't a spectacle enough by herself, she shook the chrome martini mixer like it owed her money. I could feel something stirring inside me, causing any sense of priority, even the proximity of our entrapment in 1988, to be forgotten.

"Are you thinking what I'm thinking?" said Kenn.

"I doubt it," I said, still captivated by our bartender, "unless you're thinking that we need to come to jazz bars more or," as I pointed toward the bartender, "that she's gonna shake the chrome plating off that thing before we get our drinks." Again, I left Kenn to blither on about something or other while my mind was set adrift.

"Hey, what the fuck is the matter with you? I said, *Isn't that Lisbeth Salander?*" Kenn repeated his previous question, which I apparently hadn't heard. Kenn was now leaning toward me speaking in a conspiratorial tone shaking me out of my reverie.

"Who?" I sort of shrugged, only half paying attention to the question, more curious about Kenn's body language than his words.

"Lisbeth Salander. The chick with the Trogdor ink."

"You mean the book *The Girl with the Dragon Tattoo*? Or Trogdor, the dragon sketch from the *Strong Bad* episode?" I tried to clarify, but instinctively knowing that clarity and a night of drinks, rock 'n' roll, being trapped in the wrong time, and now sitting in a jazz bar with Kenn precluded clarity, even being a distant relative of any guests that we might have.

"There was a book? I meant the movie, not the Daniel Craig one, but the original Swiss one," Kenn added.

"OK, probably not, but what difference does it make?" I asked, concerned about the direction that this was heading. Kenn often found his way along paths that were both ridiculous and reckless, especially with girls and even more so when he elected to express his views. It wasn't so much that he had strong opinions, but that he had no filter when expressing them.

"Probably not a book?" Kenn asked, now leaning away from me and distractedly playing with a candle, as though the dancing wick and molten wax held the answers to his inquiry.

"No," I said with rising incredulity and more than a little agitation, "probably not Lisbeth Salander. Never mind. What difference does it make?" At the same time, I was thinking, *where were our drinks* and *how were we getting home?* Still our drinks were in the midst of some type of domestic violence reenactment starring the attractive bass player.

"She's cool, and she totally hacks shit and puts out, dude. Not only does she put out, but she does guys and girls; she's awesome," Kenn enthused, still yammering on and on about whatever he was talking about.

But there you have it, the synopsis of the male fantasy. A tough, attractive girl, with the penchant for antisocial behavior, cyber crime and who puts out. Add bisexual in there and you've got the whole bundle. The Lisbeth Salander character in the novels was sexually indiscriminate…is that bisexual, or antisocial? Presently it represented the fine line between ignorance and apathy for me. "Fuck Kenn, I don't know and I just don't care; I just want a drink and to get home." Not the least of so that this discussion with Kenn would end, but even that seemingly modest goal was not to be.

Kenn was hooked on this conversation, which I couldn't really understand, given his views about girls and our role in history.

I actually couldn't even tell if Kenn was talking about the girl in the bar now or one of the *Girl with the Dragon Tattoo* movies, but he was now running along with a fresh set of batteries. "Yeah, but Kenn, she also carries a Taser, is capable of torturing men three times her size, for hours, and could be working for the Evil. Who are you even talking about?" I added, now desperate to interdict this runaway train that Kenn was piloting, hoping that if nothing else, Kenn's overactive predilection for conspiracy would come to my aid.

"The bass player/bartender. There's no way she's with the Evil, man. She's totally anti-Evil. I'm gonna go ask her." Kenn was undeterred and sprang into action. "Besides, how bad could it be?"

"Fuck, dude." Kenn was on his feet and heading to the bar before I could finish my sentence with a cautionary "don't." Even that seems strange when you look at things objectively. Why would you need to warn someone not to be impetuous with a girl that seemed scary and reminded them of someone socially violent and inherently dangerous?

Kenn was just like that. I followed him as quickly as I could to at least bear witness if I couldn't intervene.

"Excuse me, do you have a 'dragon tattoo' somewhere on your back or that lovely arm of yours or maybe even somewhere more intimate?" Kenn asked, as if the question were as ordinary as "Excuse me, do you know when the number three bus is due?" Unfortunately, Kenn was going to catch this bus by stepping in front of it. There wasn't even time to hit the brakes.

Kenn never did see the Taser, although it probably wouldn't have made a difference. Honestly, I only saw it as the bartender was putting it away and walking back behind the bar. Where did it even come from? Her dress was so fitted that there wasn't even room for my imagination in it. A Taser? In 1988? Shocking enough for me, all the more shocking for Kenn.

A few moments later, when he started to regain consciousness, with a throbbing pain coursing through his left side and urine soaked jeans, I explained what had happened. That we were still in the bar and we hadn't gotten our drinks. (Actually, I had drunk both and paid for them with Kenn's credit card, which seemed OK. After all, he had that credit card system going.) "Yeah, dude, so it wasn't Salander after all." Being a good friend, and heroic and all, I resisted adding, *"like I told you."* "But she did have a Taser. She hit you with it twice in the left armpit."

"Why?" Kenn managed, but elongating the pronunciation like a stoned surfer. He was alternating between rubbing his tender burn marks and wincing in agony when he touched them.

"Probably because she knew that it was hot in the bar and you'd likely be sweating, and that the electric current would conduct better through your wet armpit, thus carrying a harder hit on you," I replied perhaps deliberately missing the underlying question, but also helping Kenn recover some of the details that were missed in his unconscious state. He didn't need all the details; we were "big picture" guys, and this picture was pretty clear.

"Hit me? Hit?" Kenn started, trying to understand what had transpired. "Cool...she was hitting on me? Did she rape me when I was unconscious? She's pretty hot, yeah? So, she likes me?" Kenn continued his avalanche of incredulous and hopeful questions, but clearly misunderstood what had happened. Maybe the picture wasn't that clear after all.

It was always like this with Kenn. Why? It was a recurring question really. *Why* were we still friends? *Why* did I continue to put up with his shit? *Why* did he seem impervious to basic Darwinism that seems to kill all the other stupid contingents of a species? I suppose Kenn hadn't procreated yet, and given his running success with girls it was not likely to happen, so perhaps that was enough for Darwin. I suppose that Darwinism is as patient as time itself. As patient as erosion, and it's not about the deficient member of a species dying prematurely, just dying without procreating that is important. Kenn and I were certainly well on our way to ensure that our genetic material wouldn't be passed along to future generations. But even this was a distraction that we didn't need in our current predicament.

"Sorry, dude," I started to explain. "The thought probably crossed her mind. In fact, I'm sure that's what she wanted to do all along, but probably the fact that the Taser caused you to both wet yourself and lose all muscular control probably saved you from her rapist tendencies. That, and I suppose the fact that we're in a public place that happens to be her workplace. But if nothing else, I would have stopped her and saved your dignity."

"Don't ever...," he started to say, but was still in some pain and lacked complete control over himself.

I'm not sure what had been said of the interaction or if confrontations involving Tasers are a routine occurrence in this bar or even San Francisco, but no one was paying any attention to us at all. There was one table with four guys all dressed in leather, with caps, vest, and chaps that looked like they might enjoy or at least be interested in giving the Taser a try, but they certainly weren't paying any attention to us. Maybe because of how we were dressed. It happens a lot being from Oregon.

No one offered us help or even looked our way. The jazz band wasn't that good. Maybe everyone else was just having such a great time with the people they were with that nothing else mattered, except their half empty drinks in the half full bar. Not the band, not the wine list or the décor, and certainly not the two clowns who had drifted through the doors only to have one of them Tased before the arrival of their first round of drinks. But probably it was just because people have a tendency to avoid intervening with conflict, especially conflict involving Tasers. So like the times that McCloy had pummeled Kenn or me, the violence was invisible.

The bartending bass player was certainly neither glowing nor shimmering now. She had a grin that looked like a sly little smile and a grimace. I'm sure an apt artist could have easily turned it into the classic yin/yang symbol, but lying on its side. Her expression said, "I'm a menace, I'm mysterious, and you'll never forget me."

Indeed. You wouldn't expect to forget a beautiful girl who struck you with a Taser, but for Kenn it was even different than that. I've never forgotten the look, and maybe that night it laid the foundation for me for my future experiences in San Francisco. In fact, this is where I admit that Kenn was right—there was something about this girl that was worth being Tased for.

"We've got to go back and see her again," Kenn sputtered, still trying to re-coordinate his electrically disrupted body parts. I carried him to the bathroom in the back of the bar, feeling more self-conscious than you would anticipate from someone who was ostensibly invisible. Again my self-awareness and sense of embarrassment welled up from within me. An uncontrolled emotion, that was also unwelcomed and uninvited, but also without any external source. After all, the bar dark with people huddled around tables engaged in their own intimate evenings of cocktails and Jazz. Kenn just been Tased, twice, without anyone paying any attention, and further this was the '80s in San Francisco; men accompanying each other to the bathroom wasn't particularly uncommon.

As we entered the bathroom, I felt the familiar constriction on my chest and pressure on my temples. Unless the bartender had turned her Taser on me as well, soon the room would start feeling hotter. Then ignition of a burning sensation running down my spine would commence, and we would soon be back at Kenn's.

As the constriction on my chest started to abate and my breathing became more relaxed, I heard Kenn talking behind me. He was appearing in a mass of flickering light. This must be what it looked like when we crossed back. Somehow I had never thought to even observe what this was like.

"We've got to go back and see her again," Kenn repeated, now referring to 1988 rather than up to the bar, like he had previously. I started a shower for him and opened a Mountain Dew from the fridge, and I handed it to him, noticing that I was being ignored.

"Kenn?" I started trying to regain his attention, looking at him to see if the Taser had caused more than the immediate physical damage. "What the fuck is the matter with you? You just got your ass kicked. Shower is running, dude. Drink your Dew and have a shower. You'll feel better. I'll get some grub and some clean clothes."

"Yeah, I'm good," he said with a detached coolness. "I can clean myself up. I'm good. I'll see you tomorrow. You should just leave."

"Nah, it's OK, Kenn. I'll call in some pizzas and set up a record. Maybe a little Joy Division to start things off?" I offered.

"Actually, just leave. Leave now." And with that, for the first time since I had known Kenn, I was dismissed. Excused. Told without any room for interpretation that I was being asked to leave. Once Kenn's best friend, now unbidden.

I walked home from Kenn's with songs in my head. Songs we would have listened to that night. Songs that we wouldn't listen to throughout the remainder of the evening. Songs that now spoke different messages to me. Joy Division's "Atmosphere," "Ma and Pa," by Fishbone, the Jazz Butcher's "D.R.I.N.K.," Snow Patrol playing "Those Distant Bells," and even Jonathon Richman's "You Can't Talk to the Dude." All of these songs told of my world and my experiences, with Kenn and rock 'n' roll. Now seemingly changed by a girl in a bar.

My thoughts were interrupted, a fermata or pause, as the Stone Roses erupted on my phone. Instantly, I knew that Pyrah was calling. She too bangs the drums, and my heart leapt knowing that I had connected with her. My pulse raced with the contentedness and anticipation of knowing that regardless of the music and adventures that Kenn and I would share in the future, that along the way we had both found other distractions and broadened our horizons.

Maybe girls weren't Evil at all. Maybe it's always about a girl, even when it's about a friend. Kenn and I had harkened changes into our lives through an ability to travel through time and correct history, so maybe this was our reward, being smitten by girls who weren't agents of the Evil. Changes that were vast and important that Kenn and I brought about, but coming full circle to change and enrich us.

Looking forward, and even back, I could only think of clichés and songs, but that was OK. I was a part of something. Something big. Something important. Something that changed the world.

I didn't know what would come next, but I knew that as much as things always changed, rock 'n' roll would stand. Thinking back I suppose it should have been a sign of more than how much rock 'n' roll meant to me, but I missed it. Ironically, walking towards Pyrah I was humming the Luna version of "Season of the Witch".

Disclaimer

As odd as it may seem, this is a work of fiction.

I freely admit that, to my knowledge, none of my friends or I have managed to create a means of transporting people through time and space using *Guitar Hero*. In fact I don't recall ever playing *Guitar Hero*. Ever. Not even in a fictional alternate reality.

Given that *The Death of Rock'n'roll, The Impossibility of Time Travel and Other Lies* is a work of fiction, it follows that the story is also fictional and contains fictional events and characters. However, because my imagination is limited I have utilized real events.

For example, Billy Bragg is real. It is well documented that Billy Bragg is a Clash fan and he attended *Rock Against Racism*. As far as I am aware, Billy Bragg was never Margaret Thatcher's *aide de camp*, an extreme right-wing Prime Minister of Great Britain or lured to *Rock Against Racism* by Americans who convinced him that they were in fact angels.

There is great music everywhere and it's not limited by genre or nationality. Music is like literature; worth enjoying not going to war for. So, this is a work of fiction, with some real people and some real facts, but mostly a ridiculous lark about what might happen if something else didn't occur.

In the end, I hope that you enjoy this story, and maybe I've helped remind you of an old favorite, but also with a bit of ridiculous fun.

Thank you for reading this far.

Acknowledgements

Travelling through the depths of music, song and time is an ambitious project for most, as is writing a book. It should then come as no surprise that I owe a great debt of gratitude to the many who have assisted in this work.

Regardless of the time or place that I may travel, this book would not have been written without all the people who have lent either a gentle hand or a stern suggestion to guide me.

Specifically, my wife Nicole for her endless support, proof reading and encouragement; Lord McNeil who fell in love with the story from the opening sequence and has remained passionate about it, even after the opening sequence was changed over and again; Paul Carter who has tried his damnedest to take me on the ride of being a professional author (as he is), rather than a practicing lawyer (as I am); All Things Paladar that allowed me to impose myself in a corner of Paladar Fumior Salon for days on end soaking up inspiration from the warm Brisbane sun, excellent coffee and even better company.

Tamara Dawn, coffee and axe slinger (of HITS infamy) who provided enough inane dialogue and brainstorming sessions to make this ridiculous concept come to life; C. Emery who has been a sounding board for ideas, text, cover design and a wonderful wealth of compliments; D. Youles, S. Marchand, S. Rathbone and A. Watson who provided detailed feedback that helped smooth the story line; O. Massitti; L. Steer, L. Smith, L. Muar and even my mother (after all if your mother won't turn up at the show…) provided great supportive comments that kept me flailing away at the front of the stage.

M. Zablocki (say: Em-Zed) who's knowledge of rock'n'roll lore, contemporary literature and general coolness provided significant grounds for re-working this product, including a suggestion that improved the text as well as stripped out a reliance on lyrics that I had planned to "borrow", all in the name of art (of course). As if that wasn't enough, MZ then dove off the Marshall stacks into the social media mosh pit, helping me crowd surf in a medium that I barely understand.

Support, praise and amazing cover art by Peter Wyse, who's imagination provided a "kindler gentler Death". As always the process of working with Peter has left me filled with feelings joy and hilarity.

In addition there are a number of people such as Simonnik-kieuan, Tosh, Marcel, B. Clark, N. Deyell, the Cochranes (hailing of Ottawa, Nfld, Brisbane and Melbourne – for clarity), G. Lamb, Joan and others that have allowed me to impose upon them for concept reading, all of whom graciously supported this project in a myriad of ways. Others like B. Spice who never lacked for an article or commentary written by David Bidini that proved unequivocally that I've done everything wrong, has made this a more enjoyable process.

Let's not forget everyone that cheered from the audience of a crowded bar, the roadies that set up and hauled the gear around and the performers who have created a great body of music. Finally all the rock 'n' roll bands that have ever, or will ever take to a stage to try being a rock star on. This is especially for the oft overlooked Canadian bands, unlike the characters in the novel, who aren't always right, I'm a big fan of you all from Arcade Fire right through to Young, Neil, (sorry, nothing with "Z" comes to mind).

Thank you. You guys rock! Good night [enter name of location where you're reading this text], you've been the best crowd ever!! There will be no encore, but there will be another gig!!

[*house lights come up; enter clean up staff, roadies and assorted repro-bates who've snuck in here under the guise of helping out*]

Made in the USA
San Bernardino, CA
05 December 2013